CW00548727

ANOMALY

LEONA DEAKIN

Fisher King Publishing

Anomaly

Copyright © Leona Deakin 2013

ISBN 978-1-906377-82-3

Fisher King Publishing Ltd

The Studio

Arthington Lane

Pool-in-Wharfedale

LS21 1JZ

England

For my brave first readers, Lilly, Lady, Alice, Dom and Mum, thanks for your invaluable kindness and critique!

Thanks to the Fisher King Publishing team and to my Dad for sending them my manuscript. Also, a big thanks to proof-reader, Liz Obee, for all that time and effort.

Finally, thanks to Richard for letting me spend all those hours writing and to the rest of my family and friends for not laughing!

Chapter One

William leant forward a little more. The wind blowing up from the valley shook the leaves on the trees and made waves in the long grass. When it reached him it rippled the fabric of his walking jacket and pushed the hair back from his forehead. William lifted his arms to the side. *Would he glide at all?* he wondered.

The field below glistened from recent rainfall. Wind whipped across its surface lifting tiny bubbles of spray, and spinning them in the air. William focused on the lone sheep that knelt on its front legs and munched the grass. The sheep was kneeling far enough from the base of the cliff to avoid being hit. William could not stand to hurt an animal. He imagined its head whipping to the side, its front legs snapping straight, its skittering run across the field, and smiled a rare smile. His mother always said he had a vivid imagination. In reality, the sheep would probably stop eating only long enough to check out the new bundle at the base of the cliff, before going back to its lunch.

What are you doing? William suppressed the last rational thought to break through. His decision was made. He had made it somewhere between the cold darkness of three twenty seven a.m. and his hastily written note. Before he knew it, he had been driving away from the house he no longer thought of as home, and out into the Yorkshire Dales.

He could have walked up to Ilkley Moor from the house. No doubt some drop there would suit his needs. But that felt too much like washing his dirty linen in public. Travelling to an anonymous ridge to be an anonymous man felt more fitting. After all, he had no idea who he was supposed to be anymore.

Parking in a grass verge at the side of a deserted country lane, William spotted a small footpath winding skywards in the steep hills that rose on either side. *Perfect*, he thought, trying to ignore the wind that bumped awkwardly against his car, and the rain that ran in wide, flat sheets down his windscreen.

For a moment he sat staring at his left hand. He had left the note for his mother under his wallet on the table. Not that she would be able to understand it, early onset Alzheimer's had turned her son into a stranger. He expected Sarah would find it. William had not left anything for her. Logically, he knew this was childish and cruel, but if logic ruled his decisions, he would not be about to do what he was about to do.

William tried to imagine Sarah's reaction, but could only bring to mind *that* smile. He had seen her lips form so many smiles over the years. Smiles filled with love and laughter, smiles laced with sarcasm and even anger, but this one proved indecipherable. Without warning, William's memory expanded into widescreen. He saw the leather jacket he had spent a small fortune on for her last birthday fastened snugly to her frame. And at her feet, the overnight bag she had bought for their wedding night bulged against its well-worn seams. William swallowed the bitter-tasting saliva that flooded his mouth.

Removing the platinum band from his finger, he dropped it into the ashtray.

The higher William climbed, the wilder the wind became. Even with his hood pulled over his bent head, cold shards of water stabbed his face and dripped from his nose. Thunder rumbled in the distance, and the icy wind that pierced his clothes made him shiver. If he had been a superstitious man, he might have thought the world was trying to deter him.

William trudged on regardless, discounting three potential spots as too shallow or not sheer enough to guarantee success. He needed at least a thirty-foot drop, ideally fifty, and expected the right place would jump out at him, to pardon the pun.

By the time he reached his final destination, the rain had passed and the dark grey sky had lightened to dull silver. William removed his hood.

In hindsight, he should have immediately taken a running jump. But, oh no, he had to stand at the edge and contemplate how things might go. Imagine toppling forward and gracefully gliding to his desired demise. Daydream about the reaction of the livestock and lose his footing.

William did not glide gracefully, or even drop like the dead weight he would have if he had managed to jump. Instead, he skidded, scrambled and slid. His body responded instinctively, his feet kicked up dirt and his arms grasped for something to slow him, and it all happened too fast for him to think of how to remedy that.

At the half-way point, William let out an angry shout. He was going to make it safely down. And in the seconds before his head hit the rock, he was thinking how annoying it was going to be to have to climb back up and start over.

Chapter Two

Sarah pulled into the drive, turned off the engine and took a deep breath. Will's car was gone. She had not expected that. He seemed to be home all the time these days. She did not know if she felt more relieved or disappointed. She desperately wanted to remain on good terms, but found his coldness towards her hard to take, even though she knew she deserved it. Plus, he always made her more confused. Away from this place she knew her own mind, but faced with her husband, she would once more drown in the doubts.

It had been that way for nearly a year before Sarah plucked up the courage to do something about it. She had spent months fantasising about what it would be like to be single again. To have a little flat somewhere where she could read a book all evening instead of fighting over what to watch on the TV. To have nights out with her girlfriends, drinking as many wines as she liked without having to worry about being judged. To walk hand in hand with some new lover, a man she was desperate to make love to at any given opportunity. All ideas which brought strong waves of joy that rolled through her with the thrill of potential. Then she would arrive home and see Will's eyes light up, bringing guilt and shame by the bucket-load.

Sarah had become adept at hiding the truth. She knew her role in the marriage well enough to play it with all the panache of an Oscar-winning actress. Something she felt very proud of at the time. Why worry him with stupid dreams that would probably pass? Hiding it was more mature and certainly kinder. But it would come to be her greatest regret. The deceit of it had hurt William the most, allowing him to carry on oblivious whilst she plotted her escape.

"What sort of evil bitch does that to someone they're supposed to love," he had said, but his words had not cut as deeply as the tear which rolled from his right eye. He had brushed it swiftly away and told her to get out. "I don't want to hear your excuses, Sarah. They're not going to take away the pain are they?"

Sarah unlocked the door and stepped into the kitchen. It still felt like home even after two months and she swallowed the lump in her throat. For most of her adult life, nothing had made her happier than being here with Will. She could not even articulate a reason for not wanting him anymore. She simply felt it in her gut.

She flicked through the pile of post Will had left for her at the end of the work surface, setting aside a couple of bank statements, and throwing a load of junk in the bin, before halting on a letter from her friend Jen who had moved to Australia four years ago. Under the neatly printed address her husband had scrawled, *Can you tell your friends you don't live here anymore, W.* Sarah studied the full stop after his initial. It had been made with some force, denting the surface of the envelope and covering the spot where he used to place a kiss, or his crude drawing of a whale (after Free Willy). She had always ridiculed his artwork saying it looked more like a sausage spitting fat, but he had ignored her and continued to produce it with enthusiasm. She supposed she would never see it again now.

Sarah stuffed the letter and statements into her handbag and took a deep breath. This place infected her with gloom, she needed to get out.

Half-way to her car, Sarah hesitated. Will's wallet had been on the table. She should call him. He might need it, or be worrying where it was.

In the few seconds it took for the call to connect, Sarah wandered back towards the kitchen door. From inside, she heard his mobile ringing. "Will, you idiot," she said under her breath. Unlocking the house again, she moved his wallet into the end drawer. He always preached about not leaving car keys and purses in plain view. He would know where to look.

This time Sarah made it all the way to the car before she stopped, her hand hovering just short of the door handle. Why had he left a letter addressed to Jean under his wallet? Had he gone to see her and forgotten to take it? It didn't make sense. He had little time for his mother, plus she could not read anymore, given the Alzheimer's. It wasn't her birthday, so it couldn't be a card.

The cogs turned slowly in Sarah's head as she stood in what used to be her street, outside what used to be her home.

"No, Will, you wouldn't." Her words came out in one long breath and Sarah began to run.

It was hard to recall how long into their relationship William had confided in her, but she did remember he had made her cry. The pictures in her head were always so vivid. Thirteen-year-old Will standing on the doorstep with his father, as his mother climbed into another man's car and kissed the guy hello. A lump would form in Sarah's throat when she imagined Will trying everything he could to cheer his father up, and then waking that morning to find his dad cold in the chair by the fire. Will said he had run from room to room shouting for his mum. In the panic, he had completely forgotten she did not live with them anymore. Thinking about that never failed to bring the tears for Sarah.

She knew that part of his reason for telling her the story was to flag his expectations. His mother's actions and their consequences had left William with a twisted view of women. In his opinion, it was only a matter of time before Sarah did the same. And how Sarah hated the fact he had been right. He had protected her heart and treated it with the reverence it deserved once she had given it to him. Whilst she had done exactly what he said she would do all along.

With shaking hands she opened the kitchen door for the third time. The envelope for Jean was not sealed, just folded in place. Sarah tore out the letter, not stopping to wonder whether she might be invading any privacy. She had been with Will for fifteen years, enough time to trust her gut on this.

"Oh, God." Sarah held on to the back of one of the French chairs she had found in an antiques' fair one holiday in Devon. It had taken all their spatial awareness to work out how to pack six of them into their Ford Fiesta. And each time Will had looked in the rear view mirror, he had chuckled and shaken his head at his determined wife. She loved them so much she had even considered asking if she could take them with her when she left. An idea she eventually thought better of.

Jean,

And then there was one.

No doubt you will remain clueless to this latest reduction in our family unit, which is probably for the best. If, however, there is a chance you do understand, I want you to know you will be taken care of. My savings and my half of the house should mean you can stay where you are for as long as you need.

Take care,

William.

When they first viewed this house, Sarah had dragged Will from room to room without slowing. Now she dragged nothing but her feet.

She pushed the door to the lounge as wide as she could without stepping in, and breathed a sigh of relief. Only for it to dawn on her she had seven more rooms and a garage to check.

By the time she reached the master bedroom, her hands felt clammy on the door knob and her heart raced like she had run a hundred-metre sprint. Sarah did not hesitate. She found it easier if she gave herself as little time as possible to imagine what might be behind each door.

The empty room brought another brief wave of relief, but it soon dissolved.

That left the garage.

There had been a girl at school whose brother had hanged himself in his garage. Sarah had not known the girl, although she came to know of her following this event of course. It had been the class gossip for weeks. Not *why* had he done it - none of them were really interested in that at age nine - but what he had looked like when they found him. Joey, their best artist, had even produced a painting based on their most gruesome suggestions: the boy's eyes bulging, his skin blue, his meaty tongue hanging over his chin. They had all hidden behind the sports hall to take a good look at it.

Sarah approached the utility room door. Was there anything on the ceiling in here to attach a rope to? Or had he finally thrown out all their junk so he could fit his car in and gas himself? Sarah gripped her mobile tighter - the memory of Joey's picture as clear in her head as the day she had seen it – then she pushed the door ajar.

How long had she stood in the doorway relieved and then confused, she could not say.

His car was gone. The fact had slipped her mind in all the panic. Like thirteen-year-old Will forgetting his Mum was gone. Sarah made a guttural sound she had never heard herself make before. His childhood anecdote had always been a tearjerker, but she had never appreciated the horror of it until that precise moment.

"Police, please. Hello... I... I think my husband's going to commit suicide."

It was only later she realised that in some desperate hope she had used the future tense.

Chapter Three

William felt the sun hot on his face and arms. Disorientated from his period of unconsciousness, he failed to think it strange that his jacket sleeves did not protect him from the heat. He sat slowly, his eyes taking their time to adjust to the now bright daylight. As he reached behind his head to feel the spot that ached from its hard impact, his hands brushed against long grass. *Really* long grass. He blinked a few times to speed along his vision and focused on the tall ferns rising above him. Weird how much bigger things looked down here. He glanced up at the cliff face from which he had fallen. *So green.* When he had looked down from above he had seen mostly the grey of rocks with an odd splash of purple heather. From down here, it was like another world. The whole surface was coated in a lime coloured velvet moss.

William scratched the back of his hand as he pondered his new perspective, and felt the familiar sting of sunburn. He held his arm up to his eyes and sure enough he could see the skin had reddened. He ran a fingernail down his left cheek, feeling the same sting and frowned. *It's April.* Which is when he noticed his shoes, or at least, the lack of them.

He scanned the ground around him. How had he managed to lose both securely laced walking boots? He remembered kicking at the earth beneath him as he tumbled downwards. Surely he could not have thrown them off. But he must have, what other explanation was there?

William placed his hands on the ground to push himself up and felt an unexpectedly smooth surface beneath him. Instead of rising, he shifted onto his hands and knees and found himself crouched in the centre of a perfectly flat, white disc. He smoothed his hands across it. It reminded him of marble but felt much, much colder. His fingers curled over the far edge and ran around the circumference. It sank deep into the ground. William scraped the soil away until he had revealed a good six inches of the cylinder's side.

He sat back on his heels. He had never seen anything like it before. His job took him into many different industries: manufacturing, engineering, construction and the like. More often than not, he would be given a tour of their facilities and shown their latest developments and technologies. William knew he had not seen everything, but he had seen sufficient to know this was really different: the material, the temperature, the fact someone had buried it in the ground in the middle of the Yorkshire Dales. The only possibility that made sense was something military.

William had begun his career in the army. Not as a soldier. He worked within Human Resources in a team of people responsible for recruiting and promoting military staff. A job he literally jumped out of bed in the morning to go to. Not only did his business card say, 'William York, Occupational Psychologist', which at the time had brought him endless pride, the work proved fascinating. Nowhere else in the army did such a young member of staff have access to people of such seniority, or information so sensitive. During his four-year employment, he became a respected specialist called upon by senior chiefs to help with all manner of man management issues. And when he left to join a flash consultancy, he could count at least one General as a close friend. He could also say he had never again felt so appreciated.

William rose to his feet, slipping a little on the surface in his socks and winding his fingers around the waist-high ferns to steady him. Off the disc, the ground felt surprisingly dry. How long had he been out? The rain earlier had been torrential, he expected it would have drenched this area and kept the earth moist for most of the day. He squinted up at the sun, shielding his eyes with one hand. Then again, it was a scorcher.

For the next few minutes he brushed aside ferns in search of his boots, but with no joy. *How strange*. Standing with his hands on his hips, William scanned the field. His woolly observer had disappeared. Would a sheep take shoes? He found himself smiling at the image of his footwear swinging from their laces as they were carried mischievously away. The smile froze on his face. Where was his jacket?

That could not have come off in the fall. It had still been tightly zipped to his chin following the morning's storm when he fell.

Someone had been here and taken his things.

Who would do that when they found a person knocked unconscious? Surely the first instinct would be to call an ambulance or mountain rescue, not steal the man's clothes. Not that William would have thanked a do-gooder for taking him back to his crappy life.

William sighed, realising he liked that his visitor had selected theft over rescue. What did bare feet and the lack of a jacket matter anyway? Neither would impede his climb back up to any degree. And the sprouting of blisters would not cause him any angst for long.

A flash in his peripheral vision caught his attention. William glanced to the right. Only empty fields rolled ahead of him for as far as he could see. He turned his attention back to the hillside. There was no obvious easy way up. He would have to scramble on his hands and knees.

The flash distracted him again.

This time he turned fully and held still, allowing his brain time to take in all the detail.

Like staring at a magic eye picture so popular in the nineties, a patch of hazy air began to take shape in the distance. He could still see ahead and beyond, but the view was distorted. As his eyes focused, William could not account for what he was seeing.

No more than a few hundred yards away, two humongous domes rose out of the ground, their perimeter arcs glistening in the sun and their interiors packed with smoky air.

Without any real conscious thought, William began to move towards them in fascination.

At the crest of a small hill, he hesitated and looked back. How had he missed these domes from the cliff top? Nothing would have prevented them from dominating his field of vision.

Something's wrong.

William paid little heed to the instinct. Shaking the feeling away, he continued his progress down the slope to the base of the domes.

When he reached the domes, he realised that the hazy image he had assumed to be the view ahead was in fact a reflection. Placing his hands on the surface to shield his eyes, William peered inside. He thought he could make out shapes here and there, but despite his best efforts, his eyes insisted on focusing on his own mirror image.

The curved, silver structure was the height of a five or six storey building, its sister dome an exact replica. Around the base of each, ran a smooth ring of white material a foot or so high. William crouched and brushed his finger along the surface feeling a familiar coldness.

He walked the circumference of both domes. A carpet of long grass grew up to each base, and there were no entrances. Something about the set-up put him in mind of ventilation shafts on tunnels. He tried to look inside again, this time focusing his eyes downwards, but the interior remained elusive.

It crossed his mind he could do a search on the internet. Not that there would be much information available if they were military, as he suspected. William met his own reflection in the surface. So now he planned to go home and investigate a mysterious building did he?

"Worth living for?" he asked himself as he let his eyes wander over the smooth silvery surface.

When he looked back at his reflection, a woman stood motionless behind him.

"Jesus, woman, you gave me the fright of my life," he said turning to face her.

She did not move, other than to tilt her head a little to one side. Her expression reminded William of the reaction of locals when trying to communicate abroad. In the second or so before she spoke, he took in her unusual appearance. Dressed head to foot in black, she wore a wide silver bangle on her left wrist. Her skin-tight trousers and long sleeved top hugged her frame and her shoes looked sporty, probably the latest Nike design. William felt the heat of the sun on his face; she had not dressed for the weather. A few curled strands of jet-black hair fell to below her shoulder from a messy bun and William guessed she had been exercising. Like him, she had probably set out early before the sun came out.

During his study, her silver eyes stayed as still as her body. He finished his appraisal quickly, realising he had spent too much time appreciating her athletic figure. His conclusion: hot and definitely foreign.

"Is what worth living for?" Her accent sounded like none he had heard before.

William scanned the fields around them before meeting her

steady gaze again. "Where did you come from?"

"Where did you?" Her head still tilted as if she was studying some quizzical creature.

William forced a fake smile. "I asked first."

She straightened her head and took a step towards him. "Did you?" William instinctively stepped back, his heels hitting the base of the dome. "You're hurt," she said.

"I'm fine."

"I estimate you hit your head somewhere in the last hour."

William rubbed at the lump that had formed on his head and checked his hand. No blood, so how did she know he was hurt? "What are you, psychic?"

"What is psychic?" Her quizzical expression returned.

William moved away from her to regain some personal space. "I was wondering what this was," he said, knocking on the glass.

"You were wondering?"

"Is it your habit to just repeat what people say?" Sometimes William found it hard to suppress the psychologist within.

"Is it yours to avoid answering?" she said.

Touché, he thought with a sarcastic smile. She remained serious.

"You said you were wondering what this is?" She looked above him to the dome.

"Yeh, any ideas?"

Now she smiled, but the way people do at the troubled or the mentally ill. "How hard did you hit it?"

"My head?"

"Did you hit more than your head?"

"No."

"Yes then, how hard did you hit your head?"

William placed his hands in the pockets of his walking

trousers. "I get the sense you're making fun of me."

"You are a little odd."

"*I* am." He took his left hand from his pocket and checked his wrist. *Flaming thieves*, he thought with irritation.

"Something wrong?" the woman said.

"I was robbed whilst I lay unconscious. Bastards took my shoes, my coat and even the watch from my wrist. What's the world coming to, hey?"

A brief frown crossed the woman's forehead. "Did your coat have a metal zip or metal buttons?"

"Why, you know a thief with a fetish for zips do you?"

"What type of shoes were you wearing?"

William turned to walk away. The woman was obviously unstable.

She walked alongside him. "Your coat had metal fastenings. Your shoes had metal in the heel or maybe metal eyelets. The watch you speak of, that's metal too, yes?"

William wondered if she would walk all the way to the cliff top, and what she would think when he jumped. "Do you have a point to make?" he said.

For four or five steps she said nothing. He looked across to see her frowning at her feet. "My brother is a neurological savant. I would like him to take a look at your injury," she said.

"I'm fine." William increased his pace then stopped, causing her to overshoot him. "What did you say your brother was?"

"A neurological savant."

"As in autistic?"

Her frown deepened. "No, he selected to be a savant in neurology."

"So, he's a doctor?"

The woman giggled and it made her look like a teenager. "If

you like," she said.

William clicked his tongue against the roof of his mouth. He did have a headache coming on. He shook the thought away, he had something important to do and procrastinating would not help. "Thanks but I'll pass. A doc is the last thing I need. See you around." He strode by her, his hand raised in a goodbye gesture.

The last thing he remembered was a high-pitched vibrating whistle screaming inside his head.

Chapter Four

The policewoman's radio came to life. The voices from within sounded tinny and distant, and Sarah could not make out the words.

"Have you any idea where he would go?" said the WPC.

Sarah shook her head. She had stopped crying. It had been half an hour since she called nine nine nine and she had already answered all the woman's questions once before. "Shouldn't you be out there looking for him rather than asking me the same things over and over?"

The young woman smiled. She could not be much older than twenty five and wore more black eye-liner and mascara than Sarah would on a night out. "We've alerted all officers in the region, of your husband's registration and description. But we need all the help we can get from you. I'm here to find out anything that will aid the search, okay?"

"What if he's gone outside of the region?"

"Like where? Is there somewhere he would be likely to go? A favourite place or somewhere with memories attached?"

Sarah could not think straight. Where would he go to do himself in? Would he select somewhere familiar or pick something at random? He wasn't the most organised person; she could not see him planning things out in great detail. She suspected he had done this on a whim. In which case who knows where he might have gone.

"Here you go, love." Sarah's dad placed a cup of tea on the table along with a chocolate digestive: one of Will's. She felt a little queasy. "Are you sure I can't get you anything, there's some juice in the fridge?" her dad asked PC Spencer.

"Thank you, I'm fine."

The copper probably didn't want to drink a dead man's coffee or eat his discarded biscuits thought Sarah. She looked out of the kitchen window at the rain being whipped against the garage wall by the wind. What a horrible, horrible day. "You have to find him before he does it. I couldn't live with myself if…"

"Hey, it's not your fault, love, don't start blaming yourself." Her father sat and placed an arm around her shoulders.

Sarah shrugged him off. "How can it not be my fault?"

"What makes you say that?" said Spencer.

Sarah looked at the policewoman, realising she probably should have told them this before. "His father committed suicide when William was thirteen…because his mum left them."

"Am I to take it you're having some marital problems?"

"If you mean have I left him? Yes, nine weeks ago."

"And you think because of what happened to his father he would do the same?"

Was this woman really as dim as her questions made her seem? "I think the note is the clincher," Sarah said with a sarcasm she could not suppress.

"How did the father end his life, do you know?"

"He overdosed on Paracetamols and vodka."

The officer took hold of her radio. "Where?"

Sarah blinked a couple of times trying to digest the question. "Somewhere in Bingley, I erm… can't remember the name of the street." She looked at her father for help but he shook his head.

"Was he in his car?"

"No… he was in the lounge at home."

A hint of disappointment crossed the officer's eyes before she spoke into the radio. "PC 1262 Spencer. I have some background details on our missing man, Mr York, which could be relevant."

"Go ahead," said the tinny voice.

"Father committed suicide at the family home when Mr York was a teenager. Incident took place somewhere in Bingley, address unknown." The officer moved the radio away to speak to Sarah. "Do you know whereabouts in Bingley?"

"Will drove me past once but I can't really remember. I think it was on the outskirts somewhere… there may have been a school nearby."

"Bingley Grammar or Beckfoot?"

Sarah shook her head. She had moved to Yorkshire with Will after University and was not overly familiar with the area.

"And the father's name?"

"Pete, Peter York," said Sarah.

"PC 1262 Spencer, family home may have been near to one of the schools. Father a Mr Peter York."

"Received."

"Do you think he might have gone there to do it?" Her dad was halfway through his second digestive. He did not seem phased by eating his missing son-in-law's food.

"It's hard to say, Sir, but often people return to significant places in times like these. Do you know your son-in-law well?"

"Yes, of course. He's a great guy isn't he?"

Sarah felt tears sting her eyes. She knew her parents could not understand her motivation for ending the marriage.

"Did you see him regularly, Mr Powell?" said Spencer.

"Fairly, since we moved up here from Lincoln when I retired. We thought we might be needed soon for babysitting duties-"

"Dad!"

Her father had the good grace to colour up a little at his insensitivity. "Sorry, love, I'm just being honest."

The policewoman looked at Sarah. "Had you planned to have a family at all?"

"What the hell has that got to do with it?"

"Sarah," her father said in the low voice he reserved for showing disapproval.

Sarah took a drink of the now lukewarm tea. "William was keen to be a dad, but I'm not ready yet."

"Was that the reason for the separation?" asked Spencer.

Sarah had never considered the children factor in all her decision-making, but now she came to think about it. "I suppose it might have played a part, yeh. There was no big fall out or drama. We just wanted different things that's all."

"It would probably be more truthful to say my daughter wanted different things."

"Dad!"

Her father put his arm around her shoulder again. "If you want to help him, love, we have to tell the police the truth. There's no point pretending he's alright with all of this now is there?"

Footsteps approached from the driveway. Sarah looked up as the policewoman twisted in her chair to face the open door. *Please let this be good news,* thought Sarah, but the sight of the man on William's doorstep brought her to her feet. "Don't come in," she said.

Danny stopped in the doorway then glanced at Sarah's dad and the policewoman before speaking. "Is there any news?"

"Go. You can't be here. You have to go." Sarah moved around the table to physically block his entrance into the house.

"Sarah, love, what's going on?" said her dad.

She ignored her father and pushed Danny back from the doorway.

Danny placed a hand over hers on his arm. "I wanted to check you were okay, you sounded awful on the phone."

"Just go, Danny, please. It's not right."

Danny held up both hands and stepped back into the rain. "Okay, okay, I'm going, just… call me, yeh?"

To her surprise Sarah found she could not look him in the eye, simply nodding a response. When she turned back to the kitchen table, her father and PC Spencer wore matching expressions of intrigue. Sarah walked back to her seat with her eyes on the floor.

For a minute or so no one spoke.

"Does Will know?" Her father asked the question quietly as if he were passing the time of day. But Sarah could hear the subtle combination of sadness, disappointment and anger in his words.

Sarah spoke to the Policewoman, not able to look at her father. "He's not why I left. I only started seeing Danny a month ago."

"But you met him before you went," said her Dad.

In moments like these her attraction to William's incisive nature made complete sense to Sarah. Nothing ever passed her father by. She did not respond. After all, he had not posed it as a question.

"Was your husband aware of the affair?" said the PC.

"It's not an affair, we were already separated."

The small smirk which flashed across the officer's lips told Sarah her defence was pointless. Her husband had resorted to killing himself because his bitch of a wife preferred someone else. That was all anyone was ever going to see. She saw her life span out in front of her. A life cast as the villain in the eyes of her friends and family. A life where the guilt would infect her happiness and feed on her sanity. The very life William's mother had lived.

"Was he aware?" PC Spencer asked again more assertively.

"No."

Her father huffed at her side. "I wouldn't be so sure. People tend to know, wouldn't you agree?"

"More often than not," said PC Spencer.

Sarah put her head in her hands to hide from the air of judgment saturating the kitchen. Her thoughts swung from, *How dare he do this to me, the bastard,* to, *Oh, William, I'm so sorry.*

Chapter Five

"Have you seen this, Caro? It is unusual."

"No inputs, upgrades or modifications at all."

"Have you ever seen this before?"

"Never. You?"

"No. I could ask my friends…"

"Mmm, I'm not sure it is worth the risk. He could be involved."

"But if he's not… are you thinking what I am thinking?"

"It could be useful."

"Precisely."

William heard the conversation in the distance. His eyes remained shut and his body frozen in place as the voices came closer and clearer. He tried to work out where he was but no answer came.

"He is waking." The woman's voice said next to his right ear.

"Can you tell me your name?" The man's voice had a familiar accent William could not place. William felt a hand on his forearm and heard the question repeated. The woman by the domes, that's where he had heard the accent before. William's eyes flew wide as he recalled the piercing whistle.

He half sat, half lay in a reclining chair, much like those used by dentists. Above him the white ceiling curved away in all directions. Somehow he had ended up inside another, smaller dome.

William looked left and right.

A tall, dark-haired man stood at his side. He wore something resembling a long-sleeved cycling top in grey, and his hands rested casually in the pockets of his trousers. As their eyes met, the man smiled. "I am Caro. Can you tell me your name?"

"William. Where am I?"

"You are safe, William, and your injury is not serious."

His head injury. The woman had brought him to her brother. "Your sister brought me here?"

"Yes, Sorella is very… how can I put it…"

"Insane?"

William heard the woman laugh and turned his head in her direction. There was nobody there. He craned his neck further to see behind, but apart from him and Caro the room was empty.

"I was going to say determined." The brother's response contained no hint of humour.

"Where's the woman?" William said.

"My sister is preparing you something to eat."

"No, the other woman?"

Caro held a minute disc between his thumb and forefinger. As he moved it towards William's eye, William instinctively turned away.

"It's nothing to worry about, William. I only wish to check your vision."

"My eyes are fine, thank you."

The man lowered his hand. "I am concerned about your state of confusion."

William sat upright with his legs astride the chair end. He could see the whole room now. A curved shelf ran around the circumference, on top of which sat a whole range of strange white and silver ornaments. He watched Caro place the small disc onto a tall white stand, and it dawned on him he might be looking at medical equipment. "I'm not confused. I heard you talking to a woman. I heard her laugh. It sounded like she was in the room."

"What brings you here, William?"

"Here to this room? How the hell would I know? I was just minding my own business and then your sister did whatever crazy shit she did. What was that anyway, the whistling?" He tapped his forehead.

Caro looked to William's right as he listened. William followed his eye line to a rotating tangle of white, red and orange lines hovering in mid-air. Some form of 3D projection, he figured. The luminous, moving streaks reminded him of speeded up car head and taillights, if said cars raced around spaghetti junction that was.

"Fascinating. I have never seen anything like this before. Where have you come from, William?" Caro looked back at him. "Are there more of you?"

William met the man's eyes then turned back to the rotating image as its shape dawned on him. "Is that what I think it is?" He felt his head with his hands, the panic subsiding when he felt nothing attached.

"He is becoming stressed, Caro. Tread carefully."

The woman's voice made William jump. It sounded so close he sprung from the chair and wheeled in a circle. "What the hell. Who *are* you people?"

"I apologise, William. I do not mean to worry you. Please sit. If you will answer a few of my questions I can tell you whatever you wish to know."

Something about the man's soothing tone made William nervous. Whoever the hell this Caro was, he had done this before. "You know what. I think I'm done here. Thanks for the check-up but if you would show me the way out, I have somewhere I need to be," said William.

Caro's back straightened and his eyes narrowed. "Where do you need to be?"

"That would be none of your business." William spotted the door and headed for it.

The taller man beat him to it, placing a hand on its surface. "Who are you working for?" All the kindness had left his voice. He did not ask a question, he made a demand.

The structures *must* be military, and these people must be guarding them. That would explain the weird equipment and the tone. William remembered enough from his early career to know what to do next. He looked Caro in the eye. "I work for myself, Sir. I was just out walking. I didn't mean to intrude."

"He is telling the truth." The woman's voice sounded as near as before even though William had moved across the room. He flinched but this time made no comment. It was more important to get out of here as quick as he could.

"You are sure?" Caro asked, his hand still blocking the exit.

The woman barked a laugh. "Do you doubt my skills?"

"No, Ann, but his… uniqueness makes me nervous."

Right back at ya, thought William.

The long, white corridor felt clinical and cold despite its curved ceiling and smooth lines. William followed a few steps behind Caro, keeping his eyes down and his mouth shut. He did not want to give them any reason to keep him here. He almost made it too. He could see the door just a few yards away. It stood ajar, letting in a small patch of sunlight that illuminated the grey floor.

"Caro?" Another woman's voice stopped Caro as he passed an opening on his right.

The smell of warm bread and spiced food filled the air. William walked a little quicker to find its source. He suddenly felt starving.

"Is he well?" The woman from the domes looked at William as he came into view.

The small kitchen could not have been more different from the room he had just left. A hotchpotch of free standing wooden cabinets surrounded a large white range. In the centre of the room, on top of a blue checked tablecloth, a bowl of steaming soup sat next to a newly sliced loaf.

"He is still a little confused but his injury was minor." The brother looked at William before continuing. "His name is William, and Annie found that he has no enhancements or modifications. He says he is not working for anyone and she confirmed this to be true."

William did not like how this man talked about him as if he were some experimental subject. He considered saying, *I'm standing right here you know*, but thought better of it. These military types could be tricky buggers, best they think him confused and placid. That way, they were more likely to let him go.

"None at all, not even the primary?" said the woman.

"He is completely organic… quite fascinating."

Both strangers gazed at William with what looked like wonder. William shifted uncomfortably under their scrutiny. When his eyes fell once more on the table, his stomach growled in response.

"You're hungry. Please, eat. I prepared this for you." The woman poured water into two glasses and placed one on the table by the food.

Undecided, William looked from the soup to the exit and back again.

"He wishes to leave," said Caro.

"I know he does, but he also wishes to eat." She turned her back on the two men to wipe the surface of the range with a cloth.

"Thank you, but I'd prefer to be on my way." What did hunger matter when he planned to do himself in.

Caro nodded and began to lead the way to the door.

"Trust me, William, my soup is definitely worth living for," said the woman.

William halted and looked back at her. Was he going mad or could these people read his mind? When she turned his way she had a mischievous glint in her eyes, but her smile was warm. He stepped into the room, curiosity joining forces with his hunger. "Sorry, I forget your name," he said.

"Sorella." She took a seat at the table.

William joined her. "How did you know about… that?" He found he could not say the words, and the psychologist within him sighed a knowing sigh.

"Eat, William, it will make you feel better," she said.

"I doubt that," he said but picked up the spoon anyway and took a mouthful. The thick vegetable broth had a mild hint of spice that tingled on his tongue.

The woman looked at Caro. "I'll take William back when he's ready."

"Be careful, Sorella, we have no idea who he is."

She nodded to her brother who left without another word. "Is it to your liking?" she asked, pushing the breadboard towards him.

He took a slice of the warm bread. "It's great, thanks. I didn't realise how hungry I was."

"Mmm, it often has that effect on people."

"What does?"

She frowned a little and looked at the table. "Do you have any recollection of how you…came to be here?"

"I remember the whistling, what the hell did you do to me?" Intrigue had replaced his earlier anger.

"No, I meant before that. How did you arrive in the fields?"

"You and your brother really are masters at dodging questions aren't you?"

The corners of Sorella's mouth twitched in an almost smile. "Yes well, my brother is afraid you are here to spy on us and I…"

When she did not continue William looked up to see her biting her lip. "You…?" he said.

"Don't want to make you any more anxious. You are quite adept at avoidance too I should point out."

"You think I'm anxious?"

"Yes."

"At last, a definitive answer. That wasn't so hard, was it?"

Sorella took a sip of water, her eyes fixed on his. "No it wasn't, so let's see how you fair. *Are* you here to spy on us?"

"No," he said.

Her smile was more pronounced this time.

"Let's try for more than the monosyllabic. Who are you people, I mean without telling me anything that might prevent your letting me out?"

"You think we're keeping you here?"

William smiled at her and said nothing.

"Sorry," she said realising what she had done. "We are a community of LQs. We live off the land in the main, although some have menial jobs within the hubs-"

"LQs?" William took a second slice of bread to mop up the last of his soup.

"Lower quartiles."

"What does that mean?"

"Oh, right, um… people who when tested are found to possess the slowest synaptic speeds, therefore, showing less potential."

William understood the words well enough. He had worked with concepts of mental capacity, intelligence and normal distribution curves most of his career. Even so, he found what she said difficult to comprehend. "Who tests... no, scrap that." He imagined the answer might be one of those things it was best not to know. "You and your brother aren't these LQs are you?" He thought of how they had both spoken to him, and how she had described her brother as a savant.

"No, Caro and I are..." She looked almost embarrassed for a moment. "We came here as children with our parents, and after they died we stayed. Now we try to contribute whatever we can to support the community. Are you finished?" She held out her hand.

"Yes, thank you." He handed the dish over and she carried it away along with the bread. "You lost both your parents?"

"It was a long time ago, when I was a teenager. So, where are you from?"

William hesitated for a moment as he contemplated the trauma they had in common. "Ilkley."

Sorella turned to face him, leaning against the front of the range. "And you travelled here from there?"

"Yeh, I drove out this morning to a lane just outside Kettlewell I think. Then I walked up into the hills where we met."

"Why?"

William found he did not want to explain the purpose of his trip. "I think it's my turn again."

She scowled but nodded.

"Your brother kept talking about my lack of modifications or something, what did he mean?"

"You are better at asking the questions than I. I'm revealing more, I think."

William smiled. His job depended on asking the right questions. He'd had years of practice. "Okay, answer this one for me and I'll give you three for free." He could not imagine why this woman wanted to know more about him, but he was not

31

complaining.

"Annie found you have no upgrades to your neural network, not even the primary everyone is given at birth. It's very unusual."

For a moment William stared at the woman, once more questioning her sanity. "The primary?"

"I thought I had three free now." When he made no response she took a seat and continued. "The primary is a basic modification to the brain to ensure we have the capacity to take on future enhancements."

Of course it is. Either these people dabbled in some truly crazy shit, or they were completely bonkers. William figured he may as well play along, see if he could work out which one it was. "She said it made me useful, that Annie woman. The fact I had none of this."

"Where have you been, William? ANN is not a woman she is our artificial neural network."

"A computer?" William's words sounded distant even to himself and he once more felt uneasy. He thought about his time in the previous room with the weird equipment and the hovering brain scan.

"We prefer not to use that term, it is too degrading to-"

"How did you know I'd hurt my head?"

Sorella sat back a little at his change of tone. "You promised me three questions."

"I changed my mind. How did you know I had hurt my head? How did that ANN thing know I have no... enhancements as you call them, or that I was not lying about being a spy for that matter?" William stood and moved to the doorway.

"I knew this would make you anxious. Please, William, don't be afraid, I'll explain best I can."

He checked the corridor. It was empty all the way to the exit.

They would surely have security out there. What hope did he have if he just made a run for it? These people experimented on human brains for Christ sake. They would not just let him walk out. "You people are in my head somehow, aren't you? *Aren't you*?" A sudden moment of clarity punctured his fear. If he ran they would try to stop him, no doubt by force. And wasn't that his plan for the day anyway?

Before Sorella had chance to respond, he started running.

The ten or so half marathons he had completed in recent years had made his legs strong and his lungs efficient. William reached the door in a matter of seconds, the exercise making him feel strong. Emerging into the sunlight with his arms pumping and his legs working hard, a satisfied smile crossed his lips. Now this was the way to go, like an action hero running from the enemy.

It took around three-and-a-half strides for his eyes to adjust to the brightness, at which point he came to a dead halt.

Chapter Six

Dr Stephen Morris scanned his appointments for the day on the computer screen. He had four existing NHS patients to see who were suffering from varying degrees of depression, a new private patient with a phobia of flying, and a partners' meeting last thing. As usual, a jam-packed day. He would have only half an hour in the middle for checking emails and cramming in whatever sandwich his PA chose to buy him for lunch.

The phobia patient was booked in for the two-thirty slot, he was pleased to see. It was a good thing to end on. In the main he specialised in mood disorders such as depression and mania. They had been the subject of his PhD, and were where he felt most able to achieve some sort of legacy in terms of improving a patient's quality of life. Phobias, on the other hand, were where Steve Morris had most fun.

It was not just the content of people's anxieties that made them so enjoyable, although sometimes they did verge on the ridiculous. He thought of Marjorie Hoyle who had been scared of the number eight. She would begin hyperventilating at the very sight of it. She could not use phones, computer keyboards or calculators. She sent her husband to the supermarket to avoid having to see all the price tags. And she had once had an extreme panic attack when an episode of Coronation Street displayed that subtitles were available on page eight eight eight of teletext. The only reason they could identify for this involved a boy with the number emblazoned on his football shirt pushing her over in infants' school.

No, the main reason he loved working with phobia was the pace of it. Progress could be made so quickly.

Unlike depression, typically caused by a complex combination of factors such as genetic disposition, feelings of self-worth, learned helplessness and the delicate balance of chemicals bouncing around the brain, phobia was a simple glitch in programming. A bad link forged between something that is in essence harmless, and fear. Whilst most people might not like a big spider running across their lounge floor, their fear is tempered with logic: *Something so small cannot harm me*. But the phobic person has no such perspective. They simply have, *Be afraid, be very afraid, BE TERRIFIED*, flooding their mind.

For Steve, treatment involved simply re-setting the system, outweighing their fear with logic and reason. Left to its own devices, fear could be paralysing and in the animal kingdom all-consuming. But human beings possessed the wonder of the cerebral cortex, all that extra grey matter with the capacity to control impulses and emotions. All Steve had to do was teach his clients to harness its power. A tactic which often resulted in their euphoric appreciation.

He felt more than confident that Mr R.J. Cooper would be taking the flight to his sister's wedding down under.

The phone on his desk buzzed.

"Steve, your first appointment is here, and I have Sarah York on the phone. She says she is a personal friend?" Steve had to smile at the unbelieving tone his PA would have adopted when Sarah announced who she was. Hilary was the world's best gatekeeper. She viewed everyone as a liar until proven otherwise, a fact which had saved Steve from many a sales call.

"Thanks, Hilary. Tell Mr Peters I'll be five and put Sarah through."

He waited to hear Sarah's greeting whilst drawing a circle over and over again on his note-pad. He had always liked Sarah, even fancied her for a while at University. A woman capable of in-depth philosophical debate who was still silly enough to giggle like a child at Knock Knock jokes. She also made up one half of the relationship everyone had been most envious of. She and Will not only looked good together, but they fit, in that way some couples have of making it hard to imagine them as anything but a unit. All of which had made the split even more of a shock. In the recent weeks of being there for Will, Steve had had to work hard not to show his own grief for the lost nights of drinking into the small hours. He would miss the three of them putting the world to rights, not to mention the couple's often scathing, but always supportive, feedback on his latest girlfriend. Steve could not see how his best friend would ever find another woman as fabulous as Sarah. And that was what he resented her for most.

"Stevie, have you heard from Will?"

Her affectionate address grated, but he rose above it. She sounded weird. "Not since the weekend, why?"

"Erm… I'm at the house… and…"

Steve stopped drawing and listened more carefully. Was she crying?

"He's gone somewhere… in the car to… to." Sarah took a deep breath and spoke more firmly. "Steve, he left a note for Jean."

It took a second or two for the penny to drop, by which point Sarah had begun talking again.

"The police have told me to contact his friends to see if anyone knows where he might have gone. Did he tell you anything?"

"No." Steve's spoke in barely more than a whisper and it obviously irritated Sarah.

"How did you not see this coming, you spend nearly all your time together?"

His shock quickly turned to anger. "And whose fault is that?"

"Aren't you some sort of expert in depression?" she said,

ignoring his point.

"What's that got to do with it?"

"Well, surely you can spot these things."

Steve felt his jaw clench at her insinuation. "It's not like a broken leg, Sarah."

"But you know what to look for. If he was planning this you would have seen something that made you suspicious?"

"Not if he didn't want me to." Steve thought back over his last few meetings with Will. There had been a change a few weeks back, a melancholy surrounding him that Steve assumed to be a natural move on from the denial phase. Will had lost his appetite, sure, and he looked tired, but nothing out of the ordinary for someone going through a separation. Nothing to indicate any suicidal thoughts. "How long has he been gone?"

"I don't know, longer than an hour which is when I got here, but who knows when he left. It might not even have been today. Oh, god, Steve, I can't lose him."

It's a bit too late to realise that now. Steve bit back the response. She had hurt Will but that did not make her a bad person, there must be a good reason behind her decision. After all, what do we ever really know about people's private lives? Steve knew better than most the secrets people kept hidden from the outside world.

His mind clicked into work mode. "Listen, Sarah, there's a chance he's doing this to punish you which might sound harsh but it could help. You need to write a list of places that mean something to you both... or even, just to you. Your wedding venue, favourite holiday spots, the place he proposed, that sort of thing. Give the list to the police, if he's trying to send you a message he'll pick some place significant."

"And if he's not?" Sarah had started crying again.

"That's harder, much harder. He could pick somewhere important to him still or he may just select at random. It's impossible to know." Steve was already logging off the network and powering down his computer as he spoke. "Do the list, Sarah, and I'll take a drive out to anywhere I can think of."

"Thanks, Steve."

"Just call me if you hear anything."

He buzzed for Hilary to come through. She looked shocked to see him putting his coat on.

"Sorry to do this, Hilary, but can you reschedule today's appointments. I have an emergency."

"Oh dear, is there anything I can do?"

"No, no but thank you. I doubt I'll be back in today, so can you also send my apologies to the meeting." He dashed out, avoiding eye contact with his waiting client then returned momentarily. "Hilary, if by any chance my friend William York calls, will you ask him to stay where he is, and then ring me immediately with his whereabouts."

The PA frowned a little behind her neat fringe, but nodded without asking for clarification. Another reason why Steve liked her so much: she knew when not to be nosey.

Chapter Seven

Crop fields stretched ahead for as far as he could see, and in amongst, a dozen or so people tended and harvested. On either side of him, small, stone cottages stood in neat rows, their gardens packed with gently swaying flowers. Most of the plants he did not recognise, apart from the sunflowers with their necks craned and their petals flung wide in worship. An array of fragrance filled his nose: jasmine, lavender, freshly cut grass, warm bread and Weetabix. Someone was brewing beer; the hops always reminded him of his grandma's favourite cereal.

What the…?

An impact from behind interrupted his thoughts. William staggered forward from the spot where just a moment before he had halted in his tracks. For a second, he imagined he had been shot, but it was a fleeting idea. The collision against his back came from something large, something running, something human.

He saw her falling from the corner of his eye and held out a hand to stop her, but the momentum had pushed him out of reach. Sorella hit the pathway with a dull thud, followed by a short silence and then a shriek of pain.

Was it his imagination or had the people in the field stood in unison a fraction before her scream? William pushed the feeling of unease aside and knelt beside her. "What hurts?"

"Why did you stop?" She sounded angry. "Arrgh." She grabbed her right arm below the elbow.

"Is it your arm?" William asked as Caro appeared at the door.

"Shoulder…" She moaned in pain as she rocked into a sitting position.

William could see that her arm sat too far forward on her torso. It was a familiar sight. His father had suffered from a recurring shoulder dislocation for most of Will's youth. William had been seven when he first had to pop it back into position. His Mum said she could not stand to try; said the idea made her feel sick. So with trembling hands and a racing heart, little Will had to follow the instructions spat by his father through clenched teeth. The spittle running down his Dad's chin, and the wideness of his eyes, had scared William out of his wits. And for weeks after, he would wake in panic from another dream where his dear old Dad had become the world's scariest monster. But as the years went by, it became easier to handle until he hardly even broke a sweat.

"Has this happened before?" William said, thinking she could not have hit the ground that hard. Maybe she also suffered from a recurring condition.

Sorella shook her head.

"We need to get her to the city." Caro stooped to lift his sister.

"It's dislocated, it needs to be reset." William knew that the quicker the joint went back in place the better. His father had been the victim of too long a delay, and extra damage caused whilst moving him. It was the reason the injury had returned time and time again. "Can't you do it?" he asked Caro.

Sorella screamed as Caro attempted to lift her. Her brother let her sit back down. "My expertise centres on neurology not biology. I have never treated a dislocation and knowledge alone is not enough. It is safer to have a specialist treat her."

William had stopped listening. The colour had drained from Sorella's face and she had begun to cry. He placed a hand on her good arm. "Lie down for me."

"What are you doing?" Caro asked.

An audience had gathered around them: half a dozen men and women, and a young boy with white-blond hair. The boy grasped a half-eaten stick of rhubarb in one dirty hand.

William replayed the years of doing this before through his head and tried not to think about how much time had passed since then. "Sorella, look at me." He waited for her eyes to meet his. They had lost their silvery sheen and become the damp grey of road puddles. "I've done this before, many many times-"

Caro interrupted. "No, no, you cannot do this. She needs proper care. The shoulder could be irreparably damaged-"

William held a hand up to silence Caro, but continued to look at Sorella. "Will you trust me?"

"Get him off her." Caro's voice sounded once more commanding and William felt hands encircle both his upper arms. "Jed, Lal, help me lift her."

The two tallest men stepped forward from the crowd.

"No… wait…" Sorella said.

William's captors halted but did not let go.

She looked up at him. "How many times?"

"A dozen, maybe more."

After a second or two, she nodded.

"Sorella-"

"I trust him," she said interrupting her brother's protest.

Caro stared back at her, making no response.

William moved to her side, gently taking the wrist of her injured arm. He made his voice as soothing as he could, needing her relaxed and calm. "I know it hurts and that will get worse for a moment, but as soon as I'm done it will stop okay?"

"Promise?" She let her head rest on the floor and closed her eyes. He could tell she had tensed her body.

"I promise and I need you to relax. So take a deep breath for me" He waited until she did as he asked. "Good… and relax your body as much as you can." William watched until he saw the tension leave her neck and torso then he took a breath of his own.

Please let this work. "I want you to count to ten for me, like this, one... two... three..., and by the time you reach ten it will be over."

Her chin jerked once to show she understood and then she began. "One... two..."

William counted the first two numbers with her whilst rotating her wrist so her palm faced upwards.

"Three... four..." She took a sharp gasp of breath as he began to slide her elbow towards her belly button.

"You're doing really well, keep going." With his other arm, he leant his weight against her shoulder bone.

"Five..." Her voice shook with the pain.

"If you mess this up it could cause permanent damage." Caro sounded both nervous and irritated.

"Not helping," said William continuing to build the tension in Sorella's dislocation.

Six... sev... Oh!"

William felt the humeral head pop back into its socket.

I did it. He breathed a sigh of relief. "Any pain now?"

"Yes," she said.

Oh shit.

"I knew this was not wise. Lal, inform ANN of the situation. We now have an emergency. I should not have let you do this," Caro said.

"Where? Where's the pain?" Will heard the panic in his own voice.

"My wrist." She lifted her head a little to look at his hand squeezing her lower arm.

William let go immediately with a small laugh of relief. "Sorry."

"The shoulder is not giving any pain?" said Caro, and was that a hint of disappointment in his words?

Sorella slowly sat up without putting any weight on her right hand. "It's a little sore but that's all. Thank you, William."

"My pleasure," he said.

Her expression once more became angry. "Your fault! Why did you stop?"

William shook his head in amusement. She never did say quite what he expected her to.

"I will feel better when I've checked you over myself." Caro looked at William. "I take it you are leaving now."

In all the excitement his departure had slipped his mind. William took another look around. Their audience had moved away apart from the little boy. He chewed on his rhubarb and stared at Will as if he had magical powers. William stood and ruffled the boy's hair. "Pretty cool, hey?" he said.

The boy nodded.

"Don't try it at home." William winked before turning back to Caro and Sorella. "If it's okay by you, I'd like to stay for the examination, make sure I did it right."

"Seb, come away." A woman with the same white blonde hair as the boy grabbed his arm, the motion yanking the rhubarb from his mouth. She avoided looking at William and he could hear in her voice that he made her nervous.

This place made no sense.

William caught up with Sorella as she followed her brother down the white corridor. "I'm sorry, I didn't know you were following."

"You seemed determined to leave, what stopped you?"

"It was…" He glanced at her interested eyes not sure how to explain. "Not what I expected."

"Which was?"

Caro held the door open and William hung back a little. He had no desire to return to the room where he had awoken earlier. Staying in the doorway, he watched as Caro checked his sister's arm. And if the bodiless voice had troubled him before, it positively terrified him now.

"What happened?" said the supposed computer.

"Sorella fell," said Caro.

"Because of William, he stopped unexpectedly. There was nothing I could do." Sorella flashed William a look.

"I really wish you would let me see everywhere," said the computer.

"So you could have a laugh at my expense, I think not ANN."

The computer chuckled, sending a shiver down William's spine. It had a sense of humour.

"The joint feels good to me," said Caro "Do you concur, ANNy?"

"I do. You performed a very competent procedure, William."

The use of his name made him jump. Her voice was everywhere in this room. They must be broadcasting in some kind of surround sound and it gave him the creeps. Computers were nowhere near advanced enough to communicate like this. They did not find things amusing, and they did not chat like old friends. He had read in one journal article that IBM were beginning to model systems on the brain's neural networks, but no real progress had been made. The human mind was too complex in its storage, retrieval and problem-solving capability for people to know how on earth it did what it did. And even if some advanced organisation had managed to crack it, would they really have it here in the midst of a rural community in North Yorkshire?

William almost laughed out loud at his own stupidity. He was not usually so gullible. "Excuse me," he said.

This time he heard her footsteps behind him. "William?"

When he turned she was cradling the elbow of her damaged shoulder. "You almost had me for a while there," he said. "It was pretty convincing, the whole artificial neural network thing and the brain upgrades." The woman frowned. She obviously did not like to be caught out. "Who is it intended to fool anyway? I mean it must have cost a bob or two to set it up and make it so realistic, but why? That's the bit I don't get. I suppose people with no knowledge of the brain or how computers work might believe it, and then you could what? Scare them with it? Trick them into confessing something maybe?"

"We're not doing any of those things."

"So what are you doing then? Or more importantly, who for?"

Sorella stepped a little closer, her expression concerned. "William, we are just trying to survive the best we can. We do not work for anyone other than each other."

Was it a cult? Run by some crackpot genius who had lost the plot? Caro seemed a plausible candidate. "And who exactly are *each other*?"

"Our community, the people who live here, the villagers you saw outside. We are good people, William. I trusted you when you asked me to, I only ask the same in return."

Oh my god, he had handed them the emotional blackmail they needed on a plate. Next they would be asking him to just listen and give their beliefs a good hearing before rejecting them. It would all be so reasonable, until he tried to leave of course.

"Cut the crap, Sorella. You and your brother, and that woman who's pretending to be some advanced computer, have people working in the fields whilst you wander around this place, which, quite frankly, must have cost a fortune. I take it they all had to donate something to the cause when they joined you?"

"I'm only trying to help you."

"You just keep telling yourself that, but I'm not buying it." The time had come to leave. The longer he stayed, the harder they would try to keep him. He walked towards the exit once more.

"It's you living a lie, William, not I."

He carried on walking without slowing.

"You say you live in Ilkley, but that town has not been in existence for over fifty years. You say you travelled by car and yet you arrived having lost all your metal belongings, telling me you must have used the old teleport. You have no primary, which has been compulsory for three generations, and I can only assume you have been kept away from society somehow. I understand being faced with all this must be hard to take in, but this is reality, William."

Naturally, he did not make it out of the door. He could not pin-point exactly what had stopped him. Ilkley not existing for over fifty years could have been it, or the word *teleport*.

Sorella came to his side and took hold of his hand. "Let me help you. I can make this easier if you let me."

William looked into her silver eyes and spoke with some regret. "You really are a crazy person, aren't you?" He extracted his hand from hers and walked into the dwindling daylight.

Chapter Eight

William opened his eyes to the sound of the dawn chorus and looked across the field with dismay. His limbs felt stiff from sleeping on the floor and when he stood to stretch, the pain in his feet made him sit again. He dared not remove his torn and bloodied socks, not wanting to see the damage that running without shoes had caused. The arm of his t-shirt, where he had rested his head, was also smeared red. He checked the skin underneath and then his face, finding blood caked across his cheek. His first ever nosebleed, lovely. He wiped the blood away with the bottom of his t-shirt and took a couple of deep breaths.

Rising more carefully this time, he stood for a moment until the nausea passed, and then limped across the field to the road.

He must have the wrong place. The patchwork surface of cracked tarmac was sprouting regular tufts of green undergrowth. And yet, the way the lane curved away to the left and snaked down the hill to the right felt familiar. How it nestled into the small valley of hills rising ahead of him and behind him, looked just as he remembered. He studied the landscape more carefully. The densely packed foliage that coated the hillsides he did not recall, but the underlying architecture looked right he felt sure.

William rubbed his eyes as if that might tune his vision and set the view back to what it had been.

There had to be a logical explanation. Lots of places around these hills probably looked similar. He was just disorientated. But as he set off walking down the hill, William had a horrible feeling that this stretch of now broken, deserted road was exactly where he had parked his car.

When he had left Sorella and her crazy talk behind, people had moved away from him as he walked through the village. Some did so subtly, like the woman hanging out her washing who muttered something about being late, before heading indoors. Others simply stopped and stared when he came into view, then purposefully changed course. He had seen the blond boy, Seb, standing on a doorstep and William held a hand up to wave. A moment later, an anonymous arm tugged the boy inside. It was as if they had reason to be wary of him rather than the other way around.

At the edge of a surprisingly large settlement – he must have seen at least a hundred cottages – an elderly man in a tattered old trilby sat on a garden wall. William recalled him from the group who had gathered after Sorella's fall.

"That was some fancy work you did back there," the man said as William passed by.

"Just trying to help," William said without slowing.

"She likes yer, you know. Can you tell?"

And there it was: the attempt to make him stay a little longer. Just long enough to reel him in.

"Rest of 'em'll be glad to see the back, mind," continued the old man.

Clever, make him feel that it's a tough group to get into so membership is more of an achievement. William had always been fascinated by cults. Part of him would enjoy staying to observe how they did what they did. But he knew enough to know it would take strength of character to resist. And given his recent bout of depression, staying would not be the brightest decision.

"Not you though?" William said, unable to resist discovering the old man's strategy.

"Tsk, they know diddly squat. S'all paranoia and make-believe."

William considered asking what he meant, but decided against it. Best not to get too sucked in. "Can you point me in the direction of the two domes?" he said instead.

The old man turned his rugged, weather-worn face to William. "That's quite a trek to make in yer socks."

William glanced at his feet. "I'm sure I'll manage."

The man nodded as if he expected as much. "Just follow yer nose for five or so miles and you'll see them to your left." The old man rose and walked back towards his house. "If you see anyone, might be a good idea to keep a low profile… if yer know what I mean."

William had no idea at all. He watched the old man checking flowers in his garden and wondered if he should ask why. Then he smiled to himself. Build intrigue and anxiety - *that* was the strategy. The old guy was good too, not obvious enough to raise suspicion in any unsuspecting visitors.

William set off as directed, wondering if they would be disappointed or philosophical about his departure.

By the time he reached the domes darkness had fallen. Despite the bright moonlight, William had begun to think he might miss them but he need not have worried. They loomed larger and even more menacing in their darkened state; as if gigantic scoops had been gouged in the hillside revealing nothing but blackness within.

William gave them a wide berth and came to a standstill at the base of the cliff. His feet felt a little sore from the walk, but as yet he detected no blisters. And once he had climbed up here, he would be home and dry. He estimated he had walked for no more than a few hours from the car, and for most of that he had followed a well-marked footpath. It should be easy to get back.

All thoughts of ending things had been pushed aside by a new imperative. He needed to tell someone about this group. They would no doubt be preying on the vulnerable.

He looked up at the darkened hillside. In his mind, he had remembered it as an easy climb. In reality, it was steep, sheer and impossible to see any routes up. Picking a starting point at random, William scaled a few feet off the ground. But soon his hands grabbed nothing more than moss that slid away from the rock in great chunks. He clambered down and moved a few feet along to try again. Once more, after a couple of movements, he found himself flat against the hillside with nowhere to go. In frustration, he scrambled back to the bottom, scraping the skin off his elbow as he went. He would have to find a way around.

For the next ten minutes, William jogged along the base of the cliffs, weaving in and out of the long grasses. After half a mile or so, the gradient of the hillside changed and he began to carefully pick his way up. The long ferns and grasses made for good hand holds and his shoe-free feet easily found purchase. At the top, he rested for a few minutes to catch his breath.

The glow of city lights illuminated the horizon and nothing but moonlit countryside lay in between. The beauty of it caught William unawares. The simple magnificence of nature suddenly made his sadness feel very small.

Tiredness eventually brought him to his feet. He needed a hot mug of tea and his bed. Tonight, he would not even care that he had the whole thing to himself.

He followed the ridge along looking for this morning's footpath, but it remained elusive. Assuming it must be further inland, he began to jog, snaking his way across the moor and searching for something familiar. His jog turned into a run, as he retraced his steps and tried alternative routes. The place proved unrecognisable, monotonous and vast. It stretched out in all directions with no landmarks to distinguish one part from the next.

He quickly became disorientated.

The next few hours passed slowly and painfully. The hard, uneven ground under his feet kept taking him by surprise, twisting his ankles as he stumbled over small mounds and into crevices.

By the time he spotted a familiar smooth boulder, his muscles ached as much as his bruised and blistered feet.

William remembered the distinctive large rock from his morning's climb from the car. He had paused alongside it to get his breath back, and remembered seeing his silver Audi sitting in the valley like an abandoned toy. He strained to see it now, but darkness shrouded the basin.

On his descent he fell twice. He tore his jeans and grazed his palms, but the new pains barely registered. The idea of making his way safely home brought a wave of euphoria. He even began to jog once he made it onto flat ground. Finding himself lost had scared him more than he thought.

As his eyes adjusted to the darkness and the road came into view, William slowed to make sense of what he was seeing. Or more importantly, what he could not see: his Audi.

He walked to the road and looked back at the boulder to check his bearings. It should be here. Then he looked at his feet. The tarmac should feel smooth and flat not like walking on rubble.

William fought back tears of frustration. *Where the hell am I?*

He staggered back to the foot of the hill and collapsed on a patch of soft ground. How could he still be lost?

Just take a moment to think it through and decide what to do next, he told himself, but within seconds he was asleep.

Dawn had only broken an hour or so ago, but already the sun felt hot on his face and arms. William's slow limp along the uneven surface proved uncomfortable. He tried to suppress the growing certainty that less than twenty-four hours earlier, the crumbling mess that lay before him had been a winding stretch of rain-soaked tarmac.

In the distance, he spotted an adjoining road. It looked in better condition than this one and he limped a little quicker, trying to ignore the wetness in his right sock.

He could think of only one rational explanation. Well, two actually. The first was beyond ridiculous for an atheist like William, but there was a chance he had been wrong, and that all those God-botherers had been on the money. He could actually see the humour of an Almighty who would place you in a recognisable world tipped on its head to punish your unbelieving soul. What better way to say, 'Ha, you were wrong, sucker, look what shit I can pull on your idea of reality.'

The alternative explanation he could not even bring himself to acknowledge, because it would make him crazy; a ranting, irrational fantasist, no better than the raft of alien abductees he had seen on TV documentaries, a person to be mocked, avoided and feared.

The image of Sorella's villagers scurrying away popped into his head, and William felt queasy.

"This is stupid, just get back to civilisation." The croakiness of his voice reminded him he had drunk nothing since yesterday. A realisation which brought a wave of relief. Dehydration was enough to make you think crazy thoughts and see the world wrong.

A small stream had been moving ever closer as he walked. He could hear the gurgling as it tumbled over rocks and pebbles. William left the road and crossed the field towards it. The soft grass under his feet felt good after the cracked tarmac. As the water came into view, bubbling and frothing along its narrow channel, his thirst became all-consuming. He sank to his knees by the nearest clear pool and gulped handfuls of fresh water. The cold liquid shocked his system to life and he lay flat on his belly to sink his face into the water and drink deeply.

In the midst of throwing water over his head and neck, William caught sight of movement on the road. He jumped to his feet to see the top of a vehicle pass by. The stream sat in a valley and he knew he would not be visible unless the person looked down. William began to scramble back up the field shouting and waving his arms.

If he had had his wits about him, he might have questioned why he heard no engine. But his only thought was to get high enough for them to see him.

The small white car did not slow. William followed its course up the hill and around the corner. As its profile came into view, he stopped waving and tried to process what he saw. The teardrop vehicle looked like nothing he had ever seen before. It was not just the shape, but the silence and the speed. How could something on such uneven ground move so fast, so smoothly?

One very simple question occurred to William and his new mission became to find its answer.

The way he saw it, he had three options. The first – to continue searching for where he had left his car – felt too demoralising after last night's experience, and he quickly discounted it. Despite his considered nature, he believed in the brain's ability to see clearly in critical situations. Sometimes you had to trust your gut. It was what had told him something had changed with Sarah; that it was no longer a trial separation but the end.

She had been calling once a week for her post and William had liked the contact. Even though he hated what she was doing to them – *to him* – he still needed her in his life. During the tense visits, Sarah would remain largely quiet to avoid her husband's barbed retorts. It made him feel like less of a victim to make her squirm. But that day she seemed different. Nothing obvious, Sarah was too intelligent for that. She had dressed as normal, she sported no new hairdo or extra perfume and she said nothing out of the ordinary. But the truth screamed at William across the kitchen. He could not say what the change had been. Something too insignificant to articulate, but his brain had detected it. His clever, clever brain had cut through the noise to the nub of the matter. As she sifted her mail and chatted about the weather, it whispered, *she's happy*.

That visit changed everything.

That visit brought him here.

William shook the memory away and concentrated on the matter in hand. He estimated it was a mile and a half, maybe two, down to the other road. Yesterday he had driven for a good twenty minutes without seeing a village or farmhouse. So that could be a morning's worth of walking before finding another person. Other cars might come along but he could not guarantee it. He could walk up the hill in the hope that whoever had just passed him had headed somewhere close, but that was even more of a gamble. He had no idea where this road went to. It left too much uncertainty.

'If you see anyone, might be a good idea to keep a low profile.' Why would the old guy say that? The fact that William could think of no answer, made the decision easy.

Option three it was.

William set off back to the place he had spent the night and beyond: back to where he knew he would find people.

Yesterday's footpath had completely gone. He found no sign of the wooden posts he had used to guide him, and no well-worn trail across the fields. No wonder he'd become so disorientated last night.

Every step along the route increased his unease. *So different, so quickly.*

Standing once more at the cliff edge, he saw the changes more clearly than at any other point in the last twenty-six hours. Yesterday, the cliff below had been mostly bare rock with a scattering of heather, now it was carpeted in green. Waist-high ferns crowded its base, and the field which stretched ahead no longer contained grass well-grazed by livestock, but grass that grew tall and lush. Dominating his view, two huge domes filled yesterday's empty horizon.

William felt his hands shaking. This bizarre turn of events had laid down a challenge, presenting not so much a reason to live as a deep-seated need to survive.

A light from below blinded him momentarily. When his vision cleared he saw a small figure crouching over the white column at the base of the cliff. The silver bangle on her wrist caught the sun again and bounced it in his direction.

The wave of relief he felt on seeing Sorella came as a surprise.

William retraced his steps until he was confident he could clamber down the hill without falling. Then he limped as quickly as he could back to where she stood.

She saw him coming from a few yards away and rushed over to meet him. Her eyes grew wide as she scanned the blood on his top, his torn clothing and his dirty socks. "William, you look terrible. What happened?"

"Thanks, nice to see you too." He moved to a patch of shade cast by the hillside, and wiped the sweat from his face with his t-shirt.

"Did they do this to you?" Sorella said.

"They?"

"I mean, someone… did someone hurt you?"

"No, this is all self-inflicted."

"Why on earth-"

"You said I could trust you," William interrupted as he hobbled a little closer to her.

"Yes."

"Good. I need you to answer a question for me."

"Of course."

She looked a little taken aback when he gripped the top of her arms. "What year is it?"

Confusion crossed her eyes and she began to shake her head. "I don't understand, why-"

"Why can come later, just tell me the date." He tightened his hands a fraction.

"Okay, okay. It's April 11th 2216."

William released her arms and actually staggered backwards. Although he had suspected as much, hearing it confirmed shocked him. "2216? Two... two... one... six?"

"What year did you think it was?"

"I need to sit down." He did not look for a suitable spot. He simply dropped to his knees where he was.

"What's happened to you, William? Have you been kept somewhere? Imprisoned?" When he made no response she knelt beside him. "Don't worry. I know it must be difficult to have lost track of time, but we'll take care of you. I'm sure things are not as bad as they seem."

William looked her in the eye. "I was born on June seventeeth, 1975," he said.

Sorella's expression changed from confused to anxious before she started to laugh.

Chapter Nine

"It is not beyond imagination for him to have done his research."

"But why, what would he achieve? It makes no sense."

"It makes perfect sense. They have sent him."

"Here we are again back to the spy theory."

"Yes. You are supposed to feel sorry for him, Sorella. They have designed him that way."

"They? Designed him? Who exactly is the fantasist here?"

William heard their voices in the next room, the words only just audible. It took him a moment to recall where he was. Sorella had brought him to a small room next to ANN's dome where he could rest. He sat up from the black sofa, and moved aside the blanket someone had covered him with.

"You cannot actually believe him?" Caro sounded incredulous.

"Is it any worse than believing *they* would send someone to spy on us with the cover story of being a time traveller?" said Sorella.

"It is a moot point. Either scenario is out of the question because people cannot travel through time."

"It's theoretically possible."

"But not likely."

William made slow progress towards their voices. His leg muscles ached more than they ever had following his half marathons, and his toenails were blackened with bruises.

"So your conclusion is what? He has made the whole thing up?" Sorella sounded annoyed.

"We have no way of knowing if his brain functions properly. This delusion could be symptomatic of many diseases of the mind."

William stepped into the doorway. "I would have thought with

57

all your advanced equipment you could come up with some grander theory than my being crazy?" His appearance made both Caro and Sorella jump a little.

Caro sat at a glass table. Its surface displayed pictures and documents that Caro moved around by hand. His sister stood opposite with her hands flat on the glass. She looked embarrassed that William had caught them having this conversation.

"How are you feeling now?" She stood, smoothing her hands over her waist as she addressed William.

"A little better thanks. And I really don't care if you don't believe me," he said looking at Caro. "I just need to get home."

The other man continued to organise his images. "So you admit the idea does not sound credible?"

William took a seat on a stool by the wall. It felt good to take the weight off his feet. "Sure. If someone turned up at my house saying they had been born in the seventeen hundreds I'd ring my mate Steve to have them sectioned."

"Sectioned?" Sorella said.

Caro said, "It was what they did to people they considered mad in the twenty-first century. They locked them up in depraved conditions against their will."

William gave a curt laugh. "It's not quite like that."

Sorella pulled her own stool up to the table and sat. "Tell Caro the things you told me."

At the domes, he had waited until she got a handle on her giggles before speaking. He told her all he had experienced since leaving home yesterday morning. As he spoke she fell silent, sitting beside him and staring ahead. When he finished, she did not comment, simply rising and taking his hand to pull him to his feet. He had followed her to what looked like a waltzer car with a glass roof. Inside, six seats were positioned at regular intervals, with no sign of any controls. The last of his denial dissolved away as they took their seats and he felt them move smoothly and silently towards the road. He leant against the chair back, his head beginning to pound. Which is when her questions began: an endless list of facts he knew she was requesting to corroborate his story.

"I don't think your brother is interested in things it is not beyond imagination for me to have researched."

"No I am not. Despite his lack of upgrades, your new friend is bright enough to have committed to memory that Elizabeth II was on the throne, that the government was a coalition led by David Cameron of the Conservatives and Nick Clegg of the Liberal Democrats, that the most popular mode of transport was petrol or diesel powered cars, that the USA was the world's most influential country, and that a global recession was taking place."

"So ask him something else." Sorella waved her arm across the table top.

William realised the documents formed part of a test Caro had prepared.

Caro looked at his sister for a long moment before sifting through the images. He seemed reluctant to take part, as if he considered the whole thing a farce. When he did speak, his voice sounded even more devoid of emotion than usual. "You say that for you yesterday morning was April, twenty eleven?" He held his finger on a document too small for William to see and waited for the nod of agreement. "What were the weather conditions at the time?"

"There was a storm. It started around eight thirty a.m., probably with high wind speeds recorded."

Caro flicked that document aside and focused on another. "Was twenty ten a white Christmas in Ilkley?"

"Yes."

"When did it start snowing?"

"November. Sorry not sure of the exact date." William did not hide his sarcasm. Caro ignored it.

"What shops were on The Grove in Ilkley?"

William closed his eyes to picture the main street of his home town. Working from one end to the other, he reeled off as many places he could remember then opened his eyes. "How many did I get?"

Caro flicked to another document without responding. "What stations did the Ilkley to Leeds train stop at?"

"Ben Rhydding, Burley in Wharfedale, Menston and Guiseley."

Caro was moving faster through his records. "Who owned the fuel station in Ben Rhydding?"

"Tesco."

"What happened to VAT on January fourth?"

"Increased from seventeen and a half per cent to twenty. Are we done yet?"

"What was the country's most popular television show?"

"God, I have no idea. Probably something like the X Factor or Strictly Come Dancing."

Caro halted and looked at William for the first time.

"See?" Sorella leant towards her brother.

William tried to work out what he had said.

"Are you a religious man, William?"

"No, why?"

"Have you heard enough?" Sorella asked. "Did he get anything wrong? Did he hesitate to answer anything?"

"Did I pass?"

Caro sat back from the table, a frown creasing his brow. "You make no sense."

"I thought I was quite articulate."

Caro had the good grace to smile a little at the attempted humour.

"So can *I* have a few questions answered now?" said William sitting forward.

"I am not sure we can-"

"Of course, go ahead." Sorella cut off her brother without glancing his way.

"I take it from your conversation earlier that time travel is not an everyday occurrence?"

"It is not possible," said Caro.

"Someone couldn't have invented it over the past few hundred years?"

Caro shook his head.

"Can you be certain?"

"No, but ANN can. She can link to every other neural network. If this technology had been achieved she would know."

"I take it you've checked?"

"Naturally."

William rubbed his face with his hands. So no chance of jumping in a DeLorean and typing in his time coordinates home then. "But you *can* teleport?"

"Travelling through space is more straightforward than travelling through time."

"And you thought I'd teleported?" he said to Sorella.

"There's an old teleporting base out by the hub from when they built it."

"The hub being the domes?"

Sorella nodded.

"And the base, the white column in the ground?"

"Yes," she said.

"That's where I woke up."

"Having lost all your metallic belongings," said Sorella.

"Is that relevant?"

Caro answered this time. "Due to the levels of magnetism used in the teleport, metal and anything surrounding it gets repelled. Any garments with metal on them or in their pockets would be destroyed in the process."

William looked from one of his companions to the other. "So it's pretty certain I teleported somehow?"

"There is no station there anymore, only the base. Nothing would work," said Caro to no one in particular.

"It could act as a receiver. A point of orientation for whatever William came through."

Caro considered his sister for a moment. "Like a wormhole?"

"A wormhole?" William wondered fleetingly if he had wandered on to some science fiction film set.

"Again it is a theoretical concept. ANN can you elaborate?"

"As you wish." The woman's voice sounded as loud and as close as ever.

William flinched and scanned the ceiling but could not see any speakers. "Where is that coming from?"

Sorella giggled at his question. "ANN connects to the hearing centre in your temporal lobe."

"She's in my head?"

The computer did not react to the panic in William's voice. "Wormhole is a term coined to describe a tunnel which theoretically connects two separate points in time, allowing travellers to step from one to the other. It is not a physical entity that has ever been witnessed, although, physicists have claimed success in creating miniature versions. But these are highly unstable in nature and nothing that a human being could pass through."

"Is it feasible someone might have had a breakthrough and you wouldn't know about it?" said Will.

"Someone with a protected network might be able to hide such a discovery but there is a bigger problem than that. If it were invented now in the twenty third Century, this would become point zero in time travel. People from now could move forward in time but no one could go back farther than the point at which the device was invented."

"So for me to have come through a man-made wormhole, someone in 2011 or earlier had to have invented it."

"And of course we know that no one ever did create such a thing," said ANN.

"So what then? How did I get here?"

There was a beat of silence before ANN spoke again. "There are only two plausible explanations, alien technology or natural phenomena."

"You are forgetting delusional mind and con artist," said Caro without a hint of humour.

Chapter Ten

"Your brother's not a big fan of mine is he?"

William and Sorella walked through the village towards her house. She had offered him the use of her spare room for the night. She had also cleaned and bandaged his feet and he now wore a pair of slipper-like shoes provided by Caro. The people they passed along the way did not react as badly as they had when he walked the streets alone. Most greeted Sorella warmly and cast nothing but curious glances his way.

"He takes his responsibility to the community very seriously. Everyone relies on him and it makes him very cautious. I think he might actually like you underneath. It is not often we have such interesting company."

"When you say interesting, I take it you mean strange?"

She held open a small wooden gate in the fence of a mid-terraced cottage. The path to the door ran through the centre of a traditional English country garden. On either side, a mass of tall colourful flowers filled all the available space. "I mean interesting," she said with a smile, closing the gate behind him. "Take a seat in the shade. I'll fetch us something to drink."

William sat on the garden bench as instructed and raised a hand to the woman opposite. She nodded as she wrapped a long cardigan more tightly around her then scurried inside her house. In the window upstairs, a young girl with long brown hair stared out. She looked about the age of the teenage girls who lived on William's road. He smiled as their eyes met and the girl immediately ducked out of sight.

The small lane looked similar to the others they had passed. Each contained half a dozen terraced cottages on either side, all fronted by well cared-for gardens. William had visited villages like this on walking holidays, sat in their cafés enjoying tea and cake, or outside their pubs drinking beer. The familiarity felt both reassuring and disconcerting. Should things not be *more* different?

"Hope you like lemonade." Sorella handed him a large tumbler, and joined him on the seat. "So, I expect you have a few more questions."

"Just a few," he said taking a sip. "That's lovely." The home-made drink had just the right amount of sweetness to soften the tartness of the lemons. It still made his taste buds flinch but in a pleasant way. He glanced up at the now empty window opposite. "Why is everyone scared of me?"

Sorella followed his eye line as she swirled the ice in her drink. "People here are feeling a little paranoid. They've had a rough time recently."

Paranoia and make-believe, that's what the old man had said. "How so?"

"We lost a family in tragic circumstances so people are wary of outsiders."

"What sort of circumstances?"

Sorella studied her drink for a while. "You have enough to deal with. You don't need to be worrying about our problems. People just find you difficult to read, they are…*we* are used to knowing each other's moods."

He had forgotten his early fears that this woman could somehow tell what he was thinking. "You read minds?"

"Only moods. The primary allows us to detect how others are feeling, it aids social harmony."

"How is that even possible?"

She faced him. "Do you know much about how the brain works? I'm not sure what knowledge people would have had in your day."

"I know more than most."

She looked intrigued, tilting her head and raising her eyebrows.

"I'm a psychologist by profession, occupational not clinical, but I know the basics."

She laughed a little and shook her head. "Promise me you will not tell my brother that just yet."

"Why?"

She fidgeted on the seat, crossing and uncrossing her ankles. "Let's just say it will make him even more suspicious. So I presume you know that the brain communicates using electrochemical impulses, and that different regions command different emotional and cognitive functions?"

William nodded and shared what he knew. "Higher level thinking occurs in the cerebral cortex, which is developed through experiential learning, whilst emotions are linked to the limbic system and have a more evolutionary basis."

"Exactly. So the brain activity linked to fear, anger and surprise, for instance, is relatively consistent across human beings. What triggers it may differ but the neural pathways and transmitters are -"

"The same," said William with just a degree of wonder in his voice. He knew the amygdala in the brain had been associated with fear responses, and that certain neurons fired when people felt surprised. But to be able to track them all like reading a book was in a different league.

"Well, similar enough. There is always variation, although that is reducing now."

William made a mental note to come back to her last point. "But how can you access each other's moods without some kind of brain scanner?"

"That is where the primary comes in. It is an enhancement to the limbic system that in part tracks activity and then broadcasts it to other primaries in range."

"Shit." William felt glad she had no way of detecting the extent of his anxiety at this point in time.

"I imagine this is a lot to take in. I revised my history a little whilst you were sleeping so I appreciate how…different the world today must seem."

"So you know how everyone is feeling all the time?"

She finished her lemonade and placed the glass on the floor. "Those close by, yes."

"How close?"

"It depends to some extent on the intensity. At the moment I can tune into only those in neighbouring houses, but if someone was really scared or hurt they might be a few streets away and I would feel it."

"Like when you fell?"

She absent-mindedly stroked her shoulder. "You noticed?"

"I thought I was imagining it…how quickly people reacted…but they knew you were in pain before you screamed?"

"Yes. They would have felt it. It's like the echo of an emotion. You know it's not your own, and often you know exactly whose it is."

"How?"

She shrugged. "I have no idea. I suppose it must be a little like detecting different scents or sounds. Over time, people's emotions come to have a unique essence."

William gave a small laugh of disbelief. How the hell did they not go insane with all that noise in their heads, and what about personal privacy? "How do you cope with all the interference?"

Sorella smiled then stood and began collecting flowers from

her garden. "For us it is normal. The primary is administered at birth so we don't know any different. In some of the early trials on adults the procedure led to severe mental breakdowns. I think it was too much input for minds not developed enough to cope."

"But a baby's brain is at its most flexible."

She nodded and selected some vivid purple foxgloves to go with the white, blue and yellow spray she already had in her hand. The normality of her task was incongruous with the nature of their conversation. William found himself focusing on her bouquet to help him keep it together.

"I actually find it hard to understand how *you* cope. I've read that many people were adept at hiding their true emotions and that misunderstandings were commonplace. Does it not make life very difficult to not be sure of how others are feeling?"

William thought of Sarah's admission that she had spent a year hiding her desire to leave him. "It has its moments."

Sorella finished her selection and eyed him as if she wanted to ask for elaboration. Instead, she gestured for him to follow her. "Come inside. I think it's time I made a start on something to eat."

The door opened onto another homely kitchen. A large black range filled the wall on the right and, opposite, the wooden cupboards displayed intricate carvings of plants and flowers. Under the window, a two-basin sink sat on top of a separate cabinet where Sorella now filled a vase with water for her flowers. Only a few unfamiliar gadgets hinted that this might be a home from the distant future. William once more doubted his whereabouts.

"When was your house built?" he asked, walking through the kitchen and into a small dining area. A long red sofa covered in cushions separated the two rooms.

"The whole village is between one hundred and fifty and two

hundred years old. It started as a small farming community back in your day. In fact, my range here is over three hundred years old, even older than you." Sorella watched him make his study. "Not what you expected I take it."

"Well after the talking computers and mood reading, it's a bit twenty-first century don't you think?"

She smiled. "If you must know, I have old-fashioned tastes, which is probably why I like you."

Once more William felt relieved that she had no insight into the effect of her words on him, simply flashing a smile.

"But I imagine this is more the type of thing you expected."

With no warning a rotating 3D sphere popped into existence in the space between them. As William watched, it morphed into a group of foot-high people having an argument. Then it moulded into a miniature orchestra which grew bigger and bigger until he had to take a step back. Next, the mass of musicians dissolved into ocean waves that rolled from the ceiling and crashed at his feet. Sorella smiled at his expression as the water rolled up into a sphere again.

"How does that work?" He bent to look at the floor underneath and then stared up at the ceiling, but saw nothing. "How do you operate it?"

"It responds to commands like most technology."

William looked at her. She obviously expected him to work it out for himself, but as far as he could tell she had said and done nothing.

"Is it just a demo, following a set rotation?" He reached out to the sphere and it floated away from him in response. Suddenly it burst to life again, this time morphing into an exact replica of him and Sorella standing in this kitchen. The whole thing floated in mid-air and stood no more than ten inches tall. It also rotated like the sphere.

"Oh that's cool." William bent to look at the detail and watched his mini me do the same. "You're making it do that?"

"I'm making the requests, yes."

It took another few seconds for the penny to drop. William looked at Sorella with fascination. "Mind control?"

"What was music like in your day I wonder?"

The sound of Lady Gaga's Bad Romance filled the kitchen and William cringed.

"The music of your era embarrasses you?" said Sorella.

"I thought you couldn't read my emotions."

"I can when they're obvious."

"Please make it stop," said William.

A slow haunting tune replaced the awful pop and began building in volume. Its classical undertones accompanied an unusual but pleasant melody.

"Much better," he said with a smile. "Someday I'll introduce you to the good music from my era, but to be honest it's limited. What do you use this for, other than studying yourself in miniature?"

Sorella chuckled and began to select various vegetables from a stand. "That's just a bit of fun. In the main it's used for entertainment and information, plus it connects to ANN if I need access to the wider network."

"Oh she's not here now is she?" William shivered a little for effect, although the sentiment was genuine.

Sorella chuckled again whilst chopping the onions. "No, no, only if I request her, which I rarely do. We don't have the easiest of relationships."

"She's a computer."

"Trust me ANNs are nothing like the computers you will be

used to. They are part of our social system. They are designed to think like us and cohabit with us, and as such they have personalities. It just so happens, ours has a possessive one, the object of which is my brother."

William whistled. "Crazy, crazy world," he said under his breath. He leant against the counter and watched their mini selves dissolve into the sphere and then pop out of existence. He found it an entirely mesmerising sight.

Sorella pushed all her chopped vegetables into a large pan to fry. "Can I ask how you are feeling about all of this?"

"You can."

Her lips curled a little. "How are you feeling about all of this?"

"Sorry, couldn't resist that. You always speak so correctly. It reminds me of an English teacher I had at school. If I ever went to the staffroom and said, 'Can I see Mrs Smith, please,' he would rise to his full height and boom, 'You *can*, boy, but you *may* not.' Then he would slam the door in my face. It took me two years to catch on to saying, *may I*."

Sorella had stopped stirring to listen to his little anecdote.

William shrugged. "I was a slow learner."

"I doubt that," she said holding his gaze. "Before we came here Caro and I had further enhancements because we are…" her eyes flicked away from his for a moment, "not LQs. One of these ensures our speech is grammatically correct in whichever language we are speaking."

William picked up a small egg-shaped object and spun it in the palm of his hand. "Dare I ask how many languages you speak?"

Her cheeks coloured a little. "All of them."

He stopped the spinning motion and raised his eyebrows.

"Stop avoiding my questions again, William, it is most frustrating."

"Sorry, but this is all so fascinating."

"Are you not terrified to find yourself here, so far from home?"

He thought about that. There had been moments when he had felt something close to terror, but that was more to do with concerns about his sanity than his circumstances. "No, not terrified. Not even scared really...maybe at another time in my life I might have been, but...not now."

"Does it make you sad?"

He had to laugh at that. Nothing could make him any sadder. He had reached the bottom and, as the saying goes, the only way is up. "No."

"Why is that funny?"

"No reason."

"William?"

"It really bugs you doesn't it, not knowing what's going on in here?" He tapped his forehead.

She huffed and returned to her cooking. "If I were in your shoes I would be scared and homesick."

"Being homesick implies you have something to miss." William spoke quietly and was not sure she would have heard, she did not respond at any rate.

By the time William made his way to her cosy spare room, he had enjoyed a huge portion of oriental stir-fry with egg fried rice. At least they had not taken to eating food out of toothpaste tubes in the future. He had also drunk a glass of rather good white wine. Feeling relaxed, he looked forward to his first decent sleep since landing here. He was about to be disappointed.

He awoke to find the house dark and quiet. The dream had been so vivid, so real, but then it always was every time he had it, which was all too often. They were on some holiday, a combination of ones they had had, or an imagined one that would never be. Sarah was laughing. Her head lay against his upper thigh as William half sat leaning on his forearms and resting one hand on her stomach. Her blonde hair, darkened by the sea water, dripped across her suntanned skin. He could smell coconuts from the lotion she wore and he felt happy.

That's what always surprised him when he emerged from this dream. How somewhere deep and buried in his mind he still associated her with that feeling.

He sat and let his eyes adjust to the surroundings. The small room had just enough space to house the bed he was in and, as with the kitchen, appeared quite normal.

Knowing he would struggle to sleep again, he got up and crept downstairs.

"I'll have one of those too, please."

Her voice made him jump as he filled a glass with water.

The sight of a woman had never taken William's breath away before. Not even Sarah had ever had such an effect. Oh he'd fancied her of course. She was beautiful, vibrant and fun and he could not believe his luck when she had said yes to him of all people. But there had never been a moment when he had looked at her and felt his heart hesitate, as if taking a moment to appreciate its new reason for beating.

Sorella stood on the bottom step, her dark curls falling almost to her waist. She wore a delicate white night dress that fell just short of her knees. The lace effect bordering the neckline and hem, showed hints of caramel skin beneath. "Please?" she said again when he failed to respond to her request.

"Sure." He turned quickly away, took another glass from the drainer and filled it with water. His hands felt clammy and he was horny as hell. He concentrated on forcing the feeling away as Sorella sat on the sofa and a lamp came on.

73

"You couldn't sleep?" she said as he joined her.

"Bad dream." He perched on the edge of the seat, feeling self-conscious in his t-shirt and boxers.

"I'm not surprised. It must be a huge shock to find yourself in another time." She touched his shoulder briefly.

"How come you believe me?" He turned a little to face her. "Why don't you find the idea ridiculous like your brother, what proof have I given you really?"

She curled her feet under her and studied her glass for a while. "You don't think I should?"

"*I* wouldn't." He leant against the back of the seat and closed his eyes.

Neither of them spoke for a good few moments.

"Whether you are telling the truth or not you seem in need of help and…"

He opened his eyes to look at her.

She looked away, concentrating on her glass again. "I…like how I feel around you."

"And how's that?" he asked.

Sorella glanced at him, bit her lip and took a breath. "A little anxious…a little excited." She gave a low laugh and shook her head. "This is really embarrassing. I'm used to people knowing how I feel…is it always so hard to say?"

William smiled. "Oh yes."

Their eyes met and he knew what her next question would be. He sat up and began to speak before she had chance to ask. "There's something you should know about how I came here…*why* I came here."

"You didn't travel through time?" She spoke quietly but he could hear the hint of disappointment and betrayal in her words.

"No…yes. I mean that's not the bit I'm referring to. I'm pretty certain I travelled through time. My life is in 2011 and if you are right about this being two hundred years later then I can't see any other explanation." Sorella looked relieved. "No, the thing I need to explain is …I came out to the cliff to…" He ran his hands through his hair, finding it amazingly hard to say. "You see, the thing is…" He faced her. "Ten years ago I married Sarah, my girlfriend from uni, the woman I hoped would be the mother of my children, the person I wanted to spend the rest of my life with…the love of my life if you like. Then, two months ago she decided she would be better off without me and left."

"Oh!" Sorella placed her glass on the table and held both hands over her mouth. In the corner of her eyes William was surprised to see the hint of tears.

"Thank you, I appreciate the gesture, but I'm sure my wife thinking she'd be happier without me is not quite so shocking."

Sorella shook her head, her eyes wider than he had ever seen them. "Worth living for," she said, the words muffled under her hands. She stood and paced along the side of the dining table. "That's what I heard you say when I first saw you." She looked him dead in the eye. "You came to the cliff to kill yourself."

William found it even harder to hear someone else say it, and broke eye contact.

Her curt laugh mocked him and he wished he had stayed in bed. "That's why you don't care, isn't it? Why you've no fear of being here?" Her speech sounded less precise and he guessed she must be angry with him.

"I just thought you should know the truth, that's all. There's no need to get all worked up about it."

"There's every reason to get worked up, William, you were going to throw your life away." She knelt at his feet and took hold of both his hands. "Do you still want to do it?"

Her question threw him for a moment. His mind whipped back to her appearance at the bottom of the stairs and her earlier confessions. "It?"

"Kill yourself?"

William found his mind clearer on the subject than it had been in a very long time. "No."

Sorella relaxed back on her heels and lessened her grip on his hands. "Good. You scared me, William."

"To be honest I kind of thought you'd known all along."

"What would make you think that?"

"At the domes when we first met you knew I'd hit my head and how long ago, then you made a comment about the soup being worth living for. I assumed you had some way of knowing what I was thinking."

She smiled and took a seat next to him. "I saw you rubbing your head as I approached, and from the sunburn on your arm I deduced you had been unconscious for maybe an hour or so."

"Quite the Sherlock Holmes aren't we?" William said.

"Who?"

"Really? You've never heard of Sherlock Holmes?"

Sorella shook her head.

"God you people have never lived. And the soup comment?"

She shrugged. "I suppose I just thought it was an unusual turn of phrase. I was teasing you."

He could not help smiling at the idea. "Teasing me...I see." For the next few moments as they sat in silence he could feel her watching him.

"William-"

"We should get some more sleep, don't you think?" He rose to his feet.

"Probably." She stood also.

William took both their glasses to the sink.

"You're quite the gentleman, William."

"Oh, I don't know about that."

She waited for him by the stairs. "I think you are," she said as he joined her. "I imagine most men who found themselves in your shoes would take advantage."

"How's that?"

"Recently betrayed, a long way from home where no one knows you..." Sorella took a step closer to him, "...alone with a woman who likes you."

William could not help but smile. "You think I *should* take advantage?" He knew he should not. It went against everything he believed in, every vow he had made, irrelevant of the fact Sarah had gone. Unfaithfulness wrecked lives and he viewed the people who did it as weak and worthless, like his mother and probably his wife.

Sorella brushed her hair behind her ear. "I am not sure whether you should...I just think it would be lovely if you did."

Neither of them moved and William could feel the electricity building. He only had to step away. Just one step would break it. But instead, he placed his hand on the small of her back, pulled her to him and kissed her.

He half expected it to feel wrong. He had kissed no one but Sarah in over fifteen years and had never intended to stray from that. Yet here he stood, giddy with the idea that this woman wanted him, relishing the heat of her skin under his fingers, hungry for the taste of her mouth.

They stumbled back onto the sofa. And the small part of his mind that questioned what the hell he was doing fell silent.

"Told you it would be lovely," Sorella said as he kissed her neck, and he laughed against the heat of her skin.

The next move he had in mind did not involve being thrown across the room. William landed on his side, slid across the floor and hit his head on the table leg which is when Sorella started screaming.

Chapter Eleven

Steve had no one else to call and nowhere else to try. He put his head in his hands and leant on the steering wheel. "Where are you, Will?"

He had rung all the friends he could think of, most of whom had already heard from Sarah. Then he had contacted the two companies he knew Will worked for last, neither of whom were expecting him. Next he had driven to Will's running club. He avoided telling them more than the fact Will had not been seen for a while, suggesting he may have gone for a run and fallen. Three guys about to set off for a session said they would run some of Will's favourite routes across the moors and look out for him. Steve gave them his mobile number. Finally, he had driven past all the local railway stations to check for his friend's car.

He and Will had only ever had one conversation about suicide, in the early hours of the morning in their third year of university. Sitting in their student house surrounded by discarded pizza boxes and dirty cups, Steve had finally plucked up the courage to ask.

"How did he do it, your dad?" he had said. He had wanted to ask this for over a year, ever since Will let slip that his dad had topped himself, but he could never find the right words.

Will waved the bottle of vodka at him. "And Paracetamols, coward's way out."

"You don't approve?" Steve knew it was a stupid thing to say as soon as he said it, but at eight pints of lager and quarter of a bottle of vodka down at least he had an excuse.

Will actually laughed as he topped up their glasses. "You think any child could approve of a parent doing themselves in? God you're going to make a shit psychologist, Stevie." They had both laughed before downing the next shot. "No, if it were me, I'd do

79

something more dramatic, something with a bit of oomph, ya know, like throwing myself in front of a train."

Steve looked up from his hands at the station building. According to the woman at the British Transport Police, no one had jumped today, but how far out would Will drive?

William was the first person Steve had met on his University course and the only person he had kept in touch with. It helped that they had ended up living and working in the same city, but Steve liked to believe they would have stayed friends even if they'd ended up at different ends of the country.

The day they met, Steve had found a seat on the back row of the lecture theatre in the far corner. Having quickly become bored of the making-friends element of university life, he had looked forward to finally starting to learn something. His parents did not like his choice of degree subject. They thought he should stick to real subjects like chemistry, biology or maths, but Steve knew he was going to love psychology because people were extremely fascinating.

As Steve studied the timetable, the soles of someone's trainers flicked past his head followed by a body that flopped into the seat alongside him. "Alright?" said the new guy.

"Yeh, you?" said Steve without looking up. He liked the look of Tuesdays, Social Psychology followed by the Biological Basis for Behaviour. Eight thirty a.m. on a Friday for Cognitive Psychology looked like a bitch though.

"Looks like you're gonna enjoy uni then," said the stranger.

Steve felt his face burn up, was he the only person avidly studying the course content? He quickly pushed the paper to one side. "Just checking how they plan to torture us."

"No, I mean..." His companion cocked his head to the row below where two blondes were looking their way. The girls giggled and turned to face the front when Steve caught their eyes. "They've been talking about you for the last five minutes. I was sat behind them." The new guy leaned in and cupped his hand around his mouth. "Apparently you're just sooo hot."

Steve's face burned crimson now. "Hmm first I've heard," he said. This was not entirely true. His last year of A levels had seen him elevated in the eyes of the girls in his school. He could not put his finger on why. When he looked in the mirror he appeared to look no different from how he always had. Not that he was complaining, especially when the likes of Shelly Rose were asking him out.

The stranger studied him for longer than was really polite and Steve began to shuffle in his seat. "Ha, liar," the guy eventually said, slapping Steve's chest with the back of his hand. "Clever though, girls love a bit of modesty."

One of the blondes looked over again, the end of her pen poised seductively in her mouth.

"Will York," said the guy, holding his hand out for Steve.

"Steve Morris." He returned the gesture.

"Good to meet you, Stevie. I think I'm going to like hanging out with you." Will waved to the blonde and she smiled before looking away.

In fact Will never once took advantage of his new friend's powers of attraction, because less than a month later he met Sarah. He had been right about Steve though, his years at University had been awash with beautiful girl after beautiful girl. In fact, he had never really lost the habit.

And so their friendship became less to do with pulling girls and more about changing the world. They had big plans, like most student idealists. Not that you could ever really call Will an idealist, he was far too worldly-wise. Nevertheless, they planned to take the psychology world by storm. Make it less of an arty farty girls' subject and more of what it should be: a respected science that made a real difference to the world.

Big dreams for little boys.

Not that they knew it then. They thought they faced a world which eagerly awaited its next generation. Only time and the trudge of working nine to five would teach them otherwise, turning them from dreamers into doubters - guys who these days mocked the supposed bright young things for their naivety.

Steve checked his watch. It had gone seven o'clock, and it had started raining again. He did not want to admit it, but it wasn't looking good. Will might have grown into a cynical old fart, but he was no drama queen. There would be no calling for help scenarios. If he wanted out, he would get out. No messing about.

Steve felt a lump in his throat and swallowed it away. He would never in a million years tell Will he loved him, not least because of the stick his best friend would give him for the rest of their days, but he did. Like the brother he had never had, and more than any woman he had dated or lived with (briefly, very briefly). Without Will, Steve's life would become significantly worse.

Steve took a deep breath. He would just have to deal with it, because if that is what Will wanted…

"Fuck!" Steve hit the steering wheel with the heels of his hands. Why hadn't he seen things were this bad? Sarah was right; he was supposed to be an expert. He felt tears hot on his face and wiped them away with the back of his hand as his phone started to ring.

Sarah Calling.

"Please, please, please," Steve said crossing the fingers of his free hand and then answering.

Chapter Twelve

The big man's huge muscles bulged under his shirt sleeves. William had little hope of fighting him off, as he was dragged, stumbling down the street. William had lost one of Caro's shoes outside Sorella's house and blood ran down his cheek from where his forehead hit the table.

"Lal, stop, please, you're hurting him." Sorella had to trot to keep up with the big man's strides.

"Good, 'e deserves it with what 'e's done."

"I haven't done anything," said William.

The man pulled hard on William's t-shirt yanking him forward and making him stumble again.

"Please, Lal, just stop and tell me what's happened," said Sorella.

"You'll see soon enough." The big guy turned left into another street of terraced cottages where a large group of people congregated outside one doorway. It struck William that the house looked familiar but he could not think why.

Caro stepped forward from the crowd and looked from his sister to William, before focusing on Lal. "I think it would be wise to take a moment to calm down." Caro placed a hand on the big man's chest.

To William's relief they stopped and he was able to stand upright, albeit with a handful of his t-shirt still grasped in Lal's meaty fist.

"What's going on?" Sorella moved to William's side, close enough for their arms to touch. William appreciated the gesture but worried it might cause her trouble given the look on Caro's face.

"Lal, go inside and see to your family."

"No way. I wanna hear what this freak's got to say and I want Gracie to hear it too." His fist tightened the material around Will's neck.

"Think of Seb, Lal. It will not do any good to deal with things in this state. Let me help." Caro used the same commanding tone he had when William had first arrived.

Seb, the little boy with the blond hair and rhubarb - that was where William knew this house from. The boy had been standing in this very doorway yesterday when he left. Had something happened to him? Had he tried to follow William and got hurt, is that why the father had acted so irately?

"I can 'andle it." Lal dragged William towards the door, but at the last minute let go and pushed him towards Caro. "If ya wanna help, bring 'im in and hold 'im. I'll do the talking."

Caro took hold of William's bicep, partly to halt his stumble and partly as a restraint.

"What's this about?" said Sorella, blocking their way into the house. Lal had already entered and William thought he could hear someone crying.

"Grace has been missing all day. They just found her."

"Isn't that good news?" said William, but from the look of distaste on Caro's face, he gathered not.

"How is she?" said Sorella.

William did not understand the panic in Sorella's voice.

"That is what we are here to find out. What happened to him?" Caro eyed the cut above William's eye.

"Lal just burst in and started throwing his weight around. William hit his head on the table."

Caro nodded for his sister to lead the way in. "How were you not ready for him? His anger is saturating the village. You must have known he was coming your way."

"It's four o'clock in the morning, Caro, I wasn't expecting visitors."

"Wait here," Caro said in the hall. He released William then entered a room and closed the door behind him.

Lal's voice boomed from within. "Where the hell is he? I told you to keep hold of 'im."

"Sorella is with him in the hall…Oh my."

William looked across at Sorella. She bit her lip so hard he imagined it would begin bleeding at any point. "Any idea what this is about?"

"Maybe," she said without looking his way. "Are you okay…did he hurt you?"

"Have you seen the size of him, of course he hurt me. The man's an animal. Did you know he was there in the house?"

"No!"

"You couldn't feel his anger getting closer like Caro said?"

"No, I told you I had no idea until he grabbed you. In case you hadn't noticed I was a little distracted."

"What's going on, Sorella? What are you not telling me? Who the hell do these people think I am?"

Caro appeared in the doorway and Sorella barged her way past him.

"You had better come in here," Caro said to William.

William had a really bad feeling about this. He felt the tension and hostility coming from that room and had no desire to go in. But what choice did he have. Too many people stood outside for him to stand any chance of leaving. And if he ran he would look guilty of whatever they thought he had done.

He entered behind Caro keeping his back to the wall and his exit route clear. The small front room was crowded with people, and every pair of eyes fell on him. William avoided meeting them.

The silence that had fallen felt suffocating. His heart hammered in his chest, and he tried to suppress the voice in his head chanting, *get out, get out*.

On the floor sat a woman. Her long blonde hair hung over her face and into her lap. The boy, Seb, sat alongside squeezing her hand over and over as if trying to encourage a response. Seb looked up at William and his swollen, wet eyes brightened a touch.

William smiled at him.

"Don't you dare-" Lal said.

Caro stepped in front of William to block Lal's approach.

"E's making nice with my boy, the sick bastard. Do you know what you've done? D'you care?" The big man's voice choked up and he pushed away from Caro with an arm across his face.

"Oh Grace." Sorella knelt at the side of the woman and brushed the hair away.

Grace looked up, her eyes unfocused and her head lolling a little to one side. William recognised the woman who had dragged Seb away from him yesterday, the woman who had seemed afraid of him. William felt himself gasp at the change in her appearance.

"Can you tell us what happened, sweetheart?" Sorella said.

The woman did not respond. She merely blinked twice and dropped her head again, too quickly for it to not have hurt her neck.

"It's the same, it's the same," said the crying voice.

William followed the sound to the grey-haired woman from the garden opposite Sorella's house. She rocked back and forth on a chair, sobbing into the sleeves of her worn brown cardigan.

"They took her." Lal still had his arm across his mouth as he spoke. "I felt her panic and then...then...nothing."

"Are you happy now?" Sorella said to her brother. "Now your

paranoia is spreading around the village?"

"It's the same," moaned the old woman again. "No, no, no…" Her cries became muffled as she buried her head in her hands.

William looked again at Grace's slumped body and felt a chill run up his spine. This had happened before. The tragedy Sorella had mentioned. The thing that made people scared of him.

"This is not paranoia," shouted Lal. "Look at her. She won't speak. She doesn't understand…she's not Gracie anymore. They took her mind."

"Lobotomy," William said under his breath.

He knew as soon as the word left his lips it was a mistake to speak. The whole room stared at him and he could actually see the colour rising up Lal's cheeks.

"What did you do to her?" Lal lunged at William.

"Caro!" shouted Sorella.

The big man swung a punch that would no doubt have knocked William out had Caro not tackled Lal away. The two men crashed into the lounge door, splitting the wood from the middle to the floor.

"I swear I had nothing to do with this, it was just a guess," William said. How could they think this was him?

"Liar…LIAR!" shouted Lal from behind Caro's restraining arms. "You think we're stupid. You picked her out for them."

"Picked her out? No. I don't know what you're talking about. Picked her out for who?"

"You tell us," shouted a man's voice from William's left.

"We need to take Grace to ANNy, find out what has happened," said Caro to Lal as he stood and released him.

"He just told us," said the sobbing woman. She wrapped her cardigan more tightly around her, as if to keep out the evil.

"No, he said he guessed and we need to be sure," said Caro.

"So this loberty thing's real,?" said a small, blond man on William's left.

"Lobotomy," corrected Caro.

"What is it?" Lal rose to his feet again, towering above the rest of them and staring from Caro to Will.

"It is a very old and prohibited procedure. I am not sure of the detail but if that is what it is, ANN will know. Help me lift her." Caro moved to Grace's side but Lal stayed put.

"What is it?" Lal asked again.

William felt hot under the man's gaze. Why had he opened his big mouth? "I don't know."

"Tell me," demanded the man stepping closer. "Tell me what you've done."

"*I* haven't done anything. Your wife's symptoms just reminded me…Caro's right you need an expert opinion."

Lal came close enough for Will to feel the heat of the man's breath on his face. "Don't be telling me what I need. You'd better get the hell out of 'ere and tell 'em to leave us be, or else I'll get rid of you myself."

"Here, here," said at least three other male voices in the room.

"We should send *him* back damaged, see how they like it," shouted a woman, her voice full of hate.

Without warning the group closed in on William. His clear route to the exit disappeared. Abuse came thick and fast, and it became impossible to distinguish the words as the volume and pace increased to a frenzy of noise.

William stood flat against the wall with nowhere to go. He knew how quickly gang mentality could get out of hand and these people wanted blood. Forcing the panic away, he focused on each pair of eyes in turn trying to find one person he could appeal to. He found nothing but the same angry hostility.

"Hey, hey everyone stop it." Sorella pushed through their ranks to reach William. "I said STOP IT! William's no threat. He's not one of them." She flashed a look at her brother. "Whoever *they* are."

"You cannot know that." Caro said.

"Yes I can, and I do. Please, everyone just back away. This is not the way to deal with this." She held her hands out to encourage people away. "I know William is different but that does not make him guilty."

Caro spoke to his sister. "Do not make assertions you cannot qualify, it could prove dangerous." Then he turned to Lal. "But Sorella's right. This is not how we should conduct ourselves and our priority is taking care of Grace."

Lal stared hard at William for a beat or two. Then, to William's relief, the big man moved away to help carry his wife from the house. The group all stepped back in response and watched little Seb trail out behind his parents.

Then, all eyes once more fell on William.

"Who are you?" said the grey-haired woman, her eyes red raw.

"He is no one to worry about. Come on, William, let's go." Sorella strode towards the door.

"Let us be the judge of that," said a familiar voice.

William searched the group and found the weather-worn face at the far end of the room.

"You willing to vouch for him, S'rella?" said the old man William had taken directions from yesterday.

"Yes, Mart, I am."

"You've been with 'im the whole time 'e's been around?"

"You know she hasn't," said William before Sorella had chance to answer. He did not know if she would lie for him, but best to be sure.

Mart fixed his gaze on William. "And where were you so desperate to get to in your socks?" The old man had lost the good-humoured tone from their previous conversation.

Most of the eyes in the room moved to William's feet, and the bandages around his shoeless left foot.

"Home."

"But you came back."

"Turns out I was further away than I thought."

The old man smiled, but not in a pleasant way. "I suggest we lend you some footwear and you try a bit harder."

"Come. Now!" Sorella took hold of William's wrist and pulled him from the room.

No one stood in the street anymore. People had presumably followed Caro and Lal with Grace. William shrugged his arm free from Sorella. He strode to the end of the street, and turned left away from her home.

She caught up with him. "Where are you going?"

"You heard them, I'm going home."

Sorella moved to block his way. "And how do you plan to do that exactly?"

He side-stepped her. "I'll find a way."

"They're just scared and angry. Let me talk to them tomorrow."

William paused at the cottage where he had first met Mart. "And why do you want me to stay exactly?"

She placed her hands on her hips. "I would have thought that was obvious."

"You mean the seduction routine? That was very clever by the way, very…convincing."

Her mouth dropped open a little.

"I heard you all that first day, saying how helpful I could be. How my lack of modifications made me *useful*. As what? A scapegoat for whatever crazy shit is going on here? Well thanks, but no thanks. I'd rather take my chances out there."

Sorella had no come-back to that he could see. Bluff called. William began walking again and left her behind in the darkness.

He felt like such an idiot falling for her crap. *I feel a little anxious and excited*, he recited using the fakest mental voice he could muster. God, he hated women and their manipulative shit. He should have run a mile as soon as he discovered all the mind tampering. It could only ever mean trouble.

The image of Grace's zombie-like face floated into his head and it once more sent a shiver down his spine. He had only ever seen people like that in old research films during his degree. Black and white images of people whose brains had been purposefully damaged to prevent psychotic or criminal behaviour. What the hell was going on here?

Crazy, fucked up world, he thought, and walked a bit faster.

The idea had come to him in the house whilst under attack. Sorella had said earlier that the teleport column might have acted as a receiver for some kind of wormhole, and if so, it could still be there. It was worth a look at least.

William had been walking for nearly fifteen minutes when the Waltzer appeared alongside. Its silent approach made him jump.

"Get in, William, I have your clothes."

He glanced at Sorella and away again.

"Please, I'll take you wherever you want to go. It'll be quicker."

"Fine." He climbed in. "Don't speak to me, though, I've had enough of your games."

She waited until the door had shut. "No deal," she said.

He took his jeans from the seat and put them on, followed by the borrowed shoe he had lost.

"I wasn't pretending," she said touching the back of his hand.

"Save it, I'm not interested." He moved his hand away. "Now let me out."

"No. You need to listen to me, and until you do you are my prisoner." She sat back in the chair

"I'm pretty sure I've been that all along."

She smiled and pulled her hair back, tying it with a band. She had not changed from her nightdress, just added sandals and a cardigan.

"You think it's funny do you, keeping me here, messing with my head?"

"I'm only pleased you are displaying some emotions I understand. Anger...paranoia...these are the things you should be feeling considering what has happened to you. You feel you've lost control and it's normal to react like this."

"Which one of us is the psychologist again?"

She clasped her hands in her lap and leant towards him. "I have two centuries of knowledge and insight on you. There is no competition."

The car swung around the side of the domes and came to a standstill. He looked over at the cliff.

"Did you imagine I wouldn't guess where you were going?"

"What do you want, Sorella?"

"I want to explain. Just hear me out. I'm not playing games despite what you think but you're right about being useful to us. And we do need your help."

"Surprise, surprise. The truth at last."

"Our world today is so far from what you know. We have no wars, no crime, no prejudice or discrimination-"

William gave a curt laugh. "So I saw."

"It is peaceful and harmonious in so many ways."

"Because you're messing with people's minds. That can't be

right."

"No that's not what we are doing. People are educated through the enhancements, made more aware of differences, given the ability to empathise. There is still freedom of choice but people no longer choose to do things which are harmful to others. It is a wonderful thing."

"Great, so you won't need me then. Can I go now?"

"A few years ago we began hearing rumours about an illness that was spreading through rural communities. It would strike members of the same family then just disappear, only to pop up elsewhere in the country. People have been told not to worry, that it is a virus which triggers a rare genetic condition." She paused for a beat. "Sufferers lose most of their cognitive functions. They can no longer communicate and their personalities change beyond recognition."

William thought of the blonde woman's unresponsiveness. "You think Grace has this?"

"Yes and no. Caro has been following the cases and something does not add up. Every incident follows the same pattern. The individuals are alone at home...or working in the fields, when a spike of panic is felt by those nearby. But when people rush to their aid they're nowhere to be found, and often missing for hours on end, before being found wandering on the outskirts of their village. And the genetic condition makes no sense. Parents and children contract it at the same time, whereas genetic factors usually predispose people to things within a given age range.

"But most worrying is that no cases of the illness have occurred outside the rural communities. My brother thinks LQs are being taken and experimented on."

And all those people back there think I'm part of it, thought William feeling sickened. "Sounds like a job for the police."

"They're not interested because there's no evidence. The people affected can't say what's happened to them and no one has ever seen anything suspicious. All that's left is conjecture. We've been told it's a medical matter."

"But if someone's doing this to them, won't the ANN things be able to see that. I thought that's why Caro was taking Grace there?"

"Yes of course, but every other village uses the public service ones. Our ANN is different. My mother acquired her many years ago and we are the only LQ community who owns their own."

William looked her way. "Let me get this straight. Your brother thinks whoever is taking these people and screwing with their minds also influences what the official bodies say is causing it. That's one hell of a conspiracy theory."

"I know, and...I've been struggling to believe him, but then you immediately concluded someone had performed this lobotomy thing on her."

"Oh, don't listen to me. I have no idea what I'm talking about, believe me."

"Well, we'll know soon enough I suppose." She faced away from him and out of the window.

"I still don't get what this has to do with me."

"I know." Her eyes narrowed a touch and thin lines formed across her forehead. When she next spoke, she kept her voice low. "If ANN finds that Caro's suspicions are correct we are faced with something new; people who are willing to ruin the lives of their fellow man, people who are powerful enough to control the public ANNs, maybe even the police... If we have any chance of stopping them we need to find out who they are and why they're doing this. Caro and ANNy have drawn up scenarios for how we could investigate, but each is flawed.

"The problem is, public ANNs monitor city buildings twenty-four-seven. As soon as people enter the vicinity they scan the primary for our identity, after which our movements are monitored. When people show any anxiety, anger or suspicion they are watched more carefully. Even if we managed to mask our emotions somehow, which would be incredibly hard, the locations we would need to visit are restricted to the general public."

She looked his way. "We need to find out what is going on without them knowing we are looking."

"They monitor your emotions and movements and you think you have freedom of choice?"

She moved to the edge of her seat. "William, you would be invisible."

"Yeh, I got that, thanks. You don't need to spell it out." He stood. "May I leave now?"

"Grace is not the first here to suffer this, you know. The woman you saw crying in there, six months ago her daughter Sammy went missing only to come back like that, then a week later the same with Sammy's youngest daughter Tilly. Two beautiful people with everything to live for turned into zombies. Sammy wrote children's stories that were read all over the world, the next we knew, she couldn't even form a sentence.

"This is not my problem." William could see her disappointment at his response, but he was past caring. He just wanted out. He had never missed home so much.

Sorella held his gaze for a moment or two then dropped her eyes. The door slid aside.

The warmth outside surprised him. Dawn had broken and sunlight bathed the lime green. It was becoming an all too familiar sight. William walked to the white disc and stood on its surface looking up. If it was still here, the wormhole had to be above him; otherwise he would step right through now, wouldn't he? He leant to the left and then the right trying to see if the air looked different in any way. He did not know what he expected to see. The only image he could bring to mind was Dr Who's Tardis spinning through a swirling spiral of space dust. And nothing like that existed here.

"You know it will be Seb next. It's always the same pattern, a parent, followed by a child. That's what happened with Sammy and Tilly, that's what's happening all over the country."

William stepped off the column and faced her. "Very nice. The appeal to my ego failed so now you resort to emotional blackmail."

"He's just a child."

"A child whose father just threatened to do away with me in case you hadn't noticed."

"He's scared, we're all scared...he didn't mean it."

"Yes he did and you know it." He pointed his finger in the direction of her home. "Those people think I'm involved in this, that I'm responsible for what happened to that poor woman. I can't stay, Sorella, and I'm in no position to help you."

She curled his outstretched finger into his fist with the flat of her hand. "Yes you are. Please I'm begging you, just come back and see if it's true."

"And risk being attacked again by your ape man, no thanks."

He would have spotted the flash of anger in her eyes even if she hadn't pushed his hand away in disgust. "You're so selfish."

He grabbed her shoulders and brought his face close to hers. "I am! Are you not asking me to risk my life for a group of people I don't know? Asking me to spy for you to find out who the hell is carving up people's brains?"

"What do you care, you were planning to kill yourself anyway."

He pushed her away and she stumbled backwards a little. "The key part of that being *myself.* I don't want to be beaten to death in the street or turned into a vegetable any more than the next man."

"I'm sorry, I shouldn't have said-"

"No, you shouldn't but at least it puts the whole, *William, you would be throwing your life away,* speech into perspective." He looked up at the cliff face. He reckoned he could climb it in the daylight. "Better you throw it away doing something for us," he said under his breath.

Sorella pulled him around to face her. "You have to be the most infuriating person I've ever met. I don't want you to risk your life at all, not for us, not for that wife of yours, not for anyone. If you helped us we would protect you with everything we had. You have no idea how hard we would work to make sure no harm came to you."

"We? Sorella, everyone else in your village thinks I'm a freak or a monster…even your brother."

"So prove them wrong."

William shook his head and brushed her hand from his arm. It was time to see if he could find his way home.

Sorella intercepted him at the bottom of the cliff placing her hands on his chest. "Okay, okay, they might take some convincing but we *do* need you and in time they will realise that. You are the best hope we have of finding out what this is, of stopping this."

"I can't." William tried to move past her but she blocked him again.

"You know, Sammy's husband couldn't cope looking after her and Tilly. He tried for months and we all tried to help but in the end it was too much. He drowned them in the bath, William. Then he hanged himself, leaving his eldest daughter to find them." Sorella cried now. "Please…just stay a little longer, let me talk to them. I can sort this out. They are good people and you're a good man. I can see that."

Stunned for a moment by her latest revelation, William fell quiet. He had seen the eldest daughter in the upstairs window of her neighbour's house. She could not have been much older than thirteen or fourteen. Poor thing.

Sorella seemed to take his silence as a good sign. She stepped closer. "William." She wiped her eyes. "You've nowhere to go, stop being stubborn and running away. Please… I want you to stay… not just to help us, but because… I want you to stay."

William started to make some sarcastic remark, but the look in her eyes stopped him. She might not be lying and if that were the case, why make this any harder by being cruel. "I'm sorry," he said instead.

William began to scramble up the hillside on his hands and knees. A handful of grass here, a knee on a rock there and before he knew it he had climbed over half way.

"What are you doing? You'll hurt yourself." Sorella's voice sounded distant and panicked.

"It's okay I'm not going to jump," William said under his breath.

At the three-quarter point he paused for breath. He was not as fit as he thought. A lot of hillside now sat below him, probably enough. He remembered the original fall well enough to know he had nearly made it to the bottom without noticing anything strange. He shuffled along on his hands and feet, leaning back into the cliff to avoid toppling forward.

"William, stop it, this is reckless. Come down."

That's exactly what I plan to do, he thought. He now perched directly above the white disc. It seemed as good a place as any to start his trials. "Coming," he called, beginning his descent.

Within seconds he had lost all control of the fall. He clipped his heel on a rock and cried out as he lost a shoe again. As gravity took over he tried to slow himself, but the grasses slipped through his fingers like oiled spaghetti.

Even so as he neared the bottom, he felt a pang of disappointment. He had banked on this working.

Sorella began to call his name.

He never heard her finish.

Chapter Thirteen

At the bottom, William thought as his eyes flickered open.

A machine sounded a monotonous beat as he took in the large grey ceiling tiles and attached curtain rail. The smell of disinfectant filled his nostrils and a crisp sheet held him firmly in place. He knew where he was. He had worked for a Hospital Trust around three years ago and spent a lot of time visiting the wards.

"Hey, how ya doin?" a familiar but unexpected voice said.

Sarah sat by his side holding his hand. Her eyes looked red and swollen with dark rings underneath from her smudged mascara.

"What are you doing here?" His voice sounded dry and rasping.

His wife reached for some water and helped him to lift his head and take a drink.

"Really, Sarah, why are you here?" William said.

"How are you feeling? The doctor said it's only cuts and bruises, nothing serious."

"I'm fine."

His wife studied him for a moment as if trying to decide if she believed him. "What the hell were you thinking?" She still held his hand but her grip had tightened from caring to tortuous. "What a stupid, self-pitying, shitty stunt to pull. Have you any idea what we've all been through? Who the hell was supposed to take care of your mother – me? Not to mention sort out the house and the finances. I can't believe you'd be so fucking selfish."

He looked up at the ceiling again. "Is that all you're bothered about, the hassle of selling the house? And you call *me* selfish."

Sarah let go of his hand and half stood, leaning on the edge of his bed so he could see her face. "Oh, I apologise. Is that not what you wanted? Not the effect you were going for? Was I supposed to be grief-stricken and wishing I'd never left you?" She leant closer spitting the words into his face. "Well news flash, psycho boy, this just makes me think I'm well rid of you."

William looked at her swollen eyes. "Which is why you've spent the last few days crying?"

She straightened up. "Fuck off."

"My sentiments exactly."

"Hey, hey, calm it kids, there are ill people trying to sleep in here." Steve carried two Costa coffee cups and a white bag of goodies.

Delighted and relieved to see his friend, William shuffled to a sitting position. He moved the pillows behind him to lean against. "Alright Stevie?"

"Not bad, not bad." Steve handed one of the cups to Sarah who walked away from the bed and turned her back. "Apart from the big dent in my reputation caused by not spotting my mate was depressed and suicidal."

"Yeh well, you always were a joke of a psychologist. Is that for me?" William put his hand out for the cup as Steve prepared to take a drink.

Steve held it towards him. "Sure, but I've spat in it."

The smell brought a wave of nausea. "Keep it then. You could have *anything* considering the dodgy women you take home."

The two of them laughed and Steve patted Will's leg.

"How can you joke?" said Sarah. "How can you start the day trying to kill yourself and end it as if nothing's happened?" Her eyes accused Will of all manner of crimes.

"Are you still here?" William said. God, how he loved the effect of his verbal slaps on her. Once upon a time seeing such hurt in her eyes would have broken his heart and had him scurrying to her aid. Now it felt undeniably pleasant.

Steve looked Sarah's way and gave her a small nod and half smile of support. It surprised William. His friend had been totally on his side since the split and almost as angry with Sarah as him. William took note again of his wife's puffy eyes. The last few days must have been hard on her. So hard, she had won Steve's sympathy.

"Look guys, I'm sorry for what you've been through. This wasn't about..." Something Sarah had said stopped his train of thought. He looked between the two of them, feeling his heart rate increase in time with the beeps. "What day is it?"

The confused expression on Steve's face reminded him of Sorella's when he had asked her the same question. "Tuesday. Are you feeling alright bud, d'ya want me to get the doc?"

"That's not possible." He had left home on Tuesday morning and been away for two nights. "It should be Thursday."

His wife and friend swapped a look which said, *Ah oh.*

Sarah came closer. "What are you talking about?"

"I was there for two days and two nights."

His wife scoffed. "If that were true you wouldn't be here at all. The paramedics said you'd have died from hypothermia left for much longer. You were out cold and soaking wet from the storm. You were damn lucky that farmer found you."

"I need to see my feet." William began to shuffle out of the covers. The tightly bound sheets proved a struggle to escape from and his movements became more frantic.

"What are you doing?" said Sarah. "Stop it. Will, stop it." She grabbed both his hands. "What is wrong with you?"

"I ran through the night without any shoes. I cut my feet and bruised my toes." He shrugged her off and continued tugging his way out.

"Oh my God," she said stepping away. "Why would you do

that?"

"I didn't do it on purpose. I was lost and trying to get home." The sheets loosened and he threw them aside revealing four blackened toes and the trace of antiseptic cream around his cuts. He breathed a sigh of relief. He was not going crazy.

"So you left home Monday night?" said Steve.

Will shook his head. "Tuesday morning."

"But it's only Tuesday night now... well, Wednesday morning." Sarah said after checking her watch "So you can't have been running through the night."

"Like I said, it should be Thursday."

"I think I should get the doctor." Steve stared at Will's injuries. His coffee remained untouched.

Dr Rajiv Patel had the longest fingers William had ever seen. The small thin man wore a mint green shirt from which he picked non-existent fluff as he spoke.

"I wouldn't get these injuries from falling down a hillside, you admit that?" William insisted that they see sense. The doctor seemed stuck on the idea that his bang to the head explained everything.

Patel took a cursory glance at William's feet. "Walking or running the few miles from your car was the most likely cause of this."

"No, I was in walking boots. I could only have cut my feet like this whilst barefoot."

"But you *were* barefoot," said Sarah.

"Yes, I know I was when they found me, but I didn't lose my boots until after the fall."

The trio of standing observers swapped further worried glances.

"Mate, you went out there without your shoes," said Steve.

"Or a flaming coat!" Sarah looked annoyed again. "In this weather! You really were determined to be a goner weren't you?" she said under her breath.

William sat up straight. "No. I went out there in walking boots and my waterproof."

"Well they found you with neither, how do you explain that?"

He turned to his wife. "When I woke, after the fall they were gone...I thought someone had taken them at first, but then..." He stopped knowing he would sound even more crazy if he just blurted it out. He needed to establish some facts first to corroborate his story. "My coat and boots weren't with me, nearby? I mean, did anyone look?"

"Will," Steve looked worried again.

"Look when I slipped at the top of the cliff I had my boots on and my coat zipped up."

"When you slipped?" Sarah looked at the doctor, her eyes wide. "Can't you do something, he's obviously confused. Are you sure there's no serious damage? What about the nose bleeds?"

"We gave him an MRI scan and it was clear. A little disorientation is to be expected after a period of unconsciousness."

"This isn't disorientation, its denial!" She focused on her husband, her eyes blazing. "Will you set off this morning in only a t-shirt and jeans with the full intention of killing yourself. You left a suicide note for your mother, for Christ's sake."

"Sarah..." Steve put his hand on her arm.

"You drove to the middle of nowhere, walked five miles in a storm and jumped off a flaming cliff!"

Steve looked irritated. "Sarah, this is not helping."

"So what *is* going to help, hey Steve? What do you suggest we do? Play along and then find he's done it again, only not been so damn lucky?" She had started to cry and Steve put his arm around her shoulder. "I'm fine, I'm fine!" She stepped away from him.

William watched the drama play out with an increasing sense of shame. "Sarah, look at me," he said sitting up on the side of the bed. "Please?"

She shook her head. She obviously wanted to hide her emotions from him, which he could understand. He stood. His feet did not feel as tender as they had been; the wounds were healing. He made a mental note to speak to Patel about that. The wires attached to his hand prevented him from moving too far from the bed, so he reached out for her with his other hand. "Hey, it's okay. *I'm* okay." It felt strange to touch her arm. The gesture would not have raised a second thought at any point in the last fifteen years, but now he felt it was not his place. The realisation brought a wave of the same sadness that had taken him to the cliff edge. He forced it away.

When he had her attention, he dropped the hand. "You're right, I did intend to jump. I'm not going to deny that…"

Sarah placed a hand over her mouth to mask a small cry.

"But the truth is I fell before I had the chance. And I promise… I *swear*… I'm not going to try it again. Something happened to me out there and it brought me to my senses. I don't want to…"

Throw your life away? The words came to him in her voice not his. He paused as the memory of Sorella kneeling at his feet caught him unawares. The vivid image brought an unexpected twang of regret. How could he miss a woman he had known for barely two days? He blinked a few times feeling disorientated before realising Sarah still waited for him to finish.

He focused on his wife's tear-stained face. "I don't want to do that to you all. You're right it was stupid and selfish and I'm sorry. Truly I am."

"I don't know if I can believe you. I want to…but should I? What if you change your mind again?" Sarah's eyes were still unnaturally wide.

"I won't."

Patel coughed. "Well if that is all, I'd better get on to my other patients."

"Wait," William said before the doctor could escape. "The cuts on my feet, are they not healing a bit too quickly for me to have cut them today?" He sat back on the bed and lifted his un-bandaged foot so the doctor could see. The cuts were over twenty-four hours old now; surely the medic could see that.

"I would not say so."

"Well, take a closer look."

"Will, leave it for now hey?" said Steve.

"Come on Doc, what harm can it do?"

"Mr York, if you say these cuts occurred prior to today then I believe you. Let's just be thankful you are feeling better and healing well."

Patronising bastard, thought William, but he could see the point. Where would it get him to establish the cuts were older than today, really? Another thought occurred to him. "When they found me my feet were bandaged weren't they?"

The doctor looked thrown at that. "I couldn't say."

"You didn't treat me when I arrived?"

"Yes I did, but your wet clothes were removed by the paramedics to warm you up. As I understand it, they were beginning to freeze."

"Are the paramedics available, can I speak to them?"

Patel's eyes flicked out to the corridor as if he hoped someone would come and save him. "Oh, I'm not sure… erm."

"I'd like to say thank you, if that's okay."

The doctor hesitated, no doubt seeing through the lie. "I'll see what I can do."

"When can I take him home?" said Sarah.

William exchanged a quick look with Steve.

"Once the nurse has been in for a final check, he is free to go," Patel said.

"Thanks," said William as the doctor left.

"I can take you back if you like? I could do with picking up those running shoes I left." Steve was not much of a runner which Sarah knew very well, but William felt grateful for his friend's effort.

Sarah looked at William. "Are you sure, I don't mind taking you."

William smiled at his wife. "If Steve needs to get his shoes I suppose it makes sense…"

Sarah nodded and if he was not mistaken, she looked as relieved about the decision as William was.

William unlocked the door with the spare key he had collected from his neighbour - his own had been in his jacket pocket - and stepped into the kitchen. It felt good to be home, which considering he had not expected to see the place ever again surprised him. Two dirty mugs, a glass and a packet of half-eaten biscuits sat on the table, alongside the letter for his mother. William lifted it up and read it as Steve filled the kettle.

"You really shit her up," Steve said.

William folded the note and tore it in half. "I know."

"Is that why you did it?"

He threw the note in the bin. "No."

Steve leant against the sink with his hands in his pockets. He still wore his shirt and tie from work. "Did you mean it, like you said in the hospital? Were you really going to do it?"

"I'm going to get changed," said William, ignoring the question. Sarah had brought clothes to the hospital for him, but the jeans no longer fit given the weight he had lost.

In the bedroom, he found his wardrobe door open. He imagined his wife grabbing his things in panic on hearing he had been found, relieved but still crying. If he had wanted revenge, it had been served. But he had not.

William paused after closing the wardrobe door. Or had he?

He looked at the photograph from their wedding day that still hung on the wall. Sarah's favourite picture. In it, white roses from the bush behind framed his new wife as he leant in to kiss her. It was a completely natural moment, not choreographed by the photographer but stolen. An instant when they had thought they were alone. William had considered it too soppy to be displayed anywhere public in the house, hence it ending up here. If truth be known he had never understood why she loved it so much until now. And it broke his heart she had chosen to leave it behind when she left.

"Stevie, I need help."

His friend looked up from the copy of Runner's World he had been flicking through. "Okay. I can sort something out for you, my colleague Jason is really good and I'm sure he would be happy to see you. Let me speak to him in the morning and make some arrangements."

"Not professional help, you twerp. I need to find out all I can about time travel."

"Of course you do," said Steve.

"I'm serious. Something weird happened out there… something unbelievable and amazing…"

"Were you really going to do it?"

"And I met this woman who was incredible. I mean really, really hot. Probably right up your street, but then again a bit too bright for your tastes…"

"Were you really going to do it?"

"She wanted me to stay and help with some real crazy shit, but I was angry and scared, so I scarpered… but… I didn't expect it to work, you know… I didn't think I'd be back here and now I don't know what to do."

"Will! Were you?"

William blinked at his friend a few times wondering what the hell Steve demanded of him. When it came to him, William averted his eyes. "Yes."

"Shit."

"But I'm over it now. I've got other things on my mind. Don't worry about it."

Steve laughed a bitter laugh. "How can I not worry about it? You tried to top yourself and now you're having some sort of manic episode. You're right, Will, you do need help. Help is exactly what you need."

Chapter Fourteen

"I spoke to Jason and he's happy to see you whenever you like." It had been a week since Will's suicide attempt, and Steve had failed to make any progress getting through to him.

"I'm fine, I don't need to see him," said William.

They sat in the corner of the busy pub, crushed around a tiny table by the toilets. Steve moved his chair to let a couple of guys pass. "Well, just humour me then."

William smirked and lifted his pint to his lips. He was not going to cave. Steve knew he had no choice but to take it on himself.

"Try and see it from my perspective. Do you remember at Uni how we planned to change the face of Psychology? How we wanted to make it credible and more than just a pseudoscience-" said Steve

"And you think I'm disillusioned with my life and career because I've managed nothing of the sort. I studied the subject too you know," interrupted William.

"No, I don't think you're disillusioned. I think you're delusional."

William choked a little on his drink. "Whoa, aren't you supposed to tread more carefully than that? Is blurting it out really the most advisable route to take with a suicidal person?"

"Yeh, well it turns out you're too damn stubborn to take the subtle route."

William grinned. "Ha, touché!"

Steve moved his drink aside and rested his hands on the table. "This future you visited with its computers who think like humans and its brain upgrades. You say that these advances in psychological understanding have resulted in a world with no war, no crime, no prejudice and discrimination?"

"Well, no *I* didn't say that. She did."

"Can you see my point though?"

William scratched his head theatrically. "I think you might have to spell it out."

Steve moved his seat to let a lady pass to the loos. "Fine. Your denial only makes me more convinced I'm right."

"And there we have it, the Catch-22. The more convinced I am I'm right, the more crazy I am. Yeh?"

"You're telling me you went to a future where psychology has become not only a major science, but *the* major science. Is that not a bit coincidental?"

William rolled his eyes and took a handful of peanuts.

"Okay so let's look at the weather then. You said it was hot, continental temperatures even though it was only April. Along the lines of what people would have us expect from global warming?"

"So you think the fact I experienced a future which is consistent with weather predictions today, is further proof I've made it up? I take it my finding the place in the midst of an ice-age would have been more convincing for you."

Steve shook his head and tried not to react to the sarcasm. No need to let Will get to him. "No, I was thinking more about the foxgloves."

His friend paused mid-drink. "What?"

"You said this woman was picking foxgloves in her garden, but isn't that odd? Foxgloves grow in abundance today, in the current climate. Would they still be going strong if that had changed significantly? Do you ever see foxgloves in hot countries?"

"Steve, mate, you're trying too hard. Foxgloves grow all over Europe and even in Asia."

"Yes but when, in what season?"

William shrugged. "Your question is irrelevant."

"How do you make that out?"

William stood and picked up both empty glasses. "She was growing them in her garden. Another drink?"

Steve nodded and watched Will walk away. She grew them in her garden, where she could keep them shaded and watered. The guy had an answer for everything. Steve felt dismayed at how deep Will's delusion appeared to be. He had nowhere else to go. He had to tackle the big one. But could he really do this with Will? It seemed to Steve that anyone else in the world would have been an easier subject.

But he could not let his closest friend persist with this thing, could he? A good friend would not indulge the fantasy. Steve became aware that he was frantically tapping his foot and concentrated on stilling it. He just needed to do it as he would with a client. It would be easy. He ran through the points in his head. He just needed to ask the right questions, watch that his tone sounded in no way judgmental and make Will do the thinking.

"So the woman," Steve said as William sat and handed him a drink. He saw his friend's jaw tighten and knew his instinct was bang on. He had hit the deep seated need at the core of the delusion.

"What about her?"

Steve realised he had started in the wrong place and decided to back track. "Have you heard from Sarah?"

William frowned at the change of subject, but as Steve expected did not object. "She called three or four times to make sure I'm not cliff diving."

"Has she been to see you?"

William shook his head. "Course not. She thinks I did this to guilt her into coming back. There's no way she'd give me the satisfaction."

"Don't you miss her though?"

A look of sadness passed across Will's eyes, and Steve wondered if this was too soon. After a moment's hesitation he concluded, only one way to find out. "So she's wrong? You didn't do it to get her back?"

"God no. She's just being typical Sarah, suspicious and cynical."

Steve had to laugh at that, and the look of surprise his reaction gained from Will made him laugh even harder. "Do you remember what Sarah was like when we met her? Such a dreamer, so free-spirited and happy-go-lucky. Isn't that why we all liked her so much? All the years with you made her suspicious and cynical, you've only got yourself to blame for that."

"Cheers. Is this how they teach you to build confidence and self-esteem?"

Steve knew he could not stay detached enough to treat Will as a client. He found it too hard not to pass comments like that. He had to tackle it as a friend and hope to God he didn't make things worse.

"I've got to be honest with you, Will, I think the woman you say you met is proof none of it happened. Can it really be a coincidence she is everything Sarah is not? Dark haired, athletic, wanting you as a lover, needing you to be her hero. A role, I might add, which she says you, and only you, are able to fill."

Steve waited for a reaction. He knew from experience such direct challenge could result in anything from anger to tears.

"She was real."

Steve sighed. For William, continued denial it was going to be. "Real is the one thing she is not. Even if you did somehow travel to the future to meet her, here and now, in 2011, she is no more real than Jessica flaming Rabbit."

William did not react at all and the two of them sat in silence for the next five minutes, finishing their beers.

"Do you have much work on?" Steve asked when he could not stand the atmosphere any longer.

"Nah, I'm not really interested." William's tone bordered on angry.

"I know, but you need to work. There's a guy at my golf club who runs a wool factory. He's just got a massive new contract and needs a load more staff but his track record of recruiting has been disastrous. He says he's got a real bunch of numpties working for him. I gave him your number and told him you could help with the interviews."

"Right."

"It'll be good for you."

William fixed Steve in a steady gaze, his mouth in a tight line. "And how the hell would you know what's good for me, Steve? You who's never had a relationship last more than three shags."

"I think you'll find the average is closer to five." He leant across the table and touched Will's arm. "And I know because it's my job to know."

The corners of Will's mouth twitched. "Can I get you some biscuits for that cheese?"

"Sweaty camembert?"

William chuckled now. "More like a stinky slab of stilton you've left festering in your fridge."

Steve sat back in his chair and raised his glass to his best friend. "It's good to hear you laugh, mate."

Chapter Fifteen

The deserted moor stretched ahead as far as he could see. William checked his Garmin for the distance. Six miles done, four to go. He tried to ignore the blister forming on the arch of his foot and concentrated on the horizon. Three days of constant rain had made the ground soggy and Will could feel mud splashing up his legs as he ran. His chest hurt with the effort and his feet kept slipping in the sludge. Not so long ago he would have bounded up here without a second thought, but it had been over three months since he had run anywhere near this distance.

At the top of the hill he felt overcome with the urge to stop and catch his breath. He forced the idea aside, replacing it with an all too familiar image. One he knew would keep him working hard. It had changed over the past week he knew. Each time he brought her to mind, he needed more and more reconstruction: was her hair longer, her eyes more silver, her voice deeper? He knew whatever he saw in his head now bore little resemblance to reality at all.

The whole experience had faded to such a degree it felt like a dream. The certainty of those first days had dwindled and, whilst he fought it, Steve's hypothesis made more and more sense every day.

He could try to go back, but was proving it real a good enough reason? He had no desire to be an outcast in a future where he did not belong. And he had no interest in being their hero, which is where Stevie's theory fell short. No, the only reason he would be going back would be to see her again. It would be nothing more than an ego trip.

So why could he not sleep? And why when he did manage a few moments of rest, did he dream of wives drowned in baths and children walking the streets like zombies? Because he felt guilty, that's why. Guilty for scaring them in the first place, and guilty for running away when they needed him. Now he was away from there and calm, he understood their attack on him, this stranger who had turned up for no apparent reason. And Steve was right about one thing; William's unique ability to help was an almost unbelievable coincidence. But was that reason enough to dismiss it?

Plus, she had wanted him.

His final thought irritated him. Sigmund Freud had been spot on. Under the surface of every man's worthy intentions, swam the basest of desires, a pulsating beast looking for any opportunity to feed its need. *Go back and get laid*, was he really that shallow?

And what if he could not get back? If he scrambled down that cliff and found himself nowhere more exotic than the bottom, what then? Could he really be sure he had not been hallucinating? He knew the mind was powerful enough to create alternative realities, it was clear to see in the average dream. He could have spent hours running around the countryside in that storm, imagining himself elsewhere. He could have lost his shoes and jacket somehow, maybe even taken them off himself and bandaged his own feet then fabricated an elaborate fantasy for how it all happened.

William pushed his confusion aside and made one final push to finish in a decent time. The downhill helped, but by the time he stopped with his hands on his thighs and his eyes closed, he felt pretty close to throwing up.

"Good to see ya back, Yorkie," club secretary, Stuart Lane said. The committee man loved nothing more than playing at being the boss. Will supposed it made up for being a less than average runner.

"Cheers," William managed to say.

"Coming for a pint after? We're off to The Vaults."

Will stood with his hands on his hips and took a few deep breaths. He wanted nothing more than to crawl home and continue hiding from the world, but knew he should make the effort. "Sure, see you there."

By the time William had showered and headed over, the usual Thursday night crowd already sitting in the pub. He checked if anyone needed a drink then went to the bar. He arrived at the same time as a guy in an expensive-looking suit and open-necked shirt.

"Bottle of Rioja and two glasses, please?" The guy beat William to the order then looked his way. "Sorry, did I push in?"

"No, it's okay I only just arrived." William checked in his pocket for change. He needed some kind of snack too. He could feel the beginnings of a carb craving. When he looked up, the suited guy glanced away. He had obviously been staring.

"Do you run with the club then?" Suit-man kept his eyes to the front as he asked his question. He had that tanned, chiselled look William associated with Alpha males.

"Yeh, when I can. You?" Will had not seen the suited man before, but the club frequently acquired new members.

Suit-man laughed. "Not likely. I'm more of your gentle stroller." The barman opened the wine bottle and sat it next to the glasses. Suit-man held out a crisp twenty-pound note and collected his drinks. "Nice to meet you anyway."

William nodded. "Pint of orange squash and a bag of dry roasted, please." Once served, he took his drink to the table and squeezed into a spot next to Stuart.

"Tough run, Will? I can't believe I beat you. That's a first, hey? You losing your touch?" Phil Waverley, or Wavo, as he liked to be called, was one of the club's newest members. He had not been running long, but liked to feel he was moving up the ranks.

Stuart coughed and shook his head.

Wavo frowned and mouthed, "What?"

"He means to say, take it easy coz my wife's left me," said William before drinking half of the juice in one go.

"Shit, sorry man." Wavo suddenly found his packet of crisps thoroughly fascinating.

"Don't worry about it. I get to spend more time training now there's no ball and chain keeping me in the house."

"You'd think you'd be getting better then," called a voice from across the table. Davey Foster, the club's star fell runner grinned at William. On the road he was not a patch on Will, but up in the hills the man was fearless. On numerous occasions he had jumped right over Will's head as he made his way cautiously down a steep decline.

"Watch this space, Davey," said William.

"Is that a challenge I hear before me?"

William laughed; something told him he might be just a little more fearless these days. "You're damn right it is."

A blonde in a figure-hugging red dress with a plunging neckline crossed the pub and kissed the suited man full on the lips.

The smile froze on William's face.

"Isn't that your wife?" said Stuart.

William rose from his stool as his neighbour placed a restraining hand on his arm. "It's fine, Stuart. I can handle this." It was a lie, of course. William had no idea if he could handle it. In a split second he had gone from peaceful fatigue to a blistering tumult of rage and jealousy. He didn't know what he wanted to do more, rip the guy's head off or drag his wife home and rip her clothes off.

Stuart let go but looked worried. No one else in the group

appeared to have noticed.

"Mine's a pint, Yorkie," Davey shouted as William stepped away from the table.

The use of his nickname caught Sarah's attention. She broke from the kiss to look Will's way, her face becoming instantly paler.

"It's nice to meet me?" William said to Suit-man on reaching them.

Sarah looked confused. "Will, calm down okay. Don't start any trouble." She leant away from her new man, but he had his hand on her waist and was not letting go.

"Sorry, I wasn't sure what I should say," said Suit-man.

"Of course. I suppose, 'hi I'm the guy banging your wife' might have been a touch forthright."

"Will please." Sarah stared at him hard but he ignored her.

"I'm William," he said holding out his hand.

Suit-man still held the wine and glasses in his free hand so had no choice but to let go of Sarah to return the gesture. Which was the point of course. "Danny."

"Well nice to meet you too, Danny. Oh I'm the guy who used to bang your girlfriend by the way."

"Stop it, Will," said Sarah.

"New dress?"

She pulled the edges of the neckline together as his eyes took in her cleavage.

"S'alright, Sarah, nothing I haven't seen before."

"Don't be an arse."

William raised his eyebrows at his wife. "You're kidding right?" Then he squeezed Danny's arm just a little tighter than was necessary. "Listen, do you mind if I have a few minutes in private with my wife?"

Danny looked at Sarah.

"I'll be fine," she said touching her lover's other arm.

"Yeh, don't worry, Dan, I won't take her near any significant drops." William walked to the back door and turned to check Sarah followed. He saw her mouth, 'sorry', to her new man and roll her eyes. When had she become such a bitch?

The road at the side of the pub led to a small copse and William led the way into the trees without slowing.

"Where are we going? I'm wearing heels for Christ sake," said Sarah.

"I can carry you if you like."

Sarah made a huff of disgust. "I'll manage thanks."

"Somehow I thought you'd say that." The ground felt moist underneath, not good news for her recently purchased shoes. That would piss her off.

"How much further?" demanded Sarah.

William stopped and faced her. "Do you know where we are?"

Her eyes darted around the small clearing. "Stop messing around, Will, or I'm going back. If there's something you want to say just get on with it."

He placed his hand on the trunk of a large oak tree. "This not familiar?" he said drumming his fingers against it.

Sarah stiffened and took another look at the small woodland scene.

"I bought you tickets for the Ilkley Literature Festival the year we graduated, do you remember?"

Her eyes met his but she did not answer.

He stepped towards her. "We got a little tipsy and made our way here... right to this spot. Is it coming back to you yet?"

"Stop it."

"Come see," he said walking to the trunk and looking closely at it. She didn't move so he held his position. After what seemed like an age, he heard her sigh and come to his side. Before she had time to react, he had her pinned to the tree.

Sarah wriggled beneath him and pushed her hands against his sides. "You're not funny."

"You wanted me to make love to you right here… begged me in fact." He traced the neckline of her dress as it plunged southwards and she wriggled even more.

"Stop it, Will."

He pressed against her and whispered in her ear. "You begged me until I thought I was going crazy." He kissed the soft skin of her neck and breathed in her familiar perfume. "Would you return the favour now… if *I* begged?" He walked his fingers up the material of her dress and raised the hem a fraction.

Sarah hit him in the kidneys. "If you try anything, I *will* scream."

"Mmm I remember the screaming from last time." William pressed his lips to her skin one last time, then released her from his weight. "You still send me weak at the knees even now. Even after everything you've done." He stepped clear away from her. "I'm sorry if I scared you. I just needed to be sure."

She straightened her dress. "What d'you mean, sure?"

William put his hands in his pockets and took a long look at his wife. She always did look gorgeous in red. "That it's all gone for you. That the idea of me touching you… making love to you, makes your skin crawl."

She stepped away from the tree. "No, Will, it's not like that, I swear."

"Thanks for the sentiment, but your actions speak a little louder than your words." He turned and walked away. "Say bye to Dan for me," he said raising his hand.

"Will... William?" Sarah called, her voice breaking, but he did not look back.

"He'll be alright, I'm sure. It's not like he didn't know I existed."

Sarah picked small pieces of bread off her roll and avoided Danny's eyes.

"Oh, Sarah, I thought we agreed?"

Danny had been at pains to point out she should be up front with Will about their relationship. *I'm not prepared to be your dirty little secret*, he had said.

"The deal was if he asked me directly, I'd tell him, but he never did." Her words sounded childlike and petulant even to her.

Danny sighed. "No. The deal was if he asks you directly you mustn't lie, not, only tell him if he asks. That's twisting things, Sarah. He has a right to know."

"I'm sorry." She rested her forehead on her hand. Hard as she tried she could not get the look in Will's eyes out of her head.

"Hey come on. Don't let it spoil our night. He knows now and he'll deal with it I'm sure." Danny took her hand away from her head, smiled at her and then kissed it. "Although it's a shame it had to happen when you're looking like that. Poor bastard."

Sarah took her hand back. "Don't talk about him like that."

Danny's eyes narrowed. "Let's change the subject," he said and immediately began chatting about his day.

She had first met Danny at a conference in Geneva where he had given a talk on product development in Australasia. His speech stood out a mile. Not only because he had paced the stage without any notes, but because he was funny. It looked like he had stood up and started speaking without any preparation. Sarah knew better now. As a total perfectionist, Danny would have spent hours crafting his message in order to have the desired effect. He just hated the idea of boring people.

Their international finance company employer had seconded Danny to oversee their Australian launch three years earlier. As Head of International Marketing, Sarah partially managed two members of Danny's team, and needed to introduce herself at this event. In her head, she imagined herself coming over as professional and impressive, not sitting on the floor covered in blackcurrant juice. Her flight out had been delayed and she had pretty much missed a night's sleep, so she felt tired and distracted as she left the conference hall to find a drink. The large jugs of juice sat alongside the coffee machine and she had inadvertently thrown the strap of her handbag over one as she made her espresso. When she grabbed the bag and walked away, the jug followed. First it hit her back making her jump, and then it splashed down her legs and under her feet. She slipped and landed in a heap on the floor.

"I can't actually believe you managed to save the coffee."

Sarah looked at the still full cup of espresso in her hand, and then up at Danny's amused face.

He held his hand out. "Ya, didn't hurt yourself did you?" His accent had a very slight Australian twang.

"No. Thanks. I'm okay, I'm not sure…" She looked back at the table trying to suss out what the hell just happened. Her hip felt sore and she imagined she would have a bruise by bedtime.

"Sarah York isn't it?"

Oh God, he knew who she was. Not embarrassing at all. "Yeh, I planned to make a better first impression than that."

He laughed loudly. "I tell you what, that's the best first impression anyone ever made. There's no way I'll be forgetting you in a hurry."

Nothing had happened between them at that point, or at all prior to her leaving Will. She did have some morals. But within a few months of the conference, Danny had been transferred back to the UK and she found herself in his company more and more. At first, she felt embarrassed by how he looked at her, then annoyed, before finding herself hunting him down just to experience the thrill of it. Will had become more and more bitter and contemptuous as the years went by and Danny was like the antidote. He could be as silly as he was impressive, once arranging a tournament of races down the hallway of the third floor on wheeled office chairs. Sarah had won, to the sound of his whoops and cheers, after which he made her stand on a chair to receive her medal, an item fashioned from office string and a pad of post-it notes. As he hung it over her bowed head, he had kissed her cheek to the sound of everyone's applause. She had blushed like a teenager and hung her head lower so he could not see. As everyone moved back to their desks, he helped her down and whispered. "God, you're like the perfect woman or something." At which point she knew her marriage was over.

"So what are you having? Sarah?... Sarah?"

She came out of her daydream to find Danny and the waiter both waiting for her selection. The menu rested in her hands but she had not read a word. She had no appetite anyway.

"I'm sorry, I need to go." She returned the menu to the table and scraped out her chair. A couple nearby looked over at the sound.

"Are you coming back?" said Danny.

Sarah shook her head.

Danny began to take his wallet from the inside pocket of his jacket. "I'll just pay for the drinks, please."

She had made it almost halfway back to the small flat she

rented when Danny caught her up. "Do you mind if I have a bit of time alone?" she said.

"Sure, babe. Let me walk you home though." He placed his arm around her shoulder and she let him pull her close.

"You can't stay... not tonight. It wouldn't feel right," said Sarah.

Danny said nothing.

"I'm sorry."

"No need to apologise, you still care about him, I get it."

"I still love him," she said quietly leaning her head against Danny's chest. They walked like that to her door in silence. He made no comment about her admission. He simply planted a lingering kiss on her lips and left.

Chapter Sixteen

William's visit to the run-down factory of Peacock Wools proved an entirely depressing affair. A case study in why he was so damned disillusioned with his career. Clive Peacock pranced around the building in a manner most fitting for his name, clucking about his staff being feckless wasters. William sighed inside. He saw no sign of fecklessness or wastery. Every person looked to be applying themselves diligently. He had met this type of manager many times before.

"The other shrink said you could work some magic. Read the minds of the applicants and pick the ones with a bit of get up and go," Peacock said at the end of the tour.

"Shrinks are psychiatrists, medical doctors. Steve and I are Psychologists."

"He still deals with the mentals though, doesn't he? But he did say you were different. My wife's into all this hockery pockery, reads the horoscopes like they're a user's guide to life. Load of guff if you ask me, although I'll hazard a guess you'll put me straight on that," said Peacock.

"Horoscopes are astrology. Psychology is the science of the mind and why people behave as they do."

"Grand. Well you just find me some brains full of good old-fashioned gumption and I'll pay you a bonus, Billy my lad." The man actually hit William hard on the back, almost winding him. William had not even given a quote yet and it occurred to him he could price himself out of the job.

After the hour from hell, he left with a promise to come back to Peacock with a proposal on price by tomorrow. Now he sat at his desk, four hours later, with little progress made. It was not only that working for this ignorant man would be painful that made production of the document hard. It was also the distraction of the World Wide Web.

William found the number of credible science websites which came up in a Google search of time travel amazing. Articles in the likes of the Guardian and Independent newspapers, write-ups in New Scientist magazine, papers by academic institutions, and informed comments by the likes of Stephen Hawkings and NASA.

Admittedly, most reported how theoretically possible and yet practically unlikely it was. Exactly as Caro had said. William made a mental note to speak to Steve about that. How could he have imagined this reaction in Caro if, until now, he'd had no such insight himself? He bit the end of his pen as he thought about that. His friend would no doubt claim Will must have absorbed such knowledge subliminally. It made him wonder how crazy the crazy people ever really were, when psychiatrists and psychologists could explain everything away.

William looked deeper into the concept of wormholes. He discovered that two physicists from Steklov Mathematical Institute in Moscow had predicted they might be formed by the Large Hadron Collider. The LHC in Switzerland had first been used in March 2010. It aimed to increase understanding of the fundamental structure of the universe. William read all the articles he could find on the topic. He found references to ANN's year zero theory: the idea that travelling back in time could only go as far as the date on which the first time tunnel was created, another theory of physics that was new to him, and began to feel excited. Could ANNy have been wrong? Was it possible that a wormhole had actually been created here and now, in his time, that no one knew about?

The gist of the reports, however, said that even if such wormholes were created they would be at the sub-atomic level and brief. No human would be passing through those. But despite this general trashing of the wormhole concept, everything he read corroborated the conversation between Caro, Sorella and ANN. Even down to their comment that wormholes for humans were unlikely.

"This really did happen," he said to his office walls. No matter how Steve might interpret it, William knew he could not have subliminally absorbed such accurate detail.

Maybe it had been something else out in those hills that transported him. Some natural phenomenon or alien technology as ANN suggested. He needed to speak to an expert, someone he could describe his experience to and receive an opinion on its feasibility. And he knew just who to ask.

The doorbell rang as he pressed 'dial'. William aborted the call and went to answer. Dusk had fallen whilst he ferreted away at his computer and he tripped over some shoes on the landing. "Shit," he said under his breath as he caught hold of the banister and prevented what could have been a painful fall down the stairs. He flicked the lights on and checked his watch. It was eight thirty. That would explain the hunger. He had eaten nothing since breakfast. There were some eggs and mushrooms in the fridge. Once he had dealt with this, he would make an omelette.

The familiar face at the door was the last he expected to see, and all his thoughts of hunger disappeared.

"You don't really think he believes he went to the future, though?"

Steve sat back in Jason's consulting chair and stared up at the lemon ceiling. Research in years gone by had indicated that patients found the colour relaxing. "I think he wants to believe it. I think he feels there's nothing to live for. His wife's gone, his business is struggling and more than that he's come to hate the work. He's at a typical crisis point but unfortunately happens to come from a family of depressives. I reckon he needs this bit of fantasy to give him hope or something."

"So you're not thinking an actual delusion. He doesn't think he's there now?" said Jason.

"Oh no. He thinks he went there and back through some wormhole."

"Any chance he was hallucinating?"

Steve considered that. "Could be… could be. He's not the sort to take drugs, too sensible for that… although he was trying to top himself."

"Yeh, but hallucinogens wouldn't be the typical drug of choice for a depressive."

Steve sat up. "He took a bad knock to the head. Paramedics found him unconscious at the bottom of some cliff he said he had fallen down. They estimated he'd been out for a few hours. He thinks he was gone two days."

Jason frowned. "Well you know as well as I do, there's not a common link between mood disorders such as depression and psychotic episodes such as hallucinations or thought disorders. Is there any history of schizophrenia in his family?"

"Not that I know of," said Steve with a shake of his head.

"Any signs of paranoia or auditory hallucinations?"

"Not that I've noticed."

Jason placed his hands together and tapped the side of them against his pursed lips. "So the most likely hypothesis is he experienced a vivid dream whilst unconscious and has convinced himself it was real. To provide some hope as you say. It may even be feeding his sense of control."

Steve shuffled forward in the chair. "Making him feel he can change his lot if he wishes, by going back?"

"Could be," said Jason.

"So what do I do?"

"Well, considering he's refusing to come in and face this head on, I think your only option is to provide a good level of support and keep him focused on the here and now. Do you know the wife well?"

"Sarah? Yes, we all went to university together," said Steve.

"Any chance you can have a word and make sure she gives him as much stability as possible in the coming weeks. No dumping divorce papers just yet."

"Sarah?"

His wife stood on the doorstep with her bag hugged tightly to her chest. "Can I come in?" she said.

William stood back and let her past. "I'm pretty sure the law would say you could use your key. The house is still half yours."

"I wasn't sure if you'd have company."

The idea made him laugh. "Oh yeh, my dancing girls just left."

Sarah flashed him a quick smile. "Looks like I timed it well then."

They stood in the hall for an uncomfortable moment; his wife staring at the floor.

"Can I get you a drink or something?" said William.

She reached into her bag and lifted out a bottle of red. "I brought my own, hope that's okay?"

"Right," said William feeling nervous about her motives. "You better come through."

In the kitchen, he handed her the bottle opener from the drawer and reached down two glasses. "So is that a bribe or Dutch courage?"

"Neither." Sarah removed the cork and began pouring wine into the glass Will held out. "Both."

He rested against the counter top. "Go on then, you have my attention."

His wife took a large gulp of wine then stared into the glass as she spoke. "Do you know what I loved about you most when we first met?"

"I'm not really in the mood for character assassination."

"No," she said looking up, "that's not what I'm doing."

"Okay then, if it's a genuine question, I believe someone once told me it was something to do with my eyes."

Sarah laughed a little and glanced away. "Yeh, they are lovely. But I was thinking more about your attitude to life. That boyish enthusiasm you had for everything new. Don't get me wrong you could be a sarcastic bastard-"

"Cheers, I thought this wasn't character assassination."

"Let me finish. *But*, you threw yourself into things with so much passion, your degree, your sports, your career. I always envied how much energy you had for the stuff you loved."

William fidgeted feeling uncomfortable receiving her compliments. "Is there a point to this?"

"I wanted to know where he went."

Ouch. Build me up to knock me down, nice move, Sarah. He did not credit her insult with a response.

"I'm sorry. That must sound like a huge dig."

William put down his wine, not in the mood to socialise anymore. "It wasn't all my fault you know? You changed too. We all grow up and lose things along the way. That's just life."

"I just really miss the man I married," Sarah said.

"Not as much as I miss the woman I did." William could not help the smirk; she had walked right into that one. "Was there something you wanted, Sarah?"

She drank more wine and scanned the room. "It's incredibly tidy in here."

William took in the clean surfaces, lack of dirty dishes and recently swept floor. Had she thought he'd be unable to cope? "One advantage of not having to clean up after you."

"Are there others? Advantages to my not being here I mean?"

He looked out of the darkened window, once more refusing to answer. There were no advantages at all to her not being here. He would happily put up with her messy streak for ever-more rather than live this half-life.

"I've been doing a lot of thinking since the other night... outside the pub." Sarah twisted the stem of her glass back and forth and watched the swirling wine.

"Oh, yeh?"

She took a deep breath. "Particularly the part where you said you think it makes my skin crawl when you touch me."

"Thanks for reminding me. I was trying to repress that new piece of insight."

Sarah lifted her head. "You're wrong."

It looked like she meant it, but then William remembered her wriggling and hitting him and threatening to scream. "Look, I was just trying to make a point. It was a shitty way to go about it I know, so I'm sorry. But seeing you with that guy..." He gripped the edge of the work surface with both hands and concentrated on the floor tiles.

Sarah came to stand in front of him, making him raise his eyes. "I keep thinking about me and you against that tree...can't stop thinking about it actually." The blush rose up her cheeks. "It was sexy as hell."

"Oh we were young and horny, not to mention drunk."

"I wasn't talking about the first time."

William felt his eyes widen and his mouth drop open a tad. She was winding him up, had to be, although how the hell she thought this was funny?

Sarah put down her glass and placed both hands flat on his chest.

"What are you doing?" he said.

"You asked me if I would return the favour if you begged." She stepped closer. "But you left before I could answer."

"Stop it, Sarah," William said grabbing her wrists. "It's not funny and there is no way in hell I will ever be begging you for anything."

She rotated her hands out of his grip and grabbed at his t-shirt. "I miss you, Will."

He moved away pulling his top from her hands. "I think it's time you went back to lover boy."

"Do you want *me* to beg?"

"No!" He ran his hands through his hair. "I want you to stop torturing me."

They stared at each other for a beat.

"Fine." Sarah snatched her bag off the side and bolted for the door.

Will went after her and seized her arm. "Why? Why did you come here? Why are you doing this?"

He could see from her face she was angry and embarrassed. "Because I feel bad, because I hurt you, because you scared the crap out of me trying to kill yourself and because no matter how hard I try I can't get over you." She started to cry.

"But you want to?"

"I don't know."

"Sarah, I'm not the person to help you with this, you know that don't you."

Next he knew, she had flung her arms around his neck to kiss him. It took all his will-power to push her away. "This is not a good idea."

"Please," she said pressing her body back up to his and grabbing his hair.

"No, Sarah. You need to…"

She cut off his words with a kiss and he knew she would be well aware of the effect she was having on him.

He moved his mouth from hers, but before he had chance to speak she took his face in her hands. "Please, Will. I miss you, I want you."

She did not have to ask again.

It started with him ripping off her blouse and ended with her naked on the hall carpet, head flung back and moaning his name.

"Oh God, Will. Oh, yes. Yes, Will… Oh Christ! Will, yes, yes, YES!"

It would have been funny were it not him making her do this.

When they collapsed into each other, sweating and breathing hard, she laughed. "Wow, I really needed that."

He nearly made some barbed remark about her new man not keeping her satisfied, but instead he told the truth. "Yeh, me too."

As her breathing returned to normal, William began to feel anxious. He knew he needed to brace himself for the rejection coming, and shit was it going to hurt.

"Will?"

"Ah ha?" He found himself unable to formulate a proper word, his heart hammering against his rib cage.

"Shall we go to bed?"

This time their love-making was slow and intense. They moved around each other with the familiarity of years and stared into each other's eyes. Despite the intimacy, William did not respond when she pulled his arms around her and whispered that she loved him. But as he fell asleep with the scent of her hair filling his head and the feel of her skin against his body, his decision surprised him. He had thought he would never be able to forgive her for being unfaithful, that they were well and truly over, but there was no question about it: he was going to take her back.

Chapter Seventeen

Sarah turned the pen top over and over in her hands and stared at her unanswered emails. Her coffee sat cold at her side and she was completely unaware of her ringing telephone. Only when she heard him shouting did she come to her senses. She looked up to see him striding towards her with a face like thunder. He shouted her name and she had never seen him so angry. The whole office stared at him and Sarah jumped to her feet.

"Steve, what are you doing here?" It was a stupid question. She knew exactly why he had come.

For the first thirty seconds or so after she awoke, all was well. Sarah lay in her own bed with her sleeping husband's arms around her. Everything in its right place.

And then it began: the panic. It sizzled and spat within her, growing stronger and louder as she lay listening to Will's steady breaths. She had achieved so much, made it so far. She had battled through the hardest decisions and the toughest conversations only to wipe it all out with one thoughtless action. Well, two actually. She looked over at her husband. God he had been amazing, though. She could not remember the last time he had loved her like that. But she found it changed nothing. She still wanted out, she still wanted more, and she still wanted Danny.

Will always looked so attractive when he slept. His features relaxed and as they should be. She wished he could stay this way, but she knew he would turn ugly as hell when he woke. Her muscles felt tighter by the second as she stared at the ceiling.

When William's eyes fluttered open and he did not speak, Sarah felt a flush of hope: maybe he thought it had been a mistake too.

"This is nice," he said without the edge to his voice that had been ever present since her leaving.

Sarah ripped herself from his arms and stood in one swift motion. "This was a mistake," she said needing the truth to be out as fast as possible. She fled to the bathroom expecting him to follow, but he did not. She splashed water on her face and ran downstairs to collect her clothes. Nothing but silence came from the bedroom. Where was his rage, the insults and the name calling she had expected? She watched the top of the stairs as she did up her blouse. She had three buttons missing but did not bother to look for them on the carpet. She grabbed her bag and hunted for her car keys whilst putting on her shoes. It would only take her twenty minutes to get home and shower.

Sarah paused with her hand on the door handle. Had he misunderstood or not heard her right?

William lay exactly where she had left him, with one hand above his head and the other in the space she had left. He did not look at her when she walked in.

"Will, promise me you won't do anything silly…anything to hurt yourself."

"I don't think you're worth it anymore, do you?" He remained staring at the ceiling.

"I never was."

He turned her way and his eyes were cold. "So it seems."

"I'm so sorry, really. I don't know what I was thinking."

William faced the ceiling again and made no further comment. And that is how she had left him.

"You total bitch," said Steve.

"Get in here, Steve." Sarah pulled him into her office and closed the door. Not that it would do much good, the glass walls were not exactly soundproof. A handful of people had stood up from their desks, their neck's craning to see what drama unfolded in their boss's office. Sarah spotted her PA Jenny pick up the phone and felt disappointed; she never had the girl down as a gossip.

"Are you trying to drive him to it? Are you?" shouted Steve.

"Calm down, this is my workplace."

Steve's laugh sounded closer to a sneer as he got right in her face. "Calm down! Are you flaming kidding me?"

"This is none of your business." She would not cry, not here. Better to get angry.

"Oh, that's where you're wrong, because unlike you I care about what happens to him, what he does to himself."

Sarah moved away. "You have no idea how I feel about him, and he's not going to hurt himself again. He told me I wasn't worth it." She began shuffling papers on her desk as a cue for him to go.

Steve grabbed her arm, squeezing it painfully. "And you believed him? How stupid are you, Sarah? He's suicidal because he's depressed. Oh you were the cause, of course, you and your inability to stay in your knickers." He yanked her towards him. "But, this is a disease. He's not going to just snap out of it because he decides to."

"What the hell is going on in here?" Danny dragged Steve free of Sarah and squared up to him. "Who are you?"

Sarah glanced out at Jenny who looked pleased with herself, *stupid girl.*

"Are you her boss?" Steve looked around Danny to Sarah. "Is this your boss?"

"No matter who I am, who are you and what do you think you are doing pushing ladies around." Danny had pulled himself up to his full height and spoke with all his directorial authority.

"She's no lady," said Steve.

"This is Steve, William's friend. He was just leaving."

"Oh *you* wish." Steve stepped away from Danny who had backed off a little at the sound of William's name. "And I'm just Will's friend now am I? Cutting me out too, Sarah?"

"Danny, could you give us a minute?" She could not let him find out about last night. She felt bad enough about Will seeing her as the bad guy, she could not stand that from Danny too.

"You know I really used to envy, Will. I thought he was so lucky to have married you," said Steve, making no move to leave.

"Is this about Tuesday in the pub?" said Danny.

Sarah began to push Danny to the door. "This is nothing to do with you."

"It is, if he's sending his friends round to hassle you now." Danny resisted her attempts to move him and spoke to Steve. "Look, Sarah is really sorry this came as a shock to him, we both are, but this sort of behaviour is not going to change anything."

Steve looked from Danny to Sarah in silence and Sarah felt the heat burning up her neck.

"Steve -"

Steve held his hand up to stop her. "I take it he doesn't know."

"Yes, he saw us together earlier this week," said Danny completely missing the point.

Steve smirked at Sarah. "You couldn't make a bigger mess of this if you tried could you?"

"Steve, please, let me handle this okay?" said Sarah.

It seemed to take him an age to decide, and all the time her heart pounded in her ears.

"I don't want anything more to do with your sordid little secrets, Sarah." Steve spoke in a low voice and she hoped Danny did not detect her sigh of relief. "But I'm here to warn you to stay away from now on. I don't care what you're going through or what doubts you have, Will needs stability and he is the last person who can help you. Am I making myself clear?"

Sarah could feel Danny's eyes on her as she straightened her back. "Crystal." This was over, Steve was going and he had not said anything she could not explain away.

Steve opened the door, stopped and half turned his head. "No contact, Sarah. No calls, no texts, no emails and certainly no turning up at night with bottles of wine." He walked out and left her open-mouthed and unable to look Danny's way.

Her lover moved to the office door, closed it and faced her.

"I can explain," she said.

"Save your breath, Sarah. I'm pretty good at reading between the lines."

She felt the tears finally begin to well in her eyes. "I was confused… I can't stand how much he hates me… what I've done to him."

"And how about what you've done to me?"

Sarah could not help the small laugh that escaped her. "You're fine. You got the girl. You didn't get your heart crushed by someone you thought loved you. You have no idea."

Danny nodded and pursed his lips. "He was right your friend there, wasn't he? You couldn't make more of a mess of this." He walked towards her and brushed a stray piece of hair behind her ear. "Because you're wrong, Sarah. So, so wrong. I have every idea what your husband is going through and I'm not fine, you know why?"

Sarah shook her head, unable to speak.

"Because I didn't get the girl did I? Well not the girl I thought I had anyway." Danny's laugh sounded bitter. "And, I absolutely did get my heart crushed by someone I thought loved me." He forced her to look into his eyes. "Didn't I?"

"I'm sorry, Danny." She reached up to his face. "I do love you, I promise."

He moved her hands away from him. "Do you even know what it means?" he said, then walked out without looking back.

Steve headed for the house, his hands sweaty on the steering wheel. He should not have gone to see Sarah. He should have come straight here. But he had needed to vent his anger before he could be of any help to Will. Now it had been two hours since his friend had called and Steve could get no reply from Will's house phone or mobile.

Shit, shit, shit, Steve recited in his head as he jumped a red light and took the corner into Will's road far too fast. His hatred for Sarah was tinged with self-loathing. Why hadn't he come straight here? Why did he have to be so fucking selfish and take care of his own emotions first? Steve screeched to a halt at the side of the house and undid his seatbelt whilst opening the door. Will's car was sitting in the drive. Steve had taken him to collect it after his suicide attempt. If that was here, why did Will not answer any phones. Steve bolted to the house feeling sick with panic.

Will had sounded dazed and broken on the phone. Steve knew it was the first time he had really let his guard down. The first time Steve had heard Will's vulnerability in all its glory. He should have known to come here first.

Steve rounded the side of the house and exhaled a relieved breath.

William was sitting on the garden wall unlacing his running shoes.

"Alright?" Steve said.

Will looked up and, to Steve's surprise, smiled. "Good thanks, you?"

"Good?" He took a seat next to his friend whose skin was wet and smelled of sweat.

"Well, you know, as good as can be expected." Will removed one shoe and set it aside before untying the next. When Steve did not speak, William looked his way. "Really, mate. Stop being an old woman. You couldn't get me a pint of water could you?" He took the door key from the pocket of his shorts and handed it over.

Two wine glasses stood upside down on the drainer and the wine had been re-corked. Steve filled the pint glass and watched his friend through the kitchen window. Was he really okay? Steve was determined not to miss the signs again.

"Here."

"Cheers, you'll make someone a lovely husband someday," Will said with a cheeky grin Steve had not seen in longer than he could remember.

"So, you're over it, are you?" said Steve.

William shrugged. "What can I do, Ste, it's done now. I can't change it."

"What have you done with my friend?" Steve sat to the sound of Will's laughter. "I went to see her."

William stopped drinking and wiped his mouth. "You didn't need to do that."

"I wanted to. The bitch needed a wake up call."

His friend looked his way. "It's not your responsibility."

"Maybe not, but she can't just turn up here like that and then change her mind. It's plain cruel."

A car drove past the drive with its windows down and music blaring. The sun was out and it felt like the start of summer; another reason why Steve felt worried. There were more reported suicides in spring than any other time of year; something about the world feeling happy made the depressed more depressed.

"I could tell she didn't mean it," said Will.

Steve's heart sank. That's why he seemed so chipper, he thought she was coming back. Steve patted his friend's back. "I'm afraid she did mate. She's at work now with that guy and she *did not* want him finding out about last night."

"They work together?" William frowned up at the sky. "Figures," he said, then smiled at Steve. "What I meant was, I knew she didn't mean it last night. I should have stopped her…I tried at first. It was all about the guilt I knew, and I really, really should have thrown her out, but…" He sighed. "It's hard to explain."

"Hey, I get it. It's hard for all of us when it's handed on a plate."

William rested his clasped hands on his thighs and nodded. "Don't get me wrong, I'll admit there was a moment there when I thought maybe, just maybe… but it was no real shock this morning."

"I'm sorry mate."

William stood and stretched his calf muscles against the wall. "How do you fancy a drive out on Saturday? I thought it would be good to take a walk or something and I'd really like some company."

"Sure, we can go today if you like. I've rearranged my clients now."

William swapped legs. "Sorry about that."

"Don't give it a second thought. I'm beginning to like these impromptu days off."

They swapped a smile.

"No, I need to finish my proposal for your wool man today," said Will.

A good sign Steve thought, but he did not want to take any

chances. William was good at impression management. "How about the pub then later, or a take-away?"

"I can't, I'm catching the train down to London to have dinner with an old colleague."

"Really?"

William chuckled. "Yeh, really."

"When was that arranged?" said Steve.

"What are you? My mother?"

"Your mother never took this much interest."

William laughed again. "So true. I spoke to him before my run, he's going to put me up tonight then take me to meet another guy tomorrow morning. So you can stop worrying, I will not be left on my own."

"Sorry, I didn't mean to suggest...Is this work stuff then, has he got an opportunity for you?"

"Something like that. Right I need to get a shower and you need to bugger off." William collected his running shoes, arched his back and then looked at his friend. "Did you tell him?"

"The boyfriend?"

Will nodded.

"Not directly. She asked me to leave it to her, but let's just say I dropped a heavy hint."

"So you ruined her day?"

"From the look on the guy's face when I left, I think I ruined more than that."

"Ah finally, something to smile about." Will patted Steve's arm. "Cheers mate, you're a genius."

"Don't you forget it," Steve called as he walked to his car.

Chapter Eighteen

General Mike Tallet was approaching retirement but still looked fitter than most twenty-year-olds. He had not worn his uniform today, but even so, the receptionist sat a little straighter in his presence.

"General Tallet and Mr York to see Doctor Watson."

The woman checked her log, handed William a pass on a red cord and told them to take a seat.

"Doctor Watson, seriously?" said William.

Tallet shook his head and picked up a copy of the Times. "Still suffering from that inane sense of humour I see."

"It's hanging on in there." *Just*, thought Will.

The sign on the wall said the alert status was high, and on the TV, rolling footage of the war in Afghanistan showed the devastation left by a recent bomb. William imagined those working here must possess a higher than average sense of paranoia. Porton Down was a serious place. Employees had to undergo intensive security checks and abide by strict secrecy laws to work here. Visitors were not even allowed to visit the toilet without a chaperone.

Physicist Gerald Watson looked like the archetypal eccentric scientist. His wavy grey hair grew out in all directions in large tufts. He wore a brown and orange knitted tie with a grey shirt that looked like it had never seen an iron. William had been reliably informed by Tallet that the guy was regarded to be some sort of genius. Not that you would know it from his monosyllabic speech.

"Thanks for agreeing to see me. I don't know how much you've been told about why I'm here," said William once they were seated in a small meeting room.

Watson ran his fingers through his hair then ruffled the whole lot about. William looked at Mike, who smiled.

"Okay," Will said, "I want to speak to you about the accuracy of information on time travel within a schizophrenic's delusions."

"Why?"

"It's the topic of my PhD." It was strange how easily the lie came out.

"Why?" Watson leant forward.

For a second Will imagined the scientist could see through him. He shuffled in his seat and stumbled to find the words. "They say you should study something of interest... as it's such a lengthy process... and I'm interested in this."

"Schizophrenia?"

"Schizophrenic delusions to be exact, and the impact of intellect on their content."

Watson frowned and sat back in the chair, messing with his hair again.

Will took that as a cue to continue. "The patient in question is a physicist who believes he has travelled here from the future."

"What type?"

"Erm, I think it was somewhere in the twenty-third century, twenty two hundred and something. He said it was much warmer in climate with significant advancements having been made in artificial intelligence."

"Of physicist?"

"Oh. Right. I'm not sure. Sorry." William looked at Mike who flicked through an in-house magazine.

"Did he work in Physics?"

William was not prepared for this line of questioning. "He worked for a university I believe," he said thinking on his feet.

"Role?"

"Lecturer... and researcher."

"Goes without saying. Age?"

"Thirty-five." William figured he should keep some of the content accurate in case it mattered.

"So he had a PhD?" said Watson.

William wondered how out of his depth he was getting. "Erm... yeh."

Watson rubbed his chin and nodded to himself. "Go on."

"Right, well can I tell you about what he said he experienced, see if it's plausible?"

The man stuck his finger in his ear and wiggled it about.

William opened his file and took out a list of questions. He wanted to look like a real researcher. "My first question is about his reported mode of travel. He said he fell into some kind of wormhole that was hovering on a hillside." William sensed Mike look up from his reading matter and felt a little embarrassed at how ridiculous it sounded. "Is that feasible?"

"Theoretically."

Great, thought William, *I'd gathered that much for myself.* "He said time travel was not common in this future of his, but that they could teleport. He concluded this wormhole had somehow attached itself to an old teleporting base. How plausible would you regard that to be?"

"Which bit?"

William frowned.

"Teleporting or the wormhole attachment?"

"Both... please."

"Protons have already been teleported using entanglement to overcome the Heisenberg Uncertainty Principle -"

"The Heisenburg...?"

"Uncertainty Principle... it states you can't simultaneously know the location and speed of a particle. Looking too closely at a given photon bumps and changes it. By entangling two further photons, call them B and C, *some* information about photon A can be extracted, and the remaining passed on to B by way of entanglement, and then on to photon C. The extracted information from photon A can then be applied to photon C, creating an exact replica of photon A."

"Right…" said William.

"Of course, the original proton A would then cease to exist."

William scribbled frantically and tried to keep up. Out of the corner of his eye he caught sight of Mike smirking. This was going to be a tough conversation.

"So, you just told him you wanted to speak to someone about time travel?"

Will and Steve sat on the soft grass and opened their sandwiches. They had completed three hours of walking already.

William spoke with his mouth half full. "Good grief no. He's an army General, he'd think I'd lost my marbles."

"How then?"

"I told him I was finally working on my PhD, he always said I should do one. Said I was looking into the effect of intelligence on delusions." Will took a second bite of his lunch. "I explained that one case study I was working on involved a schizophrenic physicist who believed he had travelled here from the future. And that I needed to find someone who could say how accurate his reports of time travel were."

"And he bought that?" said Steve.

William chuckled.

"Sometimes you scare me." Steve shook his head.

"Liar. I scare you all the time."

"So who was this guy?"

"Some physicist who works on defence research. Apparently there's a whole department that looks into the viability of things like teleportation," said William.

"So what did you ask him?"

"I asked him to tell me the feasibility of what I saw, heard and experienced."

"Of what you *think* you saw, heard and experienced."

William smiled at his friend's irritated tone. "Okay, if you say so." He took a long drink of water and started on the second half of his cheese roll.

Steve leant back on his elbows and looked out at the view. It was good walking weather, not too windy, not too warm and with no sign of rain. "Come on then, spit it out. I know you're just dying to tell me."

"Not if you're going to use that tone of voice."

Steve punched Will's arm. "Piss off."

They both laughed.

"To be honest he talked a lot of gobbledygook about quantum physics and Einstein's theory of relativity, most of which went right over my head. But the gist..." Will paused to take a drink.

"The gist?" said Steve.

William smirked at his friend. "He thought my delusional physicist was just that, delusional." It impressed William how well Steve hid his smugness. "He said all the usual things about time being relative and not necessarily linear. How it could theoretically wrap around on itself and join two separate points in time. How, who knows what's out there and what might be developed down the line. Some basic forms of teleportation have already been achieved today for instance. But in essence, whilst my experience did not contradict the physics there was nothing in there to prove it was genuine either."

"Bummer," said Steve.

"I know. You must be gutted for me."

Steve looked up at the sky, fighting a smile. "I can't believe you actually are a mental."

"Are you really this unprofessional?" said William.

His friend sat up straight. "Oh my god, I have to get on Facebook and tell Paul and Dobs. They always said there was something odd about you."

"Traitor."

"Nutter," said Steve with a smirk.

"Tosser."

Yet another busy day lay ahead for Steve but he felt good about it. He had his final session with Robert Cooper this afternoon and planned on taking his client to Leeds Bradford Airport to see if he could finally climb aboard a plane without having a panic attack. Steve felt confident it would go well. Then, after work, he had a date with Michelle.

Steve's latest love interest was an anaesthetist he had met in the queue for Costa Coffee during Will's hospital stay. They had been on four dates and had yet to spend a night together, most unusual for Steve. He felt different around her, sort of nervous and self-conscious. More than a match for his intellect, Michelle took none of his crap. She laughed in his face if he said anything she regarded to be even remotely cheesy. And to top it all off, she was this petite, delicate-looking thing with strawberry blonde hair and porcelain skin. She looked more like a beautician than a doctor which Steve found fascinating. She was an endless source of surprise.

"Coffee?" said Jason as he entered the kitchen. The smell in the small room made all other options redundant. They had recently invested in a good quality coffee machine.

"Cheers. Good weekend?" Steve reached the milk from the fridge as Jason filled two large mugs.

"Not bad. The kids wanted a trip out to the zoo of all places, so we took them over to Knowsley Safari Park. Have you been?" said Jason.

"Yeh. Years ago now, though. I think a monkey ripped my wing mirror off."

Jason sniggered. "Susie wouldn't let us drive through the gibbons section. You could see the little buggers swinging off people's windscreen wipers." He slid Steve's mug towards him. "How about you?"

"Good, yeh. Will and I walked up Whernside on Saturday. You've done the Three Peaks haven't you?"

Jason nodded. "He's doing better then?"

"Oh he's doing great. I can't quite believe it. He's running every day, has his appetite back and even managed to find proof that he hadn't time travelled for himself." Steve gave a small laugh. "You know I never thought I'd say this, but I think his wife did him a favour last week."

Jason nodded and shrugged. "Makes you wonder how much we really know about the human mind, doesn't it."

"There's nowt so queer as folk," said Steve.

"Aye, lad you're not wrong there." Jason adopted his best Yorkshire accent which always sounded funny coming from the Welshman.

Hilary appeared in the doorway. "Steve, Mrs Forrest is here and there's been a special delivery parcel for you. I popped it on your desk."

"Thanks, Hilary. No rest for the wicked, aye? See you later," Steve said to Jason.

Steve walked back to his room, collecting his client on the way. Mrs. Forrest had received counselling from him for over six months on her manic depression. She was a nice lady, only about four foot tall and a little on the large side. When in a manic phase she reminded him of a Catherine Wheel, all round and lively, popping and jumping all over the place. Today she sat with her head in her hands.

Steve collected his pad of paper from the desk, moving the parcel aside as he did. It would be the end of the day before he gave it another thought.

"How did it go?" said Hilary as Steve raced back in to the office.

The journey from the airport had taken longer than he thought and now he was running late. "Good, he got on without any panic and sat in the cockpit with George Peters."

Hilary put her coat on. "Is he the co-pilot guy?"

"Captain now, promoted last month." George was an absolutely dream for Steve. His mother had suffered from a phobia of flying until a clinical psychologist cured her, so he was more than happy to help.

Mr. Cooper's fear came from a bad flight to Ireland he had taken as a teenager. The plane landed in the midst of a storm with heavy turbulence and lightning. Whilst nothing went wrong at the time, Robert Cooper had spent the years since replaying the scene in his head, imagining a whole raft of 'what ifs'? George spent a good twenty minutes talking through the actual risks faced in bad weather and the many precautions taken. It was invaluable insight for re-educating the bad programming in a phobia sufferer's mind.

Steve replaced Mr Cooper's file in the cabinet and locked it. He checked his computer was off - it was, Hilary was ahead of the game as always – then he closed the office door.

"Don't forget this." Hilary held out his parcel.

"Thanks, I forgot all about that." Steve popped it under his arm and rushed out.

Michelle was already waiting at the bar. She had ordered a white wine for herself and a pint for him. "I thought you were standing me up," she said as he approached. "Your friend, Will, said I'd be lucky to make it to date five."

Steve had invited Will to join them for a drink on Saturday after their walk. He had not stayed long. Just long enough to take the piss it would seem.

"Sorry. I got caught in traffic from the airport." Michelle questioned him with her eyes as he took a drink. "I'll explain in a bit. Shall we get a table?" He walked to a cosy one in the window lit by candlelight. Placing the package down, he took off his jacket and hung it over the back of the chair.

Michelle sat in her seat and crossed her legs. She wore knee-high, heeled boots over her jeans, and a black chiffon blouse through which he could see a hint of her bra.

"You're looking very sexy this evening," said Steve.

"Am I?" she said looking down at herself. "Oh, I thought I'd make an effort. A few of the guys from work are coming here for a drink later. I like to look good for the competition."

"Oh, right." Sometimes she surprised him in not so pleasant ways.

She leant across the table with her glass in her hand. "You're so easy to wind up." She chinked his drink. "It's all for you lover."

"Hmmm, technically... I'm not really your lover."

Michelle's eyes danced in the candlelight as she moved her drink to one side and kissed his lips. "Yet," she said and sat back in her seat. "So tell me about your day."

Steve hung his head and chuckled. "Just give me a minute to collect my thoughts." His eyes rested on the parcel and for the first time he spotted the sender's details. He sat up straight and looked at Michelle.

"What?" she said.

"I need to... open this." His heart rate accelerated and his hands felt unsteady as he prised the package apart.

"Are you okay, you've gone really pale?"

Steve pulled out a stack of papers and flicked through the various documents. The parcel still felt heavy and he tipped it up spilling the remaining contents onto the table.

"Are they car keys?" said Michelle.

He picked up the key-ring. "And house keys," he said and he could hear a tremor in his voice.

Steve skimmed the contents of the hand-written letter then stood. "I have to go."

"Where? Why?"

"I'm sorry I'll call you later." Steve kissed Michelle on her cheek.

"Steve?" she called after him but he did not hear her.

Chapter Nineteen

In the weeks since his suicide attempt William had attended every club run, struggling to keep up at first but quickly improving. It had been a great strategy. The exercise not only made him want to eat, it also made him sleep. And he finally felt fit again. Almost as good as he had before Sarah left. The whole process had cleared his mind and built his stamina. He would not have bounced back so well from his wife's latest rejection without it.

As he lay in the wake of his wife's departure, a familiar crushing weight had tried to squeeze the life out of him. Only this time, he had the good sense to do something to stop it. Ringing Steve had been one tactic. If he let someone know how he felt, it was less likely to engulf him. Ringing Mike Tallet was another.

In truth, he had made up his mind in those moments following Sarah's escape. What did he have to lose, after all? Why battle here with some half-life that would never live up to what he had lost, when he had the chance to be someone else, somewhere else? Confirming the whole thing plausible would only make it easier. And Dr Watson had not disappointed on that score.

"What you have to ask yourself is why your physicist didn't want to prove it," Watson had said as William stood to shake the man's hand.

"Wasn't that what he was doing? Like you said, his account is in the realms of the possible, he didn't stray into the fantastical." William had exaggerated somewhat when he recounted the tale to Steve. He wanted to reduce his friend's babysitting regime for a while.

"Not to others, to himself." Watson fluffed up his hair once more. "As a physicist, his instinct should have been to test his hypothesis. Doctors were telling him he was crazy... why not find out for sure, go back through, take witnesses, predict something from his past, that's still in our future? Isn't that the difference between the scientist and the fantasist... preparedness to face the proof good or bad?"

William had not anticipated rain. It had been clear skies and sunshine when he set off on his cycle ride. He stopped by the side of the road. His shoe-lace had come undone and the wet fabric proved hard to re-tie. He hung his head low to keep the rain out of his eyes as he worked. At least he'd had the foresight to bring extra clothes in his rucksack.

William continued walking, making good progress along the familiar route. He had no idea what he was letting himself in for, but it felt good to have made a decision.

After a couple of miles the rain faded to nothing more than a light spray, and the sun began to break through the patches of cloud. The fields to his left were pregnant with crops, and beyond them the dense forest stood dark and still.

William saw two things simultaneously and slowed to make sense of them. In the middle of a field of corn, a child sat with his arms wrapped around his knees. At the edge of the same field, two figures emerged from between the trees and began walking towards the boy.

William had thought long and hard during his runs about the time travelling experience. And the blond-haired boy with a cheeky smile was one of the things he kept coming back to. Seb was exactly the type of child he had hoped he and Sarah might have someday. He could still picture the lad with his mouth crammed full of rhubarb. An image which invariably led to that of Grace's dead eyes and Sorella's desperate plea, "*You know it will be Seb next.*"

So the boy had finally clinched it for him. Sorella's appeal was significant, but Seb provided the extra motivation needed. Seb and other children like him.

To find he had not left it too long was a relief. William crossed the road, cupped his hands around his mouth and shouted into the cornfield. "Seb? Hey Seb?"

In the distance, the two figures halted in unison. William hoped they stood far enough away not to detect he was different.

The boy looked up from his knees and William beckoned him over. "Can you give me a hand?" He waited to see if the boy would remember him well enough to come. Seb had seemed fascinated with William before, but three weeks was long time in the life of a child.

Without hesitation, Seb got to his feet and wiped his face.

The two figures began to move.

William walked towards the field with his hand out. "Come on, lad, I haven't got all day." If he ran he reckoned he could make it to Seb first. But then what?

The figures stopped again and William made a point not to look in their direction. Instinct told him it was better they think him oblivious to their presence.

Seb trotted until he was a few feet from the road then slowed.

"Hi, it's Will, William. Do you remember me?" William kept his voice low so only the boy would hear.

Seb nodded.

"Are you with your dad?"

The boy shook his head. His puffy eyes still swam with the tears that had streaked through the dirt on his face.

"I need to see him, can you take me home? I can't remember how to get there." Lal was the last person William wanted to see, but convincing the boy to come with him was the priority. Something about those figures gave William the creeps.

After a moment's thought, Seb climbed up onto the road and took Will's hand.

Lal Pickles could not think straight. The boy had been missing for over three hours and he knew it didn't look good. He could throttle Casey Taylor and her stupid friends. The girl knew how important it was to watch Seb, her dad, Callum, had set up the whole flaming rota.

Since Grace's abduction the village had been on high alert. Caro had set things up so ANN could monitor comings and goings around the village. Lal was no fan of the fake brains, but he had to admit it felt safer knowing she was on the lookout.

Grace needed around-the-clock-care, meaning Lal had to rely on his neighbours to help with the boy. And until Casey decided to have her little gang around, it had worked great. The four girls had left Seb in the Taylors' garden whilst they practiced doing each other's hair. They could not even say what time they last saw him. All they knew was when Casey went to check on him at eleven a.m. he was gone.

ANN said she had sensed him in the village for a further fifteen minutes and then nothing; like he disappeared into thin air.

The search party reconvened on the green to decide what to do next. They had searched all the houses and combed the surrounding fields. Now they needed to decide who went where next.

"Lal, I have to ask again. Do you know of any places Seb might go to play outside the village?" Caro sat on the bench projecting an image of the local area into the space between him and Lal.

"I've told ya before. The boy knows not to go out. They've taken him."

"No one felt any panic or fear this time, Lal," said Sorella. "Not like with Grace or the others. That's a good sign. Casey would have known if he had been taken."

Lal scoffed at that. "The girl wouldn't know if her own head was on fire."

"Well ANN would have known then," said Sorella.

Margot piped up. "None of us felt him out and about, though. What does that mean?" The woman wrapped that ruddy great cardigan around her more tightly. Lal wanted to rip it off her and burn it. She glanced up at him. "You got a problem, Lal?"

"No, woman, I'm worried. You'd think you'd know the difference at your age." He knew he should be more sensitive given all Margot had lost, but he didn't care. All that mattered at this point was finding the boy.

"He might just be out of our range, Margot. He's young and fit. He could get quite a long way in a few hours," said Caro.

"But why?" Lal shouted, throwing his hands in the air. The boy knew he needed to help with his mother and he knew everyone was going out of their way to watch him. If the child had run away, Lal would give him what for and no doubt about it.

Margot said, "And how did he get by ANN? If he'd walked out of the village she'd have known in what direction, but she said he was 'ere one minute gone the next. How's that possible?"

"I don't know." Caro looked unusually baffled. "Last she knew he was in Fallow Lane right in the centre of the village."

"He could've gone through the tunnel," said a timid voice.

Everyone including Lal turned to look at Davey Rowe.

"Reggie, Degs and I found it when we were kids, in the rocks at the end of Fallow Lane. You can crawl all the way through. It gets dark in the middle and is only big enough for a kid..." The teenager's cheeks glowed as he babbled at the many scowling faces.

"Why did none of you mention it before?" Lal had become an equally glowing shade of red.

"I… I'd forgotten about it 'til now when…when you said he was in Fallow Lane."

"Could Seb have known about this place?" said Sorella.

"All the kids know about it," said Davey.

"Let's widen the search. I have split the next five-mile perimeter into twelve zones. Each group is to take a zone and…" Caro stopped mid-sentence.

Lal felt the man's surprise followed by panic.

Caro looked Lal's way. "ANN says Seb is back."

"Where is he?"

"She says he is talking to someone."

Lal scanned the group. Everyone was here as far as he could see. "Who found him, who's with him?"

Caro closed down the map and stood. "She detects no other brain activity."

Lal placed his hands over his mouth to stop the cry fighting to come out. Gracie babbled to empty rooms and un-listening ears. They'd got to him, his boy. Lal felt all the strength go out of his legs. *My boy, my poor boy*.

But when his son appeared around the corner, he was not alone.

For a second or two, Lal felt so incensed he could not move. Over the past weeks, all his energy had been taken up with caring for his wife. There had been no opportunity to let the anger he felt out of its box. But now rage blistered through him. How had that evil bastard had the nerve to come back here. Parade what he'd done like he was proud of it. No way would he get away with it. Lal would make sure he paid for Seb, for Grace, for all of them.

Lal began to move then hesitated.

Why would the boy be happy? It made no sense. Lal could feel a tremor of trepidation from his son, but nothing like the fear he had expected.

The explanation took a second to come and when it arrived, Lal moved swiftly.

They had messed with his boy's head so bad, he didn't even know to be frightened. The rage consumed Lal and he lunged for Seb. "Get him off my boy! Get the bastard off my boy!"

William enjoyed the walk with Seb. The rain had reduced to a drizzle and the kid was entertaining.

"You're funny," the boy said as they walked hand in hand through the puddles.

"Funny weird or funny ha ha?" asked Will.

Seb took his time to think about it. "Funny weird."

"Coz you can't feel what I feel?"

"A bit… but more coz you've got funny hair and your clothes are all old."

You have no idea, thought William as he chuckled at the boy's insult. Seb wore khaki green trousers and a long-sleeved top. They were close fitting and similar in style to those worn by Sorella when William had first met her.

"So what you doin' out here on your own?" They were still two miles or so from the village and Seb dragged his feet.

The boy jumped in a deep puddle instead of answering, splashing them both.

"Thanks for that, Seb."

"You're already wet."

"Yes, I know but…" The boy jumped in the next puddle. "Never mind. Does your dad know you're out here?" It seemed unlikely the boy would have been allowed to come this far alone, even without some threat of abduction hanging over him.

Seb shook his head and swung Will's arm with his own.

"How old are you, Seb?"

"Eight in June. How old are you?"

William smiled at the memory of always wanting to be the next age up. "I'm thirty-five."

Seb actually whistled, as if William had admitted to being in his eighties or something. "That's old."

"Yeh, to be honest I'm struggling to keep walking," said William.

Seb did not comment or even laugh. He obviously thought this entirely plausible.

William checked behind them again to make sure no one followed. He had seen the two figures leave but thought it best to remain vigilant.

"So, did you walk out here on your own?" said William, satisfied that they were alone for now.

"Yep."

"Did you tell anyone where you were going?"

Seb avoided answering again, trailing his hand along the hedge and grabbing a fistful of leaves.

"No one knows I'm here either, you know. I sort of ran away."

Seb looked up at him. "Why?"

William looked at the boy's tear-stained cheeks. "I suppose I wasn't very happy and thought I'd be better on my own."

"My mum says I shouldn't speak to strange men."

Some things never change, thought William. "That's good advice, Seb, your Mum's a clever lady. I'm not strange though am I? You met me before with Sorella."

"Daddy tried to hit you."

"Yes he did." *Probably will again*, William thought. "He was just worried about your mum. You ever feel like running away like me, Seb?"

The boy looked up at him and William guessed his tactics had been spotted. "Sometimes," said Seb.

"Why?"

Seb shrugged.

"It'll be good to get home though, won't it? Your mum and dad will be missing you."

"Mum doesn't speak to me anymore."

William ruffled the boy's hair with his free hand.

As they approached the village boundary, Seb walked slower and slower. William started to feel like he was dragging the boy along.

"How ya doin, Seb? Looking forward to seeing your Dad?"

The boy shook his head.

"He'll be missing you."

"He's angry."

William looked at the frown on the boy's face. "You can feel that?"

"Yes."

The first few houses looked deserted and William found it odd that no one was working in any of the fields or gardens.

"Is he feeling anything else?" said William checking down another street and finding it empty and still. Had he returned too late after all? Is that why Seb wandered the fields alone? William felt a wave of panic as he considered what might have become of Sorella.

Seb scratched his cheek and held William's hand a little tighter. "He's scared… and sad."

William tried to be logical for the sake of the boy if nothing else. "Because he thinks he's lost you probably. You know, mums and dads can feel angry sometimes when you scare them. Does that make sense?"

Seb didn't answer.

"Your dad loves you though doesn't he? You feel that a lot."

"Yes."

William squeezed the boy's hand. "So however angry he is now it's only because he misses you."

In the last few moments before they turned the corner on to the green, Seb walked a little quicker.

And then all hell broke loose.

The number of people crowded onto the village green must have been in excess of two hundred. They all turned to look at him and Seb in unison. William had time to see a few familiar faces before they attacked. He saw Lal move and then falter, a look of confusion crossing his face. He saw Caro, standing on higher ground, no doubt holding court. And he saw Sorella.

He had only milliseconds to take it in. Sorella looked even more striking than he remembered. She had her hair tied to one side, and the dark curls fell thick and long over her sand-coloured top. She looked taller, more athletic, and he liked how her eyes widened just a touch on seeing him. And then he saw the guy on her left; a tall, blond pretty boy not much older than twenty five. Sorella was holding his hand.

Figures, William just had time to think before a group of men tackled him to the ground.

Chapter Twenty

As soon as she heard ANN say no brain activity could be detected, Sorella felt her pulse quicken. *It can't be.*

She had seen him disappear. Not like in the teleporting stations where people were there one instant and gone the next. Bit by bit from his feet up, as if he fell into some invisible container. Sorella had run to the base to look up, but nothing rose above her except for the cliff side. Slowly she had reached her hand in the air. And when she felt a slight tingle in her finger tips, she snatched it back. If that thing was what William said it was, she had no intention of going anywhere near it.

Caro said they should keep what she had witnessed between themselves and ANNy. It would only increase the villagers' fears during an already anxious time. Plus, they did not want the curious going out there and experimenting. So in the minds of her community, William remained the villain they had driven away. At first, she kept imagining she had seen him - her mysterious stranger - walking through the fields, or sitting on a garden wall. But it was only a trick of the mind. She knew he had gone for good.

When he had walked around the corner with Seb, Sorella found herself frozen to the spot. Events unfolded in slow motion. Lal shouted and the men closest to him moved in synch. Seb's eyes widened and he looked up at William before Lal grabbed the boy around the waist and yanked him away. William did not notice the boy's glance. He was looking at her. A smile had begun to form on his lips and then faltered.

Maddox and Wallace Flynn reached him first. The twins were big men and they had no trouble tackling William to the ground. Joe Falk grabbed both William's legs and held them down and

Tyler Bo unclipped his work knife from his belt.

Sorella heard her brother sigh. Even with all the anger and panic saturating the air, he could not miss her reaction. Their eyes met and Caro nodded. Despite his own reservations, his sister was the most important thing in the world to him.

"Wait!" Caro shouted, loud enough to ensure that the men would hear. "Tyler, put that away. I need to speak to William straight away. Maddox, Flynn, bring him through to ANN. Lal, how is Seb?"

Lal knelt on the grass holding his son's head in his hands. He looked Caro's way, his emotions confused but relieved. "He seems okay, so far. He can talk."

The twins hauled William to his feet.

"Lal, bring Seb too. We need to hear from both of them," Caro said.

The fall had winded William and he gasped for breath as two burley men pulled him to his feet. His escorts held him by each bicep, their large hands wrapping all the way around. Then they walked in long strides, probably to make it hard for him to keep up but William managed. He might not be as muscular, but he was tall.

Sorella trotted to his side. "You came back?"

William found he could not look her in the eye. "Obviously."

The white domed building looked smaller than he remembered. It was much lower than the surrounding cottages and built from some kind of opaque glass. The long corridor, with its arched ceiling, extended from one side. And the whole thing reminded William of an igloo with a much longer nose. As they passed the spot where he had fixed Sorella's shoulder, he glanced her way. She looked him in the eye and he focused once more to the front. *How old are you, twelve?* he chastised himself.

The small group entered the corridor and walked silently to the dome.

"We meet again, William," said ANNy.

William had forgotten how loud the voice had been in his head and it made him jump. ANN sniggered.

"Take a seat, William. Thanks for your help," Caro said to the beefcakes. "Maddox could you ask Lal and Seb to wait next door, I want to speak to William first."

"Can ANNy tell us if he did it, to Grace and Sammy and Tilly?" said the larger of the two meatheads.

"I will know if he lies," ANN replied.

The guy in the blue top nodded, apparently happy with that, then exited the room with his companion. William guessed they were brothers from their similar thick black hair, flat noses and matching expressions of disgust.

"I thought Sorella said I was invisible to you..." He nearly said *things* then stopped himself. No need to antagonise her.

"If you are inside the hub, ANN can access your neural network and determine basic emotional responses," said Caro.

So not invisible at all then. This might have been a mistake. "Would that be the case for all of your...kind?"

"I think we need to ask the questions at this stage, William. What are you doing here?" Caro stood by William's feet so he could see both his target's facial reactions and his brain scan. The projection to William's left had sprung into life as soon as he entered the room.

"I was under the impression you might need my help," said William.

Caro glanced at his sister who did not react. "And where have you been since your last visit?"

"Home."

"Which is?"

William held the man's eye contact. "Ilkley, twenty eleven."

"ANN?"

"He speaks the truth."

Caro sighed. "Fine, we'll deal with that later. Why did you have Seb?"

"I found him sitting in the middle of a cornfield. I thought it was wise not to leave him there - considering..."

"Considering?"

William smiled. "Do you two not talk much?" He looked at Sorella and then back at Caro. "Your sister told me he was in danger after what happened to his mother."

"The boy is why you came back." ANN said this as a statement not a question. *How much of his mind could this thing read?*

"What makes you say that?" said William.

"You had a strong emotional reaction when you said he was in danger."

Fair enough, he did feel protective towards the child. "He's a nice kid."

"Tell me exactly where you found him and when," Caro said.

William did just that, relaying as much detail as possible bar a couple of specifics. He wanted to know if ANN would pick up that he omitted to tell them something. She did not.

Caro gestured for William to leave the room. "Okay, let us speak to Seb. Sorella, stay with William until we are sure."

Sorella led the way to the small kitchen where he had eaten soup on his original visit. "Water?" she asked already filling a glass for him.

"Thank you."

She watched him down it in one then refilled it for him. "You have shoes this time."

"Well, you live and learn."

"And you brought a bag?"

William had forgotten the rucksack on his back. He unhooked it. "Yeh, it was a bit of a gamble but I figured it was worth a try. I threw it down the hill a few times until it disappeared, that way I knew where the passage was. Plus, I get a change of clothes as a bonus. Speaking of which..." He lifted his still soaking top from his skin.

"There's a bathroom, I'll take you." Sorella showed him to a small cloakroom complete with shower further down the corridor. "There should be a clean towel under the sink."

When she had left, William removed his wet clothes and stepped under the hot water to get warm. The air conditioning in here had chilled his water-logged outfit. As he prepared to switch the water off, he noticed red droplets splashing onto the floor. He tilted his head back and squeezed the bridge of his nose. How worried should he be about these bleeds, he wondered.

Once the bleed had stopped, he dried up and dressed. Sorella sat on the floor opposite the door with her arms around her legs. The same way Seb had been seated in the field.

She stood as Caro, Lal and Seb emerged from the dome and headed their way.

"Seb likes you," Sorella said.

William watched Seb trying to match his father's strides with exaggerated ones of his own. "One down, only a few hundred villagers to go."

"Two down," Sorella said with a smile before addressing the group. "Is he in the clear?"

William noticed Lal clench his jaw before speaking. The man was still not a fan. "The lad says you talked him into coming home. So I suppose I owe you an apology."

"Don't mention it. I understand you were worried." William looked at Seb. "How about these clothes, still funny weird?"

The boy wrinkled up his nose. "Funny ha ha."

William and Seb laughed.

"Come on your mother will want to see you." Lal placed an arm across his son's shoulders.

William watched them leave. "There's something you should know," he said as the door closed behind father and son. "When I found Seb, there were two people at the other side of the field. I think they were coming for him."

"What makes you say that?" said Caro.

"Something about them gave me the creeps. I couldn't really see them, but they didn't look like they were out for a stroll."

Caro placed his hands on his hips. "Why did you not mention this before?"

"I don't think Seb saw them and wasn't sure he should be told."

Caro looked irritated.

"But that's your call, of course."

"You are telling me you happened to turn up just at the point he was about to be taken. Is that not something of a coincidence?"

"Caro," Sorella cautioned.

"It's okay, he's right to be suspicious," said William. "You can trust me, though. I give you my word, I am who I say I am."

"We do trust you, William. Caro, you know what I saw when William left us. He was not lying about the wormhole." Sorella looked at William. "Caro and ANN checked the hillside after you left. They found a large electro-magnetic field, unlike anything anyone's ever seen."

"*They* could be using it to send him," said Caro.

Sorella shook her head. "ANN said William was not lying

about going home to twenty eleven."

Caro looked at his sister. "We still do not know what these people are capable of. What if they can fool ANNy?"

"I tell you what they can do," said William. "They can disappear in the blink of an eye."

Brother and sister both stared at William.

"When Seb came out of the field to join me, they just disappeared into thin air."

"Mobile teleportation?" Caro's voice had a far off quality as if he spoke only to himself.

"Is that possible?" said Sorella.

"ANNy says some experiments have been done…this could be bigger than we thought." Caro frowned and looked at William for a long moment. "I will give you the benefit of the doubt, William. If you are as trustworthy as you say, my sister is right, you could be invaluable to us. How long do you plan to stay?"

William had not thought about going back. "As long as you need me I suppose."

Caro nodded. "You will need somewhere to stay."

"He can stay with me," said Sorella.

"I'm not sure that's a good idea." William caught her reaction to his words out of the corner of his eye.

Caro watched his sister. "I agree. You can stay with me. I need to speak to ANNy about what you saw, Sorella will take you there and get you settled."

"Thanks."

Caro held out his hand. "Do not let me down, William."

William shook it. "Call me, Will, and I'll try my best not to."

Chapter Twenty One

The minimalist black and white interior of Caro's house looked not too dissimilar from that of the dome. In the kitchen, plain black cabinets and white plastic chairs surrounded a glass table giving a functional air. And the lack of any personal touches such as pictures and ornaments made the place feel sparse.

"He doesn't play host much I take it." William looked inside the bare living room which contained nothing more than two high-backed black chairs.

Sorella smiled and began her tour of the kitchen. "My brother has little time for anything but work." She pointed out the kettle and oven, which William imagined he would need a degree in physics to operate, then she held open the door to the fridge. "There is food and fresh milk, so help yourself to whatever you need."

"Were those guys going to kill me?"

"No." Sorella spun to face him. "They were just restraining you."

William raised his eyebrows. "With a knife? I thought you said people didn't hurt each other these days… no crime, no violence etcetera etcetera."

"That is true in the main, although the LQ communities are a little different. These people only receive the most basic of upgrades, just enough to empathise with each other's emotions. They still experience misunderstandings and arguments, whereas the rest of the population is developed to such an extent that conflict is rare."

"How so?" William wanted to learn all he could about what he had let himself in for.

"The educational modules provide knowledge and insight

about different experiences and perceptions. It means that in general people are more open-minded and tolerant of each other."

"But here they still attack with knives?"

"It was his work knife. I'm sure he would not have used it to do anything more than scare you. Even here, we do not have serious conflicts. People feel each other's emotions sufficiently enough to know when to back off."

"Telepathic fight and flight." William pondered the realities of a world where people could feel who was the most angry, aggressive or scared without waiting for them to physically respond.

"I didn't think you would come back," said Sorella.

William placed both hands on the end of the work surface. The black material felt cool to the touch. "Neither did I."

"So why? For Seb?"

William's eyes met hers. "He's a significant factor, him and others like him. If I can help stop him becoming like Grace, it seems like a worthy pursuit."

"You seem different."

"How so?"

Sorella walked to where he stood and ran a finger down his bare forearm. "You hurt yourself?"

The scratch ran from his inner elbow to his wrist. "It's nothing."

"Let me clean it."

"It'll be fine. I rinsed it in the shower." William had caught his arm on some brambles whilst securing a safe place to leave his bike. He wanted to hide it out of sight so no one would inadvertently take it, either before he had chance to return or until Steve turned up. He wondered how Steve had reacted to his letter. Had he been angry or disappointed to be fooled again? Did he feel annoyed at the request to become custodian of Will's old life?

Sorella returned to the room with a bottle and a cloth. The ointment stung and William flinched as she applied it to his cut. "It's a good thing Tyler didn't cut you if you're this much of a baby."

"I thought you said he wouldn't have- Ouch! What *is* that stuff?"

Sorella held his wrist flat on the worktop with her free hand. "It should stop any infection." The fluid left a faint orange stain across his skin and burned even after she stopped applying it. "It's good to see you, Will." She looked up with a smile. "Am I allowed to call you that also?"

"Why not," he said feeling uncomfortable that she had moved from holding his wrist to holding his hand.

"I'd forgotten how infuriating it is to not know how you're feeling."

William looked at his hand in hers. "And how would your boyfriend feel about you holding someone else's hand?"

Her laugh sounded surprised. "Boyfriend?"

"The pretty blond lad you were with on the green."

"You mean, Jessie?"

William closed his hand a little around hers and lifted both up. "Yes how would Jessie feel about this?"

Sorella studied his face for a moment, no doubt hearing the judgment in his words. "Jessie wouldn't mind."

"Really? Is that what you women tell yourselves? Don't worry he won't mind?" Why would she be any different? At least it explained how a woman so stunning could be interested in him. She obviously liked men no matter who they were. William pulled his hand free.

"You're angry with me," said Sorella.

"More disappointed actually."

Caro entered the kitchen, pausing in the doorway. "Am I interrupting something?"

"No," said Will.

"Yes," said Sorella.

"I can give you a few moments alone." Caro turned to leave.

"No, I'd like to hear more about how I can help. I want to get on with things."

Sorella stared at William for a moment then shook her head in disgust and walked out.

Caro smiled. "I must say, it is most amusing the effect you have on my sister." He beckoned for William to move through to the lounge. "Shall we sit?"

The large square room in the village hall housed a low stage, in the middle of which Caro stood behind two empty chairs talking to a small, thin man with wispy blond hair and rosy cheeks. Along the right-hand side of the room, two women served refreshments, the older of whom William remembered from Lal's living room. Around the walls, intricate carvings adorned the wood panelling and brightly coloured blinds half covered the large windows. In front of the stage, fifteen rows of chairs had been laid out and people began to file in to take a seat. William hovered at the edge of the stage and tried to ignore everyone's stares.

"Nice threads."

Seb's comment made William jump as the boy appeared at his side. William looked down at the clothes he had borrowed from Caro. Thankfully he had managed to dodge the really tight-fitting stuff in favour of something resembling walking trousers and a collarless shirt. "Good to see you, Seb. Are you here with your dad?"

"And my mum." Seb nodded towards the entrance where Lal was coaxing Grace to walk down a row of seats with one arm around her waist. The woman's hair had been tied back in a ponytail, but her head still hung low and her chin rested on her chest. She slumped forward in her chair and Lal straightened her up before kissing her head.

William turned to Seb who entertained himself with some kind of virtual ball. "How's she doin your Mum?"

The boy shrugged and continued tossing the orb from hand to hand.

Caro had said that, as with Sammy and Tilly, the woman's brain damage had affected her higher functions including the ability to communicate. Whatever caused it was not an invasive procedure. Unlike a lobotomy, where tissue in the frontal lobe was physically damaged to pacify schizophrenics, Caro said Grace and the others had experienced some form of accelerated decay. ANN hypothesised a chemical had most likely been introduced, although no trace of anything could be found.

"What is that thing?" said William.

Seb threw the ball to William who caught it and immediately felt a low tingling in his palm. When he released his grip, the orb hovered above his hand. William threw it across to his other hand where it wobbled from side to side an inch or so above then stabilised.

"It's a Worb. You can have it, I've got three more."

William smiled at Seb's cherubic face. "Thanks, but I think I need to look serious for this. Best I don't have a toy. It's totally great though."

Seb reached up, inserted his hand into the shimmering ball and clicked his fingers. The ball disappeared and a small black marble fell into Will's palm. "When you want it big, just clap your hand over it like this." The boy demonstrated with his own hands.

William did not know how to respond to his new friend's gift. In the face of everyone else's suspicion, he felt hugely touched. He placed the marble in his pocket and winked at Seb, who beamed back then skipped away. William watched the boy dart across to the refreshments table and squeeze his arm between two adults to sneak a cake. He took it over to his parents and placed it in his mum's lap.

"Where did you get that?" William heard Lal say. "Did you pay for it?" Seb dropped his head and Lal looked over to one of the refreshment women and mouthed sorry.

The room was pretty full now. The two brothers who had wrestled William to the ground sat in the front row, accompanied by women he assumed to be their wives. All four wore stern expressions as they stared his way. William averted his gaze and noticed the old man, Mart, entering alongside Sorella's Jessie and the chap who had pulled his knife. William glanced at Caro feeling nervous. He hoped the man knew what he was doing.

The two of them had spent the whole of the previous evening talking things through. Caro had told William what he knew about the abductions, what they had learned from Grace's condition and how he and ANN thought it best to proceed. The man did not discuss any of their plans in detail, which William could understand. He would no doubt wait for William to earn some trust before revealing too much.

Caro had sold today's meeting as a chance to set the record straight, to ensure that William would not come under further attack, but William was savvy enough to know the truth. Caro wanted to see how William coped under the scrutiny of the whole community. It was an age-old trick used in many a police press conference. Put your suspect in the spotlight; see if he cracks under pressure.

Caro's blond companion came William's way with his arm outstretched. William remembered him from Lal's lounge.

"Mr York, Callum Taylor. I assist Caro with community matters and would like to extend my welcome."

"Thanks. I think you might be the only one who feels that way," said William. The brothers Grim still eyeballed him from the front row.

Callum patted Will's arm. "I'm sure that's not the case. We have a very supportive group here."

William wondered if the man had taken a look around the room lately. "Have you lived here long?" William asked thinking it best to make conversation.

Taylor glanced behind William then made his excuses, leaving William momentarily confused, until he turned to find Sorella and Jessie waiting to speak to him. His heart sank. He would rather ignore this unfortunate reality.

"I wanted you to meet Jessie," Sorella said placing a hand on her boyfriend's arm, "as you were so worried about him."

Was that a hint of sarcasm? William could not be sure. He held out his hand knowing he had to behave impeccably with all the judging eyes on him. The woman knew how to pick her moments. "Nice to meet you, Jessie. I'm William."

The young man's handshake felt soft and limp. William concentrated on not showing surprise. Jessie was a strapping lad, and William had been expecting another Mr Macho given the townsfolk he had already met.

"My name is Jessie." The man spoke with an obvious slur and childlike pitch causing William to look at Sorella.

"Jessie is a very special boy, aren't you my love." Her use of the word boy when addressing her six-foot companion confirmed

Will's suspicions.

"I have chickens, do you want to see?" Jessie spoke with all the enthusiasm of a toddler.

William tried hard to smile to cover his embarrassment. "That would be great, thanks… maybe some other time though?"

"They lay eggs. Lots and lots and lots of eggs," said Jessie.

"Come now, Jessie, William has work to do. I'll take you back to your dad." Sorella stroked the man's arm and took hold of his hand. "Good luck," she said to William.

He watched her walk Jessie back to the owner of the knife. The older man took Jessie's hand as he sat down. William felt a mixture of shame and relief. He considered going after Sorella to apologise, but then Caro called for order.

"Thank you for coming everyone. I want to introduce you to William York and put your minds at ease about who he is and why he is here. William, would you join me?"

William walked onto the stage keeping his eyes focused on the empty seat. The packed room had at least two rows of people standing at the back and he could hear nothing but breathing. William hoped Caro was well practised at keeping order.

"As you know, William visited us before at the time of Grace's unfortunate incident. ANN and I have spoken to him and are satisfied he was in no way involved. Nor was he party to Seb's disappearance. The boy ran away of his own free will as we were all prone to at that age. William was lucky enough to cross paths with him and convinced him to come home, for which Lal and Grace are very grateful I know."

"Who is he then?"

William saw the larger of the two brothers had stood on the front row.

"That is a good question, Maddox. William finds himself a

long way from home and in need of a place to stay-"

"Can't he speak for 'imself?" the woman next to Maddox shouted out.

Caro looked at William who nodded and took a deep breath. They had agreed the truth about how he came to be here would be too hard for people to accept. Caro had concocted an alternative version to share; one plausible enough for the community to believe. William hoped he was able to pull it off.

He swivelled in his seat and looked out at the faces. Eye contact would be important if they were going to accept his story. "Hi, I'm William as Caro said, or Will. You've probably noticed I'm different... I've no primary as I understand it's called. I grew up a long way from here in a place where such things just didn't happen."

"How is that possible, we've had the primary since our grandparents were born?" Jessie's father called out.

"My ancestors were a religious community who wanted to protect their families from secularisation. They set up home for us on Hale Island. We've been entirely self-sustainable there for over four generations. None of us ever came to the mainland until now."

The room fell silent again and William looked for Sorella on the front row. She smiled. The biggest lie was over. Caro assured him this version of his past would allow him to talk freely about much of his real life experience. It was a story based on popular rumour within LQ communities that people lived in secret around the world. Hopefully it would make it easier for them to swallow his differences.

"You religious?" asked Mart.

William shook his head. "No, not many of my people are these days."

The lack of religion within all but the smallest sectors of society had been one of the biggest surprises to come from Caro's briefing. The fact that a good ninety per cent of the world's population received an advanced insight into science via the standard educational upgrades, had all but wiped it out.

"Why come here?" said the woman with Maddox. The skinny red-head looked to suffer from a nervous condition given the state of her pock-marked skin.

"It was by accident the first time. I had fallen and hit my head. Sorella found me and brought me to see Caro to check I was okay."

"But you knew what they did to Grace?" called the crying woman from Lal's house. A handful of people jeered in support.

William found her eyes. This was the woman who had lost a whole family. "I didn't really. I once saw something similar in an old film but Caro says what happened to Grace was not the same thing." They had also agreed it was not wise to tell people he was a psychologist. Partly because psychologists today were a whole different ball game in terms of knowledge and expertise, but also because they tended to be in positions of power.

"Is this true?" the woman asked Caro.

"Yes, Margot. William was wrong when he guessed what had happened to Grace."

"Where 'ave you been since then?" Mart shouted from the back of the room.

"I went home as you said I should. I knew I wasn't welcome and could tell I scared you as much as you scared me." He scanned the unsmiling faces. "So, you'll no doubt want to know why I came back. The truth is my home isn't really what it was anymore. All the people I love have moved on in one way or another, so I no longer... fit."

"Why come back here?" said Margot.

"When I came across Seb he was a good few miles away and alone. I thought it best to bring him home."

"Why should we believe you?" said Maddox's brother from the front row. He spoke quietly as if not really asking a question.

William leant towards him and dropped his own voice. "You don't have to. If you don't want me staying, I'll go." He sensed Caro stiffen in his chair, they had not discussed this, but Will had no desire to continue as their scapegoat. He needed to call their bluff.

A ripple of conversation ran through the room.

"Can we trust him?" Maddox had stood again. "How'd we know 'e's not here to pick someone else?"

A rumble of agreement ran around the room.

Ah oh, here we go, thought Will.

"We do not. But I for one would rather take him at his word until he proves us wrong," Caro said.

"And then what?" the other brother piped up, louder this time.

Caro looked William's way. "Let us hope it will not come to that."

"He did well."

Caro smiled at Sorella. "Not without help I noticed."

"It wasn't only me, Seb likes him too," she said.

"Yes, but Seb does not have quite the same influence on people as you do."

Sorella tutted, her brother could be so judgmental. "It would not have made any difference to your test would it, because William was oblivious?"

"They probably gave him an easier ride."

"You think?" Sorella looked over to where Maddox and

Wallace had William cornered.

"It is good for them to see the whites of his eyes," said her brother.

Lal headed for the exit with one arm around his wife, and the other around his son. Sorella waved and watched them go. "Why have they waited until now to come for Seb? Tilly was taken within a matter of days like the children have been everywhere else."

"I think they had to wait for him to be alone. We have protected him very well," said Caro.

"But how would they know? Only the police have the authority to monitor outside of the cities and then they would need justifiable cause."

Caro stepped back into the corner where they stood. "If what William says is correct and they teleported in and out without a station, we are looking at highly advanced technology. It would take a lot of money and the best minds in the country to achieve."

Sorella lowered her voice. "You really think the government is doing this?"

"I don't know who else would have the power and the access. If they were monitoring Seb, they would know that until yesterday he was always accompanied. It cannot be a coincidence they came when they did."

"And William would have been invisible to them." Sorella glanced at him. "Do you think they noticed?"

Caro shook hands with Tyler and Jessie as they passed. "I hope they assumed he was out of range. I am not sure they would reach the conclusion that he is entirely natural."

William was still fending off the Flynn boys' questions.

"Can you at least try and control your feelings, it is most distracting." Caro smirked as he followed her gaze to William.

She gave her brother a dirty look. "What have you told him?"

Caro lost the smile. "Nothing specific, only why what happened to Grace and the others is more likely to be intervention than disease, although he seemed to know some of that."

Sorella did not respond to the critical look.

Caro continued. "I said we have some ideas about how to proceed, but that first we needed to make sure people are comfortable with him staying, hence this." He waved his hand at the room.

"Caro, there have been three more families struck down in the last month, two in Scotland and one in Cornwall. It's getting more frequent and the longer you take to test William the more time we waste." Her brother knew she was right, otherwise he would argue the point. "I should go and help him."

"You should tell him."

Sorella hesitated and glanced at William. "It's none of your business, plus I doubt he feels the same."

Caro sniggered; her brother could be such a child. "That is not what I meant. You should tell him the consequences. You asked him to do this for us. You should make sure he understands the risks."

"It took a lot of bravery to come back through that thing… to come back here after being attacked. He'll be fine."

"I do not disagree, Sorella, but if this is as big as we fear and they catch him it is likely he will be incarcerated, or worse still they will attempt to integrate him."

"I know, I know."

Her brother placed a hand on her shoulder. "If your affection for him is genuine, you have to tell him the truth. If you do not, he may never forgive you."

"I'll tell him," she said leaving her brother behind to join

William and his new fan club.

"Where is it, I've never heard of Hale Island?" Maddox said as she approached.

"Like I said, it's off the grid. Our ancestors wanted somewhere we could live in isolation."

Sorella smiled, William was quite the liar. She would have to remember that.

"So it's an island?" Maddox frowned like this was the most incredulous idea.

"Ah ha, off the Scottish coastline." William's eyes flicked to Sorella and quickly away. She guessed her presence would make him more self-conscious about the story.

"That's why his accent's funny," said Wallace to his brother.

"Practising your interrogation skills, Maddie?" said Sorella.

Flynn's eyes flashed with the irritation she sensed him feeling. "I don't know why *you* like 'im so much. I thought rural boys weren't good enough for you."

Caro was right; she needed to control her emotions around others.

She ignored the jibe. "Will you excuse us? I need to introduce William to some others."

The brothers took the hint and went back to their wives. They did not bother to say goodbye. She would need to keep a check on Maddox. Out of everyone in the room, he felt the most suspicious. She expected he did not like having a stranger in their midst, especially one she felt such warmth towards. Wallace was less of a worry. He felt angry and tense, but that was normal and his brother was good at keeping him in line.

"Sorry, they're not all so rude. Let me show why we're worthy of your help," Sorella said.

"Before you do, I think I owe you an apology…about Jessie,"

said William.

"So I don't disappoint you anymore?"

The corner of William's lips curled in a most pleasing way. "Hmmm, there's still the matter of your thinking rural boys are not good enough for you, to consider."

She leant in and whispered. "You're not really a rural boy, remember."

"How do you know?"

Sorella blinked at him a few times, trying to recall why she had been so sure of that. "Are you?"

William chuckled. "No, but I am their unofficial champion so, be nice if you can."

"This is going to go to your head isn't it?"

"Oh, without a doubt," he said with a grin.

Chapter Twenty Two

"Despite operating to all intents and purposes exactly like the human mind, ANNs have no sensory input. They cannot see, hear, taste, smell or touch like we can. All they have is the electro-chemical activity coming from the primaries. So you simply will not exist for them." Caro had served a basic meal of roast chicken and salad. It had been significantly improved by the freshly baked bread Sorella brought along as a gift from Callum Taylor's wife Rose.

Since this morning's village meeting, most people's attitude toward William had shifted from suspicion to pity. Many of them had expressed genuine concern about how he might cope with the modern world. It was a concern he shared.

"Is your ANNy different then?" William said.

"No. Everything changes if you are inside the hub that houses an Artificial Neural Network. Then the electrical impulses in your brain would become as visible as ours, it would be like touching a blind person on the arm."

"So don't go inside any domes."

"Exactly. But that should not be a problem. We only want you to access the library for us, the place where information is stored digitally as a backup."

"So why can't any of you do that?"

Sorella answered this time. "The data we want is only available to those with level five security clearance. Only the most senior officials have this, and all facilities are protected by ANNs."

"If one of us were to walk through the door, an alarm would sound to show we are out of bounds," Caro said. "We expect you will be able to simply walk in."

William smiled. "You expect?"

"We have never had the opportunity to test this, obviously. We are working from a hypothesis. But there are no physical barriers to the building. Scanning is too successful for it to be needed. If we can make sure no humans notice you are different we should be fine." Caro collected their plates and placed them on the kitchen worktop.

"How do we do that? Won't everyone know immediately, like the folks here?" said William.

Caro tapped the table surface, bringing a 3D map of the city to life. "Not if you stay in crowds as much as possible. The perceptual skills of the human brain are limited to a certain volume of information, as long as you are with-"

"Seven people or more," William said remembering people typically find it hard to process above seven items of information at a time.

Caro raised his eyebrows then smiled. "I forget how much of this you will know."

"Believe me, the stuff I know is the tip of the iceberg." William placed his hands under his chin and leant on the table. A four-storey building now rotated in front of him. "And when I'm inside… no crowds there I assume?"

"No, that will require good old-fashioned stealth. ANNy has accessed the entry system and found on average five people are in the data library at any one time. There are twelve portals, these are the areas where you access different domains, so you should be able to avoid other people if you keep your wits about you."

"The ANNs won't be watching then?"

"Not in the way you're thinking," said Caro. "Visual surveillance can be enabled but it is rarely used or needed. Sight is *our* dominant sense but ANNs can sense and connect with any person in their vicinity without it. It is only activated on human request, or if the ANN thinks there is something people need to see."

"But won't it know someone is accessing the data?"

"The digital files are a back-up system for reference only, and as such totally independent of the ANNs. The idea is if something were to happen to the neural networks, the digital files would be safe. Even so, we will be taking you there in the evening when there are no administrative staff on site who might be monitoring who is looking at what."

"We're organising a trip to the theatre which is in the same district," said Sorella. "That way we can get you most of the way to the building."

"Why can't you just take me to the door?"

"Unfortunately we cannot risk the group knowing what we are up to. It might make them feel anxious which would attract attention. The ANN's pick up on alert emotions… anger, suspicion, nervousness," said Caro.

Sorella picked at her salad. "So we have to let the group think you are coming to the show with us. And you'll need to be back in the theatre when the curtains close."

"Gotcha. So, what am I looking for?"

"ANNy's been investigating what she can for the last twelve months. She's found nothing of any value in any of the networks, except for one thing, a word… Silverwire. It keeps popping up in government documents but no details are ever provided and it is only referenced at level five. Usually such project names are easy for ANNy to uncover, someone slips up, leaks details or the thing just becomes less crucial to protect. But this has appeared in over five years' worth of papers, never anything more than a word."

"So you need to know what it is," said William.

"It could be nothing but it is the only lead we have. We would not ask you to do this if we had anything else to go on," said Caro.

"Sure, I understand." William tried to commit as much of the floor plan as he could to memory. "You'd better tell me how I find what you need."

Caro spent the next thirty minutes running through the detail, using floor plans of the building to illustrate the best routes and potential hiding places. "If you find anything we cannot risk your carrying notes, so how is your memory."

William knew it was important to be honest. "It's probably seen better days."

"Fine, ANNy will run through some mnemonics with you tomorrow. Help you to use codes, acronyms and images to store and recall. It will be tiring, so I suggest you get some rest." Caro stood and began clearing the kitchen. "I think I should walk you back, Sorella. We don't want to take any risks if they are watching."

"Actually, could William walk with me? I still need to speak to him," said Sorella.

A flash of irritation crossed Caro's face before he nodded.

It only took a few minutes to walk to Sorella's house. On reaching the garden gate, William stopped and looked up at the familiar building.

Sorella led the way up the garden path. "Come in, I'll get you a drink."

"Do you mind if I don't. Like Caro said, I should get some rest."

Sorella took a couple of steps back to him. "Bad memories?"

William's eyes found hers. "Not all of them."

She came closer, a brief smile crossing her lips, and then she was serious. "I have a confession."

"Don't worry about it. You did what you had to do to get my

attention."

She frowned and began to shake her head before the penny dropped. "You credit my skills much too highly, William. Unlike you, I'm not a master in deception."

"Unlike me?"

"What else would you call this morning's performance?" The smile on her lips softened the sentiment, but still...

"I'm just doing what you asked me to do. It's not my fault you think your neighbours can't be trusted with the truth."

"Why do you always react as if I am attacking you?"

"Because you are."

"No, I'm not. Teasing maybe..." She tilted her head and smiled.

She stood far too close. William felt the electricity building again, only this time his will-power proved stronger. "Look, I just want to do the job you need me to do and not mess it up." He stepped away. "I should go, I'll see you tomorrow."

"Wait," she touched his arm, "you still need to hear what I have to say."

"Can it wait? I don't want any complications. It's not that you're not... or that I don't..." The words failed him. All those weeks of thinking about her, of wondering what he would do if by the slimmest chance it transpired she really was attracted to him. And here she stood in the moonlight, once more breathtaking and about to make some confession.

"It's about the job." She held her hand out to the bench. "I only need a minute."

William tried to mask the slight disappointment he felt and took a seat.

"This is a really amazing thing you're doing for us, very brave..."

"Oh, I don't know about that," he interrupted.

"Coming back here has already taken courage, Will, and I'm sure it has not passed you by that what we ask of you is not legal."

William moved the small pebbles about under his feet. It made for a good distraction from how close she sat.

"If we're caught… if *you* are caught, there'll be a punishment. A trial, imprisonment..."

"I guessed as much."

Sorella took a moment before speaking again. "But that would be the best case scenario."

William looked up at her.

"Do you remember I told you what happened when they tried to embed the primary in adult brains?"

He turned his attention back to the pebbles. "I see."

"They suffered horrible consequences… extreme paranoia, phobias, delusions, hallucinations. You find that amusing?" She had spotted his smile.

"No, just ironic. I'm sorry, go on."

Sorella hesitated as if she considered asking for an explanation. "We would understand if this is too much of a risk for you."

William sat up straight and focused on her. "What other options do you have?"

"We'll think of something. We know they are probably watching us now to get people alone, so at the very least we can keep ourselves safe."

He took a breath and gave the matter some thought, looking out over her moonlit flowers. Dozens of foxgloves lined the fence to his left. "What happens if you don't find out what this is?"

"I suppose it will keep happening." She chewed the nail of her thumb. "I know I said the world had vastly improved, and it has in the main... for the majority. But I suppose every society had its underclass and now it's the Lower Quartiles. The people deemed too slow to cope with anything but the primary."

"How is that decided?"

"It's a basic test of mental processing speed. Those who fall in the bottom ten per cent are given the primary and it is left at that. When it started, the parents of such people were encouraged to set up home in rural villages, places where manual work was needed to farm crops. And it's self-perpetuating of course. LQs have children who are also of lower processing speeds, and there's little cross-breeding."

"And now they're so different, they're not afforded the same respect?" said William.

"I'd hoped that was not the case. But I'm afraid now that Caro is right and they're being targeted."

"As someone's lab rats?"

Sorella turned her head away, and he did not need a primary to detect her emotion.

"Thank you for the warning, but I said I would help and I will. Whatever you need." He had come back because he wanted to do something valuable and worthwhile. Because for some unfathomable reason he had landed in this place with a unique ability to help.

William saw tears in her eyes when she turned his way. "You don't still have a death wish do you?"

He laughed. "No, but thanks for checking."

The walk back to Caro's took William past a small alley running between the houses. He did not spot the figure lurking there, or even hear the footsteps as they approached. Only when an arm grabbed him around the throat did he have the first clue he was under attack.

Chapter Twenty Three

"Who are you?" The grip around Will's throat tightened. "What d'ya want eh?"

William clawed at the muscular arm. The overpowering smell of sweat and beer had him fighting simultaneous urges to gasp for air and hold his breath. "Can't…" The word came out as no more than a choked gurgle. His assailant realised the problem, but before releasing the neck hold, punched William hard in the kidneys. Will's knees buckled and he fell to the floor with a cry of pain. He crouched there on hands and knees waiting for the feeling to pass. Before it did, a heavy boot swung into his stomach and knocked him onto his side in the dirt. William held his hand up. "Stop, stop… please."

Maddox Flynn stepped into William's line of vision and crouched on his haunches. "You don't belong 'ere, you 'ear me?" Flynn took hold of Will's shirt and dragged him along the ground until he came close enough to smell the beer on Flynn's breath again. "We don't want you 'ere, freak. None of us wants you. So I'm tellin ya, take your sob story to some other suckers." He yanked Will closer. "Or next time, ya won't be let off so easy. Get me?"

William had had enough of these bullies pushing him around. "I'm not leaving," he said, surprised his voice sounded so strong.

Obviously not used to such disobedience, Flynn's eyes widened and his jaw locked. "What'd you say?"

William sat up and pulled his shirt from the man's hands. "Caro invited me to stay and I'll stay until he tells me to go." Only an idiot would have missed who the boss here was. Caro had taken charge on every occasion.

"You think you're clever?" Flynn spat the words in Will's face.

William rose to his feet brushing the dirt from his palms. "Not at all," he said.

Maddox threw another punch. It hit William under the left eye and knocked him off his feet.

William rolled onto his side holding his face. "Shit." *The guy's an animal.*

"I'll be watchin," said Flynn before walking away.

Maddox looked across the aisle of the shuttle at Lal Pickles. He felt sorry for the guy. Seb had insisted they come on this trip, and not because he had any interest in seeing the show, he just wanted to be wherever the freak was. Maddox hated seeing the big man making nice because he felt he owed Freak for finding Seb.

He looked at Freak's face. A patch of purply grey had formed where Maddox's fist had made contact. It had been something of a new experience; not feeling any emotion from his victim. Flynn found it surprisingly enjoyable. It put the freak closer to an animal than a man in his book.

Caro had come over to the house the day after, of course. Harping on about how Maddox should show some self-restraint. How he should feel some compassion for those in need of help. Maddox thought it all bullshit. He knew Freak was up to something. Probably came here to find a woman to take back to freakville for him and his freaky friends. Look at him now, staring out of the window like some kid seeing its first ever sweet shop. *It's a city, Freakboy, get used to it.*

"Please come to the show, Maddie." Lola wound her arm around his and looked up at him.

"No chance. Me 'n' Wallace are off drinking. I don't wanna watch blokes prancing around in dresses, I wanna drink beer."

Lola punched his arm affectionately. His wife knew too well

Maddox would never agree. He didn't know why she bothered asking.

Sorella pointed something out to the freak. Her wide eyes would have betrayed her excitement if Maddox could not feel it suffocating him. For a second, he panicked at the sight of her knee touching Freak's leg then he saw it did not. But Maddox felt no real relief. Look at how close she sat to him, how comfortable she felt with him.

It would be her wouldn't it? Of all the women in the village, Freak would target her.

Oh yes, Maddox would be watching.

The city of Leeds had quadrupled in size, swallowing up the likes of Bradford, Huddersfield, Harrogate and Ilkley as it went. Only York had maintained its separate status owing to the smaller city's historical value.

William found the place unrecognisable. If any buildings remained from his day, they were now buried amidst the curved lines and curious shapes of new shiny skyscrapers. One boasted two separate towers spiralling around each other as they rose into the sky. The closest he had ever seen to anything like it was on a visit to New York. He and Sarah had spent the whole holiday staring up at the unbelievable skyline. He wondered what on earth that place looked like now.

"Is that the canal?" he asked spotting a familiar stretch of water.

"Yes," said Sorella looking below them. "Was that...?" She stopped herself, remembering the others sat close by.

William nodded. "I'm surprised it's in such good condition, it must be hundreds of years old now."

"It had something of a revival when the ANNs were first built.

The country realised it had this amazing network of transport links that had been left to decay, so they put it back into service."

"Cool," said William watching the water glisten between gaps in the buildings.

The shuttle train pulled into the station after only a ten-minute journey; phenomenal considering they had travelled a good thirty miles. William followed the group through the new station building and out onto a packed street. Fifteen villagers had come along including Lal and Seb, Caro, Callum Taylor, whose wife cared for Grace, and the Flynn families. William avoided making eye contact with Maddox. He did not want any more trouble. He felt relieved when the brothers veered off in a different direction saying they would meet the group back there at nine.

On the face of it, Sorella's civilised new world did not look too different. People still rushed about the place, some in groups, some alone. William knew the ANNs were aware of every person, and ready to deal with any aggressive or suspicious intention, but it felt no different to the presence of CCTV in his day. He had expected a Big Brother-like atmosphere of control and compliance, but experienced nothing of the kind. If anything, the place felt friendly. The only difference he did spot on the short walk was the lack of any beggars.

"That's one of my favourite buildings," Sorella said at the theatre doorway, pointing out the square, black box that was the council building. "It's so minimalist."

"I see what you mean," he said following her indoors.

William sat on the end of the row next to Sorella, and chatted with the group as they waited for the lights to go down. It was seven o'clock and the show finished at eight forty-five. He would have nearly two hours. Plenty of time.

As the room darkened he leant close to Sorella and whispered in her ear, "Back in a sec."

In the lobby, he hung back until the three staff members busied themselves with customers. Caro had said so long as he did not attract attention, people might not notice he was different. And even if they did, they may not give it much thought. Some people did not experience very extreme emotion. With any luck they would assume William to be one of those. *Best to be cautious, though*, he thought, given none of them really knew how people would react.

Once outside, William walked across the pedestrian area to the council building. He tried not to think too much about what he was doing, not wanting to give the nerves chance to set in. He concentrated instead on putting one foot in front of the other, and remained completely oblivious to the watching pair of eyes.

William passed the entrance. He wanted to see if many people loitered inside, but the opaque glass doors revealed nothing. If he triggered the alarm he had to be ready to run. He needed a plan. He would step through the doors and count to five. If the alarm sounded he could make it back out quick enough to avoid capture - hopefully. He looked at the comfy shoes he was wearing, feeling grateful for his hosts' forward planning. Whilst he had been practising his memory skills yesterday, Caro and Sorella had shopped on his behalf. They had dressed him in a smart pair of tan trousers and a short-sleeved, smock-like shirt, similar to that worn by government officials.

William took a deep breath and went for it.

The doors opened onto a wide lobby with an impressive transparent escalator to his left and a large stairway to his right. A man and a woman deep in conversation walked down the latter, but other than that the space was empty.

One, two, three, four, five.

When he heard no sound, William headed for the escalator. Five of them ran side by side, each to a separate floor. He selected the middle one, needing the information point on floor three. As the moving stairway approached its destination, he noticed just in time that it took a sharp right turn, and grabbed the rail to steady himself.

The large library index stood in the corner at the far end of the room. In front of it stooped a tall white-haired man, and in between lay nothing more than a handful of empty tables. William took a detour to the toilet. The adrenaline in his system made him nervous but he avoided using the facilities. Who knew what methods they had for tracing people these days? After standing behind the door for a minute or two, William peeked out. The tall man was nowhere to be seen.

William approached the index board. The large black rectangle sat at a forty-five degree angle on its stand. It reminded William of a draughtsman's table. He tapped the surface resulting in a dozen or so 3D icons coming to life. As instructed by ANNy, he searched for the rotating P, for portals. When selected, twelve separate cubes sprang into view each displaying a list of contents. It was exactly as ANNy had predicted. William looked for where level five information could be accessed and found it listed on portals two, six and eleven. As he selected the exit option something caught his attention. He opened up the portal lists again and read the small red letters at the bottom of portals two and six: Closed for maintenance. William exited the menu and walked away. Portal eleven it was.

This time he took the stairs, keeping his footfalls as quiet as possible. A further screening would take place on the fifth floor where small rooms around the perimeter housed the various portals. ANNy predicted that if William had managed to walk into the building, he would be invisible to all scans, but there was no guarantee and the nerves made his mouth dry. As he climbed the final few steps, William heard voices and slowed. The white-haired man from downstairs stood with his back to the stairs and thankfully blocked his companion's view. William crept across the landing and stood out of sight to listen and wait.

"I am supposed to be meeting Sheree in the club at seven thirty and I still need to check this out. I could do without it as you know."

"I can take over for you."

"No, no, it will not take long. Thank you, Lionel."

After a beat of silence, William peered around the door to see the men heading into different portals. His heart sank on seeing white hair enter eleven, pausing at the door until a voice said, 'Welcome, Mr Shaw.'

William decided practice makes perfect. Once both men were out of sight, he carefully moved across to portal five. This room stood directly opposite eleven so he should be able to see Shaw leave. As he crossed the threshold of the small room, his muscles tensed in anticipation, but no alarms went off or greetings were made.

The compact space with its bare walls and lack of windows contained only one thing: a tall black oblong in the centre of the room. William circled the structure to find the entrance on the far side. The cubicle contained a whole series of touch screens displaying the same rotating P5 symbol. When he touched each, the same menu appeared listing the portal's contents.

William practised searching through different items, periodically checking on the opposite room.

When Dr Shaw finally exited and headed for the stairs, it was ten to eight. William waited for a second at the doorway of his room until he felt sure he was alone. The other man had departed ten minutes earlier leaving the whole floor to William. It was now or never.

He crossed the corridor.

It occurred to him as he stepped into portal eleven that there might be extra security here given the level five contents. But when nothing happened, William felt his first rush of adrenaline. He was going to pull this off. He swung round to the portal opening, accessed the menu and selected his first document.

A moment later, a high-pitched alarm sounded in the distance. And before William could react, a metal door slammed shut over the portal entrance, sealing him in.

Chapter Twenty Four

Maddox Flynn's nose pressed painfully into the floor. He kicked out with his feet until the arm that was held up his back twisted again and he fell still.

"What's happening?" The voice from above echoed around the room.

"Unauthorised access, Sir," said the owner of the hand on his arm.

"Get him up."

The guard pulled Maddox to his feet, still holding his arm up his back. An older guard walked towards them looking Maddox up and down. "This is a restricted building, you cannot enter."

"I was followin' someone. He came in 'ere half an hour ago and hasn't come out. What is this place?" Maddox looked around seeing no clues to his whereabouts.

"Who did you follow?" The older guard felt important, Maddox sensed.

"A guy staying in our village, says he's from some island… proper freak he is."

The guard sniffed as if he had smelt something bad. "Only authorised personnel enter here." He looked at his companion holding Maddox. "LQ?"

"Yes, Sir," the first guard said.

"Get him out… and switch that damn alarm off, it gives me a headache." The older guard began walking away.

"Yes, Sir." Flynn's restrainer moved him to the door. "ANN the incursion has been dealt with thank you."

"Wait, 'e came in 'ere I tell you," said Maddox. "What's 'e doing here? What's this place for?"

The senior guard strode back in double-quick time. "I suggest that is none of your business." He came closer and sniffed again. "Have you been drinking?"

"I had one. I'm telling ya something's not right." Maddox fought against the guy holding him and once more found himself face down on the floor.

"ANN please confirm all entrants to the building in the last hour." The older guard listened then knelt to eyeball Maddox. "No unauthorised access apart from you. Now, do I need to call for the police or will you be gone?"

William decided to take advantage of his imprisonment to memorise all he could find on Silverwire. He discovered that someone called Professor Sharma headed up the project which was currently in its research and diagnostics phase. Documents indicated its findings were of paramount importance to the commercial viability of the UK. William began to think it was completely unrelated to the abductions until he came across an appendix document detailing a disease of the brain afflicting rural communities. It read like an instruction manual on what to say in response to questions from families of the afflicted, medics and the press.

William began to search quicker, finding the project had an unlimited budget and sign off at the highest levels of government. The Prime Minister's signature appeared on at least three contract documents. But he could find no details of exactly what Silverwire did or why. He found one report stating that a selective sampling methodology had been authorised, meaning that participants would be hand-picked. But when he tried to uncover more detail he came across the same problem each time: documents restricted to level seven personnel only. William did manage to unearth a list of who had such security access, finding only six names listed, one being the Prime Minister, Stella Montoya, and another Professor Sharma.

By the time the alarm stopped and the barrier began to rise, William had spent a good fifteen minutes in portal eleven. He knew enough about computers to know they would be able to see what he had been looking at, so to cover his tracks he had opened as many items as possible. Clicking randomly on other screens as he read through relevant documents and constantly changing the screen used for level five data. Hopefully this provided enough of a smoke screen for him to keep the information in his head a secret. He closed down all the open documents and returned the six screens to their menus. Then he braced himself for whoever waited outside.

When the shutter rose to reveal an empty top floor, William did not wait around to question why. He crossed to the stairs and walked briskly down to the lobby.

At the top of the last flight, he spotted two men by the exit. They were dressed in grey uniforms and deep in conversation. William could see no way around them and they showed no intention of moving any time soon. He checked his watch, it was gone eight fifteen. Time was running out.

Caro had pointed out that the building had a service lift at the back. He could use that to get to the ground floor, but then what? He would still have to walk by the guards to get out. Could he distract them somehow? Attract their attention away from the door and make a run for it? The truth was William had no idea. He felt completely out of his depth. All he knew was the information he had found could prove invaluable to his new friends. He had to try whatever he could to ensure he passed it on.

He still had thirty minutes, what were the chances they would stand there that long? Patience was all he needed. He would move back up a flight of stairs and into the hallway of floor one. From there he could watch the guards through the window and wait.

He had only moved two steps when a man's voice echoed around the building.

"Hey, you there?"

Sorella fidgeted in her seat. The final scene of the light-hearted musical played out and she could not stop herself from glancing at the empty seat beside her. What if they had been wrong and William was not invisible to the ANNs. He could have been in trouble all this time and they would have had no idea, sitting here watching this trash.

"Keep calm," whispered Caro in her ear.

How could he sit there feeling nothing? She knew her brother controlled his emotion better than most, as did she under normal circumstances, but this was William; a man who had no business doing their dirty work for them. What benefit was there for him?

"Sorella!" Caro said through gritted teeth.

She inhaled deeply and concentrated on the dancing, watching the steps to distract herself. The final chorus played out and the audience stood to clap the performers. The dancing girls and the children came out to bow, followed by the supporting actors and the leads. The curtain closed. Sorella checked her watch and the empty seat before it opened again for a second round of applause.

When the lights went up she looked at Caro.

"Just act normal. We cannot help him if we fall under suspicion."

Sorella understood the logic but hated the sentiment. She wanted to run across the street and demand to be told where her friend was.

"Where's Will?" Seb said.

Sorella ignored the boy's question pretending she had not heard, and joined the line of people in the aisle.

"What a show, hey?" Lola Flynn was a big theatre fan. It always fascinated Sorella that she had ended up married to Maddox the meathead. Not that Sorella had been immune to his manly charms herself once upon a time. But that was a long time ago when she was too young to know any better.

"Those children, they're so talented," Tabby Flynn dabbed her eyes with a dainty blue handkerchief. She had ideas above her station, that one, always playing the lady with her affectations and accessories.

"Have 'em training from toddlers they do," said Lal. "No life for a child, hey Seb? You'd rather be running in the fields wouldn't ya?"

"Where's Will?" the boy asked again.

"My favourite was the woman, the one playing Sally. What a voice!" said Lola.

Sorella tried to screen out their conversation as she scoured the theatre lobby. It was impossible to see if William was there. Too many people jostled their way to the exit. She knew what would happen next. Caro would want them to go home and consult with ANN, check police records and any reported incidents in the library. By which point William could be beyond saving and she would have to live with that. She had promised him they would do all they could to protect him, but all they had done was sit aside and let him take all the risks.

"Did I miss the end?"

Sorella spun at the sound of his voice and without thinking threw her arms around him.

William laughed and moved her away rolling his eyes at the group. "I only went to the loo."

She dropped her arms and felt her face burning under everyone's attention. They all knew she liked him, of course. She was not that good at controlling her emotion, but still, this must seem really out of place. She forced herself to laugh. "I'm just getting into the spirit of the place. Isn't that how theatre people greet each other?"

"Any luck?" said Caro to William when the group had gone back to debriefing the show.

William nodded and opened his mouth to speak then his eyes widened. "It may just have run out though."

Sorella and her brother followed his gaze. At the exit, Maddox stood with two police officers. All three men had their necks craned searching the crowd.

"Idiot," said Caro under his breath. He took hold of Sorella and Will's arms turning them away from the door. "Take William and go."

"Where?" Sorella said, looking back into the nearly empty theatre.

"There must be a stage door. Get him out of the building and as far from the city as you can, then tell me where you are. Go. Now."

Sorella took hold of William's hand and pulled him with her.

"Will, did you like it?" Seb asked as they passed.

She did not see whether William responded, she only heard her brother tell the boy he needed his help.

Chapter Twenty Five

William and Sorella stepped into the buzzing back-stage area. Racks of clothes lined the corridor ahead, people gathered in pairs or small groups, and children chased each other in and out of door-ways. Further down, singing and laughter could be heard from the dressing rooms.

"Follow me and try not to catch anyone's attention." Sorella led the way down the crowded corridor.

A man exited the first doorway on the left as they approached. William took in the guy's no-nonsense haircut, jeans and plain, dark t-shirt. Unlike the others, he wore a serious expression and moved with purpose. William caught his eye and followed a hunch. "Excuse me, can you tell me where the stage door is?" He sensed Sorella tense at his side and knew she would be irritated by his recklessness. Maybe these primaries were not so bizarre. They simply amplified existing insights rather than introducing something new.

"End of here, turn left and it's the red door." The man spoke without hesitation and continued past them.

"What was that?" Sorella said as they exited onto a quiet back-street.

"I did some work for a theatre a few years back and got to know a bit about how it works. My guess… he was a stage manager and would have assumed we were agents." The narrow street of large brick buildings looked immaculately clean like all the others they had walked along earlier. No litter lined the curbs and no graffiti adorned the span of windowless walls.

"How did you know he wouldn't be suspicious… about you, I mean?"

"People are rarely paying full attention when they're busy.

Plus, if the guards at the library let me pass with nothing more than a goodnight, I figured…"

The guard's shout had not been for William. Another uniformed man had appeared on the escalators resulting in twenty minutes' worth of good-humoured banter between the three colleagues. William watched from his hiding place. As it drew closer to quarter to eight, he realised the guards were not going anywhere soon. The chances of making a convincing distraction were low. He doubted it would result in anything other than drawing attention to himself. So, he decided to brazen it out.

He walked down the stairs not bothering to keep his footsteps quiet or his movements discreet. If this was going to work he needed to look as unsuspicious as possible. Hiding in plain sight had proven a successful tactic for many a conman and criminal for many a year. The men stood in a huddle a metre or so from the door. As William approached, the smallest of the three glanced his way. William raised his hand in a good-bye gesture.

The guard nodded. "Good night, Sir," he said causing his two companions to look over too.

"Goodnight," said William without slowing.

And then he was out, down the steps and halfway across the plaza. No voices shouted for him to stop, no heavy footsteps followed from behind and no alarms sounded. Why had he not done that half an hour ago?

"They let you walk right by them?" Sorella looked genuinely blown away by the idea.

"I know, A-Maze-Ing, hey? So, where do we go?" They had reached a cross-roads at the end of the street. William could see streams of people walking across the brightly lit square to their left: the rest of the audience making their exit. Ahead, the narrow street widened with what looked to be a pub or restaurant half way down, and to the right the road curved out of view.

Sorella looked around them at the limited options. "We should avoid the main routes, just in case, who knows what Maddox has told them... we should probably avoid the shuttle too." She bit her lip as she concentrated then grabbed his wrist and pulled him to the right. "The canal, we can follow the tow path."

They walked in just short of a jog along the streets, only slowing to a more normal pace whenever people came into view. None of the roads looked familiar to William and he hated to think how he would fare without his guide. "How far is it?"

"We're nearly there." Sorella turned left and entered a large tunnel.

A few feet in, William stopped. The curved ceiling and cobbled floor felt familiar. He studied the deep alcoves lining the tunnel wall.

"Will?" Sorella had stopped to wait for him.

"The dark arches." He sensed the look of surprise he knew she would see on his face. "These are the dark arches under the station."

"No the station is across the city."

"Not your station, *mine*. I used to come here. There were market stalls at one time, then bars and a really good fish restaurant. I ate there once with Sar-" He stopped himself from saying her name and glanced around again. "Shit, that's spooky."

The place looked dilapidated now, nothing more than a smelly old short cut to the start of the canal. The river still ran underneath and William paused on the bridge to take a look. It was not as deep as it had been in his day and he wondered if the warmer climate had caused that.

The canal itself had hardly changed, the restoration having kept everything in good condition. As they made their way along to the path, William could almost have been back in his own time. So long as he avoided looking up at the skyline, that was.

They walked swiftly for quarter of a mile or so with Sorella setting the pace. William tried to take in as much of his surroundings as possible. Skyscrapers bordered the canal on both sides; huge black, white and silver monoliths sweeping and curving and pointing their way skywards. He was staring up at a white cone-shaped one, when Sorella grabbed his arm and dragged him into a narrow passageway.

"What's-"

She placed a finger on his lips, and spoke in a whisper. "Police… coming down the path."

William peered out and saw two figures in the distance. They walked slowly and in synch and he could hear the soft mumbles of their conversation.

"My hands are shaking," Sorella said when he looked back at her. She held them up to show him.

He took a few steps more into the darkness and she followed. "They won't see us if we keep still and quiet," he whispered.

"I'm scared, Will, they'll feel that." She looked further down the passage but it came to a dead end.

"We'll be fine. If you stop feeling scared, there's nothing to be scared of is there?"

"Don't you think I know that?"

He could tell from her snappy response she was panicking. "Just take a deep breath or something."

The light was not good enough to see her expression in detail, but William caught the gist. It was one commonly accompanied by a phrase ending in *off*.

She glanced at the tow path. "Kiss me."

William swallowed a laugh. "Is that not a bit of a cliché? Do the police ever really fall for that?"

"I need a distraction." She pulled his face down by his shirt and pressed her lips against his. He began to laugh and she pulled away. "If they sense a woman feeling scared and panicked down an alley with a man, what conclusion do you think they'll draw?"

"And my kissing you will help that how?"

Sorella glanced towards the canal once more. "You'll just have to trust me on that one. Now please, kiss me like you mean it."

Why was he such a sucker when women did that whole *please* thing? This was how he ended up getting his heart mangled. Then again, if it was necessary for him to do this, he may as well enjoy it.

"They've gone."

"Huh?" Sorella's arms still clung around his neck and her breathing sounded a little erratic.

William smiled. "The police, they've gone."

She released him. "Oh… I see…" She pushed her hair behind her ears. "Come on then." She led the way back to the canal path, walking ahead of him again.

"Do we need to talk about that?" he asked.

"Only if you were faking." She paused a little as they emerged from under a bridge, checking the area to the right, then resumed her previous pace.

"Good point. Let's not talk about it."

Sorella stopped dead and William almost knocked her over. He held on to her shoulders to steady himself.

"You know last time one of us did that, someone got their shoulder dislocated."

She twisted to face him. "Were you?"

"Were you?"

"I asked first."

"Did you?" he said with a smirk mimicking her words from when they first met.

Her eyes pinned him to the spot as if she was trying to burrow into his brain. "Were you faking?"

"Would it matter? It worked didn't it?"

She let out an exasperated breath and set off walking again. "It matters to me," she said under her breath.

William did not respond.

Her walk sped up into a jog, and then a run until before he knew it they were sprinting along the narrow path. She was good too. Not many women could keep this pace for long. He was a strong runner but he was pretty sure he would not be able to lose her if he tried.

They ran like that for over an hour, in silence. The city began spreading out, and the buildings become more distant and lower. After travelling what must have been nearly ten miles, the canal path widened where it was crossed by a road. Sorella stopped and walked in slow circles to catch her breath.

"You're one hell of a runner," William said, wishing they had water. Running in warm weather had never been a favourite of his.

She walked a few steps away from him. "Hi, it's me. We'll wait here."

William thought she was talking to him at first. It was only when she answered a question it dawned on him she was making a call – of sorts. "How does that work?" he asked.

Sorella sat on a low wall without responding.

"The primary incorporates telecoms?"

She did not answer, taking a band from her wrist and using it to tie up her hair.

"So you're not speaking to me now?"

"What is there to say?"

"How about, how did you get on, William? Find anything useful for us on your spying mission?"

She frowned at the floor then looked up. "Of course, sorry. What did you find?" Her voice sounded flat and devoid of any real interest.

William stretched out his calf muscles. No complications, that's what he had promised himself and it was a good plan. One he should stick to for as long as he could. "Your brother was right. Silverwire is something to do with what happened to Grace and the others…and it's big. Your Prime Minister sanctioned it."

"What is it?"

He stood straight and arched his back. "It's hard to say. There was no detail on what and why, that's all restricted to level seven…"

"Level seven?" she interrupted. "But five is the highest security level."

William shrugged. "Not anymore."

Sorella looked totally deflated. "So we still don't know who's doing it and why?"

"I found out who. There are six people with level seven access. It seems a Professor Sharma is the project leader, ring any bells?"

Sorella shook her head.

"Level seven could not be accessed in that place, but there was reference to where it can be… somewhere called Caltonville?"

"I've heard of that, it's a military base in Lancashire."

"I thought there were no wars anymore, why the need for a military base?"

She smiled like he was a little slow. "We may be peaceful, but we're not stupid."

It was not long before they saw Caro approaching in the

waltzer car. Sorella stood and walked to the side of the road. "William?"

"Yep?" He went to her side and she looked at him for a long moment.

"Never mind."

Caro stopped and opened the door for them. "You covered good ground."

"We ran," said his sister, sitting and looking out of the window. "What happened with Maddox?"

The door closed and Caro instructed the vehicle to take them home. *So cool*, thought William. The relief at having completed his task successfully made him feel a little euphoric.

"It seems he was carrying out a little spy operation of his own. He followed William to the library and even went in after him."

That explained the alarm and the shutter, William thought.

"When the guards sent him away, he went to the police and told them all about William having no primary and going into a restricted building."

Sorella looked furious when she turned to her brother.

"Don't worry. I explained to the officers that this was nothing more than fantasy. I told them William was a new member of our community who Maddox had taken against."

"And they bought that?" said William.

"Oh yes, Callum and Lal backed me up that there had already been a physical attack on you. I took the officers aside and told them you and he were in a dispute over a woman."

"You told them I have a thing with his wife?" William felt more irritated than he should have, given it was only a story to pacify the police.

"I did not specify the woman." Caro glanced at Sorella and she looked out of the window again. "Society does not think so highly of our communities. It imagines that LQs lack certain morals. In the end, they accepted this was nothing more than Flynn's latest attempt to stir up trouble. Maddox protested, naturally, and I offered to go and find you for them, but they were not really interested. They were happy that this was a local matter and that I should deal with it."

"I'm impressed."

"Thank you, William, but I think we should be the impressed ones. You said the visit had been worthwhile?"

For the rest of the journey, William filled Caro in on everything he had found.

Lola Flynn's head ached. She wondered if it would be possible to shut her husband up if she swung the pan at him really hard.

"Don't you get angry with me," he spat sensing her annoyance. "I'm the one in the right here. You heard Caro spouting all that crap. He pretty much denied freak boy had no primary and made me look like an idiot. He's never liked me."

Lola exhaled loudly. "I'm sure Caro didn't do it because he doesn't like you. He was just trying to stop you embarrassing us. No one wants the police 'ere, snooping round us." It had been such a fun evening until her hot-headed husband had turned up shouting the odds. Sometimes she thought her mother might have been right about him.

"He's up to something I tell you. He was in that building, I watched him go in with my own eyes."

"Well you wouldn't watch him with someone else's would you?" Lola had always found that expression irritating.

"You think this is funny?"

"No, Maddox, I think it's tragic." She switched the lights off in the living room to encourage the end of the day to come quicker.

"Why can't you ever stick by me? Why d'ya always have to be so awkward? You're supposed to be my wife."

That was it, the last straw. She could hold her temper no longer. Lola felt pleased to see her husband flinch at the power of it, before she let rip. "*Me* stick by you? Maybe if you stopped obsessing about *her* I would. How do you think it makes me feel every time you lust after her. She's not interested, she never was and she never will be and I'm beginning to think she's got a bloody good point." Lola pushed her husband as hard as she could to get some of the frustration out. "Everyone knows the only reason you hate him is because she doesn't." Her voice sounded shrill. "I'm going to bed. You can sleep down here."

As she climbed the stairs Lola's anger gave way to despair. He never even tried to deny it.

Chapter Twenty Six

William had hoped his self-control would last a good while longer yet, but he was more out of his depth than he knew. The day after his successful visit to portal eleven, he awoke to the sound of voices in the kitchen below. Another warm, sunny day waited outside and he could not help admiring the benefits of global warming.

He had showered on arriving back last night, feeling sticky from the run, so now he dressed quickly and headed to the bathroom to brush his teeth and freshen up. Caro had provided toiletries including a surprisingly ordinary looking toothbrush and razor. William ran his hands through his hair and went in search of coffee.

Sorella sat at the table with her brother. She wore a dusky pink sundress and had fastened her hair in a messy bun. If William had been less used to managing his reactions around her, he might have given himself away.

"Morning, sleepyhead," she said.

He checked the clock on the wall. It was half past ten. "Blimey, I haven't slept that late since I was a teenager."

"It was a busy day yesterday," said Caro handing him a large mug of strong coffee. For all his stuffiness, the man sure knew how to brew caffeine.

"I'm taking you for a picnic," said Sorella as he eyed the wicker basket at her feet. "Caro and ANNy want to plan the next steps, but I thought you deserved a reward. I'm going to show you my favourite place to relax and soak up the sun." She smiled but her eyes had a cautious look. "Will you come?"

He had done a better job of pulling off disinterested than he thought. "I'd love to." She looked so happy with his response, he almost kissed her then. He should have known this was the day the truth would come out.

The lush patch of grass she took him to, about a mile east of the village, bordered a large lake and was surrounded by trees. It smelled of honeysuckle and something sweeter he could not place. They sat on a square rug and ate fresh salad and cheeses with homemade bread and her lemonade. She had insisted he apply sun lotion and the smell of it, combined with their surroundings, made him feel he was on some exotic holiday.

"What's it like being here?" Sorella asked sucking the last of some soft cheese off the end of her finger.

William nodded. "The picnic's good, the location beautiful and the company's... okay I suppose."

She smiled. "You know what I mean."

William leant back on his elbows. "Not as weird as you'd think. It still feels like the world... just a bit different. Like I imagine a visitor from the Third World would feel coming to the west."

"Third World?"

William had to snigger. Her question showed just how different things really were here. "Countries deprived of any real economy or quality of life, sadly common in my day."

Sorella selected a piece of cucumber to eat. "Was it true what you said about all the people you love having gone away? Is that really why you came back?"

"Partly."

"We have more in common than you think, you know. When Caro and I came here we left all our friends behind and the villagers were less than welcoming. You might have noticed we're also quite different."

"If you mean the fact your brother is a proper smart arse..."

She giggled and propped herself on one arm. "We seemed so strange to them, but our parents were determined we would be better off here. It was a really long time until I accepted that. Even now, I sometimes wonder if I would fit better in that other world."

"Why did they think that?"

"When Caro became a neurological savant, my parents were appalled by the effect it had on him. I love my brother but he is somewhat obsessive about his work and nothing else gets a look in. They didn't want the same for me."

"So he chose to be a savant, he wasn't born that way?"

"He was born with a mental processing speed faster than ninety per cent of the population, but becoming a savant is a choice. Basically everyone receives educational inputs on a range of knowledge areas throughout childhood. Talent and potential is examined along the way and people are developed to make full use of their personal qualities. But those in the top ten per cent can forgo all other enhancements in order to become a genius within their chosen field."

"Seriously?"

"Which is why my brother is somewhat lacking in social skills. My parents couldn't face doing that to me."

"You're top ten percent too?"

Sorella picked a small lettuce leaf from the bowl and threw it at him. "Easy on the tone of surprise, average boy."

William raised his eyebrows. "I take it you're not guessing I'm average."

"No, I'm not… and if I'm truthful, you might be a little above average."

"How little?"

She shook her head with a smirk. "Ah, men and their egos."

"So does that mean there's no schooling going on?"

"No, children still attend school but the emphasis is on developing skills and experience rather than acquiring knowledge. The enhancements provide factual input and data very quickly. As you'll know the brain is good at remembering facts, but even better at developing behavioural habits, pathways that connect what we know to what we do. You said much of your job is concerned with improving how people manage. These days, those who work in management are experts. A natural talent for such work would have been spotted early, or an interest expressed, after which the person is developed to their fullest potential."

"Unless they're deemed too slow."

Sorella frowned. "It's a matter of how well an individual could cope with the inputs. The lower the brain's processing speed, the harder it would be and the higher the potential for difficulties."

"Really? Is it not because humans still need to feel in some way superior to others? By keeping a portion of the population less capable, does that not boost the egos of the rest of you?"

"I only had a couple of upgrades, William, so that certainly wouldn't apply to me."

"I'm not having a go. I'm just saying some aspects of the human character are what they are, irrelevant of progress. How about people using the differences they see in others to define themselves? A lot of stereotyping and prejudice comes from seeing the competition as different and somehow wrong, thereby validating who you are in comparison."

"No. Most prejudice stems from misunderstanding and lack of insight, the tendency to generalise qualities across a whole group, be they good or bad. People still compare themselves with others, of course they do, like you say, it's human nature. But now they focus on what's different about themselves in a positive way."

"You're telling me outside of communities such as yours, people don't see any negatives in the attitudes and actions of their fellow man anymore? Sounds a bit too good to be true."

"People are given such insight into the human condition and its varying beliefs and perspectives, they can see things from another's point of view. We can not only empathise on an emotional level because we feel how others feel, we can rationalise intellectually about why they might react that way. Differences are embraced because they are understood and no longer anything to be feared. It makes for a much happier life."

"And yet, you deny a significant number of people the full benefits. Do you really believe those around you couldn't take it?"

"Yes." Her expression failed to match her answer. William could see he was making her think.

"Did they ever try?" He made his voice softer, to take away any judgment.

She looked at him for a long moment. "I don't know."

William sat up to select more bread and cheese. He wanted to give her some time to digest his point of view. It seemed to him hugely unfair, not only to ostracise the LQs, but to label them in such a derogatory way in the first place. On the face of it, it sounded logical and scientific, but he saw it for what it really was: discrimination.

He poured her more lemonade.

"Thanks," she said quietly without looking his way.

He touched her hand and smiled warmly when she gave him her attention. "You okay?"

She sat up straight and collected more food for herself. "Yes… thank you."

"How old were you when you came here?" he asked, to change the subject.

"Eight. My parents were under a lot of pressure to go down the savant route with me too, from myself as much as the education system. I wanted to be an astrophysicist and explore the stars. I hated them for a good three years. In fact, I'd only just forgiven them when they died. And now I sort of hate myself for that."

"Do you mind my asking what happened?"

She shook her head. "They both worked with the ANNs. My mother was an expert in neuron development and my father an architect working on the dome constructions. They had been to a conference together in Austria when their plane crashed. We're not sure why, nothing was conclusive."

"That must have been tough."

She frowned a little. "We had each other and from that point on we sort of became everyone's children. The villagers became our family. And I was educated the old-fashioned way, by reading and researching. I never had any further inputs. When we restored ANNy, she offered to source some for me. I was fifteen so still young enough to handle it, but by then I liked doing it for myself.

"You restored ANNy?"

"Have I not mentioned that? She was an old system, one of the early models that were quickly bypassed. My mother kept her for research purposes but only as a partially operating system. Caro has made it his life's work to restore and develop her, hence her total obsession with him."

"It's like listening to science fiction." He lay flat on his back and closed his eyes. "Sometimes when you're talking I just have to tell myself you're a little bit crazy."

For a while they fell into a companionable silence. William enjoyed the sun on his face and pondered on how, despite it being more tragic, he almost envied her the fact her parents had not left by choice.

"I can understand your not wanting to get too attached to this place." Sorella's voice sounded softer when she spoke again. "I was thinking about yesterday on the canal and I'm sorry for my behaviour. It's too easy for me to forget you'll be wanting to go home soon."

"I have no intention of going back." The words were out before he really gave much thought to the consequences. When she made no response he opened his eyes to see her staring across the water. "I thought you might be the one person pleased to hear that..." She still made no response and he half sat to see her expression. "Suppose I'll have to hold out for Seb." She twisted away, but not before he caught a glimpse. He moved to her side with a hand on her shoulder. "Hey, what did I say?"

She shook her head and wiped both hands across her cheeks. "Sorry, I was... not expecting... I was bracing myself for something else that's all." When she faced him she laughed a little and rubbed her arms. "You know you said sometimes you think I'm a little crazy..."

"I know my messages are all mixed, but it's been a rough year. It's self-preservation."

"These things are so much easier when you know how the other person is feeling. With you, it's like navigating in the dark. I'm always trying to guess if you're happy or sad, pleased to see me, irritated or bored."

"I've never been bored," William said with a chuckle.

Her smile had all the vulnerability of a child. It made William realise he was being unfair. She had been nothing but honest about liking him from the start. He was the one playing all the games he proclaimed to despise so much.

"You really want to know?"

Sorella shrugged. "Only if it's good. If it's bad, let's just eat more cheese," she said.

William's amused laugh was accompanied by her nervous one as he leant in to kiss her. Just before their lips touched, he hesitated and glanced away from her eyes. "The cheese *is* good though…" Then he kissed her mouth for a long moment. "The only faking from me," he said keeping his face close to hers, "has been omitting to mention my real reason for coming back was you."

And there it was: the truth will out.

Her responding kiss contained just enough heat to stir him up. "When you said this place was secluded, how secluded are we talking?" he said.

She placed a hand on his thigh and smiled. "Now *that* emotion I can read easily. I'm pretty sure we won't be disturbed this time."

And they were not.

To say she was a sensual lover would have been something of an understatement. All his normal rules of operation failed to apply. There was no chance of him keeping his cool and holding back until he was sure his woman was satisfied. The way she kissed and caressed and moved on his body had him completely at her mercy, lost in the moment and giving in to all his urges. It was indisputably the best sex of his life.

Sorella lay on her back with the sun warming her skin and William drawing patterns on her stomach with his finger tips. He lay on his side, one arm around her shoulders holding her hand, and one leg hitched over hers.

It had been a while since she had been with a man, and never one she regarded as an equal: one she respected, admired and tried to impress. Living in this community was filled with benefits, but access to suitable men was not one of them. Her early flings here had been fun and even passionate, but it was never long before she bored of the conversation. And when she tried to date men from outside the village, they always came to view her as a novelty. The simple truth was, she was too different in both worlds.

"I have to ask," said William, "what on earth does a woman like you see in me?"

"Funny, I was just thinking that."

"Ah oh."

She turned her head and kissed his mouth. "Not like that."

He rolled her closer for another kiss and she felt her heart flutter. She had no idea how he did that but she liked it, *a lot*.

"Compatible men are not an easy find for me. The villagers are often lovely but if I'm honest I find them a bit boring... that must sound awful." William made no comment, continuing to trace circles across her skin. "And my intellectual peers are all focused, career-driven professionals not really interested in a farm girl."

"So, what you're saying is, I'm a little less boring and a little less bright than the competition." His voice contained the trace of humour she found so attractive.

"Exactly," she said squeezing his hand. "It helps that you're sexy too."

He laughed into her hair. "Yeh, sometimes I wish women could see past the sexy to the real me, you know."

She moved her head away to look at him. "You don't think women find you sexy?"

"I *know* they don't," he said with a smirk. "I've had about twenty years' worth of experience in the matter."

"Well, I do... obviously," she said stroking her free hand across his chest.

He kissed her cheek. "Yes, but we already agreed, you're a bit crazy."

Sorella closed her eyes and faced the sun. "I never felt I had anything in common with anyone before, but it feels like that with you. Right from the first moment I saw you, I felt it. You looked a little lost and alone and I know how that feels."

"You're surrounded by people who adore you."

"I know," she looked at him, "but this is the first time I've really had a friend."

"If it's friendship you wanted I could have saved myself a lot of energy just now."

She smiled. "Any regrets?"

He shook his head. "You know my friend, Steve, thought my description of you proved I'd lost my mind. He said, 'Don't you realise you've created your ideal woman then made her want you as her lover?' He didn't think that was very likely."

"I'm interested to hear this description."

"Really?" William made a point of looking thoughtful. "Okay… I think I said you were average, well if I'm honest a little more than average."

She punched his stomach playfully and he chuckled. It dawned on her he was the most comfortable he had ever been in her company. For the first time he was sharing something of himself. She decided to take advantage and satisfy her curiosity. "What happened when you went home?"

He sat away a little and propped himself up. "What do you want to know?"

Sorella wondered if she had spoilt the mood. "Anything… everything. I suppose I want to understand what's happened to you, who you are…"

"Is that all?" he said with a grin.

"Sorry, you don't have to tell me anything, I don't mean to pry."

He rolled a little so he was looking down on her. "Sorella?" He stopped and lifted his head. "Does everyone always call you by your full name?"

"Yes. My father used to call me Ella, but no one else shortens it."

"Ella," he said trying it out.

The sound brought a flood of different emotions. She heard her father's voice in her head and felt overwhelmed by how much she still missed him.

William's eyes studied her. "Too weird?"

"No, it's just a long time since I heard it. It sounds nice when you say it."

His kiss once more sent her heart rate soaring and she felt glad this man had no idea how she was feeling. The intensity scared her and she had no doubt it would have the same effect on him.

"Ella, I will tell you anything you want to know… just be sure you really want to know."

What did that mean? "How will I know that until I've heard the answer?"

"I'm sure you're bright enough to work it out, ten per cent girl."

She thought about that for a moment as William wound the curls of her hair around his finger. "Is it the suicide or your wife you think I should avoid?"

"Oh, you are quick aren't you?"

She waited for him to elaborate.

Eventually, he stopped fiddling with her hair and focused on her eyes. "They're not exactly discrete topics."

"You tried to kill yourself because you'd lost her?"

"I never actually tried to kill myself."

"Technicalities, William."

He smiled at that. "When I was thirteen, my father committed suicide because my mother left him."

For a moment Sorella was stunned into silence. Then she realised he was waiting for some response. "That's… awful… I'm sorry. Is that the right thing to say, sorry?"

"There's no wrong thing to say. It is what it is. I thought I'd dealt with it a long time ago but it turns out it was my 'go to' solution when I found myself in the same boat." He gave a dry laugh and scratched his head. "To be honest it freaks me out a bit when I think about it now, like it happened to another person."

"Does she know what you tried to do, your wife?"

"Oh yeh, she was waiting to give me both barrels when I woke in hospital. I recall the phrases *Selfish bastard,* and the rather charming, *This proves how right I was to leave you*, or something along those lines."

"She sounds lovely."

William's eyes flashed with something Sorella did not have chance to read. "She had her moments."

"Wait, why were you in hospital?"

"Going through that thing is no picnic. Not so bad when you end up here passed out in the warm climate, but in my day it was freezing cold and raining. Luckily a farmer found me, so no harm done."

She stroked his arm. "Did you see her again, erm..?"

"Sarah?"

It was the first time he had said her name, and it made the woman strangely more real. Sorella nodded.

"A couple of times, yeh."

If she was not always obsessing about how he felt she might have missed the evasive look. The next question tumbled out on instinct. "Do you still love her?"

"Yes."

His response was so instant it felt like a physical punch in her stomach. Sorella tried to mask it but it was too late.

"I did warn you," said William watching her.

"You could have lied."

He smiled and kissed her nose. "And where would that have got us?"

Her breathing felt heavy as she tried to fight the urge to get up, dress and walk away. She did not want this to end before it had even begun.

"I don't *want* her anymore, she hurt me too much for that, and now... I'm not sure I even need her. But the fact is I've loved Sarah for fifteen years and that's hard to turn off."

"Would you go back if she wanted you to?"

"How would I ever know?"

The swell of envy Sorella felt towards this woman grew larger by the second. "Theoretically," she said unable to mask her irritation.

William met her gaze. "No."

Another unequivocal answer, this time in her favour. The swell stabilised.

"I have one last question then I think we should change the subject."

"Okay."

She kissed him again before he had chance to smash away all her hopes. After all, losing this woman he still loved had left him desperate enough to try and take his own life. The chances she could compete were depressingly low. "Do you think there is any chance..." She found herself having to look away as she said it. "...you might be able to feel that way about someone ever again?"

"Did you have someone in mind?"

When she looked his way he was smiling and Sorella felt her

face burning.

He took her in his arms and pulled her close. "I wouldn't be here otherwise would I? Now, this change of subject you had in mind, does it need to include conversation?"

Her answer certainly had no words in it.

Chapter Twenty Seven

ANNy had gathered all the data she could find on Caltonville military base. She talked them through it as Caro, Sorella and William concentrated on the rotating 3D image in the centre of the dome. "Their ANN scans the buildings and the entrance. The site is purely a training barracks where troops come to learn field operations. There is a skeleton staff of eight living on the base, the most senior of which is General Talbert and a further thirteen specialist trainers who are there during specific modules. As you will see we have the living quarters, the training facilities and the offices at the front of the site, behind which is the open ground used for manoeuvres." The 3D image zoomed in to the left of the site. "To the left of the training centre is an old water tower. On first look it appears derelict, but a friend of mine who keeps track of military installations tells me that four years ago plans were submitted to convert the interior."

"And this is where the level seven records are held?" said Caro, leaning in to look at the structure.

"That is my conclusion." ANNy zoomed in on the water tower until it was the only building in view. The tall metal structure reminded William of Lincolnshire's abandoned windmills. The exterior looked dirty, with chipped paintwork and a single door bolted shut with what looked to be a rusty padlock.

"Old school," said William.

"Tricks to make it look deserted I expect," said ANNy.

William was starting to get used to the weird voice in his head and nodded in agreement.

"Why house it there?" asked Sorella. She stood at William's side, holding his hand. Neither her brother nor ANNy had passed comment on the apparent development in their relationship.

"From the data William gathered it seems we are faced with a small but very powerful group. And they are hiding their activities well. From what I can gather, no public ANNs have level seven access. They appear to be churning out some given script and turning a blind eye. But I have identified an isolated ANN attached to the government which appears to have no specified role in any listed activities. She came into existence three months before the first references to Silverwire appeared and is not on the open network. I assume the portal in Caltonville is her digital backup, hidden from view. My friend confirmed the submitted plans would be consistent with that."

"So how do we get in?" William said.

"Sorella?" Caro looked at his sister.

"It's possible I can get us on site, I'll have to do some research. ANNy can you let me have all the trade records relating to Caltonville?"

"I have them ready."

William felt completely lost. "Sorry, what's happening?"

It was Caro who answered. "My sister manages all trade between the rural communities and, well, everyone else. She has been crucial in ensuring fair and profitable contracts with distributors. Thanks to her, LQs have a much improved standard of living." Her brother sounded proud.

William looked at Sorella.

"Did you think I sat around all day making lemonade?" She smiled and began flicking through the documents ANNy had provided.

"What sort of trade?" William asked.

"It used to be crops in the main, but now we have an increasing number of goods from fine wine to furniture. Our communities may be slower but they are hugely resourceful and hard working."

She flicked a few documents aside and began to study another.

"How many communities are we talking about?" William said.

"Nationally? Erm…" Sorella looked up at Caro. "In excess of five hundred."

"Jesus." That was like running a major PLC. "You can't do that all on your own."

Sorella stopped reading to look at him, her expression amused. "I'm not sure if I should be flattered or insulted by your shock, William. But you're right I oversee the process, check the contracts and assist with the more difficult negotiations. Each community has its own trade representatives. Here we have Callum Taylor, Lola Flynn and a few others managing things day to day."

"Wow."

"Mmm." She smiled at him for a little longer then squeezed his hand and went back to work. After ten minutes or so, she sat back and addressed the group. "As far as I can see, the site's requirements are not huge as they only have a small population living in. We have no direct contracts with them for foodstuffs as these go centrally to the Army and are distributed from there. The only opportunity I see, is that three months ago the General personally bought some handmade furniture from the Whickam How community in Lancashire. I'll make contact and see if he is in the market for any more."

Two hours later, Sorella gathered the group back together. They were joined by Lal and a tall thin guy William remembered from the day Sorella hurt her arm.

"We have an appointment to show General and Mrs Talbert some furniture next Tuesday morning on the Caltonville military base and we need your help. As Caro has told you, William is helping us to establish the truth behind the abductions. You probably heard that two more occurred this week. I trust we are all still keeping an eye on Seb?" Sorella said.

Lal nodded, his mouth set in a firm line.

"Essentially, we need to get William on site and in a position to access this building, which houses classified information on the topic." She pointed to the water tower. "As he has no primary he will be invisible to the ANN, but we still have to find a way to hide him from the soldiers. So… this is my plan.

"We will take the small furniture carrier which will house three or four examples of kitchen cabinets which is what Mrs Talbert wishes to see. Behind the seats, we need to build a box large enough for you to hide in, Jed. As you are a similar build to William, I want you both in matching clothes and hats. Lal and William you will sit directly in front of where Jed is hiding and when we arrive at the gates you need to be having a petty argument. In particular, you, Lal, need to be throwing insults at Jed, the type of things you know will get a reaction. That way, the guards should detect the anger of two arguing men and will naturally assume one of those is Will."

"Clever," said Caro with a nod.

Sorella glanced his way but did not break her flow. "Once inside, we will park here at the edge of the General's living quarters. It is next to this passage through which William can reach the main building and beyond. The three of us will exit the van and greet the couple, and in the meantime Jed will come out of his hiding place and wait. When Lal and Will go to collect the furniture to show to the Talberts, you two will swap places, and William can head to the water tower."

"How long will I have?" said William.

"About half an hour, is that enough?"

William nodded.

"Why can't he go in the box?" said Jed.

"That's a good point, I forgot to mention. William is going to be vulnerable to being spotted as he moves across the site and I want him to have been seen with us."

"And if I'm stopped I can say I'm lost." William had been on enough military sites to know the drill.

Sorella smiled a little and he guessed she was pleased he was ahead of the game. "I can say I sent you on an errand. If you're not back at the carrier when we're done, we will delay best we can."

The group ran through the plan and expected timings a few more times before breaking.

"It is probably best if we do not shout about what we are doing to the others," said Caro as they walked to the doorway.

Caro and William walked side by side to the base of the cliff. They had left the village just before dawn to avoid anyone enquiring about what they were up to.

"So they are Artificial Neural Networks?" William said. The two huge domes cast long oval shadows on the grass where they walked.

Caro glanced at the domes. "Yes. They are part of the public network. Fifteen structures such as this are positioned around the country. They house the ANNs responsible for public services."

"That's why they're so big?"

"The human brain is a phenomenal thing is it not? All that thinking capability within the folds of something no larger than a melon. We are still not able to create anywhere near such intricacy. If we require more brain power, we have to make bigger ANNs."

"So yours is limited in capacity?" asked William.

"ANNy is more than we will ever need. She is similar in size to that owned by private businesses and we are the only LQ community to have our own."

"Because of your parents?"

Caro looked a little taken aback with how informed William was. "Yes. It is true to say they left us financially secure enough to have lived our lives without working, but neither of us felt that is what they would have wanted. I built ANNy from our mother's equipment so we could pursue more fulfilling occupations."

They had reached the bottom of the cliff and Caro set out ANNy's scanner next to the teleporting base. "When I came out here with Sorella, we detected a lot of electro-magnetic energy in the area. This time ANNy is going to show us what this thing looks like. All set ANNy?" Caro looked up for a second. "Clear skies and little if any breeze."

"How does that work?"

"The scanner?" Caro knelt beside the spherical object.

"No, communicating with ANNy. You can hear her out here and she can hear you?"

Caro smoothed his hands over the sphere, rotating its position a touch. "The primary allows her to access the hearing centre of my brain. She can speak directly into that, as she can with you when you are within her dome. And she can hear my spoken words."

"So she can't read your mind?"

"Not really. The cognitive activities of each brain are hugely idiosyncratic. Without studying someone for a long time, she could not link any particular synaptic activity with a given thought."

"But she knew I was not lying?"

"Lies typically stimulate some emotional or physiological activity which can be detected. Even in the well-practised liar,

ANNy would see something."

"You said not really. I take it she has spent sufficient time with you to stand a good chance of guessing *your* thoughts?"

Caro smiled and stood again.

"Is that how it works with the rest of you too, when Sorella called you from Leeds?"

"It is a similar process. But only Sorella and I have the communications enhancement. None of the villagers can contact each other that way."

"Which is why you couldn't just call up Seb?"

"Yes." Caro looked up at the hillside and took a few steps back.

"Do you think it's right that some people are regarded too slow for anything more than the primary?"

"From your tone, I take it you do not?"

"It's something I'm finding hard to balance with the idea of a fair and equitable world."

Caro said. "It is more a matter of economics than equitability. When it dawned on the human race that it knew more about the universe than the workings of the human mind, an opportunity was spotted. Investment in raising our understanding was high, on the basis that what was discovered might provide significant competitive advantage.

"Then in the spirit of true science, those who developed ANN technology released it worldwide. They believed, as did many of their predecessors, that such knowledge should be for the good of all. The result was a race to adopt and capitalise on the technology. Within forty years the primary was developed and equivalents in use across the globe. Nations could not afford to hold back on an advancing world. But it was an expensive business. Cuts had to be made where they could be."

Now, this sounded like a more credible reason, thought William. How often things came down to the simple matter of money. "So, the whole *LQ people are not up to it* story is a fake?"

Caro placed his hands on his hips. "No, no. It is true that the slower the brain processes information the less successful the input. It became a matter of return on investment."

"So if the ANNs can't read your minds how does the mind control work?"

Caro frowned clearly not understanding.

"The car and the entertainment systems. You don't have to speak to them, so how does that work?"

Caro glanced William's way for the first time, a hint of a smile crossing his lips. "It takes a lot of practice and patience. The technology in such devices is different to the ANNs. It has more in common with your computers in that it follows set commands. Most people speak these aloud but it is possible to train the devices to respond to rehearsed thought patterns, like training a dog to sit in response to a hand gesture. So, if you consistently press your thumb and forefinger together when requesting the car door open, eventually it will respond just to imagining that action. It is a simple conditioning effect."

Impressive, thought William. It might not be true mind reading but it was a damn sight closer to anything he ever expected to come across.

"ANNy is ready to show us what it looks like," said Caro.

William stepped back to fall in line with Caro as a projected image of the hillside came out of the sphere. It fit perfectly over the real thing, making it impossible for his mind to distinguish between the two. Above them, an orange scar now slashed across the cliffside. Its deep bronze centre lightened to a golden brown by the time it reached the uneven edges. The shape reminded

William of an aerial photograph he had once seen of Lake Windermere. The circumference curved one way and then the other with narrower sections at each end.

"It is approximately four metres long and two and a half metres across at its widest point," said Caro.

"But what is it?"

"No idea. Our best guess is a point of friction which has torn a hole between your time and ours."

William recalled his lesson in physics from Dr Watson. "So if time wraps around itself like tangled strings, this would be where two strings come into contact?"

"That is the thinking, yes. We have no way of knowing for sure, but it would appear to be the most logical explanation."

"And this," William said tapping the white disc, "does this have anything to do with it?"

Caro shrugged. "Maybe, maybe not. It could be the cause. There will be a significant amount of magnetism within the teleporting base. When operational, it would have been covered and contained, but now it is free to attract. Its very presence may have caused the friction. Alternatively, it may be pure coincidence."

"But the fact that I lost any clothes with metal in them indicates some form of teleportation is involved?"

Caro studied him for a few seconds. "This base alone could not teleport. It is one small element of a sophisticated process, the rest of which has been removed. Plus, you personally could not teleport without harm. A living thing requires certain preparation first." He looked back at the scar. "No. I think whatever this is, it possesses its own magnetic properties and they are the reason for your missing belongings."

William considered the scar. He found it simultaneously

beautiful and scary as hell. "If this is creating such a lot of electro-magnetic activity, won't people know it's here. I mean, the military would pick up on something like this wouldn't they?"

"Not with those here." Caro tilted his head at the domes. "They produce so much activity it has been hard for ANNy to filter this out. If you had not tipped us off to its presence it would have blended in."

Not back in my time though, thought William. No domes to mask it there. How long before some satellite picked it up and people came to investigate? He decided not to voice his concerns to Caro. They had enough going on here without worrying about the chances of more people coming through.

"ANNy is picking up a small amount of radiation, which would explain your nose bleeds." Caro looked his way. "It is probably not a good idea to make a habit of going through this."

"Right." For the first time William considered the very real possibility that this thing had done him harm, not only due to the physical effects but because of the lost time. He decided to sound his genius companion out on it. "One thing I can't work out is the first time I came here, I stayed for two and a half days, but when I got back, only a day had passed."

Caro regarded him. "Really?"

"How is that possible? Why would I lose over thirty hours when I went back through this thing? Is time moving quicker here than in my day?"

A frown formed deep crevices across Caro's brow. "Talk me through it."

"Well, I left home on Tuesday morning to come to the hillside, fell through this thing and woke here a few hours later. I spent that first night searching for my car, and left in the middle of the following night. When I was found back in my own time it was still Tuesday evening."

"I see."

"Do you?"

Caro gave a quick smile. "You are asking the wrong questions William that is all."

William waited for Caro to expand. "You can explain it?" he said when the man did not.

"I can see the most logical hypothesis. It is unlikely that your time and ours is travelling at different speeds. It is also unlikely that you would lose so many hours travelling back in time yet none travelling forward."

"So?"

Caro studied William. "I am interested to see how long it takes you to ask the right question."

"Still testing me?" William could not help feeling irritated given the lengths he had gone to help these people.

"It is obvious you want an answer to this. Now I have told you there is one, a part of your brain will already be working on it. Whether you invest any concerted effort on it or not, at some point the right question will occur to you. After which, you will see the most logical conclusion. I do not expect it will take you long." Caro studied the hillside once more, his head cocked to one side.

William ran through what Caro had said but no questions occurred to him. He felt infuriated to know he was missing something that this man found so damn obvious.

Chapter Twenty Eight

Maddox Flynn downed the last of his fourth beer. The taste had become increasingly bitter. He hated these village affairs at the best of times. Clapping and cheering a bunch of kids playing amateur music and then dodging his wife's attempts to make him dance. Not that it would be much of a problem tonight. Lola had been grumpy as hell the past week. She sat with Wallace's Tabby now, throwing him dirty looks he pretended not to notice.

What had really got his back up was seeing Sorella with the freak. They arrived half an hour ago holding hands, and now they stood giggling in the corner like frickin kids. The sight of Freak brushing her hair off her shoulder and stroking her arm made Maddox's blood boil. She'd better not think of doing it with him, who knows what diseases the freak carried.

Maddox watched Sorella whisper something in Freak's ear and then walk across the room. Normally, he would have taken the time to appreciate how her black dress clung to her cleavage and showed off her long legs, but tonight he could not. He could not take his eyes off the freak. The guy bit his lower lip as he watched Sorella walk away, and the look in his eyes filled Maddox with rage.

Maddox strode across to the corner, not noticing his wife sit up straight as he passed, or Jessie Bo holding his hand up to get Maddox's attention. The freak had no idea what hit him. He was too busy lusting after Sorella to see Flynn's approach.

"Whoa!" Freak staggered back from the force of Maddox's shove, and hit his head against the wall. Two chairs clattered to the floor and Maddox kicked them away to get to his target.

Lal and Old Man Mart grabbed each of Maddox's arms and tried to pull him away, but Maddox shrugged them off easily. He could hear Lola shouting his name, but nothing mattered except making sure this weirdo kept his frickin hands off Flynn's girl.

In truth, she had only been his girl for a few weeks one summer when they were seventeen, but to Maddox no one else ever came close. Not Lola, nor any of the women from other villages he used to distract himself. Sorella was the only one worth bothering about as far as he was concerned.

She was also stood in front of him.

"What are you doing?" Sorella planted both hands on his chest, blocking his way to the freak.

Maddox looked around her. "Gonna let her fight your battles are you?"

Freak had stood now and moved to Sorella's side. "I have no desire to fight you, Maddox."

Flynn took his chance, swinging a punch in the freak's stomach and knocking the wind out of him.

"No!" shouted Sorella going to the freak.

"Maddox!" Lola spun him to face her and Maddox could feel her fury. "We're going home."

"I'm not going anywhere." Maddox clenched his fists. He felt ready to finish this piece of crap off.

"Will, are you okay?" said Sorella.

"Listen to your wife, lad," said Mart.

Flynn gave the old goat a long hard look. Who the hell did he think he was telling Maddox what to do? Maddox heard the freak saying he was fine, but the guy held his stomach like it hurt. Good. Flynn stepped towards him, but once more Sorella got in his way.

"What's got into you, Maddie?"

Her use of his nickname stopped him and he focused all his emotion on her. Lola gasped at his side. But his wife's pain paled into insignificance against the heat of Sorella's anger.

Sorella shook her head. "You have a wife who loves you and no right whatsoever to be jealous."

"It's wrong you being with him," Maddox said.

"That's none of your business."

"He's a freak, a weirdo… you don't know where's he's bin, what you could catch."

Sorella actually began to laugh. Maddox stared at her unable to find anything funny about the matter at all. Then she stopped laughing and looked him straight in the eye. "It takes one to know one, Maddox."

"Please, Maddie, let's go home," said Lola.

Maddox felt his wife's embarrassment and wondered how long before another emotion took over. He did not bother to respond to her plea. Instead, he leant in close to Sorella, so close he could have kissed her if he didn't think she would knee him in the balls. He had experience of that from a previous occasion, the night before his wedding if he remembered rightly. "You don't even know if he's for real or if he's just trying to bed you."

Maddox knew from the swell of pleasure Sorella quickly suppressed, it was too late on that score. Then he watched in horror as she turned away and kissed the freak on the mouth. Not just a peck, but a full-on moment of passion with her body pressed up against him. Maddox had never seen her be like that with anyone and the shock was enough to enable Lola to drag him away.

William smiled as she stepped away and straightened her dress, but she could see the insight in his eyes. She was starting to enjoy reading the signs now she was getting better at it.

"You and Maddox, hey?" he said.

Sorella smiled at having guessed his assessment right. "It was a very long time ago."

"Not for him." William's eyes were full of humour and, if she was not mistaken, a hint of pride.

Most people had moved swiftly away once Flynn had gone, only Mart remained nearby. "I bet he winded ya, lad?"

"He sure did. What's the guy built from? Granite?"

Mart's low chuckle accompanied a pat on Will's back. "Watch yerself, he's a persistent little bugger that one." Mart turned to Sorella. "Nice to see you've found some happiness me love," he said, squeezing her wrist and then wandering off towards the bar.

"He's changed his tune," said William watching Mart go. "I thought he wanted me run out of town."

Sorella took hold of his hand. "Are you really okay?"

"Mmm fine, that kiss did wonders for my injuries," he said with a smirk.

They stood up the fallen chairs and sat. "Mart's always been like a granddad to me. I know he speaks his mind and often a bit too quickly, but he cares. He'll be fine with you now, unless you wrong me of course."

"And how might I do that?" William pulled his chair closer and placed an arm around her shoulder.

"Leaving me, telling me lies, taking me for granted, being too possessive, making a fool of me, *not* falling madly in love with me, that kind of thing."

"That's quite a list," he said kissing her cheek.

"Oh and sleeping with other women."

William brought his lips level with her ear. "I think you might have spoilt me on that score."

Sorella tried to ignore the fact that her heartbeat attempted to drown out all other sounds. "Why do you say that?" she said.

William smiled at her. "Why do you think?"

As she gazed at William, wondering if he had any clue how in love with him she was, Sorella completely forgot where they were. Only when the music started did she snap back to reality. She sat up in her chair and quickly scanned to see how many people had been watching. Most of them, she found.

"The show's starting." She twisted a little to face the stage and leant against William's body. He wrapped both arms around her waist.

He whispered in her ear. "So you and Mad boy ever…?" Sorella fidgeted in the seat and William sniggered. "I'll take that as a yes."

"Why would you want to know that?"

"Because it's interesting…and I want to know everything about what's happened to you and who you are."

She looked his way and rolled her eyes.

"So come on then, how many lovers have you had?"

"William!" she said looking to see who sat closest.

He chuckled again. "No one can hear us."

"No, but they'll know I'm embarrassed about something."

"Ah, man up, girl. It's nothing to be embarrassed about." He gave her a squeeze. "You can't say you wouldn't like to know the same of me."

She twisted to look at him. "No, actually I wouldn't."

"Liar," he said kissing her forehead.

She faced the front again and sighed. "Okay, maybe I'm lying a bit."

William made a satisfied sound and pulled her back to lean against him again. Casey Taylor finished her flute solo and everyone applauded.

"Are you going to tell me then?" she said when he said

nothing.

"Is this a trade agreement?"

She smiled. "Okay, but you first."

"Three…or maybe four. Does a blow job count?"

Sorella stifled a laugh. "Yes."

"Four then."

She took a quick glance around just in case anyone was in earshot. "Eight."

"Such a hussy."

"Do you mind, I haven't been married for years."

"Ever come close?"

Sorella shook her head. William was the only man she had ever wanted to spend more than a week or two with.

"Who was your first?" he said.

She did not answer, concentrating on Seb as he prepared to play the piano.

"Ella?"

"Seb's about to start."

She felt William look away and then back again. "It wasn't mad dog Maddox was it?"

"Can we stop talking about this now?" She tried to sit up more but William held her too tight.

"Wow, no wonder he's protective."

"I was seventeen, I didn't know any better. Your first was all sensible and well-thought through was it?"

He laughed and rested his head against hers. "Mine was a blow job in the park from my mate's big sister, Stacey. She was good too. Well as good as you need to be with a horny fifteen-year-old."

His honesty made her giggle and she gave him a kiss as a reward.

"Any parks nearby?" he asked when she moved away.

"Shush, stop it now, Seb is on."

Within seconds of Seb starting to play, William appeared to have forgotten their saucy conversation. He sat up and rested his arms on his legs. Sorella watched his fascination grow as Seb's playing became faster and more complex. It reminded her how much she took the boy's talents for granted.

"How old is he? Eight?" said William glancing her way. "And he can play like that. God I hate him." William smiled and craned his neck to see Seb's fingers flying across the keys.

"You really like him, don't you?" said Sorella.

"He's a lovely kid. Where'd he learn to play like that?"

"I think Grace taught him, although she was never this good." Sorella looked over at Seb's Mum who for the first time since her abduction sat up of her own accord. She could almost have passed for her old self. Sorella looked at Seb and then back at Grace. His mother knew he was playing.

"I always thought we'd have a kid like that, a little blonde heartbreaker."

Sorella looked at William staring at Seb and then quickly away. She did not want to make a big deal of his words.

After a second or two, William slumped back in his chair and dropped his head. "I'm sorry," he said looking her way. "I was thinking out loud."

She took hold of his hand. "Don't worry about it, you're just being honest and that's good... not always easy, but good." She smiled and he lifted his head to smile back. Sorella looked away to watch Seb. "At least I don't need to ask what colour hair your wife has now."

Seb finished and everyone in the room stood and went crazy. The boy came to the front of the stage and gave a bow, all the time grinning at William. It seemed the adoration was mutual.

"If you practised you could be good at that," said William when Seb wandered over to them.

"Nah, it's too boring." Seb slapped William's upheld hand. "Where's your Worb?"

William took the marble from his pocket and clapped it into life. Sorella watched with amusement as they tried to catch each other out by throwing it out of reach. Eventually, she bored of their game and went in search of food and drink. When she returned with a plate to share and two glasses of wine, Lal had joined the throwing game. It was good to see him and Will laughing together. She expected that Caro revealing how William was helping them, might have resulted in such a change of attitude.

"You've got a good 'un there, S'rella," said the big man before taking his son away.

"This looks tasty." William selected an olive from the plate and popped it into his mouth. "Fancy eating outside?"

"We're not going to the park," Sorella said taking a bite of celery.

William grinned at her. "Spoil-sport."

Chapter Twenty Nine

General Talbert looked almost casual in his green trousers and short-sleeved shirt. Only the rank signified on his epaulettes hinted at any formality. His taut, muscular forearms and trim build were those of a young man, but the white hair and wrinkled skin around his neck told a different story. His wife fluttered around him clearing cups from the table and adjusting any vases or ornaments she thought looked out of place. She wore a floral apron over her navy blue dress and had her short hair set in regimented waves.

"Ms Sorella Grey, your reputation precedes you. Thank you for coming along personally," said the General with a firm handshake.

They stood in the Talberts' spacious kitchen - a modern and minimalist space which Sorella imagined was the similar to those in all the surrounding residences.

"It's my pleasure, General, Mrs Talbert." She shook the wife's hand too, before the other woman brushed something invisible off the table top. "I thought the men might appreciate my assistance. I think coming to a military base is a little unnerving for them." She needed to explain any anxiety coming from Lal and Jed.

When she had made the appointment, the General told her the couple were in the process of renovating their retirement home. Fed up with army-issued interiors, Mrs Talbert was keen to furnish her own home with handmade country furniture. Lal had selected three styles of kitchen door to show her and two free standing dressers, the first of which he and Jed carried in now. As they placed the cabinet on the floor, Lal gave Sorella a quick nod.

So far so good.

Their entrance to the site had been hassle free. Lal's attack on Jed had the two soldiers at the gate rolling their eyes and showing no suspicion of William. When they reached the Talbert residence, William had pulled his hat down as the General came out to greet them, and headed straight for the rear of the vehicle. Talbert barely glanced William's way as he cast an appreciative eye over Sorella. She knew he had something of a reputation with the ladies so she had dressed accordingly, smart with just a hint of sexy.

Mrs Talbert cooed over the carved wooden doors whilst her husband banged his fist against different parts of the interior. Sorella checked the large, no-frills clock on the wall - ten minutes gone.

"This is wonderful artwork," said Mrs Talbert.

Lal stood proudly at the side of his product. "My missus designed all of that, and I carved it meself."

"We can custom-make whichever design you like to fit the space, or produce it in free-standing format. Do you have a date in mind for when you would want them?" asked Sorella.

"Barnaby retires in September, but I hope to have the house ready by August. Would that be possible?"

"Erm, we've not agreed to buy anything yet, dear." The General examined the dovetail joints in the base of a drawer he had removed as he spoke.

"Would you like us to give you a moment to discuss it in private?" said Sorella.

"No, don't be silly," said Mrs Talbert. "He's just trying to keep you on your toes, prides himself on being a good negotiator. I told him, this woman does it for a living, Barnaby, it's no good using your daft tricks on her."

Sorella smiled at the General. The colour had risen a little on his cheeks but she felt only a hint of embarrassment. Here was a man well-practised at controlling his reactions. "I'm always open to some healthy negotiation, so long as my people receive suitable reward for their work," Sorella said.

"Quite right," said the General. "Perhaps you could give us a few moments."

Sorella, Lal and Jed made their way to the front garden and waited. It looked like a pretty depressing place to live. The box-shaped houses and uniformed gardens lacked any character. Even the neatly trimmed conifer bushes lining the Talberts' pathway gave the impression of six on-guard sentries.

"Be a bonus if they buy," said Lal chewing on his finger. "You know we can't do any new designs since..."

"I know." Sorella patted Lal's arm. He and Grace had been a formidable team. Sorella sometimes had to encourage them to slow down. Their use of resources was often out of balance with their sales opportunities, but she could not fault their passion.

The General appeared in the doorway with a wide smile. Sorella walked towards him preparing herself for the negotiation process. But then, Talbert paused and the smile slid from his lips. "Lucille, stay indoors and lock up." The General strode by his three visitors. "I suggest you join my wife. I'm afraid we have a small incident."

Sorella kept pace with the General. "What sort of incident?" She tried desperately not to feel a suspicious level of panic.

"Army business, nothing to worry about. I'll be back as soon as I can."

"Barnaby, what's going on?"

The General glanced back at his wife. "We have a breach and a man down. Take these folks indoors and stay put."

William started well. His entrance to the site went without a hitch, his swap over with Jed proved smooth and unseen, and his progress to the water tower was unheeded. After which things got weird, *really* weird.

A lone soldier stood in the area between William and the tower. Not a major problem. They had anticipated as much and prepared accordingly.

"Do you remember the first day we met when you'd hit your head?" Sorella said as they made their way towards the base. She held what looked to be a mascara wand. "Ever wonder how I got you back to the village?"

"The whistling in my head?"

"This is a sleep inducer. Point it at any part of the body and press here." She showed William the button on the side. "It will render your target unconscious for between twenty minutes and half an hour depending on their size."

"How the hell did you lift me?" He took the stick from her and turned it over in his hand.

"I called Caro."

Just as her brother had predicted, out of nowhere the question popped into his head. William placed a hand on Sorella's arm. "What day was that when you found me?"

"Not this again," she said with a smirk.

"Not the date, the day. Can you remember?"

"Of course, it was Monday afternoon."

Of course, William repeated silently. "You're absolutely sure?" She nodded.

"And this time when I came back, what day was that."

"Thursday," she and Lal said in unison.

William gave a small laugh and shook his head. Caro had worked it out quicker because he had more information. As soon as William had said he left home on Tuesday morning, Caro would have seen the answer. He had pretty much told Will too, or given a ruddy great hint at least. It was unlikely time would be lost going one way and not the other, the man had said. William had left home on Tuesday morning and arrived here on Monday afternoon, left here Wednesday night and arrived back Tuesday night. Left home again on Friday and arrived here Thursday. He had lost over twelve hours of time in both directions.

What happened to that time was not something he wanted to spend too much time thinking about.

William stepped out of the soldier's eye-line and removed the sleep inducer from his trouser pocket. The range was only a few feet. He needed to get significantly closer. The ground from the training centre to the tower was too open to cross without being seen. He would have to loop around and approach from the back.

Keeping low, he skirted around the outside of the building, ducking under the large picture windows. There were no groups in today, ANNy had checked, but he was not taking any chances. Once he had made it to the other end, with the back of the tower now in front of him, all he could see of the soldier was his shadow stretching across the grass. William moved swiftly, crossing the field and pressing his back against the rear of the tower. As he paused to stir up some courage, he could hear his own breathing echoing in his head. He took more shallow breaths to dampen the noise.

Despite lacking a primary, William knew the soldier's senses would be honed to perfection when it came to detecting a presence. Creeping around to zap him would probably result in William drawing attention to himself before he was ready. It would be much more effective to act swiftly and give the man little chance to react.

William stood straight and exhaled. *Just do it, man*, he told himself before walking four steps to the right and aiming his weapon.

It all happened too fast for William to make sense of it. At the very instant he lifted his arm, two figures appeared between him and the soldier. They came out of nowhere, literally materialising in the space in front of him. Both wore black uniforms and faced the other way. If he had not been so psyched up to deal with the soldier, he might have been able to stop himself from pressing the trigger. He might even have crept away unseen.

"Sergeant Holden-," one black figure managed to say before the sleep inducer hit his back and he dropped to the floor. His companion jumped to the left, revealing William to the soldier who raised his weapon. It was nothing like any firearm William had ever seen. It didn't even look like a gun. For a start it was white and its curved form appeared flimsy and lightweight.

"Drop your weapon and put your hands where I can see them," said the soldier.

William let go of the stick and held his hands up. He was not taking any chances.

"ANN, inform General Talbert we have a situation at the water tower, three unauthorised personnel and one man down." The soldier kept his weird weapon aimed as he spoke.

The second black clad figure spoke as he knelt to check his colleague's pulse. "Sergeant, this man was trying to access a restricted area." Satisfied his companion was not harmed, he stood to face William. "How did you get here without our knowing?"

"I was lost. I haven't hurt him." William could not think of anything else to say.

The soldier stepped towards William. "What business do you have you here?"

"I will take care of this," said the stranger.

The Sergeant held up his hand. "I'm sorry, Sir, this is military ground. You will let me handle this. In fact, who are you and what are you doing here?"

The man in black smiled in a patronising manner. "You're not authorised to know who I am. But I can tell you we came to intercept this man." He took William by the arm and moved him a few steps away. "And he is no longer your problem." He crouched once more in front of his sleeping colleague, and when he stood the man on the floor was gone.

The soldier took a few steps back. "What the..." He now trained his weapon on the stranger. "Who *are* you people?"

"No more needs to be said. We have what we need." The stranger clamped something cold and heavy around William's wrist. Across its surface scrolled hieroglyphic-like images and it emitted a low vibration.

"No. Stop. WAIT!" Sorella ran from the training building, passing a surprised-looking General as she went. Behind her, Lal and Jed followed. "He's not the one you want, he can't tell you anything, he's only following my orders."

William's captor paused.

"What on earth is going on here?" demanded the General.

"General Talbert, this man was attempting to access restricted level seven data but as you can see the situation is in hand," said the man holding William.

"What authority-"

"I am Silverwire, Sir."

Talbert stiffened at that and gave a small nod.

"Listen, I'm the only one who can tell you anything useful," Sorella said. "My name is Sorella Grey. My father was Montague Grey, my mother Ophelia. They were advanced scientists and I am upper quartile. I'm the one wanting what's in there." She nodded at the tower.

"She doesn't know any more than I do," said William.

Sorella flashed him a cold look. "You will keep quiet unless I tell you to speak." She looked at William's captor and tapped her forehead. "Jessie is our village idiot, not much going on up there. He can't tell you anything. I've only given him limited information."

"I'll take my chances." The stranger took hold of Will's wrist strap.

Sorella stepped closer. "Just check if what I'm saying is true. My name is Sorella Grey, he is Jessie Bo. Check it," she demanded.

William gave her a hard stare. "My name is William York." He would not let these animals take her.

She scoffed. "Okay, Jessie, whatever you say. Why don't you check out who William York is whilst you're at it?"

"Sorella don't-" William said.

She returned his stare. "I'm not going to tell you again. Shut up."

Mr Silverwire considered Sorella for a moment then spoke off to one side. "I need a check on the status of Sorella Grey, Jessie Bo and William York."

William shook his head at Sorella as she watched.

"Received," said Mr Silverwire.

The man moved fluidly without hesitation. William had no time to react. The strap was off his wrist, on Sorella's and she and her captor were gone in the blink of an eye.

"No!" Will grasped at the air where seconds before she had been and fell to his knees. *What the hell just happened?*

"Where is Caro? He said he'd come." Jed paced back and forth in the small holding cell. He had managed to send a message to

Caro on a tiny hand-held device before the General marched them over here.

"Why would she do that?" said William. He sat on the cold dirt floor with his back against the wall.

William's two cell mates did not answer. They had told him he needed to stay quiet and act dumb. All their lives depended on it. Sorella had been quite clear on the matter. They needed to pass William off as Jessie. If people thought he was slow, they would not question his lack of emotion.

"Why not let them take me?" William said.

Lal and Jed exchanged glances.

"They were the guys who came for Seb," William said to Lal.

"Huh?"

"The day I found Seb in the field, I saw two figures in black appear out of nowhere and then disappear again."

The big man clenched his fists. "Why did no one tell me?"

"I imagine they didn't want you to worry about how close he'd come." William dragged his fingers across the floor, feeling the dirt wedge under his nails. "And now they have Sorella." The thought of her alone with those people, of them hurting her or doing to her what they had done to Grace, was enough to drive him crazy. He stood in an attempt to shake off the dread crawling through his body. "She should've let them take me."

"She could not," said a familiar voice.

The trio turned to see Caro in the doorway. A few feet behind him, the General stood with his arms folded.

William fell silent. Despite the questions bouncing around his head, Sorella had given him a chance to get out of here. The least he could do was not mess it up.

"Can we go now?" said Jed.

"Yes." Caro glanced at Talbert. "I explained to the General that you were being used as a cover. He understands this initiative was planned by my sister. He is happy to leave any further action to the proper authorities."

William noticed how Caro avoided telling any outright lies. He had said just enough to give the impression Sorella had worked alone. No doubt done to keep the ANN here from detecting anything suspicious.

The General did not look pleased with the decision, but he opened the cell door to let them out.

"Jed, you take the carrier back. Jessie, Lal you come with me." Caro led the way back to the Talbert residence, waiting until the General was out of earshot before speaking again. "We need to get to ANNy, tell her what you saw."

"It's the same ones who came for Seb who've got her," said Lal.

Caro glanced at William and then back to Lal.

"You should've told me. I had a right to know," said the big man.

Caro opened the door of the car and stood aside. "I did not see what good it would do. But I apologise."

William checked the location of the General. He was speaking to his wife on the porch of their house. "What did you mean when you said she couldn't let them take me?" William said quietly.

"If you had teleported without a primary there would have been no way for your brain to be restored. You would have arrived on the other side no more than a vegetable. Teleporting is not a physical movement it is a copy. Your system is erased at point A and simultaneously recreated at point B. As the most complex organ in your body, your brain is impossible to replicate unless it has been primed. My sister just saved your life."

"In return for her own?" said William, feeling sick.

Caro stared into the distance. "She obviously felt that was a fair trade."

William paced. "But why? I'm nobody. Why would she do that?"

"Because she loves ya, lad," said Lal climbing into the car. "I thought you'd have spotted that by now."

William leant his head and arms against the side of Talberts' house and swore under his breath.

"William, come, there might still be time to help her," said Caro.

How could her robot brother stay so damn calm? "Was she scared?" William said.

When there was no answer, he looked Lal in the eye and spoke louder. "Was she scared?"

The big man shuffled in his seat. "S'rella's the most resourceful young woman I've ever met. If anyone can handle this she can."

William pushed away from the wall and took his seat in the car. "I'll take that as a yes."

Chapter Thirty

Sorella hoped she had done enough to secure William's safety. She had instructed Jed to call her brother as they followed the General through the site. If anyone could get them out, Caro could.

Her skin tingled from the teleportation. She had only experienced the mode of travel once before when she was a child. On that occasion, the sensation had made her cry. Her father tried to calm her, saying how lucky she was to have had the experience. How most people would never be able to afford it. But Sorella had not been convinced. Later, when she learnt more of what the process entailed she felt even more resistant to it. Becoming a whole new person in the blink of an eye - every cell replaced, every memory copied - struck her as the most unnatural of concepts. Even when Caro explained that ageing operates in exactly the same way, that the body continually replicates old cells with new, it did not alter her perspective.

Her companion removed the strap from her arm as she looked up at the large sphere rising above her. Its exterior looked weather-worn and old. The walkway around its widest point was broken with large sections missing. Behind it, a tall brick chimney towered overhead. Wherever she was, it was old, industrial and deserted. It was also near the sea, she could smell it in the salty air.

"Come." The man took hold of her arm just above the elbow and led her down a cracked pavement towards a large white building. The few windows it had were smeared with dirt, and what had once been a lawned perimeter now grew long and unruly with weeds. The man held one side of a double door open and indicated for her to go in.

Inside, an elevated metal walkway ran along a tubular corridor. Through the gaps in the metal, Sorella could see the bottom of the tube curving under them. Around its walls, the faded images of people working in blue plastic suits and face masks only added to her confusion. She tried to take in something that would give a clue to her location, but the man dragged her along too quickly. It was a wasted effort anyway. Across the archway at the end of the tunnel, an elaborate mosaic announced where she was.

The tunnel exited into an enormous hangar housing huge cylindrical objects. Sections of each had been removed and dismantled to show the bizarre workings within. For a brief moment, fascination replaced Sorella's fear. She had never seen anything like it in her life. Her brother would love to see this.

"Impressive huh?"

The man's words snapped her back to reality and she focused on the large tent dominating the centre of the room. This was it then. Adrenaline sizzled in her veins and she fought the urge to pull away from her captor and run.

As they approached, she could see a red-haired man inside. He wore a white apron and his waistline spread over his hips in a flabby roll. Her captor pushed her into the tent.

"Ms Sorella Grey. Welcome." As the red-haired man spoke, he placed a syringe on the tray at his side then turned his blotchy, pock-marked face towards her. She did not need to feel his enjoyment in her head. She could read it in his smug smile.

It was pointless pretending she was not terrified. And she could see he knew that from the continued smirk. But it did not render her defenceless.

"Professor Sharma?" she said, pleased her voice sounded strong.

The smirk disappeared.

Her courier placed a hand flat on Sorella's back and pushed her further into the tent as he spoke. "The intel was correct. They were attempting to access the portal. She says she is their ring leader, insisted I bring her."

Intel? Sorella thought in shock. Someone had told these people what they were doing? That made no sense.

"Thank you, Mr Faber. You may leave us," said Sharma.

"Sir." Faber lifted the tent flap and exited.

"Please take a seat." Sharma held his hand out to the examination chair. "Our ANN informs me you and your brother slum it with the lowliest, despite your credentials."

"I'm fine standing, thank you. And our community is by no means lowly."

"You see yourself as their champion do you?"

Patronising creep, thought Sorella. "No. I see myself as their friend and I'm not the only one. We know what you're doing and we will stop you."

The man smirked once more. "Big words for a little lady out of her depth. Would you like to take a seat of your own accord, or would you prefer that I make you?"

Sorella straightened her back. "Do your worst."

"That is the plan, although we have to await my colleague for the real fun to begin. She would like to know what you know and how that is possible."

"Maybe you're not as clever as you think you are."

The professor took a few steps her way. "Oh, I doubt that, Ms Grey. I doubt that is the case at all."

As soon as she heard the high-pitched whistle, she knew there was no more she could do.

"This is ridiculous, it's been hours and you're telling me you have absolutely no idea where she is." William paced back and forth. He had been doing this the whole time he and Lal had briefed ANNy on the chain of events.

Numerous attempts had been made to contact Sorella by both Caro and ANNy. Wherever she had been taken, all communications were being blocked.

"There is nothing to go on. There were no locations linked to Silverwire in all the data you brought back from the city. All we have is the military base," said ANNy.

"And it's obvious nothing active was happening there. The General looked as shocked as we were. How did Silverwire know what we were doing?" said William.

"Maybe the General is more involved than we think. You said he recognised the authority of Silverwire. He could have alerted them to the appointment Sorella made." Caro made a third sift of all the searches ANNy had done on Will's initial information.

"So why beam in and out like that, why not be there waiting?" said William.

"They could have been monitoring us. If they discovered the trip was planned they might have put two and two together," said ANNy.

"How would they do that, tap the phones?" said William.

ANNy had a small laugh at that. "They would not need to. They could simply monitor conversations."

William felt a little stupid for not guessing as much. "How?"

Caro answered. "The primary allows ANNs to pick up on speech. They cannot detect what people are thinking at a cognitive level but they do hear spoken words. It is what allows them to communicate with us."

Lal stood from his position leaning against the counter. "So they can just listen in whenever they want?" He appeared as shocked by the idea as Will.

"It is not legal outside of authorised areas" said ANNy. "We can monitor specified buildings or regions so long as people are made aware."

"But if the police had cause to suspect criminal activity, they can enable covert monitoring anywhere," said Caro.

"And Silverwire is bigger than the police," said William.

"There would need to be a physical amplifier in place if they were monitoring," said Caro. "And ANNy would know because she would pick up the speech too."

"Not since Seb went missing," said ANNy.

Caro stopped what he was doing. "Because we still have ours up." He looked annoyed. "I will get it taken down."

William placed his hands on the table in front of Caro. "That's all well and good, but what about finding your sister?"

"If there is an amplifier, we can look at its technology and determine where it was made. Then we can track who might have commissioned or purchased it."

"And how long is that going to take? We may already be too late. Lal how long was Grace miss-" William stopped mid-sentence and looked at the two men. "Grace. Why didn't I think of that before? Lal, we need your wife."

"Gracie can't help. She's not with us anymore." Lal made no attempt to move.

"Your wife is the only person who knows where they have taken Sorella, because she's been there. She's the only chance we have." William began to pace again as he thought it through.

"But she cannot communicate," said Caro.

William was surprised the supposed genius was not keeping up. "That doesn't mean she can't remember. Go, Lal, bring her here quick as you can, and bring Seb too. I have a job for him."

The big man started to leave.

"Oh and does Seb have any paints or inks?" asked William.

"I've got a load in the workshop," said Lal.

William patted the big man's arm. "Good. Bring a pot back with you, preferably black. Caro we're going to need paper."

By the time Lal returned with his wife and son, William had explained his plan to Caro and ANNy who were on standby to help. His first job was to get Seb making the prints. William took him into the side room. "Ready to help us, buddy?"

Seb nodded and took a seat at the table, eying the paper and paint with interest.

"Okay, I need you to make me six different prints. I'll do the first one to show you how." William took a piece of paper, folded it in half vertically, creased the fold and re-opened it. Then he selected the smallest brush Lal had provided, dipped it in the paint and splashed a few random dots across one side of the page. "So, once you've done that - and you don't need any more splashes than that, okay?"

The boy nodded.

"You fold the paper in half like this, press it flat," William smoothed the palm of his hand across the page, "and re-open." The piece of paper now displayed a symmetrical black and white pattern. William held it up in front of Seb. "What can you see?"

The boy studied it for a moment with a frown, and then smiled. "A bird and a pineapple."

William turned the paper around and studied it. "If you say so, buddy." He ruffled Seb's hair. "So, more of those please."

"Yep." Seb had already folded his first page in half by the time William left.

Grace sat in the upright examination chair. Her head hung low as usual so William had to kneel at her feet to see her face.

"Hello, Grace. My name is William. You probably won't remember me, but I'm a good friend of Sorella's and she needs your help."

"She can't understand ya," said Lal.

William ignored him. "I'm going to say a word to you and I want you to tell me the first thing that comes into your head. Can you do that?"

Grace gave no response.

"Okay, well let's just give it a go." William took hold of the woman's limp hand. "Seb," he said pronouncing the word clearly.

The woman remained silent and motionless.

William squeezed her hand. "Seb," he repeated keeping the same emphasis on the word.

Still no response came.

"Seb." William dipped his head to look in her eyes. "Just the first word you think of Grace. Seb."

She made no noise but William felt her hand twitch.

"Good, that's good Grace. Can you say it out loud for me? Seb." He knew success with these things relied on positive reinforcement.

"Oie." The sound Grace made had a rasping quality that made it hard to interpret.

William squeezed her hand. "Fantastic Grace, and again... Seb."

"Oie," Grace responded.

"She makes no sense see." Lal sounded defeated.

"She said the same thing twice, though, didn't you, Grace," said William. "The same word. What is it? What are you thinking? Can you say it clearer for me... Seb."

The woman's lips shook as she attempted to press them together. "Beee."

"Now that was completely different," said Lal.

William looked up at her husband with a smile. "Oh I don't think so. She's just struggling to form the letter." He concentrated on Grace again. "One more time, Grace, even clearer for me... Seb."

Grace lifted her head a fraction and made an exaggerated mouth movement. "Be..oie"

William shuffled closer to her. "Boy?"

The single nod from Grace resulted in simultaneous gasps from Caro and Lal.

"What's going on ANNy?" William asked.

"You were correct, William. There is activity in the memory centre of her brain."

William pulled up a seat in front of Grace. "Okay, Grace. Now I need you to help me find out what you know. We will do the same thing with a whole bunch of words. Each time you just tell me what pops into your head, okay?"

The woman made no response but she held her head higher and kept eye contact.

"Seb," said William.

"Beoy," replied Grace without hesitation. Lal once again gasped at her side.

William squeezed her hand. "Boy," he said using the same tone and intonation he had with the word Seb. Hopefully she would detect that he wanted her to now respond to this word.

"Lor," said Grace. The woman was bright, despite her condition.

"Again for me, clearer... Boy."

Grace stuck her tongue out in an exaggerated manner. "Lorve."

"Love?"

Grace nodded once.

"You've got the idea. Now I need to take you back to the time you were taken. It might not be nice, Grace, but Sorella really needs you. We think she's in the same place and we need to find out where that is." William spoke to Lal. "Where was your wife when they took her, do you know?"

"She was picking corn."

Seb's choice of hiding place took on a whole new connotation, but William did not have time to think about that now. "Here we go then," he said taking a deep breath. "Cornfield."

"No!" Grace's answer caused both William and Lal to lean away. She shouted the word as her face contorted in an obvious expression of anger.

"I guess she remembers," William said glancing at the woman's husband.

Lal pulled up a chair and took his wife's other hand. "She's flaming terrified."

"I know you don't want to remember, Grace, but it's really important." She did not blink as she stared at William. He was not sure if that was a good sign or not. "Cornfield," he tried again.

Grace squeezed his hand so tight it hurt. "Duk."

"Again. Clearer," he requested. "*Cornfield*."

"Durk."

He took a guess. "Dark?"

"Daarrk," she said.

"Was it dark where you were?"

Grace did not respond.

Maybe not, Will thought and returned to the plan. "Dark."

"Bzzzz"

"Good, that's good. Again for me… Dark."

"Bzzz."

"Bus?" asked William.

"Bzzz." This time Grace let go of their hands and waggled her fingers as she said it.

"Buzz, buzzing, like a vibration?" William remembered the feel of the teleporting strap on his wrist.

Grace nodded once.

"You have to teach me how to do this," said Lal taking his wife's hand again and staring at her in wonder.

"It's the closest thing we have to mind reading where I come from," William said. "Can you collect all of Seb's pictures so far? Then it might be best to take the lad home, this might get a bit tough."

Caro placed a hand on Lal's arm. "I'll take him back to Rose. You stay with Grace." A moment later, Caro returned to hand William the pictures.

"Thanks." William placed them on his lap. "Grace, we're going to do that again and then I'm going to show you a picture and I want you to tell me what you see."

This time she nodded to his instruction. The practice was making her quicker.

"Cornfield," William said, wanting to track back to her first thought processes.

"Bluck," Grace said this time.

Black, she had been trying to say black with dark. He needed to remember to think of synonyms. "Black."

"Bzzz," said Grace

"*Buzz*," prompted Will.

"Ton," said Grace.

"Ton?"

"Ton… ton," said Grace.

He was obviously wrong. He ran through options in his head, *ton, tonal, tone*.

"Ton..." Grace repeated. She made another exaggerated movement with her mouth. "Ton..el."

"Tunnel?"

She nodded.

"You were in a tunnel?"

"Ton… all."

William picked up the first print and showed it to her. "What do you see?"

Her eyes scanned the page and then stopped. "Ball."

"Show me." He placed the image flat and she traced one shaky finger around a circular blob. He showed her another print. "What now?"

This time she ran her hand across the surface. Caro returned to the room and stood in the corner. "Ball," she said again circling a patch of paint that looked more egg shaped than ball-like, but it was probably the closest to a circle on the page.

"Does she mean a dome?" asked Lal.

"Ball." Grace stabbed the page again.

"Good, Grace, good. I don't think so," he said to Lal. He turned the prints over. "Let's go back to the words, Grace. Seb."

"Boy."

Good, she understood his request. "Ball," he said.

"Sell… green… s… seller, seller." She gripped Will's hand. "Seller green."

"Is she saying seller or Sorella?" said Lal.

"Or cellar, as in dungeon?" offered Caro.

William showed her the rest of the prints. "Do you see it? The place they took you. Do you see it?"

Grace snatched the pages from William's hand and jumped clumsily from the chair. She knelt over them on the floor and moved all six images around each other, tapping on some as she studied them and moving them again.

"Get her a pen," said Lal. "She used to draw her designs sitting like that."

Caro placed one down and Grace snatched it up and began tracing around the shapes.

"What's that? A chair?" said William leaning over to see.

Lal got down on the floor next to his wife. He picked up each page to study as his wife discarded it. "I think we have a chair." He rotated the page. "Maybe a person?" He turned the paper round to show William and Caro and they nodded in agreement. Lal flicked to the next page and the next and then he stopped, his eyes widening a fraction. "This is a needle." He handed the sheet to William and the shape of a syringe was clear to see. When they looked back at Grace she had begun to draw her own images in the free spaces on the paper.

"If they administered a chemical as we think, that would explain a needle," said Caro.

"She's drawing her own designs now." Lal sat back on his heels watching his wife's furious efforts.

William studied the images she had traced in his abstract prints. Some were indistinguishable no matter which way up he held the page, and others were as Lal had seen. This woman remembered where she had been taken, but getting useful detail out of her was proving tricky. He wished he had Steve to call on for advice, someone with experience of using these techniques in real life. All he had to go on was what he remembered from University.

Grace still drew flowers, animals and woodland scenes in every space she could find on the last piece of paper. Some looked like those on Sorella's kitchen cabinets and William felt a lump in his throat. She might never see them again.

As he struggled to get a grip on his emotion, a thought struck him. Something about how Grace drew her pictures... William flicked back to one of the prints and twisted it on its side. Then he compared a previously unclear outline to how Grace held her pencil. "They made her draw. Look... we have a chair, a person, a needle and this is her hand holding a pen." He threw each of the pages onto the side as he spoke. Lal and Caro both came to look. In the final image, Grace had turned a long streak of paint into two fingers wrapped around the barrel of a pen.

"D'ya think she's showing us what she drew?" Lal watched his wife again.

"Caro-" started ANNy.

"I know. Find all the details you can on every person abducted and in particular if they had any special talents."

"What are you thinking?" asked William.

"You said the documents referred to Silverwire having something to do with the commercial viability of the country. After three generations of educational upgrades our population is becoming more homogenous. Everyone is thinking more and more consistently as time goes on."

William recalled Sorella mentioning this on his first visit. Something about how the emotional pathways of human brains had some natural variance, but that this was reducing. "Too many people who think alike so...what...not enough creativity or innovation?"

"Or maybe a simple loss of individual talent. After all, is that not what has always given certain people a competitive edge?" Caro looked at Grace. "She and Sammy were without doubt the most naturally talented artists here. You said Silverwire was using selective sampling, picking out the most suitable subjects to research. If they wanted to know how a creative mind works, who better to pick than those two and their talented offspring."

"They took her coz she was talented and then left her like this?" Lal had one arm around his wife now, coaxing her to stop drawing.

"They are only interested in finding commonalities across the research population. Each individual participant is irrelevant." Caro checked himself. "I mean to them, Lal, not to us."

"Why do this to them, though?" William indicated to Grace and her condition. "Were they covering their tracks?"

"Quite literally," said ANNy. "The quickest way of finding where a talent resides would be to destroy sections of the brain and see if the talent persists."

"You mean destroy it whilst they're conscious?" said William feeling the kind of revulsion reserved for extreme acts of cruelty.

"It would be the easiest way," said ANNy.

"My God, that's barbaric." William looked at all of Grace's artwork. "That's why they kept her drawing?"

"But she can still draw," said Lal.

"It may be they are only interested in the creative spark as opposed to an acquired skill," said ANNy. "Grace's ability to draw may be left untouched if what they were looking to isolate was how new ideas are formed. She may never be able to draw anything new.

"Professor Sharma wrote an article ten years ago entitled, Spark of Genius: why the world's best thinkers relied on more than intellect."

William threw his hands up. "And you didn't think to mention this before?"

"He is a savant in psychology. All his writings relate to some aspect of the mind. It was impossible to know which was related to Silverwire until now."

Caro looked as if he had aged five years. "And LQ communities are the only place where such sparks of inspiration are isolated from intellect. They are a clean research population."

"I suppose it would take too long to research it any other way," said William.

"Prime Minister Montoya is up for election again in three years," ANNy said.

"Huh, things don't change. Everything always boils down to power and politics. I need some air." William made it no further than the small kitchen. Standing in the doorway, he felt an overwhelming urge to run anywhere and everywhere. To be doing something purposeful to find her, but what was the sense in doing the pointless? If he had been a little faster at the base maybe he could have taken both Silverwire men down. If he had waited behind the tower just a minute longer, he could have avoided any confrontation at all. If he had just insisted that the man did not listen to her.

If, if, if…

He slumped into a chair. What was happening to her now? Were they destroying sections of her brain whilst he flailed around not knowing what to do?

He grabbed paper and pencil from the side. There had to be something in what Grace had said which could help them. He wrote down all her words: dark, black, buzz, tunnel, ball, seller, cellar, Sorella, green. He underlined the three seller words and green. She had been most animated when she said these, and it was the only two word phrase. He tried different word combinations:

Cellar Green

Sorella Green

Seller Green

Green Cellar

Dark Cellar

Black Ball

Green Ball

Dark Tunnel

Black Tunnel

Dark Black

He paused after the final pairing, *synonyms*. Sometimes when the mind is damaged, words and their meanings become muddled like crossed wires. He wrote all the alternatives he could think of for all of Grace's words, then sat back and looked at the crowded page.

And there it was. So simple and so obvious.

He ran back to ANNy and told her what he had found. "Find me an image of the place."

"What's this?" said Caro looking up from his study of Grace's drawings.

"I think it's where Grace was taken."

"The most recent image I can find is from 2098 when the site was fully decommissioned and closed," said ANNy.

"Show us," said William.

A 2D image appeared on the surface of the wall. The aerial photograph showed a large industrial plant with in excess of a thousand buildings packed onto the coastal site. Concrete cooling towers, brick chimneys, huge warehouses and metal pylons lined the coastline. And in its centre, a large metal ball dominated the landscape.

"Grace, is this where you were?" said William.

Lal lifted his wife to her feet and brought her towards the image. After two steps she halted and made a low guttural sound.

Caro looked at William. "Where is this place?"

"Sellafield. It's a nuclear power plant on the west coast, near Whitehaven. She was trying to tell us the name, she just had field and green mixed up."

"ANN?" said Caro.

"It has been vacant for the past eighty years. It opened briefly as a museum in early 2134, but closed two years later due to lack of visitors. People did not trust the safety of such old-fashioned technology."

"That ball," Caro said pointing to the large structure, "could that contain an ANN?"

"The diameter and curvature would suggest it is possible," said ANNy.

"So they have hidden Silverwire in a dormant power plant. A place considered too dangerous to enter by most of the population." Caro studied the image closely.

"What are we waiting for?" said William.

Chapter Thirty One

"Sorella? Sorella, can you hear me?" The voice spoke in slow motion and Sorella found it impossible to determine if it came from a male or a female.

"Yes," Sorella replied, her voice coming out in a similar low drawl.

"I am Commander Smith. We need to have a little chat."

Sorella opened her eyes and a woman's face slowly came into focus. She wore her white-blonde hair closely cut to her scalp and it emphasised her chiselled, angular features. Sitting on a high stool to her left, the Professor looked relaxed and calm with his hands clasped in his lap.

"How did you know about the portal at Caltonville?" the Commander asked.

"I didn't."

"Lie," said the ANN. It had a deeper voice than ANNy, more asexual.

Worth a shot, Sorella thought. She tried to sit a little higher in the chair, but her wrists and feet were strapped down.

"Shall we try that again? How did you know?"

Sorella stayed quiet. They may be able to tell if she was lying, but they could not force her to speak the truth.

"Did you know what was in there?"

Sorella met the woman's eyes and held them.

"I really wish you were not going to be difficult. This would be so much easier on all of us if you cooperated." The woman leant back to sit upright. "There is something that bothers me, Ms Grey. Why would you insist on your being brought here in place of one of your men? Is he someone you are protecting?"

Sorella remained quiet.

The Commander smiled. "It makes no logical sense, you see. Why not let us take him so you could continue to manage your little operation... or are you not really the ring leader?"

Sorella decided to deflect this one. "It makes perfect sense. I don't see why someone else should suffer just for following my instructions."

"Even someone like that?" The Professor's tone sounded incredulous. They had obviously checked out the name Jessie Bo and discovered his condition.

"*Especially* someone like that. Jessie doesn't know any better."

"But you were happy to use him for your own ends," said Smith.

"I knew I could protect him."

"I don't see why you'd bother," said the Professor, picking something from between his teeth.

Sorella looked his way. "We clearly have quite different morals."

Sharma's eyes narrowed in time with the spike of irritation Sorella felt from him. "I think you'll find most of the population share the same morals. Is that not the point of the education process? It is you who differ, Ms Grey."

"Is that why you've kept what you're doing a secret? Because you know people would think you sick and immoral?"

Sorella felt the Professor's anger as his cheeks exploded with colour. "Do you have any idea how this country will suffer if things continue as they are. It was British scientists who first discovered ANN technology. And instead of capitalizing on that and profiting for themselves, they insisted the knowledge was shared freely for the good of the world's population. They are responsible for the tremendous steps in civilised existence we are all now benefiting from. But the UK does not have the size to compete trade-wise with the larger land mass countries. It is being increasingly weakened and marginalised. Within one more generation, our influence on world matters will have dropped to lower than average status. Not to mention our standard of living."

Sorella had no idea how this was relevant but it obviously was. She took a punt to see if he would bite. "And you think that justifies what you're doing?"

The man placed his hands over her clamped wrists and brought his face close. "What made Britain great was its capacity for invention and inspired insight. Do you know how many of the world's greatest ideas came from us? The electric engine, the jet engine, the fax machine, the television, the telephone, penicillin and so much more, until our final triumph: artificial neural networking. And since then, nothing. We are no more successful than the rest of the world."

"I think you've said enough, Professor." The Commander folded her arms. "My colleague is very... passionate about our work as you can see."

Sorella tried to piece things together in her mind. She could not see how abducting members of the LQ community would help the country become more inspired. She wanted to ask, but hesitated to give away how little she knew. Letting them think she had discovered more than she had, might prove a useful trump card.

"As a skilled tradesperson and negotiator, I think you will agree we have been more than open with you. It is now time for some reciprocity," said Smith. "How did you know about Caltonville?"

"Someone told me." Sorella decided to give the impression of cooperating without revealing too much.

"Who?"

"A man who recently came to our village and said he wanted to help us."

"She speaks the truth," said the ANN.

"Good. Now we are getting somewhere. Who was this man, what was his name?" said Smith.

"He left very soon after arriving and just disappeared. I discovered very little about him before that." Sorella chose her words carefully, not wanting ANN to pick up on any signs of falsehood.

"And he gave you no name?"

"He seemed nervous and scared about something. He was very keen to get away again," she said dodging the question.

"So this man just came to your village and told you about Caltonville?" The disbelief was clear in the Commander's voice.

"He knew we were suspicious about the abductions."

"Did he tell you how he came by this information?"

Sorella decided the truth would not give them anything but a false lead. "He said he knew from documents within the level five portals in Leeds." She was pleased to see a look of concern pass between Smith and Sharma. Let them think they had a mole, keep them paranoid. If that was all she could do, it was something at least.

The Commander stood. "What did this man look like?"

"Oh... erm... tallish, brown hair, sort of average really." Sorella suppressed a smile.

"You liked this man?"

She needed to avoid thinking about him. "Why wouldn't I? He gave me what I wanted. He led me here to the truth."

"What were you expecting to achieve?" The woman placed her hands behind her back.

"Initially, to discover who was abducting our people and why.

Ultimately, to stop you."

The Professor laughed. "Would you consider yourself a success?"

"Don't be naive, Sharma, she's not working alone. Her brother is a savant," said Smith.

Her two captors paused, listening. Their ANN must be communicating in confidence.

"Intruders?" said the Professor.

Sorella shifted in her chair.

The Commander smirked. "Just some local idiots who take this for a football ground. ANN, send Faber and Rowe to exit them." She met Sorella's gaze. "You weren't hoping for rescue were you? I am afraid no one will find you here."

This woman was a smug bitch. Sorella didn't bother suppressing her distaste as she addressed the Commander. "How many more people do you plan to abuse?"

"It's not abuse. These people have little quality of life. They're not losing a fraction of what there is to gain," said the Professor.

Sorella pulled against her restraints to sit as far forward as she could. "They have families, people who love them, lives to live... lives *worth* living. You should be ashamed."

The Professor gave no more reaction than a small twitch of his lips. If she could have left her chair, she would have knocked him off his.

"How many more?" she demanded.

Smith stopped pacing and put her hands on her hips. "What makes you think we will tell you anything?"

"Because you have nothing to lose, seeing as you'll be getting rid of me anyway."

"We do not plan to take your life," Smith said.

"Just my mind?"

The Commander dropped her head with a smile. "There is an alternative." She made eye contact. "We are always in need of good people to complement the Silverwire team. With your intellect and your contacts you could prove very useful."

"You want me to help you?" Sorella felt sick at the thought.

"You would be well rewarded. Achieve a much improved standard of living, life in the city, intellectual stimulation. And you could speed up the selection process no-end with what you know of these communities."

"I'd rather lose my mind."

"Shame." Smith nodded at the Professor and then focused on Sorella. "Your wish is our command."

Sharma selected his syringe and checked for air bubbles.

Sorella wriggled in the chair but there was no escaping. "My brother won't let you get away with this."

Smith laughed as the professor injected an ice-cold chemical into Sorella's neck. "I think Caro will be too busy caring for his only sister twenty-four hours a day, to be meddling in that which does not concern him. Goodbye, Ms Grey."

Sorella felt her heart begin to beat faster. The anxiety she had been feeling during the entire conversation heightened into full-blown fear. Her whole body felt cold and her muscles tensed. She tried to relax, but only heard her breathing getting faster and faster.

"I'll take her back myself, Professor. You may return to your business. ANN can you provide the porting coordinates?" Smith's voice sounded like it was at the end of a tunnel and blackness began to descend. It felt darker than closing her eyes; in fact her eyes were still open. Sorella blinked a couple of times to prove it to herself.

How long she lay there like that, she had no idea. But in the last moments, she realised this was what terror felt like. The fighting instinct to stay alive at all costs, washed from her brain by the full and certain knowledge it was too late.

"But that's impossible!" Smith's words were the last thing Sorella heard before her mind locked itself from the world for good.

William and Caro stood at the edge of a dirt track. The rest of the group waited by the vehicles: six strong men willing and waiting to aid Sorella. Lal and Jed were joined by Tyler, Callum and even the Flynn brothers. They were relying on Maddox's desire for Sorella's safety to stop him causing trouble, and so far so good.

"There's the ball," said William. The large structure loomed in the distance.

"If that houses an ANN, none of us can step onto this site without her knowing. None of us but you." Caro handed William a small silver oblong. "We need you to find out what we are up against, how many people and where they are. I expect if that is an ANN, they will be housed within. See if you can get a look inside without crossing the threshold. Remember, as soon as you step inside the hub you will become visible to her. When you have a clear idea of things then – and only then – switch this on here." He showed William a small indent at the side of the object which he slid his thumb over. "As soon as you switch on it will connect to me."

"At which point they'll know I'm there?"

"Yes. The ANN will detect the device as soon as it is operational. Give me as much information as you can, as quick as you can then switch this thing off and get yourself out of there."

William nodded but he would not be doing any running away.

He was here for Sorella and until she was found he would be looking. "I'll be as quick as I can."

"We will cause a distraction. See if we can help make your route clear. William?" Caro stopped him at the gate. "Take these." He handed over the sleep inducer and what looked to be a gun.

"Is this..." William felt the weight of it and saw the safety switch.

Caro nodded. "They are outlawed these days, considering we can disarm people without injury. This was my great-grandfathers. I thought you might appreciate something familiar in terms of defence." He touched William's arm. "Not that I am suggesting you are an experienced gunman."

"Well I'm no novice."

Caro looked genuinely shocked, his mouth dropping open a little.

"I started my career in the British Army as a civilian. One of the perks was getting to play on their shooting range. Don't worry it will be a last resort." William placed the gun in his jacket pocket. "Thank you." He patted Caro's upper arm.

Four or five dilapidated buildings lay between William and the sphere. Jogging across the grass to a low wall, he crouched behind and surveyed the ground ahead. This place was not a very impressive legacy from his time. The square concrete structures lacked any aesthetic design.

He could see no people ahead of him. But from behind, he heard shouts coming from Maddox and Wallace. The distraction had begun.

The strong scent of salt and fish filled his nostrils. A smell he associated with day trips. He had a feeling if this did not go to plan, he may never regard it so pleasantly again.

Keeping low, William ran over the open ground to the first

building. The one-story concrete construction had no windows. He peered around the edge. There was no one in sight. ANNy had suggested Silverwire might consider the presence of their ANN to be all the security they needed. It certainly meant they could keep the number of people in the loop to a minimum. But William found the lack of security weird. He had expected the place to be crawling. Maybe they had moved on and taken Sorella somewhere different. William pushed the idea aside. No point being defeatist now.

The ground to his left opened out into fields. Despite the lack of people, he kept close to the buildings to stay as hidden as possible and did not pause until he reached the final construction. The old office block ended with a glass enclosed staircase coated in green sludge. William made sure not to touch it as he listened for any signs of life. He heard nothing but the sound of Caro's distant diversion.

The derelict sphere now towered above him. Its cracked patchwork of tiles had large sections missing and around its circumference ran a broken metal walkway, the railings bowed and jagged where they came to an abrupt end. The smaller buildings attached to the rear and sides all looked to be in an equal state of disrepair.

William checked for people one more time then stepped into the open. He examined the base of the sphere but could see no way in. Next he circled the attached buildings, finding only boarded-up doors. Through the windows he saw the spaces contained nothing more than crumbling walls and broken floorboards. If this was a cover up, it was pretty extreme.

Was there another way into the dome… underground maybe? Grace had mentioned a tunnel.

"Smoothly enough, yes, smoothly enough," a male voice said

in the distance.

William stopped where he was and strained to listen.

"I'm heading back now, yes."

William followed an overgrown passageway towards the speaker. The path ran between two buildings behind the sphere. At the end, it opened onto an old road, and, opposite, stood a red-brick warehouse with large windows evenly spaced along its length.

"Smith is waiting for the process to run its course and then she will deposit the article in the normal manner," the voice said from beyond.

William took a quick glance left and right then darted across to look through the nearest window. Through the adjacent wall, he saw a rotund ginger man walking his way. Behind the man, a set of double doors stood ajar in an enormous white building.

"I'll see you in five." The rotund man picked up his pace.

William looked to his left. Any second now the man would cross the road where William stood. He looked right, the brick building stretched as far as he could see. There was nowhere to hide. He looked back at the passage. That would risk stepping into the man's eye line.

Shit, you idiot.

William had no option but to stay where he was. He moved to the space between the windows, and pressed his back flat against the wall.

The man's footsteps came closer.

All it would take was a glance to the left and William would be seen. He held his breath and concentrated on staying still. An itch began in his nose. He gritted his teeth and dug his nails into his palms as it became more insistent.

The short man came into view. He wore an unflattering pair of creased white trousers. Not a good colour for a man of his girth and not at all helped by the cream shirt tucked tightly in. His waistband clinched his middle like an elastic band around an overstuffed cushion. A few steps past William, he stopped to check his wrist strap.

Will's fingers curled around the sleep inducer in his pocket.

The man swore under his breath and fiddled with the teleporting strap some more. His fleshy middle rippled in response. One more minute and William would zap him. He had heard this man say Smith was waiting for the process to complete before depositing the article. And William had a hunch the article in question was Sorella.

He needed to get into that building fast.

The ginger man straightened and continued on.

William leant his head against the wall and exhaled. The itch had disappeared. His body had a sick sense of humour it seemed. He counted to ten in his head before moving to the corner of the warehouse and looking out. There was no longer anyone to be seen.

William ran to the open door. She was in here, he knew it. And the sight of the tubular entrance hall strengthened his conviction. His eyes rested on the sign at the end.

Welcome to Sellafield.

This was Grace's tunnel.

He kept his footsteps light as he jogged along the walkway and emerged into a massive exhibition hall. Partially dismantled turbines and reactors dominated the space, but he paid them no attention. He focused instead on the ceiling-high, white tent in the centre of the room.

William scanned for any dome structures but the room was open and square. If they had an ANN, it was not here. And there was still no sign of any guards. Their arrogance had made them complacent.

William passed behind two turbines, taking a wide line towards the tent. Through a gap in the material, he could see a blonde woman. She stood with her back to him dressed in military uniform. In front of her, slumped in a chair, was Sorella.

Please, God, don't let me be too late.

William returned the sleep enhancer to his pocket, and removed the gun.

The blonde woman half turned as he stepped into the space behind her. "But that's impossible," she said, her eyes widening as she took in his weapon. "How did you get in here?"

There was no one else in the room. This woman must be Smith.

"What have you done to her?" His glance at Sorella was quick. She was out cold, and it would only distract him to think about that too much.

The woman backed away a few steps, her eyes still unnaturally wide and focused on the gun. "Who are you?"

William waggled the firearm at her. "I'll be the one asking the questions I think. What have you done to her?"

Smith lunged to her left and grabbed a wrist strap from the table.

William shot her in the leg.

She fell to the floor with a cry of pain, dropping the strap and clutching her injured limb. The bullet had hit her above the right knee. His aim was still good he was pleased to find.

"*What* have you done to her?" William squatted to see the woman's face.

"ANN we have an intruder-"

William put pressure on her right calf with his hand.

"Aarrgg…" She gritted her teeth and looked at him. "I'm telling you we have an intruder. He just shot me. Get-"

William held the gun to her temple. "What makes you think I won't do it again? Now for the last time, what have you done to her?"

"You can't stop it," she said, grimacing as he adjusted his hold on her leg.

"Stop what? What is it? What does it do?" He pressed the gun harder into her head.

Smith said nothing.

"Tell me what you've given her."

The woman closed her eyes and swayed a little. Probably due to the pain.

"TELL ME," William shouted in her face.

"No!" She opened her eyes. "I don't know." She looked over at Sorella, her expression becoming shocked. "Is she okay?"

William immediately looked, as Smith obviously knew he would. The next he knew, the woman had booted him away with a foot in his stomach. He slid backwards along the tiled floor and dropped the gun. Scrambling to his knees, he retrieved it and aimed it her way, but Smith and the teleporting strap were gone.

He needed to get out of here fast. The ANN may have picked up on his voice through Smith's ears. It wouldn't be long before one of them sent someone in here.

He pocketed the gun and removed the restraints from Sorella's wrists and ankles. He was about to lift her, when he noticed the syringe. It lay discarded in the bin. Moving as quickly as he could, he took some paper from the table, formed a makeshift envelope and put the syringe inside. If Caro knew what she had been given, he might be able to find the antidote.

Sorella made no sound when he lifted her from the seat. Her

head rolled against his chest and he kissed it before carrying her out to her brother.

Chapter Thirty Two

Caro checked the time again. William had only been gone fifteen minutes but it felt like a lifetime. Dusk was beginning to fall and the last of the sun's heat had dropped out of sight behind the mass of buildings. Caro had never seen anything like this place with its old-fashioned pylons and over-sized constructions. At any other time he would have been genuinely fascinated and could have spent many a happy hour walking the site, working out what everything once did and imagining the teams of people going about their daily tasks. Now it was a place of horror and he felt useless trapped here with no option but to wait.

"Here they come," said Lal at his side. The man then patted Caro's shoulder as he sensed the hope spike and dissipate.

Maddox, Wallace, Callum and Jed jogged up the road to where Caro and Lal waited.

"Two bastards put out of their misery for a while," said Maddox as they reached the vehicle.

"Is that all that came?" said Lal.

"Yep, and they never knew what hit 'em," said Wallace proudly. "We let 'em chase us off site then we jumped 'em. They're bound and gagged as you said, they won't be getting out in a hurry."

Caro nodded. Hopefully it would take some time for the ANN to work out what had happened and even longer for them to be rescued.

Callum came to Caro's side. "Any news?"

Caro and Lal both shook their heads.

"We watched the site for a while longer before coming back but no one else came," said Callum.

Caro closed his eyes and inhaled deeply. The sea air filled his mouth with salt. He tried to fight the doubts clouding his mind knowing if his sister knew of them she would be appalled. Her love for William was more powerful than any emotion he had ever felt in her, and the man had proven himself both dedicated and trustworthy. And yet... what if? What if everything had been leading to this, to getting him, Sorella and the village's strongest men to this place? What if William's role had been to lead them here so their investigations could be halted? After all, William had been the one who alerted them to Caltonville, then miraculously drew what they needed from Grace, identifying Sellafield as Silverwire's location. How much of that could he have influenced? Caro could not recall exactly how William had worked things out and was angry at himself for not paying more attention. He could have led them all to a trap.

"Caro!"

The distant shout jolted Caro from his thoughts. Across the wasteland ahead, William ran with Sorella in his arms. Her head lay against his chest but her arms hung loosely and bounced with the motion. She was unconscious.

Caro started towards them until both Lal and Callum stopped him with a hand on each arm.

"No need for 'em to know there's anyone helping 'im," said Lal.

Caro knew the man was right but waiting was agony. "Everyone, in the car," he said. They needed to get out of here fast. Who knew what would be following hot on William's heels.

William ran onto the road. "They gave her something. I think I got the syringe. Hopefully there's enough of a trace to work out what it was." William slowed to a walk as he reached Caro. "What?"

Caro had actually taken a step back as William approached, so fierce was the fear. He looked at his sister's lover then he looked at his sister and felt the tears well. "Get in," he said to William forcing himself to focus on getting them all to safety.

William was running on adrenaline. For the first half of the journey he talked incessantly as Caro navigated their route cross-country, making sure to avoid any cities or sites protected by ANNs. Only when William had run dry his story of nearly getting seen and shooting a commander called Smith in the leg, did he seem to notice the atmosphere. Not one of the six men had asked William a question or commented on his account. In fact, not one of them had spoken a word from the moment they came into contact with Sorella.

As Caro took the decision to take a shortcut across the fields, William took a moment to look at every member of the group.

"Is someone going to tell me what's going on?" William said.

But no one could bring themselves to answer.

Sorella lay on the small bed looking serene. Her brother wiped her brow with the back of his hand and kissed her cheek. Outside in the corridor, Lal tried his hardest to calm Maddox who was shouting and punching the walls.

William sat on the floor with his back against the side of the dome. "There must be something else you can do?"

Caro shook his head. He had not spoken a word in the last ten minutes.

"ANNy?"

"I am sorry, William. We have tried everything and all we are doing now is prolonging the suffering. It is best to let it run its course."

William looked at Sorella's face and found it hard to believe such horror was going on inside her head. ANNy had analysed the serum from the syringe and found it did nothing more complicated than stimulate the fear response. It flooded the brain with a paralysing terror that slowly destroyed the mind. And it was self-perpetuating. The serum itself was completely absent from her system by the time they arrived back. But it had triggered a chain reaction that proved impossible to stop. Caro had injected his sister with all manner of endorphins and inhibitors to break the cycle, but each time the reprieve was brief. Like pulling someone from the water only to drop them back and let them drown again.

"Why can't you stop it?" said William.

"Fear is such a powerful emotion," said ANNy. "It floods the whole system, washing through every synapse and triggering a whole manner of physiological changes. Heart rate and blood pressure increases, blood is removed from the surface of the skin to protect major organs, vitamin K is released to aid clotting and hairs are raised on the arms. All of these things then perpetuate the fear. Each time we try to interrupt it, there is enough residual alarm in her system to trigger a fresh bout."

"And nothing can counteract it?"

"Nothing is as powerful as fear. It is part of your survival mechanism. If there is a reason to be afraid it makes sense that no other emotion can distract you from that."

"What about reason and logic, all the things that make us intelligent and not reliant on our emotions?"

ANNy continued. "That would require her to be awake and for all intents and purposes she is in a coma. She is locked in a dream state where her emotions can run wild. If anything, her fear will be influencing what she is thinking not the other way around."

William looked at the screen showing Sorella's brain activity. It was a mass of synaptic firing. Caro hypothesised she was experiencing nightmare upon nightmare. "How long?"

"It is hard to say," ANNy said. "It could end any moment or it could go on for hours. With all this activity it is impossible to know what damage has already been done with any certainty. Grace had a traumatic loss of neural functioning by the time it stopped, hence her current state. The mind is either shutting off to protect itself or the activity is so extreme it becomes destructive."

"But Grace also had lesions?"

"Correct, they do not appear to have conducted any experiments on Sorella. They merely administered the serum used to simulate a brain disease."

William had heard enough. "I'd like to take her home."

Caro looked at him for the first time.

"Back to her own house, somewhere comfortable and familiar. It might help."

Her brother nodded, but William could see the man had lost all hope.

"I cannot monitor what is happening if you take her away," said ANNy.

William stood and walked across to the bed. "Does it matter? It won't make any difference to her will it?"

"Do you want me to help?" said Caro, his voice flat.

William lifted Sorella from the bed. "You could make sure Maddox has gone and unlock the house."

Once back in her small cottage, William carried Sorella to the cosy bedroom he had shared with her over the last few days. Caro removed the blanket from the bed and William placed her down and brushed her hair from her eyes. Then he removed her shoes.

Her brother covered her and knelt by her side.

"She looks so peaceful," said William.

Caro leant his head against the bed and held Sorella's hand. "And yet she is not."

"I'll stay with her if that's okay?"

"Thank you." Her brother stood. "I think I need to…"

William placed a hand on Caro's shoulder. "I'll take care of her and if anything changes, you'll be the first to know." He could not imagine how hard it must be to be able to feel what she was feeling.

Caro emerged from the house to find Lal and Callum waiting. He nodded and the three of them walked in silence back to ANNy. There was nothing that could be done for Sorella now and once she was awake, his life would be changed beyond compare. He glanced at Lal and wondered how the man coped so well with such a heavy load. Caro hoped he would handle it with the same amount of stoicism.

"I know you don't want to hear it, but maybe we should have left her. We've risked the whole village now," said Callum as they entered the dome.

Caro ignored the comment but he knew Callum would have felt his disgust.

"What will they do?" said Lal.

Caro stood facing the now empty room where moments before he had watched his sister's trauma. "They do not know what we know."

"They will assume the worst," said ANNy in a low voice.

"So what do we do?" Lal placed his hands on his hips.

No one answered.

"Caro?" said Callum. "ANNy?"

"I'll train my visual scanners on the perimeter but as they can teleport in, I suggest you stay vigilant and keep watch. I may not be able to alert you quickly enough to their arrival," said ANNy.

"I'll spread the word," said Callum. "And organise a rota to watch this place and Sorella's."

"Are they watching us now, can you tell?" said Lal.

"Who knows what they can do," said Caro. Mobile teleportation, fear-inducing serums, secret labs in secret locations...this was beyond anything he had ever heard of. "But they need this kept quiet. They will want to deal with us as effectively and efficiently as possible."

"The one thing on our side is they know how they have left Sorella. They will expect us to be distracted by that," said ANNy. "It may give us time."

Once they were alone, William lay alongside Sorella and wrapped his arms around her. He positioned his mouth next to her ear. He was not sure how much truth there was in the idea that people in a coma could still hear, but it was worth a shot.

"Ella, I want you to listen to me. I know you can hear my voice, and you're safe I promise you. Whatever you're experiencing, whatever you think is going on it's all a dream, just a really bad dream. I want you to concentrate on what I'm saying, try to hear me through all the noise and fight this." He stroked her face with the back of his hand.

"You're the most incredible woman I've ever met... no scrap that, the most incredible *person* I've ever met. I won't let you go, you hear me?" He had to take a moment to control his own emotions. It would do no good for her to hear him upset. He needed to sound strong and positive.

William knew the thing that set humans apart from every other species was their ability to rationalise their emotions. He had spent many an evening listening to Steve tell of how the most extreme phobias could be overcome by harnessing the cognitive powers of the mind. If he could just awaken a little of that power in Sorella it might be enough for her to fight this. It was a long shot, he knew, but he had nothing left to lose.

"Ella, honey, it's all a dream, it's not real. *I* am real. *We* are real. Everything else is your brain playing tricks on you. And just a small part of your brain at that, a tiny little emotional part that's bullying you. You have this impressively quick mind and I know you can beat it if you try. All you have to do is think of other things - good things - things that make you feel safe and happy. I'll try to help you as much as I can, but you need to do this yourself. You need to ignore everything else and listen to me, just *please* listen to me."

For the next however many hours, William talked until he was hoarse. He talked about the times they had had together, stories she had told him, anecdotes from his own life; anything to take her focus away from the fear. When he had exhausted all his adult tales, he began to tell her about his childhood. He skirted over the bad times in favour of his most humorous memories. He told her about losing his trunks whilst showing off his diving in a school swimming lesson. About his ambitions to carve a fallen tree in his back garden into a canoe, abandoned after it took him three months to make no more than the smallest dent. He told her about winning his first sports day event doing the wheelbarrow with Julie Craig, and how in his teens he walked around with gladioli in his back pocket because he wanted to be Morrissey. Then he had to explain who Morrissey was and got a little carried away describing the genius of The Smiths.

By the time he fell into an exhausted sleep, dawn was breaking and Sorella still lay motionless in his arms.

Lola listened to Callum's briefing with a growing sense of dread. She could feel panic in the others too, but none quite as keen as her own.

She had walked across to the green barefoot having awoken to feel the familiar presence of her husband. He wasn't in the house but his despair was strong enough to reach her where she dozed on the sofa.

As she arrived at the group, Callum was explaining how people needed to stay together, that no one should be left alone and that volunteers were needed to pair up and stand guard. But his words were not the source of Lola's panic. Hers came from the sight of her husband, his eyes swollen and red and his shoulders slumped in a stance of defeat she had never before seen.

Would he feel anywhere near this distraught if something had happened to her? She guessed not.

They had been about to eat dinner when Lal had come for Maddox. Sorella had been taken, he said, and her husband had left the house without even a goodbye. In the hours that followed, Lola had paced and fretted, leaving her own meal uneaten. She had long known of her husband's feelings for Sorella, even followed him on occasion as he followed her. She had stood a small distance away as he hid from view to watch Sorella tending her garden or working. And the affection he felt took great chunks out of Lola's already battered heart.

If he could just feel a fraction of that for her, Lola would have been content.

"I've designated areas to patrol which we can spilt between us," Callum said as Lola came alongside her husband. "And it's probably a good idea to watch ANNy's place. William has taken Sorella home-"

"She's okay?" said Lola in surprise. She had assumed from how her husband felt that they had not managed to find her.

"Sadly not," said Callum.

Lola saw Maddox's jaw clench.

"We were too late to prevent them doing their worst. ANNy expects she will awake in a similar condition to Grace." Callum's eyes flicked to Lal who stood with his arms folded and did not react.

Lola felt all the strength go from her knees and gripped Maddox's arm to steady herself..

"I'm fine," her husband said misinterpreting her gesture and shrugging her hand away. "I'll watch Sorella's."

"There's a whole crowd there already including Rose. We could do with you and Wallace taking an area to patrol," said Callum.

Maddox stared hard at Callum and said nothing.

"Fine," said Callum after a beat. "Wallace, you and Jed pair up and patrol area four, that way you can keep an eye on your own homes."

Callum continued to assign various areas to people as Lola touched Maddox's arm again. He was yet to look at her. "Should I come with you?"

Maddox glanced her way, his eyes red raw but cold. "No."

Wallace placed a hand on the small of Lola's back. "Go with Tabby, we'll keep watch on you."

Lola felt tears sting her eyes. She knew everyone viewed her brother-in-law as the dumber of the two Flynns. But at least his love for Tabby was real. The woman had driven everyone else nuts at one time or another with her snobby ways, yet Wallace's devotion was unwavering.

Just as Maddie's was for Sorella, Lola thought in a moment of clarity.

Maddox's eyes were suddenly on her.

Lola felt her face burn. She buried the feeling as quickly as she could but it had been too potent and carnal to disguise. In the midst of her bitter jealousy and panic, how would her husband interpret her swell of pride?

Chapter Thirty Three

William awoke to the sound of someone banging at the door. "Ella?" he said quietly. There was no response and he carefully prised his arm from under her.

Rose Taylor stood at the door with a large pan. "I brought some soup. It was the only thing we could get Grace to eat at first. I hope that's okay?"

William took the pan. "That's really thoughtful, Rose, thanks."

"How is she?"

He noticed a whole group of people loitering in the surrounding gardens. "Much the same so far." He checked the time, it was gone nine. "I don't suppose you've seen Caro this morning have you?"

"He's with ANN. He's been there all night. I think he's still hoping to find something…" She dropped her eyes and shook her head. "Poor man."

William said goodbye and placed the still-warm soup on the range.

Back in the bedroom, Sorella lay as he had left her. He stood for a moment watching her sleep. Maybe he should get someone to come in to see if she still felt any fear.

Instead, he took his place beside her again. Just a little while longer, he decided.

"Do you want to hear something crazy," he said running his thumb across her parted lips. "I think… no, I know…" He had to laugh at himself. "See, I'm so messed up I can't even say it when you're in no position to appreciate it." He kissed her lips very gently. "I love you, Ella. No matter how this turns out, I'm going to stay with you, I promise."

Her eyes flickered open.

William half sat in surprise. "Now that was spooky. Who are you, Sleeping Beauty?"

Her eyes looked vacant and a small frown creased her forehead.

"Ella?" He moved his head from side to side to see if her eyes would track the movement. They did not. "Can you hear me?" It dawned on him she might have no clue who he was. "Sorella, sweetheart, you're safe. I'm going to get Caro."

She moved her eyes to his.

"You remember Caro, your brother?" He smiled and she did also, a little. He slid off the bed. "I'll be really quick."

He put his shoe on as he hopped across to the door. He did not want her alone for a moment longer than was necessary. Maybe he could send one of the others for Caro, one of the folks loitering outside. Then he could come back here and wait with her. Or would she prefer to be with someone she might more easily recognise? If Mart was out there, he would ask him to come in.

"You promised."

William froze in the doorway at the sound of her voice. When he looked at the bed she had turned her head towards him.

"…to stay." Her voice sounded weak but the words clear.

"Ella?" William dropped his second shoe, crossed to the bed and took her in his arms. She hugged him so tightly he could hardly breathe. "It's okay, you're home. You're safe," he said suppressing the hope. She had spoken a sentence, something Grace had no capacity to do. But repeating his words did not mean she could express her own thoughts. He held her face in his hands and braced himself for the truth. "Do you know who I am? Do you know where you are?"

"I couldn't… it was… I couldn't…" she said between gulps of air which quickly became sobs.

William pulled her against him and kissed her head, letting her squeeze him even further without complaint. "Shhh, you're safe, I'm here." He could feel her shaking and rubbed her back. She was bound to be traumatised given the night she had had. But William began to feel excited. She had tried to tell him about it. She may only have used a few words but that was so much better than he had expected, than he had been willing to deal with. Maybe his tactics had worked, or they had not given her as much serum as the others, or her mind had been too strong for its effects.

Maybe she was completely fine.

Once more, William suppressed his optimism. No harm at all was unlikely. But whatever capacity to communicate she had, he could work with that. Given what he had achieved with Grace, he felt sure he could help her regain as much ability as possible. In fact, he and Caro would make a formidable team. She could not have two more useful allies.

Sorella's body stiffened in his arms. She pulled away and her eyes were wide and alert, like a creature hunted. "They knew we were coming." Her eyes darted around the room before meeting his again.

"Hey, it's okay, you're safe."

"William, they were expecting us… at Caltonville, they said they had Intel."

The lucidness of her statement took him by surprise. "My God, you really are okay," he said with a laugh of relief.

"They know who we are."

"ANNy said there was no hope, that there was nothing we could do."

"Are you listening to me?"

William took hold of her chin. "Do you feel any dizziness, or nausea?"

"I'm fine."

"Are you... really?" He lifted her chin and looked in her eyes. "What do you remember?"

"I need to see Caro," she tried to get up but William held firm.

"Ella, do you remember what they did... to you?"

Her eyes filled with tears and she looked at her hands. They were still shaking. "I'm fine."

He took her hands in his. "Sorella, look at me."

She raised her eyes. "They know who we are."

"I don't care."

The panic in her eyes dissolved and what replaced it broke William's heart. Tears spilled onto her cheeks and she nodded. "I remember."

"Do you want to talk about it?"

She leant her head against his chest and shuffled closer, wrapping her arms around his waist.

"I want to help," he said kissing her head.

"You're here, that's enough."

In the moments that followed as they sat entwined, William held her head in his hand and fought back his own tears. He could not believe his luck – her luck. He felt the guilt he had not known he was carrying ebb away. He had not been too late. He had not ruined her life.

Sorella sat up a moment before William heard footsteps on the stairs. When her brother entered the room she smiled for the first time. "Hi," she said.

Caro blinked a couple of times as he looked between his sister and William. William smiled also.

"Am I to assume you will not be in need of my constant care?" said Caro.

Sorella glanced at William. "I have my eye on someone else

for that job, but thanks for the offer."

Caro stumbled a little against the wall where his body seemed to lose all its rigour. Sorella climbed from the bed and went to hug him.

"I'll make coffee," said William giving them some privacy.

Whilst the water boiled, he opened the door and searched the faces scattered around the street. When he found the one he was looking for, he smiled. "She's fine, as good as ever."

Maddox nodded and almost smiled to the sound of everyone's cheers. For all the hassle he had caused, William could not blame the guy for caring about her.

"William, thank you." Caro took him by surprise with a hug. "She told me how you helped her fight this and I am sorry I ever doubted your intentions."

William raised his eyebrows at Sorella. "You heard me?"

Sorella nodded.

"I have also reassured her of the lengths we have taken to make sure we are safe. There is no need for her to panic, she only needs to focus on her recovery."

William did not listen to Caro's words. "All of it?" he said to Sorella.

She held his gaze. "All the important bits."

William stepped away from her brother. "Ah, now I was getting a bit delirious by the end there. I'd missed a lot of sleep you see."

Sorella came close. "Is that so?"

"Ah ha."

She placed her arms around him. "So you don't love me then?"

William felt embarrassed under the watchful gaze of her brother. "Maybe a little," he managed to say.

"Is that a little more than a bit or a little less than a lot?"

He could tell from the look in her eyes that she was enjoying his discomfort. The realisation gave him courage and he pulled her closer. "You'll have to see if you can work it out." William glanced up and caught a look in Caro's eyes he did not understand. Sorella showed no reaction so he told himself it must be nothing. Only later would he realise his instincts had been bang on. That as he confirmed his love for Sorella, her brother had not felt happy for her, but sad.

After working their way through the crowd of well-wishers outside her house, Sorella had talked William, Caro and ANNy through all that had happened during her time with Sharma and Smith.

Every now and then she squinted and rubbed her temples. On each occasion, William and Caro exchanged a worried glance.

Caro explained how what she had been told confirmed that Silverwire was related to isolating the creative spark. He also told her about William's intervention with Grace, at which point she looked his way - clearly impressed.

"The question is who to pass all this onto," said Caro. "The way I see it, we have three choices. We could send a blanket communication out to the press, we could make an approach to the opposition party or I could circulate details via the Royal Society of Medicine."

"Send it to the press. Everyone should be told about it. It's an atrocity." Sorella's tone was hard and uncompromising.

"And cause wide-scale panic? I am not sure that is the most sensible route," said Caro.

"They have to be stopped straight away, and the quickest way of achieving that is by getting the truth out to everyone."

"Do you not think it irresponsible to tell people about

something over which they have no control? Would it not be better to find a way of ending Silverwire through official channels?"

"We can't go to the police you said that yourself. Silverwire is too powerful." Sorella tried to mask the fact she was massaging the side of her head.

Caro frowned as he clocked the movement. "That is why I suggest making an approach to the leader of the opposition or calling on the influence of the medical community. Now we have a breakdown of the serum, thanks to William's quick thinking." Caro glanced Will's way. "We can prove that the affected people have been purposefully harmed. That in itself should instigate an enquiry."

"But they could still bury it. This involves the Prime Minister after all. How can we guarantee it would stop if we don't just expose them?"

Caro turned to William. "What do you think?"

"I think you're both right. Do it all. Tell the medics and the opposition first with a caveat that if action is not taken within twenty-four hours you'll release it to the press."

Caro looked at his sister.

Sorella shrugged and nodded. "Fine by me."

"That is settled then. I will finish the documents and send them now."

"You will come to the party though?"

The village had come out in force to celebrate Sorella's remarkable recovery. At this very moment, teams of them were decorating the village hall, preparing food and arranging entertainment. William found the whole thing entirely fascinating. Having grown up in the city suburbs, he had never experienced the community spirit of a rural village.

"Of course. As soon as the documents are sent I will be there," Caro assured her. "But before you go I want ANNy to check you over."

"I'm fine."

"You say that but I would rather know for sure. Plus I need William so you cannot leave yet."

Sorella slid off the work surface where she had been perched and sat in ANNy's examination chair.

"What do you need me for?" said William.

"I want you to check a few details for me about the information you gathered from the city portal."

"Off you go then," said Sorella. "And don't keep him too long, I want some time to change."

Caro led the way down the hall to a small side room.

"Is she okay?" said William.

"She has a headache. That is why I want ANNy to check if it's anything to worry about. I hope it's tiredness in the main. She may not last long at this party."

"Is having a party really a good idea considering what's going on?" William kept his voice low. He did not want Sorella to know he disapproved.

"It will give people something to do. Everyone's feeling anxious but there is no point panicking. We need to keep control as much as we can… of ourselves, I mean."

"Does it not make us vulnerable, everyone being in the same place?"

"Silverwire cannot afford to do anything too drastic. They will have to be clever. However they respond they need to be able to explain it away and that will take some planning. Wiping out a whole village will not be an option, so everyone together is our best defence."

Really, thought William feeling sceptical but hoping the man was right. "What would you do, if you were them?"

Caro let William pass into the small room. "I would get my insider to tell me what they know."

William looked at him in surprise. "You think someone is working with them?"

Caro closed the door behind him. "To be truthful, William, I cannot believe it of anyone here, so I am not sure I want to know."

William wanted to tell the guy to man up, that everyone's safety might depend on finding out if someone had betrayed them. But Caro's expression took on the sadness William had seen in Sorella's kitchen, again halting his retort.

"When you were in Caltonville and you told them to search for William York, ANNy ran a check to see what they would find. We did not want some poor chap with the same name to fall under suspicion," said Caro.

"Right. Sorry about that." It had never crossed his mind he might be doing such a thing.

Caro gave a small shake of his head. "During her search she came across something we thought you should see." He indicated to the document on the table. "I will give you a few minutes."

William watched Caro leave. Why all the intrigue? And why would he lie to his sister? He walked to the table and spun the document with one hand. It was a newspaper article from the Guardian's science and technology section: an interview with Cambridge University physicist, and expert in time travel, Charlie Fletcher.

William pulled up a chair and sat.

'What inspired you to study time travel?'

'When I was seven, I discovered my dad was not my biological father. My real father had been my mother's first husband,

William York.'

William felt the room expand and then contract around him. He checked the date of the article, February 2042.

'He disappeared just after my Mum became pregnant and was eventually declared dead. But when I was young, William's best friend, Steve, used to tell me how my father claimed to have travelled through time. He said that on the day William disappeared, he sent Steve a note saying that he was cycling to where he had found a wormhole and was going through'

'So you decided to see if this was possible?'

'Not really. By the time I became a student I'd discarded the idea. It was a kid's story. I don't think Steve wanted me to think suicide was a family curse. My paternal grandfather had also taken his own life at a similar age. But the seed of fascination was planted, I suppose. I spent my childhood pondering on time travel so it felt like a natural place for me to focus my research.'

'So, is it possible that William York time travelled?'

'In short, no. Theoretically it could happen, but in reality we have nowhere near the capability and I'm not sure that will ever change.'

The article went on to describe Charlie's latest research on quantum entanglement in teleportation. William realised he was hunched over the table, his face inches from the text. He sat back, his hands shaking and his mouth dry.

When Caro returned, William was staring at the blank wall.

"I considered not telling you, but that seemed immoral."

"No… thanks… you did the right thing," said William.

"Will you tell Sorella?"

"I don't know." He tried to get a handle on what this meant, what it altered. Five minutes ago he was staying here for the rest of his days and now everything had changed. How could he even begin to choose?

Charlie had lived his life as someone else's son. Dismissing William as some sad, pathetic figure, too wrapped up in his own grief to consider how his actions might affect others. Exactly how William had judged his own father. Would Sarah have told him how much Will had wanted a child? Would she have been able to overcome the bitterness and guilt of his leaving to have been the bigger person? He thought not.

"What will you do?"

William looked up at Caro. "If I go back now he is yet to be born. If I stay, his life is over and I never even got to meet him."

Caro nodded as if he had known what William would do all along. "She will understand."

"You think?"

Caro placed his hands in his pockets and studied the floor. "She will be devastated to lose you, but my sister is not one to deny a child of their father. We suffered too much from that ourselves."

"Me too," said William, feeling a heavy weight of grief settle in the pit of his stomach..

"You need to speak to her."

"Speak to who?" Sorella appeared in the doorway with a smile.

Today was one of celebration for her. She had survived the horror of Silverwire, they had uncovered enough to bring it down, and she had heard him promise to stay because he loved her. This was not the time.

"Never, you mind," William said forcing a smile and getting up to kiss her. "Are you in the clear?"

"Fit and well, and ready to party."

"You're sure?" said William.

"It's just a headache, nothing to fuss about… really. Plus, we'll have safety in numbers."

"We'd better get going then." William nodded to Caro as he followed Sorella out. When the time was right he would tell her, and together they would decide what he should do.

"I will follow you over soon," said Caro.

Sorella waved a hand above her head as she made her way along the corridor. She never even glanced back at her brother. It would be one of the greatest regrets of her life.

Chapter Thirty Four

Under normal circumstances, Sorella would have felt uncomfortable with this level of attention. But somehow with William at her side it was bearable. Not that he was with her right now. He stood with Callum and Rose who wanted a blow by blow account of all that had happened, whilst Sorella danced. Lal and Seb were the first to pull her onto the dance floor, after which she joined Mart for an old-fashioned waltz, and now she danced with Davey Rowe, the nineteen-year-old singer from the village band. The whole time she twirled and swayed she knew William watched her. She could feel his eyes following her every move and the sensation brought a tingling heat to her skin.

Davey moved in close, swaying his hips against hers. He had really begun to fancy himself the past few years. Sorella tried not to smile at the look on his face. When she next glanced William's way he cut his drink short to smile and jerk his head to call her over.

"We'd never seen anything like it. There were fireworks and people singing in the street and this was, oh when Rose? Four years ago...?" Callum halted his story as Sorella approached. "How's our lovely Sorella then, having fun?"

Sorella placed an arm around Will's waist. "Actually I am. Thank you. This is really good of everyone."

"You lot'll find any excuse for a party," William said totally deadpan.

Callum's shocked expression amused Sorella. He obviously had not experienced much of Will's humour yet. "We are celebrating Sorella's recovery," the man said as Sorella felt his mild disgust.

"Like I said, *any* excuse," said William with a slight shrug.

"He's joking," Sorella said before Callum became any more upset.

"I am?"

She nudged Will. "Really, I'm very grateful. People didn't need to go to such effort."

"You're very welcome. Rose, shall we circulate?" Callum took his wife away, still feeling bemused.

"You shouldn't tease them like that."

William pulled her closer. "Says the biggest tease in the room." Under the light-hearted tone and amused expression, Sorella detected a hint of something darker.

"I saw you watching me," she said.

He made a theatrical frown. "I wasn't watching you, I was watching Seb. He's one hell of a dancer."

"I know you like him, but I would hope you wouldn't be looking at Seb that way."

When William's smile was genuine and completely for her it was a beautiful thing. She reached up and kissed him for longer than was really polite given the public setting. "I love you," she said.

He stroked her cheek with his thumb.

"I like that I can finally say that without having to worry about your running a mile."

William's smile looked almost sad as he pulled her into a hug and held her head against his chest.

"Are you okay?" she said, feeling a cold stab of intuition.

"Course. I'm just relieved you're all right. You scared the life out of me you know."

Before she had chance to check if that was the truth, Sorella's head was filled with anger. She sighed and moved from William. "Maddox is his typical cheerful self."

Maddox burst through the doors dragging Lola behind him. His wife stumbled a couple of times as they crossed the room but Maddox did not appear to notice. When they reached Sorella and William, he forced his reluctant wife forward. "Lola has something to say."

Lola squirmed and extracted her arm from his hand. "I can do this on my own."

Sorella looked at William who raised his eyebrows, as confused as she was no doubt.

"I came to apologise."

For the first time Sorella felt the other woman's shame masked under her husband's fury. "What for?"

Lola avoided her eyes. "I didn't know they would hurt you. I didn't know the people who took Grace would come. I just thought you'd get in trouble."

"And that's your excuse?" Maddox's expression turned furious, his hands almost shaking. "She could have died. She could have ended up like her." He pointed to Grace across the room.

"Yes and we all know who would have been most devastated about that." Lola flashed a look of disgust at her husband and then glanced at Will. "Sorry, William."

William held both hands up to show he took no offence.

"What exactly are you saying?" Sorella tried to put a lid on her bubbling anger.

"I heard from Jed about you going to Caltonville… that you intended to break into some secret place, so I-"

"She told the police," interrupted Maddox, disgust dripping from every word.

"*You*? *You* told them we were coming?" Sorella lost her hold on the anger. "You stupid woman, you nearly got William killed, you nearly ruined my life."

"Ella." William placed a hand on her waist.

She did not shrug him away but his caution did not halt her attack. "What were you thinking? Did you even stop to think about what we were doing and why? No, of course you didn't. You just wanted to punish me for something I've never done."

"I'm sorry. I know it was wrong, but he thinks you're this perfect woman." Lola threw a haunted look her husband's way. "And I wanted him to see that wasn't true."

"I don't encourage him you know." Sorella indicated to Maddox. "I've never done anything to encourage him."

William steered her away. "Come on. Let's get some air."

"I'm sorry, Sorella." Lola had started to cry.

"You should be ashamed," Maddox said walking away from his wife and towards the bar.

Sorella's fury made her head pound and her hands felt hot and shaky. "I can't believe she would do that."

"She's upset," said William as they walked across the green.

"*She's* upset. She should be... how can she hate me that much?" Sorella had always felt sorry for Lola. Maddox's behaviour embarrassed his wife so much, but she had never detected any bad feeling towards herself. "You do know if you had teleported it would have-"

"Turned me into a vegetable, I know, Caro told me. But that didn't happen and you're fine so don't let it upset you." William kissed her head.

"Caro was playing it down. A body can't survive with a scrambled brain. You'd have lasted minutes if that."

"But it didn't happen, El. We're both fine."

His calm tone only made her more angry. "How can you be so reasonable?" If he didn't care that this woman nearly killed him, he should at least be angry that she almost stripped Sorella of all quality of life.

"Because I know how it feels when the person you love prefers someone else."

His words stopped Sorella in her tracks. She felt embarrassed to have missed how easily he would identify with Lola.

"It can make you do crazy things," he said looking her in the eye.

The anger she felt towards Lola shifted to a new target: his wife. "You know I'm never going to do that, don't you?"

"Ella..." He dropped his head to look at the floor.

"I know you think no one can ever say this for sure." She stepped towards him and lifted his chin. "But I know I will never... *ever* hurt you like that. I've waited too long to feel this way."

William rested his forehead against hers, and spoke in a low voice. "There's something I need to tell you."

Before he had chance, she had broken free of his embrace and started running.

Lal laughed and kissed his wife's cheek. William's free association technique had opened up a whole new world for the two of them. He knew it would never become a full-blown conversation. She would never again be able to construct a full phrase or sentence. But at least it was some interaction, and that was a damn sight better than what had gone before. He enjoyed throwing random words at her to see how she would respond. When he understood her, he would be filled with joy and in turn so would she. Sometimes, like now, her responses made him laugh out loud and that brought her even more happiness.

For the first few weeks after her abduction, Grace had felt nothing more than a dull sadness. Lal was not sure he could have coped with that for the rest of their lives. He would be forever grateful for what Sorella's young man had done. Finally, he understood why Seby liked the guy so much.

Speaking of the boy…

Lal scanned the room. Jed stood talking to Callum and Rose. Everyone was here then. Jed had agreed to stay with Caro until his work was done. But Seb was nowhere to be seen.

Lal stood and checked again, but there was no sign of him. For a second, he thought the cold slice of panic he felt was his own. But then he saw the others moving out of the door, and his perception cleared,

"Gracie, hon, I'll be back in a minute."

Seb crept along behind William and Sorella. He wished he could hear what they were saying, but he didn't want to get caught. He knew he was not supposed to leave his mum and dad, but William was just too fascinating. Seb wanted to know everything about him. The man was the coolest.

Being the youngest in the village meant everyone treated Seb like a baby. But he was nearly eight. Only William spoke to him like a buddy, and laughed at his jokes when the others told him to stop fooling around. Last week, whilst Sorella worked, William had borrowed Seb's dad's bike and they had ridden to the lake and back. William even taught him how to ride down the steep footpaths his dad would never let him go on.

Seb ran along the edge of the green and hid behind the three large bushes outside of the Taylors' place. He could not hear what Sorella was saying, but he could feel she was angry. It annoyed him that she was cross at his friend.

When they stopped and got all mushy, Seb looked away. His mum and dad used to embarrass him with stuff like that.

Crouched in his hiding place, Seb felt the flash of panic just like everyone else. It took him a moment to work out who it came from. He rarely felt any strong emotion from Caro. The man was sort of flat. Not like William, from whom he never felt anything at all, more like a duller version of everyone else.

Seb stood from his hiding place as Sorella began to run. People streamed out of the centre and in the distance Seb could hear a whirring beat. He looked up searching the skies, and stepped out onto the green to see more clearly. Jed nearly crashed into him as he ran by. The man held his arms out and called sorry as Seb stumbled then righted himself.

Seb heard Maddox shouting William's name, but he did not look to see why. He was more interested in the plane. He had never seen one so low and close before and he wandered to the centre of the grass with his face turned upwards.

As everyone else scrambled by, Seb was the only one standing still, the only one looking up, and the only one to see the lightning bolt leave the undercarriage of the plane and head for the ground.

Caro finished writing up his findings on the serum whilst ANNy formulated a suitable press release. A formal paper was already complete and waiting to be sent to the Leader of the Opposition.

"It makes for powerful reading," ANNy said. "We have done people proud I think."

"It's not over yet. I want to see these people stopped and punished before celebrating."

"Is that why you are avoiding the party?" said ANNy.

"I'm not avoiding it, I'm working."

"You *are* avoiding it. Why else would you send Jed off unless you had no intention of going?"

Caro looked up even though ANNy had no face to focus on. "You know I'm not one for frivolities."

"She would like you there, though."

"She has William." Caro went back to his work.

"For now, but she will need you when he goes."

"All the more reason to give them some time alone," said Caro.

"Alone with all the villagers?"

"I thought you liked my company."

ANN chuckled. "You know I do."

Caro finished inputting the last of his data. "You think he will definitely go back?"

"I think from what we have seen of William, he is a man who believes in doing the right thing. Don't you?"

Caro nodded, knowing ANNy would pick up his agreement. He would have to think carefully about what to say to his sister when the time came. He trusted she would ultimately come to the right decision, but he felt unsure of how she would handle the news.

"Caro!"

As soon as ANNy said his name, Caro felt adrenaline surge through his system. He looked up to see she had filled the room with an image of the village from her scanner. The plane was flying low and was just minutes away.

Caro began to access the Royal Society ANN. "Send everything out, the paper and the press release."

"You need to go."

"We need my voice and fingerprints for the Medical Society."

"Caro, when that thing hits it will kill us both. If you go you can bring me back."

"This is more important."

"No, it is not!"

"I can send it and still make it out in time." Caro checked the aircraft. It was almost over the village boundary. He focused on the entry system ahead of him, selecting communications and permission to circulate to all. A silky voice filled the room.

"Welcome to the Royal Society for Medicine. Please provide your full details and password so I can authorise your request."

"Caro Grey, Neurological Savant number seven one eight two two. Password, Montague."

"I have sent everything, Caro, please go," said ANNy.

"Mr Grey, please place your hand on the pad." A rectangular object materialised in front of him and Caro placed his palm flat against it."

"Caro they are nearly here." ANN sounded panicked.

"Just a minute longer."

"You haven't got a minute, you need to go now!"

"Thank you, Mr Grey," said the silky voice. "Please provide the documents and I will circulate them first thing."

"No they need to go now. This is an emergency."

"All communication goes in the morning, Sir. Please be assured we will treat it with the utmost priority."

"Go, Caro, I can deal with this."

"I just need to send this document."

"Caro, I can do it. Go. *Now*. I beg you. You are the only one who can bring me back. You need to get out."

Caro could hear the plane above them and knew he had no more than seconds.

He began to run, skidding out of the dome and into the corridor. It seemed so much longer than it ever had before. His feet slipped on the surface and he fell forwards. He put out his hands out to stop himself falling then used them to push into a sprint for the door. The plane's dull whir filled the air and he pumped his arms.

As his hand touched the exit, his final thought was that he was actually going to make it out.

William had no idea what was going on. Sorella was already off the green and down the street before he realised she was gone. She could not possibly be running from what he had to tell her, not like that.

He heard a commotion from behind and turned to see people streaming from the centre. *What the hell?*

Then he heard Maddox.

"Stop her. William, stop her!" The muscle man tried to squeeze past the crowd at the doors of the centre.

William sprinted after Sorella. For Maddox to call on his help, something bad had to be happening. He turned the corner to the dome and almost skidded to a halt. A plane hovered above, its black undercarriage filling the sky. It made no noise other than a strange beat that sounded like no aircraft William had ever experienced.

Ahead of him, Sorella raced towards the dome as if her life depended on it. William knew he would have to draw on all his resources if he stood any chance of catching her.

Voices shouted as the crowd came closer, but all William could make out was Maddox's repetitive cry. "Stop her, William. Stop her."

A few feet from the door, he managed to get his arms around her. Sorella fought against his hold elbowing him in the stomach and stamping on his foot. William lifted her off the ground and spun her away from the dome. She kicked her legs whacking him in the shin and he swore.

"No! Put me down. Let me go." Sorella wriggled in his arms

and he nearly lost his grip. "Get off me, Will." She pushed at his arms clamped around her waist as suddenly a bright white light surrounded them and they were jolted off their feet. A loud snap split the air and Sorella's scream was blood curdling.

She kicked and scrambled and rolled away from William, managing to break free and get to her feet. "Caro!" She ran once more for the door, her hand outstretched towards it, before William was up.

Out of nowhere, Maddox ran into her side and tackled her to the ground.

"No! That's my brother." She punched Maddox's chest as he held her down.

"You touch that you die," the muscle man said.

"I need to get him out. I need to get him out." She pleaded with her eyes.

"It's too late, Sorella."

"No." She tried to wriggle backwards from under him.

Maddox strengthened his hold. "He's gone. It's too late."

"No, no, no." Her voice sounded hoarse from the screaming.

William put a hand on Maddox's shoulder. "Let her go."

The man's jaw twitched as he looked up. "There are over one hundred million volts of electricity running through that place."

William looked at the dome building. It looked the same as always, but he could see that Maddox's hair stood on end.

"I don't care, I just want my brother. Let me go." Sorella had started to cry.

"I won't let her touch it," William said to Maddox.

Flynn slowly released his hold putting himself between Sorella and the dome. She immediately sat and tried to stand but William moved quicker. He dropped to his knees and clamped his arms around her.

The devastated faces of the villagers gathered around. Crouched next to them, Maddox watched Sorella with a tortured expression. Once more, William was thankful he could not feel what she was feeling.

"What the hell was that?" he asked Maddox.

"Electricity bomb, they use them to decommission the ANNs."

"No," Sorella said shaking her head and holding on to clumps of William's shirt. "He has to be okay. I can't lose him." Her eyes begged William to tell her what she wanted to hear.

William looked at Maddox who gave a small shake of his head. Could they tell that Caro was gone? William wrapped his arms a little tighter around her. And as her makeshift family looked on, she cried into his shoulder.

Chapter Thirty Five

William set out another chair and checked the row. When he was happy it looked straight, he moved further back on the grass and began the next one. He felt a definite chill in the air today. It was the first cool weather he had experienced here, a sign that winter was approaching.

The baking summer months had passed slowly; hour by hour, day by day and week by week as he coaxed Ella back to life. The first two nights after it happened, they had not slept. They simply sat curled together on her sofa whilst she talked and cried, or rested silently against him. But gradually, he encouraged her to sleep and then eat. A few weeks on, he managed to get her walking, cycling and running; all the things that had helped him through his darkest days.

They had decided not to tell her how close Caro came to making it out. The Flynn brothers had eventually ventured into the dome. They both worked in the city hubs, so had experience of the bombs and how long it took for the area to become safe. They found her brother by the door. He would only have needed a few more seconds for everything to have been different. But she did not need to know that. It would only make it worse for her, and so they all agreed to keep that detail a secret.

They suspected he must have stayed in the dome to send out the Silverwire documents. There was plenty of time between the villagers feeling Caro's initial panic, and the lightning striking, for him to have exited the building. Most of the village had made it all the way from the community centre to the dome before the bomb hit. Caro had only needed to run down a small corridor.

Still, it had taken three weeks before they heard that Prime Minister Montoya had been arrested for her involvement in unethical human trials. Very few details were provided of her crimes. Reports merely said a further eight people had been charged for their involvement, including a renowned Professor.

It was some small comfort that Caro had not died in vain.

Maddox came to help with the chairs. "How's she doing?" Things had been a lot more civil between the two of them since the whole affair.

William moved his stack along another space. "Not too bad. She wanted some time to herself, to prepare. Any news from Lola?" Maddox's wife had fled the village following Caro's death, too guilt-ridden about her role in things to remain. She had been staying with her sister in Scotland, and the separation seemed to be suiting her husband.

"No change."

"Sorry to hear that." William fetched another stack of chairs to distribute.

Maddox shrugged. "Probably for the best."

When his last row was done, William stood and stretched his back. The whole green was laid out with chairs facing a memorial stone cloaked in red velvet. In William's opinion, it was a mediocre gesture, but the villagers appeared greatly touched. They had never been visited by royalty or any political parties before, so to have the King and the Prime Minister on the same day was creating a flurry of excitement. Children had been making flags from all manner of material for the past few weeks, and an array of colour and texture now zig-zagged across the sky.

"Are you sitting with us, Will?" Seb walked along a row of chairs, jumping the gaps between. He wore a smart shirt and waistcoat and William thought he looked adorable, although he would never say that to the boy. He knew how sensitive Seb was about being treated like a child.

William's thoughts automatically turned to Charlie. He had chosen not to mention his son to Sorella following Caro's death. But that did not mean the boy was ever far from his thoughts. In his head, he tracked Sarah's pregnancy. It was October now and if his calculations were correct Charlie would be born in February. Crunch time was fast approaching.

"You'll be with S'rella won't ya?" Lal gestured for his son to get down.

"Can we sit with you then?" Seb ignored his father's instruction, standing with his feet on two separate chairs so he was head height to Will.

"They'll be at the front, boy, now get down," said Lal.

Seb jumped from the seats and William ruffled his hair. "I'll see what I can do."

William walked through the village, past groups of people dressed in their finest. Most beamed with pride at the forthcoming visit and called out cheery hellos. He hoped Ella was not going to be offended by the lack of austerity.

Back at the house, he watched her through the kitchen window. She wore a jade green dress with her hair tied his favourite way, in a bun at the side of her neck. She stood with her back to him and in the lounge stood Caro.

The image looked so life-like if he had not known differently he would have thought her brother was really there. William was not sure how they could stand having such realistic projections of their loved ones still available after death.

In the early days, Sorella had taken to playing these things over and over, learning Caro's conversation until she could join in as if it were real. Eventually, William had to ban her from using them for a while. He could see it was doing her no good. She had fought him of course. Screamed and shouted, and then pleaded like an addict in need of a fix, but he had held firm.

"Hey," William said as he entered the house.

"Hi."

He could hear the tears in her voice as the image of her brother disappeared.

She brushed the side of her hand across her cheek and faced him with a smile. "How did you get on?"

"Yeh, everything's ready. The place looks great... as do you."

"Thanks." She began clearing away their breakfast things from earlier.

"I'll do that if you like."

"No it's okay, you need to get ready." She kept her eyes from him as she worked. A tactic he recognised well now.

William wrapped his arms around her waist and kissed her cheek. "It's going to be fine, babe." He gave her a squeeze. "*You're* going to be fine."

She exhaled and leant against him. "I don't want to cry."

"People will understand if you do."

She looked up at him. "I know, but... Caro would not have got upset...I want to be strong for him."

"That's because your brother was Mr Rational. It doesn't mean you have to be the same. He wouldn't expect you to be anything but yourself."

A faint smile touched her lips and he lifted her chin to kiss them. She twisted in his arms and for the next few moments, they lost themselves in each other as it was always so easy to do.

Sorella ended the kiss reluctantly. She did not want to come back to reality, but today she had no choice. This was for Caro.

William moved his face only a fraction away. She knew he was checking for how she was coping. When he was satisfied with what he saw, he rubbed his nose against hers. "I'd better get ready then. Fancy joining me in the shower?"

She knew he was joking, but still she was tempted. "Before you go, I've been thinking. I might speak to the Prime Minister about you, see if he will arrange citizenship."

"That's a no to the shower then?"

She slapped his arm playfully. "What do you think?"

"I don't know, El." William stepped away and leant against a kitchen chair. "Do we need to do that?"

"I just thought it would help, if you ever wanted to get a job in the city or something."

He shrugged. "I'm happy enough helping out here."

"You might not be forever. And what if we want to travel or…" She stopped herself from saying it. After all, his experience of marriage had not been great thus far.

"Or what?" he said sensing her hesitation and no doubt seeing her cheeks grow hot.

She busied herself with more tidying. "It was just an idea. I figured he would be willing to accommodate us no questions asked at the moment. We might not get another chance."

William remained silent and when she could stand it no longer she looked his way. The sight of him biting his lip and staring at the floor was all the response she needed. She was not stupid.

"Look forget it. If you prefer to leave things as they are that's fine. I should be going. I can't let the others do all the work."

"Ella." He stopped her as she tried to pass. "I think we should talk about it properly before we make any approaches."

"No. It's obvious you don't want to make things permanent." She knew she had given him a rough ride over the past months. He had been amazing, but maybe it was all too much. He had come here looking for a distraction and time to heal, not a job as a grief counsellor.

"That's not true."

She brushed his hand away. "Don't start lying to me. The one thing I could always trust you to be was honest." She walked towards the door.

William sighed. "Of course you would do this today."

Sorella aborted her exit and came back to where he stood. "What do you mean?"

He rubbed her upper arms. "This is a big day and it should be about Caro. Let's just focus on that for now." He dropped his eyes. "And when it's all done we'll take a walk out to the lake."

"And you'll tell me what's going on?"

William kissed her forehead and hugged her. "And I'll tell you what's going on."

Sorella fought back the tears. She had hoped in vain he would say there was nothing to tell.

Part of her wanted to be annoyed with William for keeping whatever he was from her, but it proved impossible today. Sorella clung tightly to his hand as they awaited Prime Minister Farrow's speech, concentrating on the feel of his thumb rubbing her skin.

There was a carnival atmosphere in the air which she had not expected. Villagers had lined the street to watch the cars drive by, and most now sat on the edge of their seats as they waited for the ceremony. She knew it was not a funeral, but she had expected some level of sombreness.

An aide stepped to the podium Lal had carved especially for the occasion, and checked the technology. The crowd fell silent. A minute after which, Reece Farrow took the aide's place. He was a tall, thin man with dark skin and a slightly oriental look. He had led the opposition party against Stella Montoya for seven years prior to this scandal, and was no doubt revelling in her demise. But he was professional enough not to show any sign of this. He had his emotions well and truly under control.

"Good afternoon, Ladies and Gentlemen. His Majesty and I are honoured to be here today to preside over this commemoration."

The King sat to the side of Farrow and nodded in agreement.

"As you will all know, Caro Grey and his sister Sorella," Farrow looked her way and smiled, "showed initiative, tenacity and bravery in their efforts to expose a great disservice against communities such as yours. And I would like to take this opportunity to give you a personal assurance that measures have been put in place to ensure such a crime can never be committed again."

A rumble of appreciation ran through the crowd.

"I also feel it my duty to apologise to all those directly affected and their families, for the atrocities they have experienced and the ongoing challenges they face. We are providing as much help and support as we can to ensure this is made as bearable as possible."

Sorella glanced at Lal, Grace and Seb sitting alongside William. Lal had refused the full-time carer offered to the family, preferring to look after his wife himself. But she knew the financial support he had received had been tremendously helpful. He looked her way and winked.

"My final words before I hand over to His Majesty are for the Grey family. I know that Montague and Ophelia were invaluable members of our society who contributed greatly, and it seems their children have followed in their footsteps. For that, I think all of us should be hugely grateful."

The cheer which went up made Sorella jump and William squeezed her hand. She kept her eyes straight ahead. *Don't cry, don't cry.*

Farrow gave way to the King who stood and applauded along with everyone else. New to the throne, only just thirty and extremely good looking, Sorella guessed he was the real reason for all the excitement around the place.

"Hello," he said with a broad smile taking his time to look people in the eye. She liked him already. "It is with much sadness that I come here today to Mr Grey's home. From what I have heard, I would very much like to have met the man about whom everyone speaks so highly. I know he was much loved by you all and especially by his sister." The King held Sorella's gaze for a moment and she felt her eyes well up. "Not to mention celebrated by rural communities and cities alike for giving his life to save others.

"This memorial is a small token of the country's appreciation. But more than that it should stand as a reminder of the values we all hold dear.

"All life is precious and worthy of protection. All people are valuable and worthy of respect. Our world is privileged to have each and every one of us, and all should be free to enjoy it without fear and persecution."

William leant in close. "Wow, *he's* good."

The King moved to the memorial and then paused. "Miss Grey, would you join me?"

Sorella had not expected this. For a second, she considered saying no, but then stood, straightened her dress and made her way to the front.

The King took her hand in both of his. "Hi, I'm Harold and you must be Sorella."

She nodded finding herself lost for words.

"I'm incredibly sorry for your loss."

She felt a tear escape her left eye. "Thank you."

"Would you help me?" He gestured for her to stand on the other side of the stone and together they unveiled the memorial to her brother.

The whole village stood to applaud. Sorella had seen it before, they had asked for her approval on wording and design. And it was exactly what she had asked for: minimalist and neat just like Caro.

Before she knew it, the King had been whisked away and her friends surrounded her. Rose, Callum and Martha arrived first each giving her a hug, Lal lifted her off her feet during his hug, and Jed simply kissed her cheek for a long moment, squeezed her hand and left. She knew he had been having a rough time with the guilt. If he had refused to leave Caro for the party, he might have got him out.

"Can I have a hug?" Maddox said from behind her.

Sorella turned and embraced him. "Thank you for everything, Maddie, for stopping me that night and for being so good with William."

"S'okay, if he makes you happy."

She moved away a little. "He really does." She found the timbre of his emotion hard to take standing so close. She wished she could make those feelings go away for him.

"Trust you to hog the squeezing, Flynn."

Sorella spun away from Maddox and flung her arms around Mart. He and his wife Lucille had taken her and Caro in when their parents died, and pretty much raised them as their own. He rocked her from side to side as they cuddled, and a few tears escaped her eyes onto his best shirt.

Over his shoulder she spotted William. He leant forward in his seat with his hands clasped together staring at the floor. Something about the sight scared her more than anything ever had before.

"You'll be alright, lass," Mart said misinterpreting her reaction. He gripped her arms and smiled in her face. "We're all going to make sure of that."

Sorella hugged him again and kissed his cheek. "Love you, Mart."

"Love you too, Chickadee."

A quiet cough sounded to their left and she found Prime Minister Farrow waiting his turn. He had no aides with him now as he took a swig from his bottle of water.

"Mr Farrow, thank you for organising all of this." She held her hand out as she spoke.

"Reece, please. And it is the least we could do."

Mart and Maddox moved away leaving the two of them alone. She checked William again but his seat was empty. Maybe she could lay some ground-work for his staying. Would he be angry if she did that?

"I have an offer to extend," said Farrow. "I want to invite you to head up a new committee I am initiating. It will act to ensure the fair and equitable treatment of lower quartile communities. I know you have already worked tirelessly on their behalf and you would certainly have the profile to do the job. Might you be interested?"

"Erm… I…" Sorella swallowed and looked for William again wanting his opinion. "I'm very flattered. Could I give it some thought?"

"Take as much time as you need. I don't have anyone else in mind who could do the job as well as you, Ms Grey."

"Sorella, please," she said and the Prime Minister smiled. "Can I ask you something whilst you're here?"

"Certainly."

Across the green she spotted William. He sat on the grass with Seb, their heads tilted towards each other. She should not do this without him. It was not what he wanted. He would definitely be angry.

Farrow still waited for her enquiry and she quickly formulated another line of questioning. "Did my brother manage to get the Silverwire information to you, is that how it was exposed?"

"Yes and no. I understand documents were sent to me, but sadly my predecessor had anticipated such a possibility. They were intercepted before they arrived. The documents sent to the press did land, but there was a degree of procrastination due to suspicions of a hoax. In truth, I think the size of it scared them. What really made the difference was the serum breakdown sent to the medical community. When they ran tests and confirmed Caro's claims, there was no way out. It was a master stroke. Silverwire never saw that coming."

Chapter Thirty Six

They made it to the point where the lake came into view walking hand in hand, both happy to discuss nothing more than the events of the day. There had been numerous invites for dinner which they had declined, heading home to change and setting off with no need for discussion.

Bronze and yellow leaves crunched under their feet. Other than that, the only noise was the faint sloshing of water and a few bursts of birdsong. William had come to love this place as much as Ella, and he found it even more stunning in its autumnal colours.

"I think he may have been right to do what he did. Caro I mean," said Sorella.

"Yeh?"

She nodded. "Farrow said it was the breakdown of the serum that brought Silverwire down. Without that it would have been our word against theirs. I think Caro knew we only had one shot."

"It was a brave thing to do."

"He was too stubborn and principled for his own good."

"Both equally fine qualities."

Sorella smiled at him. "No surprise I'm attracted to you is it."

William wrapped an arm around her shoulders and planted a kiss on her cheek. "Love you."

She freed herself and folded her arms around her body. It took William by surprise.

"What's this?" he said.

"I know... all of this was not what you expected, what you signed up for... and I know I've not been the best company. I understand if things have changed for you."

He returned his arm to her shoulder. "Happy or sad, you're

always good company, El. And for what it's worth, I'm more in love with you than ever."

She came to a standstill. "So what's going on? I know it's something bad it was written all over your face earlier, and after the ceremony you looked so distant…You're scaring me, Will."

This was it then, no more time to put off the inevitable. He took a couple of deep breaths as she watched then set off walking again. "You remember the day Caro died he asked me to look at some papers?"

She caught him up. "This is to do with Caro?"

He took hold of her hand. "Not really, he just highlighted the… issue. When we were at Caltonville ANNy ran a search on my name to see what would come up if Silverwire did the same, and they found…" He glanced her way not knowing how best to say it. He had rehearsed this conversation so many times in his head, but for the life of him he could not remember his lines. "There was an interview with a time travel expert, Charlie Fletcher. It was from my day, well a few decades after, but still in my lifetime…or what would have been my lifetime if I'd stayed. Sorry, I'm finding this really hard to say."

She wound her fingers through his. "Just say it."

"Charlie's my son."

Ella stopped, the motion pulling her hand from his. "How… I don't… how is that possible?"

William fought the urge to crack a joke about the biology of it. It was just his nerves. He replaced humour with sarcasm. "After fifteen fruitless years it appears one mistake was all it took."

He saw the realisation take hold in her eyes. "When you went back?"

"I'm guessing so, things had not been active in that department for a good many months before." He moved the leaves about under his feet. "Then Sarah turned up out of the blue and full of guilt. I knew it wasn't a good idea but she was all over me, begging and pleading. And I suppose at the time, I wanted her back so-"

Ella held her hand up to stop him. "Too much honesty, Will."

"Sorry." He could hear himself babbling but was unable to stop.

"And you've known all this time. Why haven't you said anything?"

"How could I, Ella, after Caro?"

She left the path and walked across the grass towards their picnic spot. Once there, she took one of the two blankets from his bag and laid it on the floor. Then she walked to the lake edge and stood looking out. He went to join her.

"I'm sorry," she said after a while.

"What do you have to be sorry for?"

"Your having to carry this on your own for so long. It must have been unbearable."

"To be honest, I've tried not to think about it too much. I was waiting for the right time." Her eyes widened and flashed with panic. "To tell you," he said by way of reassurance. Pointless really, he could not get away without hurting her, why delay it? "He's a physicist at Cambridge. Who knows where he got the brains from." William laughed a little but she did not join in. "He researches time travel."

"Is he trying to find you?"

"No. He appears to discount the whole idea, puts it down to a story Steve told to save him from the truth. That I am some saddo who took his own life."

Sorella reached for his hand.

"The article said he'd written a book on the topic and was

taking part in some TV documentary. Time travel that is, not the suicide."

"You're proud of him?"

William pushed some gravel off the shore line and into the water. "What do I have to be proud of? I contributed nothing to his life and who he is...other than disappointment."

Sorella's breath hitched as she inhaled. "You're going back."

William hung his head for a few moments before he had the courage to look at her. When he did, her eyes were full of tears.

She swallowed. "But I love you...you love me."

"I know..." he said softly. "But... I can't help thinking... I wouldn't be worthy of that if I stayed." He ran his free hand through his hair. "It's an impossible choice."

Ella looked at him with a shake of her head. "It's not fair..."

"No." William looked at his feet again.

She came closer until their arms touched, and faced away from him. He watched as one tear after another spilled down her cheek. Ella crying had been a familiar sight in recent times, and whilst he always found it hard, nothing had prepared him for this. He wondered if Sarah had found it anywhere near this painful to tell him she was leaving. Had she also felt sick with guilt for shattering another person's world?

"It's not impossible," she said very quietly after a while. "He's always going to need you more than I do."

William looked up, surprised. He had not expected her to say that. "I'm so sorry," he said humbled by her generosity towards this child who was nothing to her.

As the evening drew in, and they sat leaning against a tree with the spare blanket wrapped around them, William found the nerve to speak his deepest desire out loud. "You could come with me?"

Sorella leant her head against his shoulder by way of a reply.

"Ah, well it was worth a try," William said masking his disappointment best he could.

"There's too much for me here."

"I know."

"Without Caro, people need me... and I need them. I couldn't do what you've done, I couldn't leave everything... everyone behind."

"Hey, I know. I shouldn't have asked."

He was relieved to see a faint smile. "I'd have been offended if you hadn't."

William wrapped his arms a little tighter around her.

"Will you come back?"

He had given this a lot of thought: whether he could split his time between the two places, like those people who spend half a year in some holiday home. But each time he imagined the reality of it, he knew every departure would be excruciating, every visit too short. Not to mention what effect the radiation might have long term. "Do you want me to?" He would do it for her, though, if she needed him to.

"Only if you can stay for good."

He kissed her hair. The fact she chose not to pull him up on his promise to stay only made him love her more. "Agreed."

As the night drew in, they sat huddled together under the blanket watching the small waves ripple across the water and lap onto the shore. He could smell her perfume mixed with shampoo, the sweet scent of many a lovely hour spent together. Bit by bit, the sun dropped from the sky, the clear blue turning crimson in its wake. When it splashed into the horizon spreading golden streamers across the water, Ella whispered one simple word.

"When?"

Chapter Thirty Seven

The window looked out onto snow-covered fields. Thick white frosting coated every branch and rose a good ten centimetres from the window ledge. The world outside was silent, dulled by its icy blanket. Even in here people spoke in whispers. William wrapped his coat a bit tighter around him as the doors swished open across the room. A heavily pregnant woman entered with one hand cradling her stomach. Her husband carried a bag and flitted around his wife with nervous energy. William could not tell if her expression was down to pain or irritation.

He looked away and watched a robin bob across the snow, its red breast puffed up and proud.

"Mr York, you need room three two five on the third floor. The lifts are just over here."

He thanked the nurse and collected his flowers from the chair. It felt wrong to come empty handed.

This place felt more like a hotel than a hospital. He was surprised. For their whole relationship he had assumed Sarah shared his views on the NHS, but obviously not. This place had cost them a bob or two. It did not even smell clinical. When he glanced in the rooms as he passed, he saw flat screen TVs, tea and coffee making facilities and designer fabrics.

The door to three two five stood ajar and William heard voices from within as he approached.

"Holy crap," said Sarah as he walked in. She was sat up in bed, her hair scraped back from her face and the circles under her eyes dark. Yet she looked somehow radiant.

"Hi, Sarah." William glanced across to the seat by her bed. "Danny."

"What the hell are you doing here?" His wife sounded more

shocked than annoyed – for now. A tiny hand reached up from the bundle she was cradling and grabbed at the air.

"I came to see my son."

Sarah's mouth dropped open and he heard Danny cough a laugh. He had wondered if this might be the case. Charlie had found out Danny was not his dad when he was seven. Coincidentally, the number of years needed to have William declared dead. They must have checked the boy to determine what should happen to Will's estate. Or maybe he started to look too much like his real father for them to pretend any longer.

"That's not even funny. Where the hell have you been anyway? Everyone thought..." Sarah placed her finger in the outstretched hand and tiny fingers closed around it.

William took a step forward. "Who's joking?" He saw a podgy arm attached to the hand and took another step, and then another until his son came into view. "Wow."

Sarah looked down and stroked the boy's head, then she met Will's eyes. They shared a smile before she frowned and dropped her gaze.

Danny stood. "This is not funny and not the time. I suggest you head back out before I get someone to take you. He's not yours, William."

"Oh, I'm afraid he is."

"Why are you doing this?" Sarah wrapped the blankets tighter around the baby. "This is our day. It's not fair to come here and stir up trouble."

The boy smacked his lips together and a small amount of spittle dribbled onto his chin. The kid was gorgeous. William touched his baby's other hand, and the little fingers opened and closed around his. He had never felt love like it.

"You didn't work it out from the dates?" William said still

smiling at his son.

"Oh my god, that's why you're here. Who told you anyway? Steve I suppose. Look, William, I'm sorry to burst your little bubble but it's not that precise, and it was just once, which compared to Danny and I…"

William turned his head a fraction to look her in the eye. There was a time he would have enjoyed pulling her up on the once comment, but he had no inclination any more. "I hear once is all it takes." He stood straighter keeping his finger in place. "I know he's my son, Sarah. Don't ask me how, but I do. And I *will* be his dad."

"Enough now. You need to leave." Danny looked angry as he moved around the bed.

"Have you picked out a name yet?"

"Charlie, after my father," said Danny.

William actually felt sorry for the guy. "It suits him. Hey Charlie, nice to meet you. You are one lucky fella, *two* dads to spoil you." He grinned at his son.

"I said that's enough." Danny stood very close, his jaw clenched and his cheeks reddening.

William removed his hand from Charlie's as a gesture of good will. If this was going to work, it would take a lot of compromise.

"If you're trying to ruin things for us, Will, you're wasting your time. I'm with Danny now, I'm happy with him. I love him and you're not going to change that."

"I'm not trying to." William smiled at his wife. "I'm pleased you're happy. I don't want you back, Sarah. I am more than over us. I just want to be a father to my son."

Danny pulled William away from the bed and pinned him against the wall. "What is wrong with you? Don't you think you've caused Sarah enough heartache with your childish behaviour?"

"Charlie is my son whether you like it or not," said William keeping his tone calm but firm. "I suggest you get him tested then we can get on with working out how to manage this…" He handed the flowers to Danny who threw them on the floor.

"Danny, calm down," said Sarah. "He's not worth it."

Danny didn't let go for a second, and William thought the guy was going to hit him. But then he pushed William towards the door with a look of disgust. "You're an idiot. Get out of here before I really lose my temper."

William held his hands up and backed away. "I'll leave you two to discuss things. Sorry if this came as a shock."

"Wait," said Sarah as he opened the door. "What happened to you, where have you been?"

William shrugged. "Travelling," he said, closing the door on the way out.

Chapter Thirty Eight

Sorella turned her attention to the last of the documents she needed to review before tomorrow's meeting. Chairing the Fairness for All committee had given her a new lease of life. It challenged her mentally more than anything she had ever done before, and she could feel it making her stronger day by day. She had even been asked out to dinner by a rather attractive legal savant, but it was too soon. Only eight months had passed since William left and still she felt his absence everywhere. She envied him being somewhere totally different, without so many memories. It was why she liked spending so much time with the committee in London.

He had encouraged her to take up the government's job offer and provision of a new ANN before he left. He said she needed to get back to work. He did not want her moping with nothing to do.

They had made a huge effort to spend as much time as possible enjoying each other's company in the last few months. But he would not let her make any recordings of him.

"I don't want you sitting in your underwear watching those things over and over."

"Naturally you would imagine me in my underwear."

He smirked at her. "Whenever I think of you, you'll be in your underwear, if that."

"Nice to know that's the image you'll have of me for the rest of your life."

He grabbed her round the waist. "And I suppose I'll be fully clothed in all your imaginations will I?"

"Hmmm," she said with a grin. And then she had kissed him, hugging him close and holding on tight.

"Don't," he said pulling away. He had hated knowing how

desperate she was for him to stay.

When it came to his actual departure, they had selected the date at random. He wanted to go in January so he would be home in time for Charlie's birth. So they wrote the numbers twenty to thirty-one on separate pieces of paper, folded them and shook them in a jar. He picked out the twenty-fifth. A previously unremarkable date that would forever more be heart-shattering.

She could not stand to go with him; to see him disappear that way again. So, as agreed, he waited until she had fallen asleep. And it must have been near dawn because she held on to wakefulness for as long as she could. When she awoke to her new life, she sat in the faint light and unfolded the note he had left on his pillow.

My Ella,
Worth living for, now and always
William x

She shook the memory away and concentrated on her reading. She only had an hour until she was due at Lal and Grace's for tea.

The document was a final draft proposal to increase opportunities for LQ people. Her mission was to encourage more integration and halt the exclusion that had justified Silverwire's experimentation. In preparing the document, she had selected a sample of communities to visit and spent time talking to people about their hopes and ambitions for the future. Many of the parents felt protective of their way of life, but at the same time hoped for more for their children.

She read through the key recommendations one more time. They included making a variety of educational upgrades available to lower quartile children; increasing the number of job opportunities for lower quartile adults within the commercial world; and involving rural communities in local government issues. It also proposed that the LQ label be dropped. There were a few minor amendments to make, but on the whole she was happy it read well and presented strong arguments.

She could not deny that William had influenced the stance she had taken. She had never thought to question the consequences of labelling people as less intelligent. It was just the way things were. But his distaste for how a seemingly civilised world had ostracised so many of its people, changed that. And thanks to her brother, she was now in a position to do something about it. Filling her life with endeavours she knew the two men she loved most would approve of, felt like a suitable tribute.

She packed up and said goodnight to ANN. The new network was more conventional than her predecessor. There was a lot less back chat and far more collaboration with wider systems. Surprisingly, Sorella found she missed the rebellious streak in Caro's ANNy.

Seb greeted her at the door and gave her a small hug. He had become very attentive since William went away and Sorella suspected he might have been primed. In the first few days, he often turned up out of the blue with some random request for milk or butter, and then hung around to keep her company. He dragged her out into the fields saying they needed extra help preparing the land now Grace could not do it. And he even arrived on a couple of occasions to request she recommend a book for him to read. It transpired Will had encouraged him to take up the hobby to expand his mind.

She ruffled his hair as Will used to do and followed him into the kitchen. Lal had his head in the oven. He wore his sleeves rolled up and one of Grace's aprons, a frilly yellow number with pink ties. The stew he stirred filled the room with the scent of lamb and rosemary.

"Pass us the pepper, boy. Hello my love." Lal flashed her a grin as he took the pot from Seb and shook in a good measure.

"I brought some wine." She placed the bottle of red on the table. It was the last of Will's favourite and to be honest she was trying to get rid of it. Not only did the taste bring back a surprising amount of memories, the alcohol made her melancholy. It had been over two months since she last had a drink.

"Lovely." Lal gave her a kiss on the cheek. His face felt hot from the oven. He began to open the bottle. "I'll let this breathe. We're nearly ready to eat so come through. Gracie's waiting to see you."

Grace sat at the dining table drawing. Her trademark flower designs looked as good as ever. As they suspected, she never generated any new ones, but it did not appear to upset her. She looked up as Sorella entered and smiled. Then she hunched over the paper again and continued her work.

"Keeps her busy," said Lal with a wink. "Doesn't it love?" He patted his wife's shoulder as he passed. "I need to set the table now." Grace did not respond to the request until he physically stopped her from drawing and moved her hands to her lap. He crouched at her side. "Food."

She avoided his eyes, looking around the room.

"Gracie, food."

"Egg," she said.

Lal chuckled. "Yes we had egg for lunch. I've done a stew now." He placed knives and forks out in the four spaces.

Seb skipped in with a basket of bread and popped it on the table. "Ella, have you ever read the bible?" He had picked up her nickname from Will, and was the only one who used it.

"Erm, well I know what it's about."

"Will said I should read it. He said it was funny."

Sorella suppressed a smile. "Did he? You know, it's a very old and valuable belief system, Seb. They used to have wars over it. It's probably worth waiting until you're a bit older to read that."

"He's halfway through it." Lal tucked a napkin into Grace's top. "Lamb, Gracie. We're having lamb."

"Jump," said his wife.

"Yep they do that, my love, they do jump."

"And make jumpers," said Seb holding onto the back of a chair and bouncing up and down.

Seb was exactly the reason why her new job was so important. The boy was barely nine and had taken it upon himself to read a book like the bible. Proof indeed that low quartile did not mean low potential. All he had needed was someone to fire him up and inspire him.

"Have you heard from William?" Lal asked as Seb tucked into his stew like he had not eaten in weeks.

Sorella had become familiar with fielding this question. The story they had told was that Will had to return home for family reasons and would be gone a good while. But everyone felt how much she missed him and that only fuelled their curiosity.

"No, it's not easy from where he is."

"No communications at all?" Lal took a fork of his own food and then helped his wife with hers. Grace could manage to scoop it up but struggled with hand to mouth coordination. "Where is he, outer space?"

"Outa space, outa time, outa space, outa time," chanted Seb.

Sorella stopped chewing and looked Seb's way. Had William told him? Would he do that? They had spent a lot of time together, and a child's mind is more open to such ideas.

"He said he'd write to you." Seb took his fifth piece of bread and smiled at her.

Sorella smiled back, dismissing the idea. His chant was nothing more than a coincidence. "He did… and I'm sure he will when he can."

William had told her the same one morning over breakfast. "What are you going to do, send paper aeroplanes through that thing," she had said in jest and he had shaken his head with a smile. "I'll find a way." And so she had ANN scouring every type of written document from his day once a week. Newspapers, magazines, blogs anywhere he might have placed some message, but there had been nothing. She even cycled out to the hillside one morning to check for paper planes.

"It must be hard for you, but you can't mess about when there's kids involved. Seb! How much of that damn bread are you eating?" Lal slapped his son's hand away from the basket.

Sorella sighed, so much for Mart keeping her confidence. "Great, who else knows?" She felt Lal's embarrassment mixed with her own.

Lal reddened a little and shrugged. "Tis nothing to be ashamed of, him doing the right thing. I hear the mother's not around any more."

"She's not dead if that's what you mean. They split up before he came here."

Lal raised his eyebrows. "Oh, I see."

Sorella concentrated on the food. She knew what he was thinking, what they all would be thinking once this got out. Who was to say William and his wife would not rekindle things for the sake of their son. It was an idea that certainly kept her awake in the small hours.

And that night proved no different. She wriggled under the

sheets, too warm, and with too much commotion in her head for sleep to come. Plus, Lal had insisted she drank a glass of the wine and as usual it only served to amplify her misery.

She got up and paced, visiting the bathroom, fetching water from the kitchen and finally sitting in the window seat until sunrise.

As soon as the day was fully born, she showered, dressed and set off to catch the London shuttle.

It was gone nine p.m. when she returned, exhausted from the busy day and lack of sleep. Tabby Flynn dashed out of her front door as Sorella passed. Sorella hoped the woman was not planning one of her moaning sessions. She never realised how many of the villagers' complaints Caro had shielded from her.

"Sorella?"

"Hi Tabby." Sorella kept walking without slowing.

The woman trotted to her side. Despite the late hour, Tabby still wore full make-up and a pair of healed sandals. She also felt excited about something. "You had a visitor today."

Tabby's words stopped Sorella in her tracks and drove all thoughts of sleep from her mind. *William*? She glanced towards her house but it sat in darkness.

"She said she had come from Australia to see you."

The disappointment tasted bitter in Sorella's mouth as she saw confusion pass through Tabby's eyes. "She?"

"Julia Piper her name is. Real pretty thing. She said she would come again tomorrow and to tell you she has something important to speak to you about."

By the time Sorella made it back to her house, she had forgotten all about Julia Piper. She headed straight for the bedroom, removed her clothes and flopped into bed. In under a minute, she was fast asleep.

The knock on the door interrupted her dream and for a few seconds Sorella searched for its source in her imagination. She could see a door at the end of an incredibly long corridor, but no matter how hard she tried, she couldn't reach it. The knock came again, louder and she became aware of the sun on her face and the sheets curled around her. Sorella opened one eye and checked the clock. The knocking came again.

"You looking for Sorella?" Jed's voice came from outside her window.

Sorella sat up.

"Yes. Is she in do you know?" The woman's voice sounded unfamiliar.

Sorella tied a wrap around her and went downstairs.

"If she's not there, she might be with ANN. Do you want me to show you?"

Sorella opened the door to see a pretty brunette in a lilac dress. She could not be much older than twenty. Sorella could tell she was not a country girl, her nails were neatly filed and painted, and her clothes too fashionable.

"Morning," said Jed giving Sorella a wave as he went on his way. Out of the corner of her eye, Sorella spotted him glance back to appreciate the girl one more time.

"Are you Sorella Grey?" The girl's brown eyes were wide and her emotions a mixture of hope and excitement. It was too early for Sorella to try and work out what was going on.

"Sorry, I had a long day yesterday. I was sleeping."

"Oh dear, I didn't mean to wake you, sorry. I just couldn't wait to see you once I found you were really here."

It crossed Sorella's mind this girl could be some admirer of her work. She had met people fascinated by her story before, although no one had ever come to her home.

"My name is Julia." She held out her hand. "Julia Piper. This is so unreal. I can't actually believe I'm meeting you. You are beautiful too, just like he said."

Sorella ran her fingers through her hair. Goodness knows what she looked like. "Sorry," she said as Julia's words sank in. "Just like who said?"

The girl's embarrassment flashed on her cheeks. "I'm doing this all wrong. You have no idea who I am, do you?" She stroked a hand over the square box she held under one arm. "My grandfather is George York. We are direct descendants of William York and he asked us to bring you this." She held out the box and Sorella leant on the door frame for support. Julia beamed at her. "He wrote to you, just like he promised."

Chapter Thirty Nine

"So he still needs a bath and he usually goes down about six."

"Yeh, Sarah, I know."

Sarah and Danny were off on a weekend away, leaving Charlie with William from Friday until Monday. It was the longest time they would be alone together since the infamous DNA test. What a waste of time that had been too. They had only needed to wait a few months before his parentage became more than apparent.

"This last week he's nearly been sleeping through, but he might miss me, so I'd prepare a few feeds just in case."

"He knows, Sarah. Come on." Danny put his hands on her shoulders to lead her away. The man appeared to be dealing with the whole situation impressively well. Discovering her duplicity then finding Charlie was the result, would have ripped many a couples apart. But the pair of them appeared to be rock solid.

Sarah kissed Charlie's head. "Mummy will see you soon, Sweetheart. Be good for your daddy."

William looked into his son's chocolate button eyes. Both Sarah and Danny had blue eyes. By the time Charlie was nine months old they would have known he was Will's. He could not help wondering how things had gone the first time round. Even though this was also the first time round. The whole thing made his head spin if he spent too much time thinking about it.

"Now then, big man, you and me are going to have some fun." William kissed the boy's cheek and Charlie kicked his legs and punched the air. "I know, exciting isn't it?" William chuckled and picked up his son as he heard Danny's car pull away. The boy smelt divine. William inhaled a few times before lifting him above his head. Charlie giggled whilst opening and closing his fists.

"So, bath, bottle and bed, hey? Who says you don't take after your old man?" William carried Charlie and his bag up to the nursery. Sarah and Danny had gone for sit-on-the-fence yellow, having decorated before the birth, but William had gone all out blue. Cute cartoon aliens climbed the walls and a spaceship mobile complete with dangling meteors hung from the ceiling. It played David Bowie's Space Odyssey which never failed to make William smile.

He had also splashed out on a whole bathful of boats, fishes, buckets and spades. Charlie was not really old enough to appreciate the effort yet, but they kept his dad happy. When the bath was done and the nappy changed, William dressed Charlie in the Babygro Steve and Michelle had bought. They were coming over for dinner and would love to see him wearing it. As he buttoned it up, William planted a big raspberry on Charlie's tummy. "Do you like that?" He did it again making his son giggle and squirm. "That's a rumpty-fizzer that is. Your granddad used to chase me round the house to give me those."

William carried Charlie downstairs thinking how much of his father's parenting he had forgotten, or chosen not to acknowledge, after his death. Only now, did he appreciate how much fun he had been, always making toys for William and playing with him for hours. He would have made a cracking Granddad.

For the next hour, William sat on the sofa, feeding and cuddling Charlie until the little boy fell asleep. Having him to stay was the best thing in the world. William wished he could have him every night.

Once the boy was in his bed, William settled back into the arm chair. He should be making a start on the bolognese sauce, but he still had an hour until the guys arrived and they could watch him cook over a glass of red. There was something else he wanted to do first.

To the sound of Charlie's muttering and gurgling, he opened the notebook and began to write.

Friday 21ˢᵗ September 2012
Hi Ella,
This is a first. I have Charlie for the whole weekend. He's upstairs now sleeping. We had a bath and some food and then a cuddle on the sofa. He is so gorgeous, El, I wish you could see him. He has big brown eyes and the coolest little quiff of brown hair. Turns out he's not going to be a blond bombshell like Seb, too much of his dad's mousy influence!

I've been telling him a few stories about you (clean ones I promise). I told him how we met and how you saved my life, twice. I also told him you were far too beautiful for his dad, but via an amazing combination of spy skills, heroics and general brilliance I managed to win your heart. I've decided to tell it as a combination of Camelot and Bond (look it up). It's my story after all and who's going to argue.

Steve and Michelle are coming over for dinner. He finally proposed last weekend so I'm bracing myself for wedding talk. But it's good to see him so happy at last. I think I mentioned he was a bit of a bugger in the past but Michelle seems to have him under control. It does make me a little sad seeing them together

Sorry I think they just arrived, I hear a car, so I'll cut my ramblings short and write again soon.

Hope you're happy and keeping yourself out of trouble.
Love you x

Sorella finished reading and looked across the sofa at Julia. "How many of these are there?" She took in the stack of hardback journals in the box.

"Twenty-eight. All crammed full. Some with pictures."

Sorella let the girl take the book from her hands and flick on a few pages. When she handed it back there was a faded photograph of William holding a small boy. Charlie wore a party hat and a badge saying, *I am one*. Sorella put a hand over her mouth as tears stung her eyes. Charlie looked so much like Will, and he was right, the boy was gorgeous.

"That's my great, great, great, great, great-granddad and his son. Weird isn't it?"

It was all Sorella could do to nod. William had written her the equivalent of twenty-eight books charting his life. She could not take it in.

"Our family has been entrusted with this for seven generations. But after my granddad died it was all but forgotten about. I mean it should have been my Mum bringing it really, but she died giving birth to me-"

"Oh, I'm sorry," said Sorella.

The girl shook her head. "Ancient history, but thanks. So like I say, we'd forgotten all about it until a letter arrived on January twenty fifth, requesting that I collect it and deliver to you."

"And you came from Australia?" Sorella lifted the books out one by one and stacked them on the table.

"Yep, my great granddad emigrated over there. He had these transferred from the London office of our family's solicitors to their Perth one. That's where I had to pick them up from. They were really strict too. I had to take my passport and evidence of my family tree.

"But then my Pa wouldn't let me travel to England on my own until I turned twenty-one. It was my birthday last week."

"That must have cost you a fortune."

"It won't cost me a penny. William did not trust family

sentiment to get these to you. Before he died he set up an investment fund which has grown… a lot. On delivering this, my family will become very wealthy."

Before he died. Sorella forced a smile. "Sounds like William. He never did trust easily."

"My Pa thought it was some elaborate hoax set up by my Mum's grandfather. Apparently he enjoyed practical jokes. He said I was wasting my time coming to find you but I thought if there was any chance this was true you deserved to know." Julia fidgeted in her seat and Sorella felt the girl's guilt. "I hope you don't mind but I read them… I wanted to see what was so important and…" She looked up, wide-eyed. "He really was here?"

"He left on January twenty-fifth."

Sorella would not have thought it possible for the girl's eyes to grow any bigger, but they did. "Wowzers. I mean, that's unreal."

Sorella peeked inside the cover of the top book, and the sight of William's writing filled her once more with excitement and fear. She was hungry for the details but scared of how the story ended. It was easy to believe he was living his life in parallel somewhere. She had never let herself acknowledge that the moment he went back he simultaneously became a man who had been dead for one hundred and fifty years years.

"I didn't come for the money. I came because if there was a chance all of this was true, I thought you deserved to know…he tried to come back."

Sorella could feel it was her eyes which had become huge now.

"It's all there in book fifteen."

When the girl had left - with a copy of Sorella's bio statement confirming delivery - Sorella locked the door and began reading.

She knew she should start at the beginning, but she had the rest of her life to read it in order.

He had tried to come back, implying something had stopped him. She needed to know what that was.

The ringing doorbell woke Charlie and he started to scream. Damn, he should have told Steve to come straight in.

"It's open," William shouted as he passed the kitchen. "I'll just see to Charlie." He took the stairs two at a time and lifted the boy from his bed. "Ssshhh, come on little man. It's only Uncle Stevie. Noisy Uncle Stevie." He bounced the boy a little trying to keep his ear away from the screeching. Blimey he had a pair of lungs on him. He walked to the top of the stairs. "Sorry guys, I'll be down in a sec."

He expected Steve to pop his head around the kitchen door but he did not. Probably too busy necking with Michelle. Anyone would think his friend had never kissed a girl before the way he hung off her like a horny teenager.

Charlie's cries dimmed a tiny amount and William rubbed his son's back and paced. He hoped this was not a sign of things to come. He had discounted Sarah's comment about the boy missing her. It was not like he hadn't stayed over before. But maybe he could tell she was gone for a while. If so, William could be in for a bumpy weekend, not to mention a dent to his parental ego. "Ssshhh, hey, baby boy, daddy's here."

It took a few minutes longer before he felt the boy go heavy in his arms. He placed him down and stroked a hand across his head. "Night, night." William kissed him, pulled the door to and crept downstairs.

"Sorry about that, turns out the doorbell is not a good-" The sight of a policeman standing in his kitchen sent William cold.

13th June 2039

Ella,

It's taken me a long time to write this. I was hoping I would be able to surprise you but sadly it seems I have missed my chance.

A month ago, I stood in a small church in Lincolnshire and watched Charlie get married to Lisa. His half-sister, Janey, was a bridesmaid and they sat both Danny and I on the top table which was diplomatic. It was a gorgeous day, the sun was out and everyone had fun.

After the meal, Charlie asked me to take a walk with him. We took a couple of whiskies and strolled around the hotel grounds. When we were alone, he said it was time for me to be happy now. He and Lisa were settled, his Mum and Danny strong as ever and it made him sad that I had to choose. In short, he told me to go and see if there was still a chance of happiness with you.

I laughed at first, as you'd expect. I'm a sixty-three year old man, what would she want with me now. And do you know what he said? 'If she loved you as much as you loved her, isn't it worth a shot?'

Next morning, I woke at the crack of dawn realising he was right. We only live one life after all, hey? It took a while to make my arrangements, but my mind was set and I said my goodbyes.

Oh, Ella, I wanted so badly to see you one more time. Even if I turned up to find you happily married and surrounded with kids. Just one more moment would have been enough. But it is no longer possible. It has gone. I knew within my first hour on the hillside. I remembered as clear as day where that thing had been, but still I stayed until it went dark. Eight hours I was out there, scrambling about like an old fool.

So that's that. No more, maybe one days.

If you haven't already done so, you need to find someone who deserves you and live your life, El. Don't be holding on for me. It's too late and for that I am truly sorry.

I might not write again. I think I finally need to let you go.

All my love, William.

But he did not stop writing. There were thirteen more books. Sorella picked each one up, flicking through to see tales of holidays around the world, pictures of him and his grandchildren and reflections on his life. It had become his diary, an account of how he had lived his life, probably to encourage her to do the same.

She paused on the final page of the final book. The writing had become more difficult to read on previous pages, but it was once more clear.

December 2055

Dear Ella,

My father is dictating this to me as he is too weak to write just now. He says to tell you his life has been full and fulfilling and certainly worth living. And that you and I have been the highlights.

He hopes this makes its way to you and that you enjoy the read. Finally, he wants you to know...

I missed you every day. W x

The closing words written in William's own shaky hand were too much to bear. Sorella threw the books back in their box, stumbled to bed and curled up in a ball. It would be two full days before she emerged, her eyes swollen and bloodshot, to begin living her life.

Chapter Forty

William's heart drummed hard with panic. The only reason the police would come here was Sarah. Had he changed something by coming back? Was Charlie destined to live his life with only one parent?

"Mr York?"

"Yes."

"Mr William York?"

"Yes." *Oh crap, man, just say it.*

"Do you know," the police man checked his notepad, "Miss Sorella Grey?"

"What?" It crossed William's mind this could be Steve's idea of a joke. And if so, he would actually kill him.

"She insisted we bring her to you. Refused point blank to go to hospital. She said you would know who she was. Mr York?"

It can't be. "Sorry… I erm… think so."

"You think or you know?" The moustached man did not look impressed with William's floundering.

It's not possible. There's no way… but what if…? He looked the copper in the eye. "Yes, I know her."

The officer put his head out of the door, looked down to the drive and nodded. A car door opened and closed, and William realised he was holding his breath.

He had no time to see her face. She ran from under the policewoman's arm and threw her arms around his neck. "Will!" But the voice was unmistakable.

William put his arms around her. "You're freezing." Her clothes were wet and he could feel her shaking.

"She managed to get herself lost walking in the dales. We've had a paramedic check her over and she needs to get warm. Then it might be a good idea to get her to a doctor."

"Sure, okay," William said to the officer. "I'll take care of her."

The officer looked at William with a stern expression then glanced at his colleague before giving a short nod. "We'll pop by tomorrow morning, check all is well."

Ella still clung to him after the police left. William took hold of her face and looked at her for the first time. *It's really her.* He felt a rush of joy that quickly dissolved into concern. "What are you doing here, Ella?"

"You were right, about it disappearing, that's why you couldn't get back."

He shook his head. "I haven't tried to get back."

She shivered. "No, but you will… you told me in your books."

William released her and leant against a chair for support. Did she say *books*, plural?

"I took ANN's scanner to check it out and it had already shrunk dramatically. She said within days it would be too small to pass through. It was our last chance."

William listened in horror. What had he done? "No," he said.

Ella reached out towards the wall as if to steady herself and then began to fall. William caught her mid-faint. She weighed next to nothing which scared him. It was not like she had any weight to lose in the first place. He carried her upstairs and into the bathroom and laid her gently on the floor. The quickest way to warm her was in the bath. It was still full of Charlie's toys and he removed them before refilling it with hot water.

"You need to get warm and dry," he said when he sensed her sitting up. "You can stay tonight but in the morning you need to go back."

"What..why?"

"This is wrong, Ella. I don't want this." He looked her way

and her silver eyes studied him. He held her gaze to prove he was serious.

She broke eye contact. "But you said…"

"What? What did I say? That we needed to deal with this? That I would come back if I could? That you should live your life?" He found the hurt on her face excruciating.

"That you missed me every day," she said staring at her hands.

Charlie started to cry again and Ella looked towards the nursery.

William took a towel from the cupboard and handed it to her. "Get warm. I need to see to him."

The water began to cool so Sorella climbed out of the bath and wrapped the towel around her. She finally felt warm and wanted to keep it that way. It had been a shock to find the temperature so cold when she came to in the field. The sky was too overcast to see where the sun sat so she had no idea how long she had been out. William had told her how much colder things were in his day, and she had worn three layers of clothes in preparation. But the rain had soaked through to her skin. She had to get moving to get warm.

By the time she found a farmhouse and knocked on the door, she had been walking for hours.

She sat on the floor and leant against the bath. Charlie had been quiet for a while. She strained to hear what was happening, but the house was silent.

Deciding to come here had been a fast decision, not impulsive, just efficient. After monitoring the anomaly for twelve hours, ANN estimated only days were left given the speed it was shrinking. And the more Sorella thought about it the more she was certain of one thing. If she had arrived on the hillside to find it already gone she would have been devastated. She had to come.

There had not been enough time to do more than say a few goodbyes. ANN had agreed to wait until the anomaly closed before redistributing Sorella's estate across the village. She would also send out the quickly written resignation letter for Prime Minister Farrow. Sorella had tied up her life in a matter of hours. Not stopping to think for fear it might prevent her from doing what she needed to do. But of all the reasons not to come, this one would never have occurred to her. If William had turned up at her door she would have been ecstatic. Finding he was not pleased to see her was the last thing she ever expected.

A bright red droplet of blood splashed onto the white towel. Sorella leant her head back and wiped her nose. Great, this will annoy him even more. She held the bridge of her nose.

She was not even sure she could get back now. She might be stuck here forever. The thought of being stranded alone filled her with terror, and she fought back the tears.

"Here, let me." William replaced her hand with his and squeezed tight. He knelt on the floor next to her and placed some tissues in her hand.

"I'm sorry," she said.

"It'll wash out, don't worry."

She looked in his eyes. "For coming."

He took the tissues from her, wiped her top lip and handed her some more. "Here, it'll pass soon."

Sorella closed her eyes to cut off the tears.

William took her hand. "You understand why you have to go back?"

She ignored his question.

"Ella?"

There was a knock in the distance and a man called Will's

name.

"Shit." He released her nose. "I think it's stopped, sit up for me." He stood and went to the stairs. "Hi, down in a sec."

"Sure thing. Is the little terror playing up?" said the man.

"Charlie's fine. Get yourself a drink, the wine's on the side."

Thankfully, her nose had stopped bleeding. She looked up at Will as he stood in the doorway. His expression said, *what am I going to do with you*?

"Steve and Michelle are here for dinner."

Sorella glanced at the wet clothes she had hung over the chair. "Do you have something I can wear?"

"I'm not sure it's a good idea for you to meet them."

"What do you want me to do? Hide up here?"

"No, of course not." The irritation was clear in his voice. "I'll tell them to go."

Sorella stayed quiet, not her call. After a moment or so, he sighed and left the room. She went to the sink, wet a corner of the towel and cleaned the blood from her face. Everything was quaintly manual: the taps, the light switch, the toilet flush. She held her hand against the white metal radiator and smiled. She had not seen one outside of a museum before, and never a working one.

"Try these." William handed her a pile of clothes and left.

The drawstring trousers were huge, even when she pulled them as tight as they would go, they slid off her waist to the floor. She tried the shorts and they were the same. The t-shirt was better, but not long enough to wear on its own. She walked onto the landing and could hear Steve talking about some wine he had brought. She could not go down like this. She considered shouting for Will but then spotted his bedroom door was ajar.

"Anyway, Chell wanted a day out not one spent watching a

plumber fix… hello?" Steve stood at the far end of the kitchen. He looked nothing at all like Sorella had imagined. For a start, he was fair-haired and she had always pictured him dark. His fiancé leant against the sink to his side and Will stood opposite her. They each held a glass of red wine. Michelle and Will both looked her way as Steve made his greeting.

William appraised the shirt she had borrowed. It came to a modest enough length to save her dignity and she had rolled the sleeves up. "Help yourself," he said and did she imagine the smile? "Steve, Michelle, this is Ella. Ella…Steve and Michelle." He waved his hand between them as he made the introductions.

"Fuck me," said Steve his eyes wide with surprise.

"Steve!" said Michelle before coming forward with her hand outstretched. "Nice to meet you."

Steve did not move from the spot, his head flicking between Sorella and William. "Seriously, fuck me."

Michelle slapped his arm. "There's a child in the house."

"Sorry, but…" He eye-balled William. "Ella… as in *Ella*?"

"She came to visit," said William, and Steve raised his eyebrows.

"I came to stay."

William shot her a dirty look.

"Well, I did. It's the truth. It's not my fault you don't want me here."

They stared at each other until Michelle broke the tension. "Glass of wine?"

"Yes, thank you."

"Is that a good idea?" William turned to light the stove: a working gas hob, how fabulous. Sorella had not realised he lived in a time when it was still pumped to every home.

She took the glass from Michelle. "I don't see why not."

William began slicing an onion with his back to her. "You don't think you might be dehydrated?"

"Never stopped you."

He gave a bitter laugh. "That's not true and you know it. Plus I never went through two days in a row"

"And nor will I be."

"You're not staying."

"I am."

He scraped garlic and onion into the pan and faced her. "You're going home."

She shook her head. "Why?"

"I've told you, I don't want you here." The miniscule flick of his eyes told her all she needed to know. For a brief moment in the bathroom when he had held her hand, she had detected something in his voice that gave her hope.

"Liar," she said.

"Yeh? You *can* read my mind now can you?"

"Would you guys like some time alone?" Steve pulled Michelle out of the kitchen. Neither Sorella nor William responded as they disappeared to the lounge.

Sorella ignored his stare as she walked over to where he was. "What are you making?"

"Bolognese."

"Can I help?"

William added meat to the vegetables and stirred. She stood by his side, leaning against the worktop so she could see his face. He concentrated on his cooking.

"Let me see if I have this right. You think I've given up too much. That by coming here I've left my whole life behind on a whim. You think I'll regret it and be unable to cope, and you're worried what will happen if it doesn't work out for us."

He glanced her way. "I'm not worried about us...but you're spot on with the rest."

"Even though you did the same?"

"That was different?"

"How?"

"I had nothing to leave behind."

"You had your friends in there, your job, your sick mother. How is that any different?"

"I had good reason."

"And you think I don't?"

William added tomatoes and fresh herbs to his sauce and set it to simmer before placing his hands against the front of the hob. "Not a good enough one."

"Look at me, Will."

His eyes remained firmly ahead.

"Look at me."

Eventually he faced her.

"You don't think you and me are a good enough reason?"

"It's not the same. I always had the option of coming back. If you're right and that thing is disappearing as we speak you can't ever change your mind. If you miss all those people you care about, you can never see them again. Do you realise how serious this is, Sorella?"

"You only thought you were free to come back at any point. There were no guarantees. At any time it could have shrunk and you'd have been stranded there."

"I don't want you throwing your life away for me."

She walked to the door where she had dropped the small bag she had been carrying. From the inside she removed the last of his books and turned to the final page. "I didn't bring the rest of these because hopefully everything will be changing now. But this I couldn't leave behind."

He took the book from her and read the last page. Then he flicked through to earlier sections, and read the last page again.

"That's why I came, because you predicted my future... I would have missed you every day too." She placed both her hands over his and closed the book. "It doesn't have to be that way."

His expression was unreadable. She wished she could tell how he was feeling. She was pretty sure if he kissed her, she would be home and dry. But he made no move to. He only stood motionless, his hands encased in hers and his brown eyes indecipherable. Was it a mistake to show him an excerpt from the end of his life? He had always coped so well with the weirdness, but maybe that was a step too far.

Please kiss me, Will.

"Sorry to interrupt, I just wanted to grab the wine."

Steve's entrance broke the trance and William moved away. He placed the book on the side and flicked the kettle on.

"Why don't you go join them, Ella? I need to finish up here."

Steve, Michelle and Ella were already sitting around the dining table when he served up the food. It gave him the strangest feeling seeing her with his friends as if her presence was completely normal. She was asking Michelle about the wedding plans and doing a good job of keeping the other woman talking.

"So when is the big day?" said Sorella.

"August next year. We still haven't decided on the exact date. The venue has a couple free so we're sounding people out to find out which is best. We want as many of our friends there as possible, don't we?"

Steve nodded as he took his plate from Will. "Cheers."

"Are your parents still around?"

"Yes, all four will be there. I think my mother had given up on me. She's already bought her outfit, complete with hat."

William placed Ella's plate down before his own. She looked up and they shared a brief smile. "Thanks."

"Mmm this looks great, Will, thank you." Michelle tore off a piece of ciabatta.

"Have you met Charlie then?" Steve said as he served himself a generous portion of rocket and parmesan salad.

"No."

"She only got here a short while before you. He was already sleeping," said William. The truth of it was he had sat in the nursery with Charlie fighting the urge to carry him through to the bathroom. Introducing the two people he loved most in the world would have been an amazing thing. But he knew it would only make it harder to let her go.

"He's gorgeous," said Michelle, "a big bundle of loveliness."

"I've seen a few photographs. He looked a lot like Will I thought." Sorella kept her eyes firmly on Michelle.

"Poor bastard," said Steve.

Ella smiled at him. "Maybe he'll grow out of it."

A wide grin spread across Steve's face. "Well, there's hope for us all."

"Cheers, guys." William liked the way Steve winked at Ella. Was it really possible he could have this? He had spent so many months telling himself to get used to not having her around, it was proving hard to believe. He watched her turning her wine glass in circles with the stem. She had not drunk a drop nor touched her food.

"So Steve tells me you two met when Will was travelling."

Ella glanced at William when Michelle asked her question.

"Yeh, that's right," William said.

"Where?"

"Sorry?" said William.

"Where on your travels did you meet?"

"You know, Ella," interrupted Steve, "if you don't like his bolognese you're in trouble. It's the only thing he can cook with any competence."

Sorella smiled at his friend, but it failed to reach her eyes. "I'm not very hungry, that's all."

"Feeling queasy?" William had often fluctuated between nauseous and starving in the first twenty-four hours.

"A little." She sat back away from the table.

"I'll get you some water."

"No, it's okay. I'll go," she said standing. "I could do with some fresh air."

"Take my coat it's by the door, and glasses are above the sink." He watched her walk out. "And put some shoes on," he called, seeing her bare feet.

"Is she okay?" Michelle looked worried.

"She'll be fine. She just got caught in the rain today. She needs to keep warm and dry."

"And you said she was dehydrated?"

He should have known the doctor would pick up on his earlier comment. He considered lying but then thought better of it. If she started feeling worse he might need Michelle's help. "She had a nose bleed before you arrived."

"Has she had those before?"

"No, but it wasn't a bad one."

"So," said Steve twirling spaghetti around his fork. "She's here to stay?"

"I don't know." William took a drink and forced in a mouthful of food. His appetite had taken a nosedive since she arrived.

"That's progress from, *You're going home*, I suppose." Steve smirked as he did his best impression of William.

"Where does she live then? I don't recognise the accent."

The two men looked at Michelle for a moment. She stopped eating and raised her eyebrows.

"Erm-" started Steve.

"Too far away to commute," said William before Steve was tempted to give anything away. The less people who knew about this the better, he did not want her treated like some freak. Especially given what would be found if anyone ever had chance to look at her brain.

"But you don't want her to stay?" said Michelle selecting more salad.

"Of course, he does, look at him." Steve waved a fork in William's direction. "He's desperate for her to stay. He's crazy about her."

"You should let her stay then," said Michelle like it was the easiest decision in the world.

"It's not that simple." William stood. "I should check how she is."

"Hey," said Steve placing a hand on his arm. "She's great...gorgeous, don't mess up."

Ella stood in the doorway holding her arms tightly around her and rubbing them with her hands. She wore his North Face jacket over the shirt and was stepping out of a pair of his trainers. It was an adorable sight.

"How you feeling?" William asked.

"Cold. It's freezing out there."

It was actually a mild thirteen degrees, but compared to what she was used to... He held the back of his hand against her forehead. "You'll get used to it."

Ella's eyes widened a fraction. "Does that mean I'm staying?"

"Do I have any choice?"

"Of course…" The corners of her mouth twitched. "Well, no, actually."

"That's what I thought," he said with a smile. If he sent her away he had a feeling he would for evermore regret it.

She beamed back at him with a combination of relief and victory in her eyes.

"Are you feeling any better?" he said.

"Much."

"Any sickness?"

She shook her head and a curly strand of hair fell in front of her eye. He moved it aside.

"Good." He slid his hands inside the coat and pulled her close. Then, for the first time in eight months, he kissed her, and they moulded into one another as if they'd never been apart.

Chapter Forty One

William opened the door and Charlie twisted in his arms to reach out to his Mum. "Good trip?" William said.

"Lovely, thanks. Hello beautiful boy." Sarah came in a few steps and took Charlie from him.

"It was just the break she needed," Danny said stepping in behind her.

"Don't make out I'm not coping. I didn't *need* a break it was just nice to have." She kissed Charlie's head as Danny rolled his eyes at Will, who smiled. "Have you been good for daddy, Charlie?"

"He's been great. No problem at all."

"Why do you always do that?" she said throwing him a look.

"Do what?"

"Make out it's so easy taking care of him. I know how much hard work he is."

William took a couple of steps back and leant against the worktop. He knew from experience it was best not to bite.

"What did you get up to then?" Danny rubbed Sarah's back and stroked Charlie's face as he spoke.

"We had fun didn't we? We took a drive out to Burnsall and walked along the river. We fed the ducks in the park and played with a train set Uncle Stevie bought."

"Steve come over?" said Sarah still mooning over her son.

"He and Michelle came for dinner on Friday. He finally proposed."

Sarah looked up. "No way."

"Yep, last weekend. Champagne, roses, diamonds, the lot."

"It's often the last to fall who fall the hardest," said Danny.

Sarah shook her head in amazement. On seeing Ella at the far end of the room she did a double take. She looked back at William with wide eyes. "Are you going to introduce us?"

Danny glanced Ella's way and William was pleased to see his eyes widen also. She had chosen to wear another of his shirts over some tight jeans. They had been shopping and bought her plenty of her own clothes, but she said she liked this. William was not sure if she was doing it for his benefit or her own. Either way, it was damn sexy.

"Sure, Ella this is Charlie's mum, Sarah, and step-dad, Danny."

"Hello," said Ella coming a few steps closer. "You have a lovely son."

"Thanks. Ellen, did you say?"

"No, Ella… it's short for Sorella."

"Nice name," said Danny and William could tell it was not the only nice thing he could see about her.

"I didn't know you were seeing someone." Sarah hitched Charlie higher on her hip. "We'd have picked him up earlier if you'd said you were expecting company."

"She's been here all weekend."

Sarah stopped checking through Charlie's bag and stared at William. "Is that appropriate?"

"Sarah," cautioned Danny.

"No, really. I'm not happy about you having your latest shag piece over whilst you're supposed to be taking care of our son."

William laughed which made Sarah's cheeks flare with colour. "You make it sound like I have women over all the time." He looked Ella's way. "I don't," he said with a smile. Ella came to stand next to him and they put their arms around each other. "Ella lives here now."

Sarah and Danny both looked gob-smacked. William wished he could have captured the moment.

"We met whilst I was travelling. She gave me a place to stay when I needed a friend. She saved my life." William knew it was childish to say that to Sarah, but it was out of his mouth before he could stop it. And the way his ex's eyes narrowed as she glanced Ella's way was undeniably pleasant.

"We've been together for a while, so you don't need to worry about my being his latest...shag-piece was it?" Ella looked up at him. "I've not heard that before."

William grinned and kissed her cheek. "I'll tell you later."

"Well, *we've* never heard of you."

"Sarah!" Danny appeared genuinely horrified by his girlfriend's bitchy comment.

Ella smiled and gazed at William. "Saying goodbye was hard on us both, so I'm not really surprised."

William could see Sarah had no comeback to that. She turned her attention once more to checking Charlie's bag.

"So you're not from round here?" Danny said.

"Actually I grew up not far away near to Burnsall."

"That's why we took a trip out there," William said. They had agreed she should keep as much truth to her story as possible.

"When Will heard about Charlie and came home, I thought my friends and my job would be enough, but..." She hugged him a little tighter. "Turns out I couldn't live without him."

Sarah had paused her activities to listen to Ella.

Danny glanced Sarah's way. "Well then, we should make a move."

William took Charlie back for a final cuddle. The boy smacked his dad's face with one hand and William took hold of the fist and kissed it. "Ya big bully. Say bye bye to Ella." He turned the boy her way and was delighted to see his son beam at her. She had been incredible all weekend, helping out and playing as much as he wanted, but also giving him and Charlie time to themselves.

"See you soon, Charlie." Ella also kissed his hand. "Next time we can talk more about physics."

William gave her a look and shook his head. She shrugged.

"Are you a physicist?" said Danny.

"No, she's just a smart arse," said William.

"I'm fascinated by it myself," Danny continued as if William had not spoken. "We should compare thoughts sometime."

Oh yeh? I think one of my women is enough, pal. William saw the same irritation cross Sarah's face.

"Come on." Sarah took Charlie back. "Thanks," she said to William. "Nice to meet you," she said to Ella without making eye contact.

When they were gone, Ella stood in front of him with her hands on his waist. "You enjoyed that didn't you?"

"Oh yes," he said with a smirk. "Too childish... too immature?"

She shook her head. "I quite enjoyed it myself."

William raised his eyebrows.

"You never said I had to like the woman."

"No I didn't... just don't ever let on to Charlie."

She kissed him.

"You do know if it wasn't for Sarah, we wouldn't have met," he said.

"Don't judge her negative actions by their coincidentally positive outcome."

William leant back a little. "You really don't like her do you?"

"She obviously loves Charlie, but I have no idea what you saw in her."

He chuckled. "Is this the green-eyed monster I see before me?"

Ella dismissed his comment, pushing away from him and

checking the clock. It was one pm. "Let's go exploring."

He pulled her to him by the front of his shirt and undid the top button. "I can think of something to explore."

"Have you not had enough?" she said, letting him draw her closer.

"Of you?" He brought his face close to hers. "You do know that's never going to happen."

For a moment, as he kissed her deeply, he actually thought he had won. But he should have known better than to think he would ever be getting his own way again.

She moved away and grinned. "We have all night for your kind of exploring. I want to go and see this old world of yours... discover my new home. I want to learn how to drive a motor car, and watch one of your 2D movies at the cinema. I want to take a trip on one of your slow trains and put my own website on your internet."

"Hmmm are they euphemisms?"

"No!" She slapped his arm. "Come on." She grabbed both their coats, pushed his car keys into his hand and dragged him to the door.

"You do know we just call them trains these days, don't you?"

She giggled and kissed his cheek. Then she moved past him back into the kitchen. William watched her with fascination. Would he ever get used to seeing her here in such familiar surroundings? He was not sure.

Ella picked up the book he had left on the worktop: his final weeks and months recorded in his own hand. He had avoided looking at it again. It was one type of weird he was not sure he could handle. On the way past the bin, she threw the book inside then took his hand with a smile.

"Let's go and start your history over."

Lightning Source UK Ltd.
Milton Keynes UK
UKOW040945240513

211168UK00001B/2/P